REMOVE THE SHROUD

The King's Ranger Book 3

AC COBBLE

Cobble Publishing LLC

Keep in Touch and Extra Content

※❈※

You can find larger versions of the maps, series artwork, my newsletter, and other goodies at accobble.com. It's the best place to stay updated on when the next book is coming!

Happy reading!
AC

Chapter One

꙳ꙮ꙳

R ew stared at the rain as it swept over the dark green hills like a matron's broom across a dusty floor. Mist billowed ahead of the roaring gale, swept up from the force of the falling water and the raking strength of the wind. Great curtains of water scoured the hills. Stands of trees were alternately visible through the cloudy gray and obscured when another sheet of blowing water lashed across the land in front of him.

On the porch where he stood, cold droplets of water pattered against his face, flung by the fury of the weather. The icy liquid seeped into the thick wool of his cloak. He could feel the damp reaching his skin, and he shivered, but he stayed where he was, watching the storm.

He reached up and wiped his hand across his freshly shaven pate, brushing away the cold water, knowing more would accumulate there in a handful of breaths. Distant thunder rumbled, barely audible over the roar of the wind, a portend that the storm was far from finished.

Rew had spent the last decade outside in the wilderness. He'd spent many a day holed up and watching the rain, but in the forest, he had the protection of the trees. Out there, south of Spinesend, it was all open, sprawling hills, and there was nothing to stop the wailing onslaught of wind and water. It was impressive, watching the violent weather, seeing that ancient magic unleash its fury upon the world. Rew did not enjoy getting rained on, but he gave respect where it was due, and nature had long since earned his respect.

"Any break?" asked Anne.

He'd heard her come out of the front door of the inn a moment ago but had not turned. He shook his head and kept his gaze out on the countryside as she joined him. He told her, "We've a few days of it, still."

Anne grunted, leaning against the railing beside him. "That's what you said a few days ago."

"It was true."

She gave a mirthless laugh and stood back up. She tugged her shawl tighter around her shoulders and complained, "King's Sake, Rew, it's wet out here."

He finally turned and grinned at her. "I know."

"Then why-are you standing out in the cold?" She waved at the torrential rain pounding down in front of them and hammering the roof of the inn like a mad drummer's beat. "Bressan's ale barrel is still half full, and I'm sure he'd enjoy your presence at the game board. He's up twenty to none against Cinda, last I heard, and Raif hasn't even finished a game with the man before tipping his king."

"You or Zaine could play him."

"Zaine doesn't know how to play Kings and Queens."

"But you do," reminded Rew.

"I know how, but I don't enjoy the game," remarked Anne. He didn't respond, and after a moment, she asked again, "What are you doing out here, Rew? We're not going anywhere until this passes over, and you're saying there's more to come... Blessed Mother, even I can see it will be days yet before the roads are passable. Travel on the highway right now would be like wading through soup. We'd need a boat just to make it the half league into Laxton."

"I know."

She moved next to him and put a hand on his shoulder. "I know you want to get farther away from Spinesend, but we can't. We're stuck here, Rew, so let's make the best of it. Have an ale. Play Bressan in Kings and Queens." She gave a short, constricted chuckle. "I cannot believe I just said that. Soak it in, Rew. That may be the very last time I ever encourage you to have an ale."

"I don't want an ale, I want to move. It's not Spinesend I'm thinking of, Anne. I'm finished hiding, and I'm finished running. My thoughts are ahead, on Carff."

"As are Raif's," remarked the empath, fussing with her shawl as the billowing mist began to soak through it. "He's thinking of his sister—rescuing her or confronting her, depending on the hour you ask him. But that's not what is on your mind, is it?"

"I've given very little thought to Kallie Fedgley, to be honest."

"You're thinking of Alsayer."

"He's part of it," acknowledged Rew.

"And… Prince Valchon?" asked Anne. "I don't understand, Rew."

Rew reached up to wipe more droplets of water off his head and told her, "Anne, it's time I face up to what's behind me, what I've been ignoring for the last decade. What I've ignored for my entire life, really. It's time that is over. I can't tell you everything, and I am sorry for that, but I cannot. I will tell you that Prince Valchon is a part of it. All of the princes are. And now that I'm done running… Pfah. This rain. I feel the need to move, to go, but you're right. We can't go anywhere until the storm passes. We'd spend more time pulling our boots out of the mud on the highway or wading across flooded streams cross-country than we would making progress. I know that, but it doesn't change how I feel. That's why I'm out here. I've finally decided to move forward, but I can't, so I'm waiting."

Anne nodded. She left unsaid that waiting inside made a fair bit more sense than waiting outside. The kind of waiting Rew was doing wasn't about comfort, not the kind of comfort that Bressan's

Inn offered. Never again, until it was over, however that might be, would he be comfortable.

They stood quietly for a long time, watching the rain, and then Anne said, "Rew, I will not leave the children. Where they go, I go."

"So you've said."

"Will you leave us, then?"

He turned to her and offered a wan smile. "No, I won't. You told me once that the children are a part of it, and you were right. More than you knew, then. More than I wanted. My past, their future, it's tied together inexorably. You can still feel the bonds, can you not?"

She nodded.

"Their fate and ours are one and the same, though in the end I don't think anyone will be thanking us for that."

"But the princes will not forget them..." murmured Anne.

Rew wrapped an arm around Anne's shoulders and drew her close. "We—both us and the children—are in terrible danger from terrible men, but so are many others. Maybe we could save ourselves. Maybe we could run far enough away and burrow deep enough into hiding to avoid what is to come, but..." He paused, unable to say it.

"But it's not just about us, is it?"

"No, it's not. Not anymore. I... For a long time, I wanted it to be. I knew it wasn't, but I wanted it to be. While I've been hiding..."

Anne pulled herself upright, straightening her back and lifting her chin to look him in the eyes. "Life isn't easy, is it? At least we know what we need to do, right?"

"We..."

She reached up and grabbed his chin, forcing his gaze to meet her own. "We. I won't leave the children, and we won't leave you."

He nodded, and the smile wavered on his face. She saw the

hesitation but did not comment. She dropped her hand and stood beside him. There was nothing else either had to say.

She was guessing that he knew what to do, that his next move had already been planned, but it wasn't. He knew what he wanted to do, which even he had to admit wasn't the same as having a plan. It was a wiser man's game, plotting out the moves, the reactions, the results. He didn't know what would happen if he was successful, but in Spinesend, he'd realized that he knew what would happen if he did nothing or if he failed. That truth lay behind him. Ahead of them was the unknown, the wilderness, and he'd been drawn to that all of his life. It was only now that he realized why.

"I'm cold out here, Rew."

He hugged her tight. "Let's go inside, then. I could do with one of Bressan's ales, and maybe I'll give him a go at Kings and Queens."

"Good luck to you," said Anne, grinning. "Better you than I. I swear that man sees three or four moves ahead."

"Perhaps," said Rew. "The best players hold the entire board in their head, you know? They see where each piece is, and what it can do. They play out several turns in their imaginations, figuring out the possibilities, the potential responses, the next logical moves. Each new position is like a book they've already read—at least that's what I'm told. I'm not a good player, but I've learned that to beat the best players, you can't challenge them at their own game. The trick is to do something they would have never imagined."

"That sounds like a way to get beat, too," murmured Anne, leading him toward the door of the inn.

"Sometimes." Rew laughed. "Sometimes, that's a way to get beat right quick, but there's another strategy, too."

She raised an eyebrow.

"When you're getting beat, and there are no moves you can make to get out of it, you flip over the board."

"ATTACK. ATTACK!" BELLOWED REW.

Zaine, twisting like an eel, slithered forward and delivered a hard thrust.

"Ouch!" cried Raif.

The big fighter dropped the linen-wrapped wooden dowel he'd been using as a practice blade and grappled with the thief. He twisted, lifting her to fling her down on the ground. As he held her high, the thief kicking and wriggling helplessly in his arms, he must have thought twice about it, because, more gently, he flopped her down and then pinned her with his body weight.

"That's unfair," cried Zaine, struggling beneath the heavy fighter. "I hit you!"

"Enough," said Rew, crouching beside the writhing pair.

Raif rose up onto his knees, breathing heavily. Zaine, from her back, tossed a handful of straw at his face.

"You gave him a good blow," said Rew, pointing to the spot Zaine's practice dagger had struck Raif, "but the big lad wears armor there. Many of your opponents will as well. But even if he wasn't armored, that strike would've punctured his lungs but missed his heart. Without Anne's help, he'd almost certainly die within a few hours, maybe a day, but he'd still have some fight left in him. With a bigger foe like Raif, it's just as important to get away after you do your damage than it is to land the blow."

Beaming, Raif stood, brushing the straw off his hands, and declared, "One for me, then."

Rew rose as well and poked the boy again in the ribs where Zaine had hit him. "Did you hear the part where I said you'd die in a few hours? It's only worth winning a fight if you live long enough to see the next sunrise."

Raif shrugged. "Winning is winning."

Rew frowned at him and shook his head. "Lad, you risk too much. When it's for real, your armor may deflect some of the damage, and Anne can heal some of the wounds the armor doesn't prevent, but sooner or later, you're going to be felled by a blow that you cannot get up from. You fight like this, and it's not a matter of if—it's when."

"What would you have me do, Ranger? I either fight to win, or I do not. We can train on maneuvers and skills, but when it's real, I only know of one way. I understand what you're saying, but once the steel is crossed, I don't hold back."

"Brave words, but mark mine. You continue like this, lad, and you're going to pay the ultimate price," warned Rew. "Don't believe me? Then go to one of those taverns the retired soldiers lurk in and tell me how many berserkers you find there. Winning is nice, but if you want to survive to be an old man, you've gotta think."

Raif's lips tightened and he shrugged.

Rew held his gaze for a moment then shook his head and pointed Raif toward the open door of the massive stables they were sparring inside of. "Why don't you go check on Anne and your sister?"

"I'd rather stay here," muttered Raif, looking out the open doors, seeing the pouring rain splashing down into the cold puddles and rivulets outside of the stables. A damp, chilly breeze whistled softly through the open doors, and Raif turned to Rew, allowing the weather to make his point for him.

"What Anne and your sister are trying is dangerous. Anne will do her best, but she's not the guide that Cinda needs. Someone needs to check on them, often."

Grumbling under his breath, Raif collected his cloak and spun it over his shoulders. "You'll owe me a mulled wine when I return, Ranger."

Rew waved the boy toward the door, and Raif strode out into the downpour.

"You think he'll ever make right on that tally of his?" questioned Zaine, rolling to her feet easily.

Rew shrugged.

Raif, feeling the pride of young nobility, had insisted that he and his sister would pay their own way on the journey to Carff. It was all well and good, except the boy and the girl didn't have more than a handful of coin between them. All of their wealth had been left in Falvar or lost in Spinesend, and now they traveled with nothing more than the clothes on their backs, Raif's greatsword, and the provisions Rew had purchased for them on the road. Someday, Raif promised, he would compensate Rew for every expense down to the individual ciders and wines. Periodically, the fighter would update Rew on what he thought was owed, and Rew would ignore him.

Zaine rubbed her backside. "It's nice that he's so generous with his imagined coin, but I wouldn't mind him having a few other considerations. The overgrown oaf doesn't know his own strength."

"He's taking it easy on you," said Rew, raising an eyebrow. "Didn't you feel him hesitate before you both went down?"

"Why would he take it easy on me? You didn't tell him to, did you? I can handle myself, Ranger."

Rew scratched his beard and glanced down at his feet.

"What?"

He didn't answer.

"What?" demanded Zaine, shuffling closer so that even with his eyes down, he couldn't avoid seeing her.

"I think that, ah, Raif is fond of you."

"Fond of me?" Zaine laughed. "What are you talking about? He's fond of—oh. But…"

"But we're on a dangerous journey, and you don't have time for that," suggested Rew. "I know. I'd talk to him, I would, but a lad his age… It's all they think of, Zaine. It's best you ignore it, and in time, it should pass."

Zaine shook her head, kicking the straw at her feet.

Rew frowned at her. "What?"

Flushing, Zaine looked away.

Rew swallowed. "Ah, Zaine, I'm old enough to be your father. Really, you're a lovely lass, but—"

The girl coughed and started gagging. She stared at him wide-eyed, shaking her head.

Rew raised a hand toward her but didn't think it appropriate to touch her just then. "Zaine, you don't need to be embarrassed. It's common that a young woman sees an older, more experienced man, and—"

"Ranger, I've no interest in men," interjected Zaine.

"Well, of course not," he said. "I only meant that wisdom can be attractive, but I feel a responsibility toward you and—"

"I like women," cried Zaine. "I'm… fond of Cinda."

The ranger and the thief stood staring at each other for a long moment. Finally, he asked her, "Does she know?"

Zaine shook her head, her face still a rosy shade of red. "Cinda's mooning all over Bressan's eldest son. Watch her. Every time he bends down to get a mug off the bottom shelves, she's staring at his backside. Why do you think she keeps ordering ales? She doesn't even drink ale. Raif keeps taking them, believing he's teasing her. I've thought about telling him just to see what he'd do, but I worry about Bressan's son. He's a good lad, and like Raif said, when it comes time to fight, what little thought Raif ever keeps in that thick skull of his flees like a hare."

"Maybe she's, ah…"

"Cinda told me what she'd like to do with the innkeeper's son." Zaine shuddered. "The only thing that's holding her back is the foolish notion that noblewomen should only lie with noblemen. Purity of the blood, you know? They put more faith in that than they do the Blessed Mother. I guess she hasn't heard the stories I have about what those lords and ladies get up to when the other isn't looking."

Rew glanced toward the open doors and the pouring rain outside. "I see."

"Does your font of wisdom, acquired after so many long years, grant you any advice you'd like to share about this situation?"

Rew coughed, scratched his beard some more, and then

declared, "I think you should talk to Anne about this sort of thing."

Zaine chortled and slid her wooden practice daggers into her belt. "Ranger, if my father was still alive, I think the two of you would have gotten along famously."

The thief turned and walked out the door, breaking into a run and splashing through the ankle-deep puddles as she dashed toward the back of the inn.

Rew sighed. A horse, one of the thoroughbreds the innkeeper Bressan raised for the races, whinnied at him.

"What do you know?" muttered Rew, scowling at the beast, before he, too, dashed out into the cold wet, running to the inn.

PALE, GREEN-TINGED WHITE LIGHT FLICKERED ON AND OFF, BATHING the corner of the common room and the hearth in an eerie, spectral wash. The glowing orange embers of a fire in the hearth seemed to pulse and fade in time with the other light, dying desperately with each burst of stark illumination.

Rew bent forward and tapped out the ash from his pipe into the fire. He exhaled slowly, sending the air of his breath over the embers. He felt the coals flare, warming his face. The fire crackled, but he stopped before the charred wood caught flame again. It was night. He was tired, and it was time for the fire to die.

He glanced at Cinda, her face alternately lit and then dark as she practiced summoning her funeral fire, the cold white and green flame dancing across her fingertips and then winking out.

Rew told her, "I'm off to bed. You?"

She shrugged. "I'm finding I don't desire sleep as often as I used to. When I asked Anne about it, she turned away. What is happening to me, Ranger?"

Rew sighed and settled back down in his chair. "In dreams, your physical body rests and is restored. It is a time of regeneration and healing. But also in dreams, your mind is freer of your physical form than when you're awake. We're closer to the plane of death when we dream. As your powers develop, you'll, well, you won't need to sleep. Not for your mind, at least. Your body will still require rest to restore itself, but the more you use your power, the less you'll feel the desire to lie down and actually slumber."

Cinda frowned, and the funeral fire ignited on her fingers again.

"There is risk in not resting," continued Rew. "Your mind won't feel the need, but you must force yourself, or your body will suffer. There are plenty of storied necromancers who ignored the mundane concerns of their corporeal form, and that was the ironic end of them. You can summon all of the spirits you want, but your body still needs to eat."

A wan smile curled Cinda's lips, and she nodded. "That makes sense."

"You'll rest then?"

"Later."

"You'll need your strength for when we leave this place."

Cinda glanced across the dark common room to where a thick, leaded-glass window barred the wind and rain outside. They could hear the rainfall drumming on the porch of the inn, relentless, as it had been for six days now.

"When are we leaving this place?"

"As soon as we can," replied the ranger. "I know you want to leave, to go and find your sister. I understand, but we won't make it far in this weather. There's only misery out there until the storm passes."

Cinda shook her head, her eyes fixed on her hand. "It is my brother who wants to find our sister, Ranger. We all saw what Kallie did and heard what she said. I have no interest in seeing her again."

"You don't? Just a few days ago…"

Cinda let the funeral flame grow on her hand, casting its sharp light over the entire room. "In the last few days, I've had a lot of time to think. Raif may choose to ignore it, but you and I both know what will happen when we find Kallie."

Rew's lips twisted into a sour grimace.

Cinda's fire winked out again, and darkness filled the common room outside of the weak glow from the embers on the hearth. Cinda continued, "There won't be a reconciliation with Kallie, no matter what my brother hopes. All I ask, Ranger, is that when it is time to end her, you do it. You, or Anne, or Zaine, though I hate to put that on her. Do not let my brother be the one who slides the steel into our sister. He's an oaf, but he should not have to live with that. He couldn't live with that."

Rew bowed his head then looked up to meet her gaze.

She was staring at him, the orbs of her eyes gleaming in the darkness. He frowned. It was impossible to be certain in the low light of the room, but were her eyes changing, the iris turning green? Already? Rew rubbed his face with both hands then met Cinda's gaze again. He cleared his throat and said, "I will do it. You're right. Your brother does not need that on him. You both have enough of a burden already."

Cinda, looking decades beyond her years in the darkness, nodded. "What I am becoming is not your fault, Ranger. You tried to steer us away, to find us another path. I see now why you did that. It—It was kind of you, but it is too late now. We are on this road, and we must find the end of it. Do you think we will, in Carff?"

Rew shook his head slowly. "No, I'm afraid the end of this journey is not in Carff. You will have to shoulder your burden beyond there." He laughed mirthlessly. "If we survive. I suppose it's worth qualifying everything we say with that grim clause. I am sorry, Cinda. I'm sorry that we could not find another way and that I could not keep you from being drawn into this."

Cinda smiled at him, her face regaining the freshness of her youth, and he saw the girl he'd first encountered walking from Eastwatch to Falvar. "The burden was mine before we met you. I didn't know it, but it was there. My father, the princes, they put it there. If we'd never met you, we still would have been in this mess, though not for long. I don't think we would have survived Falvar without you. No, none of this is your fault."

Rew shrugged, fiddling with his empty pipe. He did not respond.

"I hope my sister is gone from Carff when we arrive. It will be better for Raif—and for me, I'll admit—if we never see her again."

"I understand."

"We have to go, though, don't we?"

"Have to... That's not entirely true," said Rew with a sigh. "There are other ways, other paths we could take. They won't lead to Kallie, and they won't lead to answers. You could run, or you could hide. It might work for a time. Maybe even a long time. But there is no changing the truth of who you are and what you're capable of."

"Then there is no choice," said Cinda. "This burden is mine, but I need your help understanding it. I need you to guide me to what it is that they expect from me, what it is they captured my father for. You know, don't you?"

"I believe so," he acknowledged.

"But you won't tell me?"

"Not now."

"You can be a frustrating man, Ranger."

"I know."

They sat quietly for a long time until the light from the fire no longer bled past the edge of the hearth.

"Cinda," said Rew. He heard her turn toward him, but he could not see her in the black of the room. He gathered himself then told her, "You should know that if we walk to the end of this road, then I will use you, much like they attempted with your father. I know what your blood is capable of, and I need it to finish something. Only you can finish this. It is not something that I can do on my own."

"But you will not tell me what this is?"

He shook his head. "I cannot. It is too much, for now. In time, you will know. Just like you now understand why I tried to avoid this to begin with, you will understand the need for secrecy."

"Eventually, I will learn everything?"

"Eventually."

"Tell me this, at least. If the end of this journey—if what you need—is not in Carff, why are we going there?" asked Cinda. "Not to assuage my brother's boyish fantasy of reconciliation with Kallie, surely?"

"It is not the end of the road we seek in Carff but the beginning," Rew told her.

Cinda grunted.

Rew reached up and felt the prickles atop his scalp. He yawned.

"You're a good man, Ranger," said Cinda suddenly, "the best I've known, I suppose, though maybe that is no grand prize. Still, I will do whatever it is you ask of me. I trust you to lead us where we need to go."

It was like a knife twisting in his guts. She didn't know. She couldn't know. By the time they were finished, it would destroy her. It would destroy him, too, and he couldn't begin to guess the calamity that might follow for Vaeldon. He couldn't tell her that, but he thought that if he did tell her, she would still agree to do it. She'd meant it when she had said she would do as he asked. There was some comfort to that. There was discomfort as well, when he wondered if it was merely a convenient story he told himself. It didn't matter, though. It was necessary. They were taking a terrible risk, embarking on this road, but it was the only gambit he had if he wanted to free the kingdom. When playing against a master of the game board, one had to do what was least expected.

He reached over and put his hand on hers.

"Wherever this road takes us, I will go," repeated Cinda quietly.

Rew stood and pulled her up as well. "Tonight, all I ask is that we both try to get some sleep. With luck, in a day or two, the weather will clear. When it does, we must be ready to travel."

Cinda chuckled. "Very well, Ranger. I'll lie down, and I will try to sleep."

"Try—that's all any of us can do."

In the black of the room, they both walked confidently to the stairs where their rooms were on the floor above. Rew, his senses attuned to his surroundings, stepped easily. Cinda, becoming a creature of the darkness, needed no light, and she followed him up the stairwell to their separate rooms.

Chapter Two

"Y ou sure I can't sell you horses?" asked Bressan, the slender innkeeper and equine breeder.

Rew, cradling a mug of coffee in his hands and leaning his elbows on the railing of the inn's porch, shook his head.

The innkeeper drew himself up, tucked his thumbs behind his belt, and blew out a puff of air, stirring the prodigious mustache that covered half of his face. "There's a reason you're staying up here and not down in Laxton beside the highway, and if it's not to purchase horseflesh, I've seen enough in my years to know what it means. You're running. It is none of my business, but wherever you're going, you'd get there a lot quicker with a horse between your legs. I can teach you to ride, if that's—"

"I know how to ride," interjected Rew, "but I choose not to."

"I've seen your purse, my man. It's not about the expense, is it?" questioned the innkeeper. "It's true that I breed the finest mounts in the Eastern Province, but they're not all so fine. If you're short on coin, I've got some mares that will be within your range. Old girls that have some spirit but aren't for the races, eh? Or I've got some nags that I'd almost give you so I can stop caring for 'em. They'll still get you to where you're going, though. Four legs are better than two, and that's the truth."

Rew shook his head. "I prefer to walk."

The innkeeper scowled at him, as if offended.

"If a man's legs can't get him where he's going, then maybe he ought not to be going there," declared Rew.

"That sounds like something a man would say after too many ales," groused the innkeeper.

"There's no need to make the hard sale, Bressan. You'll have buyers soon enough. Buyers for anything with four legs that can carry a saddle, and those folk won't be worried about how much you charge."

The innkeeper raised an eyebrow.

"There's war on the horizon," explained Rew. "It won't be long before someone comes along looking to expand their cavalry. They'll need spare mounts and won't fuss about the quality, and even those nags you mentioned can haul supplies. You'll have more business than you can handle."

"I know," replied the innkeeper sourly.

Rew glanced at him, holding his coffee mug close to inhale the rich scent.

Looking apologetic, the innkeeper added, "I hate the thought of my horses riding into war. It's terrible on them, you know? They're like my children, those horses, and I'd rather sell 'em to you for next to nothing than put them through that. Blessed Mother, I'll give them to you if you promise me you'll ride them away from this brewing madness. I've been around long enough, and my pappy and grandpappy before me, to know that when the first man comes along wanting to buy the entire herd, we sell it. They'll pay up until the fighting starts. Later, they'll just confiscate any animals we have left. You're right, could be good coin for me, but half those horses they take won't be seeing summer. They're like my children, man. It's not about the coin. You sure you won't—"

Rew smiled. "You're a good man, Bressan, but I prefer to walk. Even if I didn't, I couldn't make the promise the horses would be in any less danger with me."

Bressan nodded to the rolling hills that spread out in front of them. Mist hung like wraiths over a moor. It sparkled brilliantly with the first morning sun they'd seen in a week. A thin line of dark soil cut through the emerald and white landscape, the road leading from the inn to the village of Laxton and the highway beyond it.

"If you mean to walk, you'd best get to it. By tomorrow, if not this afternoon, there will be soldiers on that road coming up from the highway, looking for my horses. The nobles already came before the storm hit, picking over the best of my stock. Soldiers'll come next. You're good people, and if you're going to outrun whatever trouble it is that dogs you, I suggest you start right away."

Rew nodded.

"Despite how much you complained about not enjoying the game, you've given me more of a challenge on the game board these last few days than I've seen in years," continued the innkeeper. "I pride myself on my game, but I've never seen anyone play like you. You move in unexpected ways. Sometimes it works, and sometimes it don't, but you're willing to try. I respect that, and I'll keep your secrets, if anyone asks."

The innkeeper left the question hanging.

"I don't think anyone will ask."

Bressan nodded and turned back to his inn. "Regardless, you'd best be on the road as soon as you can be. I'll check about breakfast. Then, maybe that's the last I see of you?"

Rew did not respond.

"Mayhap you'd like a bit of the strong stuff you were drinking the other night for the road? Friend of mine ages it in barrels for years afore he bottles it. Finest spirits coin will buy you, here or anywhere in Vaeldon. It's wasted on the soldiers. If you won't take my horses, at least take my liquor. Can't have those fools wasting everything, can we?"

Rew laughed. "I'll raise a drink to you on the cold nights, Bressan, in memory of the shelter you've given us here and a hope for your horses. I wish you—and the beasts—luck in the next months."

"I'll have the girls pack you a couple'a bottles, then. Don't let your woman see it, though, eh? Sometimes a woman thinks she's all the comfort you need on one o' them cold nights. They don't understand that after some days, a man needs a drink. My thinking, you might have a few of those days ahead of you, friend."

Rew laughed. "And sometimes a woman is why a man needs a drink."

The innkeeper grinned and guffawed. "Ain't that the truth."

Bressan reached back and slapped Rew on the shoulder before shuffling inside. Through the open door, Rew could hear the sounds of the sedate inn waking. There hadn't been more than a dozen other travelers staying in the sprawling, comfortable inn the last week, but this morning, Bressan's staff were freshening rooms, and the ovens were fired up in the kitchen. The smell of baking bread wafted out, stirring Rew's hunger. More bread than they needed for the guests that were already there, he thought. Bressan spoke the truth. The innkeeper expected more visitors that day.

Sighing, Rew looked down the sinuous dirt tract that led to the highway. It was thick with mud, and even as it dried in the morning sun, it would be hard walking and impossible to cover their tracks. Cross country it was, then.

FOR TWO DAYS, THEY SLOGGED ACROSS THE ROLLING HILLS, THE LUSH turf sodden from the week of torrential rain. Every morning, they awoke covered in cold dew, and within minutes of starting to hike, they were soaked to the knees from striding through the tall, wet grass. The temperature wasn't freezing, but constantly damp as they were, it felt like it may as well be. Rew began making them change their socks every time they stopped for a meal, and he had Anne check everyone's toes to make sure hypothermia had not set in.

There were sparse stands of trees where they took shelter from the unrelenting wind and attempted to harvest firewood, but even when they found fallen branches, they were heavy with moisture. It made for pathetic, smoky fires that did little to warm them and much to water their eyes. Anne was able to cook a little, but after a week of Bressan's hearty fare, her best efforts in the conditions seemed meager.

The children didn't complain, and even Anne could only offer glum looks and apologetic shrugs as she dished the thin soups she managed to heat over the paltry flames. All of them knew braving the soaked road from Bressan's inn down to the highway would have been equally as bad, even if it wasn't for the risk of encountering soldiers from Spinesend.

By the second day, though, beneath clear skies and bright sun, Rew felt it safe enough to return to the highway, and he led the party through the hills until they came across the wide, dirt road. It hadn't completely dried, but after generations of traffic, the soil was compact enough that it was easy walking. The entire party breathed a sigh of relief as their boots found the road.

"This ought to make travel a lot quicker," said Zaine, scuffing a boot on the damp dirt and scowling at the thick tangle of grass they'd walked out of.

"Aye, just another four hundred leagues. We'll be there before you know it," replied Rew with a grin.

Cinda kicked her legs, trying to move the sodden wool of her skirts. "How do women travel in these? I'd rather my robes."

"Your crimson robes will tell anyone looking for us that you're a necromancer," reminded Rew.

"This garb will tell anyone that I'm a serving wench," grumbled the noblewoman, leaving the skirts alone for a moment to pull up her bodice, which was cut lower than she was used to.

"It's a good disguise until we can get further from Spinesend," responded the ranger. "Wear it until we find a village with a seamstress. Then, you can change. It's a long walk, and there will be plenty of opportunities to find more suitable travel attire. I hope we've evaded pursuit for the moment, but no reason to make it easier for anyone looking for us, eh?"

Cinda grumbled beneath her breath, but she stopped arguing.

Anne, looking down the long, empty expanse, wondered, "Do you think Bressan would have sold us some of those horses? It would have made the journey quicker. He liked you, Rew. I bet you could have talked him into a good price."

Rew shrugged and did not respond.

ALONG THE HIGHWAY, AS THE SUN CONTINUED TO SHINE DOWN, traffic increased until there was a steady flow of people and wagons. Most of them were moving north, the opposite direction the party was taking. The highway was the main thoroughfare between the capital of the Eastern Territory, Spinesend, and the much larger capital of the Eastern Province, Carff. The cities were the two largest trading hubs in the east, but along the five-hundred-league stretch, there were several other towns both large and small. The way was dotted with roadside inns and stations of varying quality to accommodate the steady stream of travelers, and the party rarely went more than half an hour without seeing someone or something.

At first, Rew and the others had been nervous, peering closely at each group they passed, twitching at anything that might signal an attack. But over the next several days, it became obvious that no one was interested in them, and that if there were watchers on the road, the party had gotten out ahead of them or had not yet found them.

That's not to say it was a relaxing stroll. The other groups they passed were heavily armed, and most of them had formed caravans for protection. Rew risked asking several of the other travelers what they were worried about, confused how the news from

Spinesend had already spread so far. But instead of political unrest, he was told people were guarding against the Dark Kind. Rew hadn't seen any sign of the creatures near Spinesend, but it seemed rumors of them had infected the land like a plague. After several serious-looking parties mentioned the narjags, Rew began to worry it was more than just rumor, but there was nothing to be done about it except to keep moving, so they did.

On foot, after months of living on the road, even the children were capable of maintaining a brisk pace most of the day, and more often than not, it was the party who was overtaking their fellow travelers. Every couple of hours, though, they would have to hop off to the side of the road as mounted men or horse-drawn carriages thundered past.

Messengers, Rew suspected, rushing to share word of what had happened in Spinesend. They could be working on behalf of merchants and the cabals such men formed, or they could have been spies for the various factions of minor nobility strewn amongst the cities bordering the highway. Rew didn't know, or much care, but he was powerfully curious at what the messengers might be relaying. Was the news about the conflagration in the tower, about Duke Eeron's flight, or had there been further disruption after they'd fled? Rew wanted to know, but given the chances some of those tidings might involve him and his friends, he couldn't bring himself to stop one of the messengers and ask.

So it was with a bit of trepidation and anticipation that they came across a carriage stopped on the side of the road ahead of them. The carriage was painted with a dark blue lacquer, trimmed in gold, and the horse standing beside it would have been the pride of Bressan's stable. A footman, garbed in a crushed velvet coat and stockings the same shade of dark blue as the carriage, was up to his knees in mud. A wheel was lying, shattered, twenty paces off the road and behind the carriage, and the vehicle had flipped on its side.

Half an hour before and half a league behind, the carriage had flown past them like the king himself was chasing it. Rew did the calculations in his head and decided the vehicle had been on its side for a quarter hour.

"They might need my help," murmured Anne. "Rew, can we..."

Rew shrugged. It was quite possible whoever was involved in a wreck at such speed might need Anne's care, and while the empath tended to any victims, he would have a chance to question the footman. The children remained silent, observing the wreck cautiously. Rew was glad that if nothing else, they'd at least learned to be careful over the last several months.

Anne, on the other hand, rushed forward and began chastising the footman and inquiring about his cargo. When Rew and the others caught up, his stomach fell. Anne was scaling the side of the overturned carriage. She looked down at the ranger.

"I'm going to need your help. There's a woman inside, and it seems she's giving birth."

"King's Sake," growled Rew. "Maybe we should keep—"

"Rew!"

"Right," he said, shrugging his pack off his back and tugging open the flap. He turned to the footman, who was standing around uselessly. It appeared the man had been trying on his own to right the carriage. Ridiculous. Snapping to get the man's attention, Rew asked, "Does your mistress have a tent that you can set up?"

The man blinked back at Rew stupidly, and the ranger decided the horse peering around the overturned vehicle showed more intelligence than the footman.

"Where did you sleep last night?"

"I, ah, underneath the carriage," mumbled the footman. "We didn't pause long enough to prepare for a proper journey. The lady doesn't even have her entourage. You asked... A tent? No, we don't have one."

Muttering under his breath, Rew glanced at the children and instructed them, "Work with him to set up... something. Use our tarps if you need to. We'll need shelter for the baby, and judging by the sounds in that carriage, we'll need it soon."

Glancing around the open hills, Zaine mentioned, "There's nothing to string a tarp from, Rew. This isn't a good place to make camp."

Rew waved his hand at her irritably. "Figure something out."

"Of course," said Raif, and he moved to the back of the carriage, likely just happy to have something to do that didn't involve helping with or listening to what was going on inside.

Steeling himself, Rew scampered up after Anne and peered down to where she was crouched inside of the overturned carriage next to a woman.

Seeing Rew, the woman tried to shove down her skirts, but Anne slapped the woman's hands away. "No time for that foolishness. He's seen worse."

Grunting, Rew dropped down into the carriage and handed Anne his packets of medicinal herbs, a few waterskins, and the spare clothing he'd pulled out to use as rags. He unstopped one of the liquor bottles Bressan had given him and drank two large gulps. Anne snatched it from him and began splashing it on her hands. Muttering to himself about how much she was using, Rew began arranging pillows beneath the sweating, screaming woman. Anne put her hands on the woman's stomach, and Rew frowned. The woman was screaming in pain.

"Anne? Are you going to—"

"I need to turn the baby," she said calmly.

"King's Sake."

The woman wailed, and Anne was quiet for another minute. Then, she declared, "No, I can't. I'm putting too much empathy into the baby, and I cannot stop. Rew, you've got to turn it."

Rew stared at her, aghast, unable to even formulate an appropriate curse.

"Wash your hands, Rew," instructed Anne. She raised an eyebrow at him. "You have touched a woman there before, correct? You know how this works?"

"I've touched a woman, aye," babbled Rew. "Not like this. I, ah... Anne, are you sure?"

"All of you men ought to do this at least once. The world would be a better place if you had some idea of what we women go through," declared Anne. "We wouldn't get asked such stupid questions, for one. Of course I am sure, Rew."

She began giving him instructions, and Rew's mind went blank.

———

THE NEXT MORNING, REW WAS STANDING OUTSIDE OF A TINY, ROAD-side way station. The way station had been back toward Spine-send, but the children hadn't managed to erect a shelter by the time the baby was born, and Anne had insisted. The empath had carried the baby, and Rew had carried the woman. Miraculously, both had survived, and Anne judged they were healthy.

That night, while stripping out of his ruined clothing before realizing many of his other garments had been sacrificed during the delivery, Rew had consumed the rest of the bottle of spirits they'd used as disinfectant and half of another. He'd wished for more, but he'd stopped at Anne's steady stare. His answering look had been anything but steady.

The mother, grateful at first for the successful birth of her child on the side of the road—within a tumped-over carriage, no less—had grown irritable and demanding several minutes after both she and infant were deposited in the simple way station. She was nobility, and it seemed she thought that meant they ought to act like her servants. For anyone who'd spent time with nobility, her attitude was not a great surprise. A minor family from Spinesend, barely landed, Raif had explained. Rew had lost interest once it became obvious the woman did not know or care who they were, so the ranger stopped paying attention to anything she said.

When he had woken the next day, Rew had hoped to send the woman on her way, but it'd been quickly apparent that wasn't going to work. Without the carriage, and the woman barely able to walk, they were days away from safety for the baby. While even Anne had started ignoring the noblewoman's shrill demands, the empath would not abandon the newborn.

None of them were heartless enough to argue with her, so they'd sent the noblewoman's footman off alone with the horse to secure transportation for his mistress while they waited with her in the way station. The structure wasn't more than three walls and a roof, with a small hole cut for smoke to escape, but there was plenty of water in a briskly running stream, and it was the only shelter nearby. The woman and her footman had the misfortune to wreck the carriage halfway between villages, and in the new mother's condition, it wasn't clear when she would be capable of making the walk.

As they settled in to wait, everyone except Anne and the noblewoman had drifted outside. The way station was too small a space to share with a woman who had such a high opinion of herself.

Once outside, Rew stretched and sipped his coffee, hoping the dark liquid would do its work to quell the pounding in his head. He was considering another cup—he could use it following the inundation of alcohol he'd subjected his body to the night before —but he didn't want to admit that to Anne, and he was growing concerned they would run out of the dry coffee beans. They'd packed lightly when departing Bressan's, knowing there were plenty of places on the highway to stop for provisions, but if they weren't moving, they weren't getting closer to any of those places. Rew was finding, given his condition, that the problem of the diminishing coffee beans was an easier thing to stew over than what else lay ahead of them.

Behind him, inside the shelter, he heard Anne's whispered instructions to the new mother, teaching the woman how to latch the child and feed it. Two dozen paces away, Raif and Zaine were working through their morning exercises, looking rather lethargic, but the ranger wasn't any peppier, and he couldn't find the energy to chide the children into more effort.

The baby was healthy, and it had the lungs of a lion. Even in his stupor the night before, Rew had not slept long and doubted that anyone else had either. The child was quiet now, biding its time, Rew was sure, for the next moment any of the adults tried to catch some sleep.

Cinda joined him, a mug cradled in her hands. She inhaled the steam rising from it and then covered a yawn with her hand. She asked him, "Back at Bressan's inn, I got to thinking I no longer needed sleep. It seems I was sorely mistaken. Maybe I don't need as many hours as I used to, but King's Sake, I need some. Are all babies like that?"

"Crying all night? Yes, I suppose they are. All the ones I've been around, at least."

"And you've been around a lot of babies in the middle of the night?"

He frowned at her.

Cinda grinned then sipped her coffee. She scowled. "Do you like the taste of this stuff? It's awfully bitter, isn't it?"

He nodded.

"At Worgon's keep, where I first drank coffee, we added sugar and milk. It made it quite good. We should have gotten sugar from Bressan before we left."

Rew didn't respond.

"You don't enjoy yours a little sweeter?" she pestered him. "It's more pleasant, and not even you can argue with that."

"There's bitter and sweet in life, lass," he told her. "You can't enjoy the sweet without the bitter. I take my coffee black in the morning so that the rest of the day is sweet."

Cinda snorted, shaking her head at him. "Still feeling the effects of that liquor from last night? I saw you trying to hide the empty bottle. Pfah, that's why we don't have any sugar, isn't it? You and the innkeeper got to be thick as thieves, and it seems it was only your luxuries that made their way into our packs."

"Black coffee is an acquired taste, and I've no doubt by the time this journey is over, you'll have acquired it," he advised her. "But for now, if you're not going to drink it, give me the rest of your cup. You ought to practice with the others. We seem to have made it out of Spinesend safely, but the world is full of danger, particularly for you."

Cinda shifted uncomfortably then responded, "I tried a bit earlier to draw power like Anne had taught me, but there wasn't much there. It was easy to draw enough for the funeral fire when we were staying at Bressan's, but here, it's like this place is... dead, I guess. That's not the right word."

Rew cackled, the sound like glass breaking on the quiet morning. "No, that's not the right word," he managed. "The opposite, in fact."

Looking around, Cinda's eyes widened. "There's nothing here, never has been, has there? No settlements, no one dying. That's why I didn't feel anything. No souls have departed here."

"There hasn't been much here at least since Spinesend was founded, which must have been a thousand years ago," remarked Rew. "In this place, there's never been more than souls simply passing through. It's not strategic, not easily defended, so I imagine whatever battles have happened in the past, did not happen near this way station."

"I can feel that," murmured Cinda, still looking up and down the road and at the stand of oak that surrounded the small station. "No one has died here in years, I think. With no one dying, there's nothing for me to grab a hold of. I have no power."

"Not much," acknowledged Rew. "Necromancers draw from the strength of departed souls, conjurers summon creatures from other planes of existence, enchanters imbue their strength into physical objects, and invokers tap their own power, utilizing arcane movements and phrases to amplify what is in their blood. Everyone has to pull from something."

"And rangers?"

"Rangers do their best to stay away from it all."

Cinda rolled her eyes. "What was that magic you cast which hid our flight from the battle between Duke Eeron and Baron Worgon's men? How did you hide us in the tower?"

Rew's lips twisted. He explained, "Low magic. Anyone can cast a bit of it if they really try, though some have more of an affinity. Most rangers can manage small illusions and extend our senses a bit. Works better in the wilderness where we can connect with the natural world. Anne's empathy is low magic as well, though what she does with it is rare."

"The fire you started on the thatch roof in Umdrac?" questioned Cinda. "Was that low magic?"

Rew coughed, nearly spilling his coffee, which would have been tragic.

"So you've a bit of high magic, then?" pressed the noblewoman. "How is that possible?"

Rew sipped his coffee, sighed, and explained, "Low magic is cast through connection. Anyone can do it, but it requires an openness to the world, which less charitable folk might say is why nobility rarely uses it. The strength of the caster of low magic grows as the connection grows. As a ranger, I've spent my time out in the wilderness communing with nature, practicing my craft. It means I can cast quite a bit more than I could when I first arrived in Eastwatch."

"And Anne practices healing," said Cinda.

"Aye, healing, but her empathy goes beyond that. We're here in this way station because of her and the connection she's forging with that new family. Same as when she ran her inn, it was about people, right? Every time she meets someone new, every time she strengthens a bond between herself and another person, through her empathy or just conversation, she increases what she's capable of. Not much, mind you, but thousands of tiny steps add up. And yes, her healing is the core of it. To get where she is now, she's had to come a long way. To heal your brother's wounds, she had to heal many, many more before him. There are few empaths who have experienced what Anne has."

"I understand," responded Cinda, frowning, "but high magic isn't like that at all, is it? It was high magic that started the fire on the roof?"

"No, high magic is not about the connection," agreed Rew, "and it was how I started that fire. High magic comes from your blood. It's similar, I suppose, in that your blood is the product of dozens of generations of men and women with talent coming together and mixing those traits until you're capable of far more than what your ancestors were capable of. I doubt your great grandfather could have banished those wraiths like that or called death's flame like you did. At least, not untrained, he couldn't."

"Interesting. So how did you—"

Rew waved away her coming question and kept talking, hoping she'd forget she meant to ask it. "Low magic, high magic, it all improves with practice. Low magic is like exercising your body, where high magic is like reading a book. Everyone knows instinctually how to move their arm, but a skilled woodworker achieves mastery after many years of practice. Not everyone knows the knowledge contained in books, though. That requires great minds sharing their learnings through the years, and it is in only rare cases that someone new can add to the corpus of general knowledge. That's why you're special, lass. You've the talent to bring something new," continued Rew. He nodded to where Raif and Zaine where working through their routine. "That should give you some idea of the difference, but it's not a perfect analogy. Just like soldiers strengthen their bodies, casters of high magic can do the same. They should do the same."

He peered at her over his cup of coffee.

"I don't see you out there training," complained Cinda.

"I'm supervising."

"I don't even know how to practice necromancy."

"There's been little death, but that doesn't mean there's been no death in this place," said Rew. "At some point through all of the years, I'm certain that someone has died here. And if not on this exact ground, then nearby on the road. It's safe, this close to

Spinesend, but nowhere is completely safe. If all nobles drive carriages like our lady with the baby and her footman, for example, then surely a few of them have perished on the highway."

Cinda grinned.

"Close your eyes, see what you can feel," suggested Rew, "and then feel for the echoes. Not just what's here in front of you like it was during the battle, but what has been here before. It's easy when you get the hang of it. Here, let me hold your coffee."

Chapter Three

While they were stuck at the way station waiting for the noblewoman's footman to return with transportation, Rew and the children spent as much time as they could outdoors. The ranger walked Raif and Zaine through complicated sparring exercises then wore them out with demanding fitness training. Cinda sat quietly, practicing drawing power from the world around her. At first, she could sense hardly anything, but by the next morning, she'd found something there, though it was not strong enough for her to cast any spells with it.

"You're moving back through time," said Rew, "through years and ages. Necromancers can pull echoes of power that way. In most cases, the farther back you go, the less you can pull from a death. What you're tapping into is the power released when the soul transitions, and that power dissipates over time. It is different from the wraiths. In their case, the necromancer is assuming control over power that is still on this plane, and that power has accumulated the longer the souls have been trapped here. Make sense? No, it will, eventually. For now, just know you'll be strongest around recent death, like the battle. The more people that die..."

Cinda, her face pale, did not respond.

Rew knew it made her uncomfortable. Necromancy, by blood and by choice, was not a common form of high magic. Between the necromancers Baron Fedgley had recruited for work in the barrowlands and the three they'd faced when Worgon was ambushed, Rew thought it might be all of the necromancers in the province. It was a shame, as Cinda could use instruction from someone who knew what they were talking about. Though, none of the necromancers they had encountered—except Fedgley himself—had been very talented. Even in the midst of hundreds of deaths, the power of the ones he and Cinda had killed had been paltry. Minor cousins of a minor noble, guessed Rew. In the right circumstances they could still be dangerous, though, which is why he suspected Duke Eeron utilized them for the ambush of Worgon. On a wave of hundreds of recent deaths all around them, even pathetic necromancers could manage significant feats.

That was the problem with necromancers. For them to obtain the power of a soul's transition, they had to engage in behaviors that were distasteful. No one wanted to be the noble who flocked to recent battlefields to harvest the power of the dead. Few wanted to locate one's keep over an ancient crypt or to stroll graveyards every evening looking for where fresh earth had been laid. And there was always the overhanging suspicion that the necromancers themselves were behind every odd death that occurred anywhere near them. They lived beneath a cloud of fear and distrust, because throughout history, plenty of necromancers had earned that fear. Not to mention, the totems of necromancy—bones, skulls, flesh-bound books, and other arcane paraphernalia—fit poorly with the stylish noblewoman's decor.

But it's what Cinda was. By blood and by talent, she was a necromancer. While most nobles with the affinity shunned that side of themselves, chose to focus on different magical skills, or to ignore high magic altogether, Cinda did not have a choice if she was going to survive.

She'd been marked by the princes and their minions, and living through the next months would require every bit of power she could pull together. Still, it made the other children nervous around her when she was practicing, and none of them wanted to mention it to the new mother inside of the way station.

When he wasn't observing Raif and Zaine flail at each other with linen-wrapped sticks, Rew spent hours talking Cinda through tapping into the thin power that surrounded them. He spoke to Cinda calmly, giving what little advice he could, serving more as a comforting presence than a helpful guide. With Raif and Zaine, he was stricter and frequently found himself barking instructions at them. The fighter took it easy on the thief, and she kept shooting glances at Cinda, who ignored them both. The unspoken, subtle tension and looks between the three made Rew grind his teeth and push them harder.

They needed it. The fighter and the thief had been practicing too much together and no longer felt the hammering excitement of combat. Rew knew he ought to spar with them himself, but he also knew that if Cinda did not gain control of her powers, then everything else they were doing was a complete waste of time.

Luckily, trapped in the small way station with nowhere to go for privacy, Rew did not have to worry about any other complications arising from all of the secretive, yearning looks. He hoped. Rubbing his face in his hands as the sun rose to mid-morning brilliance, Rew couldn't wait to get moving again, or if not moving, maybe he and Anne could swap. He sighed and discarded that thought. He'd rather be out with the children than in with the infant and its sharp-tongued mother, no matter how long they were stuck there.

It was with relief that at midday, Rew saw the footman coming down the road accompanied by a mounted soldier and a man with a cart and a donkey. It seemed the next town didn't have a proper carriage to spare, or perhaps the footman didn't have coin to hire it. They'd never learned why the woman was traveling alone so close to term, and she patently ignored any attempt to ask her. In Rew's experience, such things always came with a secret attached, and when it came to nobles, those secrets were rarely benign.

The soldier rode up first, looking over the party outside as if they were a bandit crew. Evidently deciding Rew was in charge, he raised his voice to speak to the ranger. "I'm told you are sheltering Lady Oswald?"

Rew nodded and hooked a thumb over his shoulder. The footman, not waiting for the soldier, had already directed the cart and its driver toward the way station.

"You came upon the lady by pure chance, I am told?" inquired the soldier.

Rew blinked up at the man. "Yes…"

The soldier grunted then glanced at where Raif was still sparring with Zaine. Beside the fighter, propped against a tree, was his huge greatsword. "Adventurers, are you? Mercenaries? Plenty of your kind on the road, these days."

"We're simple travelers," replied Rew.

"Coming from Spinesend?"

Rew nodded slowly.

"There are no simple travelers coming from Spinesend," said the soldier, his legs tightening reflexively on his horse, the beast shuffling closer to Rew.

Shaking his head, the ranger replied, "We left Spinesend over a week ago. We spent several days at Bressan's inn. Are you familiar with it? It must be quite popular in the region. We waited out the storms there until the roads were suitable for travel. If your lady came direct from Spinesend, she must have left days after us. She was in a carriage, after all, and we are on foot. What is it you're accusing us of?"

The soldier drew himself up, his leather armor creaking with the motion. "Nothing, nothing at all. One cannot be too cautious these days."

"What happened in Spinesend?" asked Cinda.

The man looked at her sharply but did not reply.

Behind them at the way station, Rew could hear Anne's voice

as she helped the Lady Oswald out and into the cart, which the Lady Oswald had plenty to say about. The soldier's lips tightened, but he did not comment.

Rew saw the soldier wore no livery, but his armor and his weapons showed wear. Rew questioned him, "You asked if we were mercenaries, yet I see no colors on your attire. Are you in service of the lady?"

"I'm no mercenary," spat the soldier.

Rew looked over his shoulder at where the noblewoman and the infant were being loaded into the cart. "Does the lady know you? We went to great effort to care for her these last two days, and I'm not willing to waste that work."

The soldier shifted in his saddle again then replied, "She does not know me. Look, I am sorry I approached you so brusquely, but you understand I'm right to be cautious about strangers on the road? I'm in the service of Lord Hamring, who has an interest in Lady Oswald and their—ah, her child. The lord felt it best to evacuate her from the city and arranged for it to happen. When she did not arrive as expected, he sent me to find her. You've heard the rumors of Dark Kind, no? They're not the only danger on this highway. These are grim times, and the lord was worried, so worried in fact, he asked me to remove his colors for this mission. Fortunately, I found her footman—who does know me, if you care to ask him—and he brought me here, where all seems well. Ask her man if you doubt my story. I encourage your caution."

Rew nodded, thinking that some gratitude was in order as well, but not believing he'd hear it. "I don't mean to doubt you, but as you say, it's a time for care. Tell me, why did Lord Hamring want the lady out of Spinesend? If it's a personal matter…"

The soldier fiddled awkwardly with the reins of his horse, and Rew scratched his beard. A baby the lord had an interest in… Of course it was a personal matter. He opened his mouth to apologize when the soldier spoke up. "The news will be all over the highway in days, if not already, so I suppose there's no harm. A week ago, there was a confrontation in Duke Eeron's keep. The stories are confused, but we believe that a high profile prisoner was broken out of Duke Eeron's dungeon and then assassinated the duke. Lord Hamring thinks that Spinesend is no longer safe for the nobility. I don't know if he's right or wrong, but the duke... I agreed it was best to move the lady and the child as quickly as possible."

Rew blinked. "Wait, the prisoner assassinated the duke?"

The soldier nodded. "The person in custody was broken out, and that very night, the duke was found dead in his throne room. He was seated on his chair as if he meant to hold court, but his head was sitting in his lap. There wasn't a drop of blood anywhere except for on the man himself. How does a man come to be holding his own head, and without a mess? Spellcasting, friend. The prisoner was a spellcaster, and they've had their revenge."

"Oh my," murmured Cinda.

The soldier nodded. "Indeed. Even stranger, the arcanists who ought to have been investigating the matter are dead as well. Killed in their beds, presumably so the spellcaster could cover his tracks. One got away, a man by the name of Salwart, or maybe he was taken captive, I don't know. If they can find him, perhaps he can tell what happened. If not, I don't think we'll ever know."

"What was Prince Valchon's response to the attack?" wondered Rew, unsurprised Arcanist Salwart was missing. The arcanist would have known his time was up, and he would have been out of the keep nearly as quickly as Rew if Duke Eeron hadn't immediately ordered the arcanist's arrest.

"Nothing yet," complained the soldier, shrugging. "At least, nothing that we've heard. Duke Eeron killed, obviously by high magic, though there are few in the territory who could challenge the duke's strength. Baron Fedgley gone missing after the Dark Kind assaulted Falvar. Baron Worgon rebelling against Duke Eeron and getting felled on the field of battle... You see why my lord wanted the Lady Oswald out of Spinesend, eh? Dangerous times, it is, and we're all waiting on Prince Valchon to come and sort it. Until he does... All I can offer is my sincere advice to watch your backs."

"We're ready," called the footman from where he'd settled his mistress into the cart.

The soldier offered a curt wave. The footman clambered awkwardly onto the back of his horse, and the cart driver flapped the reins, getting the donkey walking.

Rew's party gathered together and watched as Lady Oswald, her wailing baby, and the others rolled back to the road, headed away from Spinesend.

"Well," said Anne, rubbing her hands together as if to wash the presence of the noblewoman off of them. "Shall we get packed and moving again?"

"We should," said Rew, "but first there's something I've got to tell you."

FOR A WEEK, THEY HIKED SOUTH, FOLLOWING THE HIGHWAY TOWARD Carff. The terrain was easy. Gentle hills, isolated stands of trees, and small settlements speckled a day or two apart. In peaceful times, Duke Eeron would send the occasional patrol along with a magistrate, checking in with each community, settling any disputes the village councils could not, and rooting out bandits that sought to establish themselves along the road where village militias were unable to handle them. For locals, travelers, and the bandits that preyed on both, it wasn't so much the patrols that kept order but the threat of what would happen if they did not. No one, no matter what side of the law they were on, wanted to earn the duke's full attention.

Because it wasn't peaceful times, and there were no patrols keeping the bandits in check, there was a risk they would flourish. It was in the back of Rew's head as they walked, but he found it diffi-cult to focus on such an unknown risk. When he allowed himself to look ahead, he knew what waited for them in Carff, and that was enough to keep him tossing fitfully in his bedroll each night.

But when he kept himself in the present, it was impossible to ignore the lightness of the children's footsteps and their easy smiles. Their buoyant attitudes annoyed him, but after a few days, he had to admit he'd been annoyed by their frantic demands of justice for their father as well. After a few more days, he began to envy them. They seemed to dance across the highway because they weren't weighed by the same concerns that burdened him. They still believed their lot in life might be improving.

True, Zaine had nothing but the thieves' guild behind her, and by now, she knew she could never return to that life, at least not in the Eastern Territory. Raif and Cinda had lost both of their parents —their mother in front of them in Falvar and their father in front of them at the hands of their sister in Spinesend. Their lives had been upended, and they were traveling far from anything they'd ever known. They'd lost the security that a privileged childhood brought. That didn't mean the future was going to be better.

One evening, after they'd settled camp beneath a towering oak, fifty paces from a bubbling stream, Rew had taken one of the bottles Bressan had given him and sat down on the banks of the water. He pulled out a length of thread and a pin he'd stolen from Anne's pack. Rew dug up several worms and skewered one of them on the pin, bending the thin metal into a hook. He tossed the line into the stream, letting the thread drift along the surface of an eddying pool of water while the worm dangled beneath. He unstopped the bottle and sipped the fiery liquor inside.

Anne, after starting a pot of soup for their supper, came to join him. "Think you'll have enough luck I can throw something in with the stew? I've had my fill of the salted meats we brought."

Rew shrugged and pointed up at the sky. "I think it'll be an hour before they start to bite. Right at sunset."

"Then why are you fishing now?"

He smiled and did not respond.

Anne sat with him, enjoying his company.

After half an hour of silence, he told her, "I'm worried about the children."

"More so than usual?" she replied with a grin.

He glanced back where Raif and Cinda were encouraging Zaine as she fired arrows at a series of targets they'd set up. "They seem... happy."

Anne waited.

He looked at her.

"Is that it?" she asked.

"They've lost everything they ever knew. King's Sake, Raif and Cinda lost both of their parents in front of their eyes. How can they not feel sorrow at that? But look at them. They're laughing like they're flirting at a feast day."

"Rew, they are flirting."

"That's my point!"

Anne studied him for a time and then asked, "Rew, you haven't told me much of your upbringing, but did you cry when your father passed away?"

He shook his head. "He's not dead."

Anne frowned at him.

"It's different," said Rew before she could think that through. "I—My father was never really a father to me. Fedgley, though, you heard him at the end. He cared for his children. Or, their legacy, at least. That's something."

"He cared only for his legacy," corrected Anne flatly, "and if you recall, they both were rather upset when he died. But Rew, Baron Fedgley was no kind of father to those two. Not like what they deserved. He sent them away to Yarrow for three years, and they only returned to Falvar when they fled. Do you think Worgon showed the kind affection that any child craves? Cinda left Falvar when she was thirteen winters. Before that, she spent more time with Arcanist Ralcrist than Baron Fedgley. Think about this—Cinda would have barely flowered as a woman when she left for Yarrow. That's a difficult time for a girl, and her parents sent her away in the middle of it."

"I'd rather not think about that," muttered Rew.

"And Raif," continued Anne, "he was a little older when they were sent away, but it's obvious he still holds a childish fantasy of what his father was. It's because he barely spent a moment with the man. Rew, Baron Fedgley sired the children, but he did little else that earned him the title as their father."

Rew grunted and sipped his bottle of spirits.

"Before, the children were locked away, protected, and isolated," continued Anne. "They'd hardly seen anything outside of the walls of the keeps in Falvar and Yarrow, and even then only on chaperoned trips. They'd never sat down and spoken to real people or had a conversation that wasn't influenced by their titles. They never had a chance to do any flirting, because their pairings would have been arranged. And it wasn't any better for Zaine, who was under constant pressure to lay on her back for coin, rather than for love. Remember when you first met the Fedgleys? They seemed arrogant, didn't they? It's because they'd never met someone who outranked them! It's no kind of life that they've left behind. They have a reason to be happy, Rew, so let them enjoy it."

"Some people might disagree with that," complained Rew. "I think Zaine might argue that a bad father is better than no father at all, and a keep isn't the same as a prison, Anne. The ale is better, for one."

She snorted. "I'll have to take your word that the ale is no good in prisons."

"You're not worried then, about how they're reacting? I'll grant you Fedgley was not a good father, but they were safe. What we're facing now, Anne… It's like they've forgotten about it. Even Cinda. She's hardly sleeping, you know? She spends half the night questing, searching for the power of departed souls. Necromancy is grim work, Anne, but look at her right now. It's as if the shadows of her sleepless nights aren't even a memory during the day when she's with the others. She's jesting with Zaine and her brother like their tutors let them out early for the day, rather than like they're walking toward—toward what we're facing."

"They are young, and they're resilient, especially Cinda," said Anne. She waved a hand to encompass their campsite. "They may have lost family, but they've gained family as well. They march toward death and terror, but they do it with friends. I feel the bonds between the group more acutely than the rest of you, but we all know they are there. Even you, Rew. That strength we've found together means something important, and it is fulfilling them like they've never experienced. It's the grace of the Blessed Mother, and these days do not have to be all darkness and gloom. Let them enjoy what they can. It is our job to worry about what is ahead."

Rew didn't respond.

"Rew," said Anne after another minute, "I think a fish ate the worm off your hook."

He cursed, and she laughed.

Chapter Four

Three days later, Rew realized that he should, in fact, have been paying more attention and worrying about the threats ahead. Not just in Carff, but on the way there. A dozen bodies lay scattered on the road like the broken shards of a dropped glass. Rew circled the site and saw that some of them had attempted to run, others to fight, but they'd all died. Messily.

They'd been dressed in sensible travel attire, and while some of them had weapons near their bodies, others did not. Their gear was largely intact, though he saw sheaths where weapons were gone. Packs had been ripped open and the contents scattered, but little of it looked to be missing. The bodies, though, were torn apart and picked over like the carcass of a roast chicken after New Year. Flesh had been stripped away, bones broken, and worse. These people had been eaten. In the middle of the carnage, Rew spied the remains of a young family with children. He swallowed uncomfortably and glanced behind him, checking if the others had seen it.

They had. Cinda and Zaine stood next to each other, shoulders brushing, though they didn't seem to notice. Both girls were pale faced and breathing quickly. Raif had lifted a hand to clutch the hilt of the greatsword, but he didn't draw it. The threat was over.

"Narjags," said Rew, though certainly his companions had already guessed the same. Still, it had to be said. It had to be acknowledged. He cleared his throat. "Seems there was something to all of those rumors we've been hearing."

"Travelers much like us. Could have been us, if we weren't trying to keep to ourselves," remarked Anne. When the children looked at her, she added, "In the larger towns, groups form of those looking to embark on long journeys. Even in times of peace, it's safer to travel together. You can tell they're not merchants because they have no goods, and they're not wealthy because there are no professional guards among these remains. See? No one is wearing armor. At least they were killed quickly."

Anne met Rew's eyes, and he did not comment. It was better to think that these people had died fast, that some of them had not laid there, watching as their companions were disemboweled and consumed, watching while waiting their own turn. Narjags were not picky eaters. They would eat carrion as readily as a fresh kill, but in Rew's experience, they didn't wait to make that kill before feasting, either.

Raif looked as if he wanted to fight someone, but there was no one there except the dead. Zaine was carefully looking away, pretending she was scanning the land around them for some sign of the Dark Kind. Cinda wore an inscrutable look, her eyes heavily-lidded, and Rew had the uncomfortable feeling the budding necromancer was questing, feeling for the well of power that must have been released from the deaths of the travelers. She gave no outward sign she was mustering that power, but her cold stare was evidence enough. Anne glanced at Rew, a question in her eyes.

"They came from there," Rew said, pointing toward a thick stand of trees fifty paces off the road. "About two dozen of them, but I'd have to look closer to get a better count. The tracks are all muddled here where the fighting and—fighting happened. I could follow a bit and find where they rested. The signs should be obvious enough to know their numbers. Narjags don't go far on a full belly. Unfortunately, it appears they headed south, possibly moving parallel to the road."

Anne blanched.

"It's concerning they're headed in the same direction we are, but there's a good chance they'll avoid the highway," said Rew, looking around. "While they're not exactly bright creatures, they have sharp instincts, and even narjags should know that if they stay near the road or the site of the kill, they'll eventually be found. It's likely why we haven't seen any other signs yet. It appears they're on the move, and their hunger must have overwhelmed them. We're somewhat safe now that they've been sated, but obviously, we'll need to be cautious until we get out of the region. While I think they'll avoid the road, I can't be certain."

"We have to tell someone!" exclaimed Cinda.

"Who?"

"I, ah, w-who?" stammered Cinda.

Grimly, Rew shook his head. "We're far from the seat of power, but we're still within Duke Eeron's duchy. It's his men who ought to patrol this highway and keep the peace. I, for one, don't want to travel back to Spinesend, but if we did, recall what that soldier told us. I think whoever is trying to run the duchy has bigger concerns than a pack of narjags."

"But then the king must do something!" insisted Cinda. "Everywhere in Vaeldon is his land. If he doesn't act, then more people may die."

"The king is thousands of miles away in Mordenhold," mentioned Rew.

"Does he not send regular patrols?" demanded Raif. "In times of disruption, his men should be keeping the peace. Well, I suppose he's the one to blame for the disruption, but even more so that means his men should be on patrol when he knows the lords will have their hands full."

"Just a few months ago, what would you have felt about the king's black legion patrolling your family's lands? Lad, have you ever even seen the king's soldiers? The nobles don't want the king's men in their territory, and the king doesn't want to put them there. Vaisius Morden keeps his armies close and only releases them when he means to use them. I doubt there's more than a handful of his agents in the entire province. The nobility are responsible for their own domains, and when they fail in that task, the king does not support them—he replaces them. Believe me, the sort of peace the king's legions bring is not the kind of peace people want. I've seen the results of their work, and I'd rather the narjags."

"All of the people of Vaeldon are the king's people! Without the people, he has no kingdom. What about Prince Valchon? It is his province. Won't he do something?"

"He's in Carff," responded Rew. "That's a long way from here, lass."

"The king and the princes owe the people just as much as the people owe them. Someone should do something."

"The ranger is right, Cinda," said Raif. "Don't confuse what we want the world to be with what it is. If the king gave a fig for these people, he wouldn't have cast the Investiture to begin with."

"We have to do something," argued Cinda.

"We are," said Rew. "That's why we're on this journey. It's not our words the king needs to hear. It's our actions he needs to feel. You understand? What we want is not always what is, but that doesn't mean we have to accept what is. Changing the world is not an easy thing, but the first step is recognizing what needs to change. Come on. Let's get to the next town. Perhaps the villagers have formed a militia already. If not, at the very least, we can warn them of what is out here. We can't change the world in a day, but perhaps we can give the next village a chance."

The noblewoman looked at him, and he held her gaze. No one spoke. They began hiking again, walking wide of the awful death the narjags had wrought.

THE HIGHWAY GREW EMPTY, WHICH SENT A CHILL CRAWLING UP REW'S spine. If the attack on the other travelers had been an isolated incident, word should not yet have spread. The killings had been recent. He worried what the empty roads portended for their way ahead. Without doubt, the rumors of narjags had proven true, but those rumors had been widespread. Could there be more than one pack of the foul creatures roaming the empty lands between Spinesend and the villages to the south? It must have been fifty years since the area had seen a pack the size of the one that had attacked the travelers. What did it mean if there were more of them?

He walked on with grim thoughts clouding his mind, but overhead, the sun was shining and warm, so that was good.

"What is it?" asked Cinda, more nervous than ever since they'd stumbled across the remains of the other travelers. "Do you sense something?"

Rew shook his head and tried to soothe her nerves. "No. I think we're safe, for now. Attacks rarely happen on bright, sunny days. They always occur when it's dark and windy, probably cold. Could be raining. When it's a nice day, you know nothing terrible will happen."

"You've been reading too many spooky stories," called Zaine from behind them. "They just tell you that so when it starts to rain in the story, you know to get scared."

"Maybe," said Rew, scratching his beard. "Maybe."

But that day, the sun stayed bright, there were no attacks, and they saw no other signs of the Dark Kind. As they passed others on the road, they called out and told them what they'd seen. Other travelers only nodded, as if it was what they'd expected. The rumors of Dark Kind were thick on the road like midges in a wet summer, but they knew now it was not just a rumor. Narjags were out there, and as they progressed south, Rew accepted there were too many rumors from too far away for it to be just one pack of the Dark Kind.

But rumor was all that their fellows on the road shared. No

one reported kill sites to the south nor that the road was impassably dangerous. It was an ominous haze of nervous expectation, and as they moved farther, Rew found that people took his warning as just more rumor, despite his claims of what they'd seen.

One man, sitting atop a wagon piled with apples, demanded, "And did you see the narjags yourself, then? I've made my business trading on what I can see, not what some panicked tradesman told me he overheard from his drunk friend in the tavern. Unless you saw them yourself—"

Rew glared up at the man and interrupted him. "I saw the signs. I'm telling you, you're putting yourself at risk heading that way."

"Pfah!" barked the man. "That's what they'd say if I was going south, too, 'cept no one I've spoken to has actually seen a narjag—ever. There haven't been narjags in these parts for fifty years!"

"I've seen narjags!" bellowed Rew. "I'm trying to help you, man."

"Unless you're buying apples, you ain't got no help that I want, and if anything, mayhap I'm best off headed to where the narjags have been, not where they will be, eh? Didn't think of that, did you?"

The man snapped the reins he was holding, and the oxen pulling his wagon lumbered forward. Cursing to himself, Rew watched the wagon roll past.

Later that evening, as they were settling into a camp well off the road, Zaine asked, "Isn't that a good thing that no one else has seen signs of narjags? Could it be there is only the one pack of them?"

Rew, digging deep into the soft turf to make a pit to hide their fire, grunted. "We saw the aftermath, so we know they're out there, but where did they go? I'm certain they left southwest, toward Carff, but why not harass the travelers coming the other way? And if they're not harassing people south of here, why are there so many rumors? It's on every pair of lips that we pass, even those coming from the south. Remember that apple trader earlier today? People don't want to believe, but despite themselves, they do. I think it has to be because there are more of them out there."

Zaine frowned. "We've been hearing rumors since we left Yarrow."

"Aye, and you've been seeing narjags since then, too," retorted Rew. "Don't you recall that pitched battle in Falvar?"

"The ranger has more experience with these creatures than any of us. If he says there are more, then there are more," said Raif, scooting around the camp to sit beside Zaine, their knees almost touching. "If I had to guess, I'd say small groups of them are scattered all around. I suppose that's the way it always is in the wilderness, right? Something has driven them out into the open, and I think it must be intentional. Something to do with the Investiture, maybe?"

"That makes the most sense to me," said Rew, nodding at the fighter with a little bit of pride. "It worries me thinking what could be behind it, but the fact is, there are Dark Kind where there have been none in fifty years."

"So it may have nothing to do with us at all?" asked Zaine, raising a finger as if she'd caught them on a point.

"Probably not," agreed Rew. "I don't believe this is directed at us, but that doesn't mean we should not be concerned. If we come across a pack of narjags, it suddenly will have a lot to do with us. The Dark Kind should worry anyone who might stumble into their path."

"What do we do, then?" asked Raif.

Rew grimaced and admitted, "All we can do is to keep moving, but we do it carefully."

They took turns on watch that night, but at no point were more than half of them asleep. They tossed and turned and shifted restlessly. They could feel it, like a weight in the air, and toward morning, Rew realized what it was. Raif had been right. More right than he knew.

The Investiture was weighing heavily on this part of the

world. It was tugging at them and the fabric of the land around them. The king's attention had been drawn. By them, by Duke Eeron's death, by something Vyar Grund reported? Certainly Vaisius Morden would not care about a handful of Dark Kind. Lying in his bedroll, staring up at the moon and stars above, Rew offered a hope to the Blessed Mother that the king also did not care about them.

Eventually, he gave up on sleep and rose quietly two hours before dawn. He gestured for Zaine to go back to her bedroll, and the thief did so appreciatively. Alone in the silence, Rew brooded. Most of the time, identifying a source of anxiety helped him move past it, but not tonight. He knew better than anyone the king's personal attention was rarely a good thing. Whether it was them or something else occurring in the region, the king's attention was ominous.

The next day, they approached a small, nameless community that straddled the highway. A thicket of low houses was mixed with several modest inns, some other shops that looked to sell general goods, some pens where livestock were kept on the outskirts, and little else. It was the sort of place where weary travelers could pause for a few days to recover from a hard journey or to avoid bad weather. It was the kind of place that thrived on robust traffic coming down the road, and it looked empty.

Rew and the others paused five hundred yards from the settlement. They'd been avoiding such places since leaving Bressan's, either walking straight through or circling around them to avoid notice, but with the Dark Kind out there somewhere, they'd discussed stopping to learn what news they could and to make sure the villagers were alert. On the run, it was always a good idea to restock their provisions when the opportunity arose. Rew had figured that they were now far enough from Spinesend and any pursuers from there that the balance of risk and reward had tipped toward stopping, except something was wrong. The place was dead silent outside of the bleating of livestock off behind the buildings.

"This feels strange," said Zaine. "In the guild, they taught us to listen to our gut, and Ranger, my gut is screaming that we shouldn't go anywhere near that place."

"Dark Kind, you think?" questioned Raif.

"No, listen," replied Rew. "You hear the animals? They're still alive. If narjags had swept through, they would have killed the livestock just like the people."

"What, then?" wondered Raif. He frowned at the village. "There's no smoke coming up from the chimneys. A day like today, that many buildings… Half of them ought to have fires burning."

Rew stood still. Raif and Zaine were right. Something was terribly wrong in the village ahead, but it wasn't the Dark Kind. He was sure of that.

In the fading light of evening, as the sun sat and the horizon glowed pink and orange, they could see the air above the buildings was clear. Rew inhaled deeply, and he caught the faint scent of woodsmoke. There'd been fires earlier that day, but it must have been hours since anyone tended to them, and they'd all died out. There was no motion, but they could hear the animals, and there was no damage to the buildings. It didn't look like the work of narjags or bandits. Either one would have been interested in the livestock.

Rew scratched his beard. It was just the people who were missing. Tension hung in the air like fog. The king's attention was on this place. Rew was becoming sure of it. What did that mean for this village, and what should they do about it?

Cinda shifted from foot to foot, and asked, "Could they have… run off?"

Rew shrugged and did not respond. Of course it was possible everyone in the village could have all decided to pick up and run away without taking their animals with them, but he knew they hadn't.

"Should we go around?" wondered Raif.

"If someone is there and waiting," Rew told them, "they will have already seen us."

"Someone waiting for us?" asked Raif, confused.

Rew glanced at Cinda. "Do you feel anything?"

"Like recent deaths?"

He nodded.

Frowning, the noblewoman closed her eyes, and they waited. After a long moment, she shook her head. "I don't feel anything. It's like the way station. There doesn't seem to have been a death there in years."

Rew grunted, frowning at the buildings, drumming his fingers on the bone hilt of his hunting knife. No deaths in years? Not even by natural causes? That could not be the case, which meant that somehow, the power of those deaths had been leeched away. Rew shuddered.

"It will be dark in half an hour," remarked Anne. "If we're going to go around, we should start walking now, don't you think?"

"If we take time walking around the settlement, we won't get far before nightfall," mentioned Raif.

Rew stretched his hands then rattled his longsword to make sure it was loose in the sheath. He pushed back his cloak, making sure he could draw his hunting knife cleanly. Then, he bent to pat the throwing daggers tucked into his boots.

"Are you sure about this, Rew?" asked Anne.

"If someone is in there and waiting for us, they will have already seen us," he told her. "We could go around, but they'll know what we're doing, and then when we camp, we'll be up all night wondering if they'll come for us in the dark. If whatever happened here is related to us, and there's going to be a confrontation. We can't avoid it by going around. I think it best we select our time and we deal with this while we still have light. And if it has nothing to do with us, well, I'm still mighty curious about what is going on here and what it will mean for the rest of our journey."

No one objected, so he led them toward the abandoned village. As they got closer, it became even more obvious that whoever had been there was gone. Until they reached the outskirts, at least, and then it was clear that whoever had been there was dead. The scent of fresh blood filled the highway as it cut through the center of the village. Carrion birds flocked overhead, resting on the eaves of the buildings. They were drawn to the scent of death, but they couldn't reach the bodies. Those were inside, guessed Rew.

"You said you sensed nothing?" he asked Cinda. "No recent deaths, nothing at all?"

Pale-faced, she shook her head.

The necromancer might not have been able to feel the power of the departed souls, but they all knew there'd been death in the place. They'd seen too much of it, and too recently, to mistake the scent for anything else.

The ranger spun around slowly as they stepped in between the first buildings, looking for something, but there was nothing to see. The village was in good repair, but it was empty. It was clear from what his own nose detected and the presence of the carrion birds, that the dead were nearby. If it had been Dark Kind, people should have been left in the street, or the buildings would have been damaged when the creatures forced their way inside. The Dark Kind would have left signs of their presence, but there was nothing.

Even bandits wouldn't have bothered to close the doors behind them after they had ransacked the place. Rew slowed. Unless they were still there waiting in ambush. But if they were, he didn't think they would have taken so long to make their move. Were the perpetrators gone?

The victims were not. The birds smelled the dead. King's Sake. He and the others could smell the dead, but why did Cinda not sense the power from those souls? She was new to necromancy, but identifying the wells of power created by the departing souls was the one thing she'd been working assiduously on. Rew wouldn't have been surprised if she failed to cast the power she found, but could she have failed to recognize it?

Anne caught his gaze, and he could see she was thinking the same thing. There was one possibility he considered, but it was too awful to voice. Besides, it made no difference. If it was what he feared, it was too late to run, too late to do anything about it. They'd have to face it, so they may as well do it now.

As the shadows stretched across the highway, they began walking between the two dozen buildings to the other side of the village. None of them mentioned staying there or even peeking inside of the structures to see what they could find. It was taking all the courage they had just to walk through.

Halfway down the road, Rew glanced back behind him, feeling an itch growing on his spine. There was nothing there. When he turned toward the other side of the village, a dark silhouette stood barring the road. The party stopped walking. The figure was cloaked in shadow, but Rew could see the two polished wooden hilts of broad-bladed falchions sticking up above its shoulders.

"Vyar," hissed Rew, drawing his longsword.

Walking slowly, shambling, Vyar Grund strode from the shadow into the center of the road. The left side of his face gleamed white where his bone was exposed from the blow Rew had delivered back in Spinesend. His clothing was marred with dried blood, tears, and ragged cuts. His hands were covered by his gauntlets, and he'd pulled his half-mask back across his face, so only his dead eyes were visible above the scarred leather.

His dead eyes.

Rew gasped. He barked to the others, "Run!"

Shocked and confused, they did not.

Rew stepped forward, placing his body between Vyar Grund and the others.

In a voice like bones rattling in a tin pot, Vyar Grund croaked, "Do you fear me, Rew?"

"Of course I fear you," growled the ranger.

There was a soul-rending laugh as the ranger commandant chuckled. He stepped closer.

Rew held his ground, but his body trembled in fear. He called again to the others, "Run!"

Behind him, he heard Anne whispering to the children, grabbing them, trying to draw them away, but they didn't move.

"They're caught fully in the Investiture," rasped Vyar Grund, still walking closer. "They're not strong enough to resist its call. They cannot flee. Not from me."

Rew hissed.

"W-What is this?" stammered Anne.

"The empath," rasped Vyar Grund, pausing a dozen paces from Rew, looking past the ranger to Anne. "Yes, I remember you. You went to Eastwatch with Rew. You... you opened an inn. You've grown older since I last saw you. He has as well. That is good. You're more certain now, both of you. You know your purpose, finally."

Anne's breath caught.

Vyar Grund's cold eyes turned to study the rest of the party. "The youngest of Baron Fedgley's spawn. No self-assurance there. But who is that? She is not Fedgley's eldest, I would know. Who is she, Rew? She looks scared."

"She is no one," snapped the ranger, shifting his feet, preparing to... he wasn't sure. What could he do? "She's a thief from Yarrow. She traveled with the Fedgley children from there."

"There's something wrong with—" began Cinda.

"Quiet!" snapped Rew, taking a hand from his longsword to throw it up toward the girl. He did not know what was about to occur, but he knew it best if the attention stayed on him. He addressed the ranger commandant. "Have you been waiting for us?"

"Rew, I don't understand," said Anne, her voice quaking. "How... What is this?"

Vyar Grund waited motionlessly, so Rew explained, "Vyar Grund is dead, Anne. Meet King Vaisius Morden the Eighth."

Everyone was silent.

The king, masquerading as Grund, chuckled his hard, dead laugh. He advised them, "It is customary to genuflect before me."

Behind him, Rew heard the others drop to their knees, and he knew all four of them would be pressing their foreheads tight to the dirt of the highway.

"Why are you here? What do you want?" asked Rew. His heart was hammering, and sweat was pouring down his back. He forced his breath to slow and his grip to loosen on the hilt of his longsword. It did not pay to let Vaisius Morden see you nervous. It did not pay to give him reason to wonder why you trembled in his presence. Not that anyone was comfortable around the man or around his undead puppets, but he was like a hound when it came to smelling fear. He knew its flavors, and he would chase relentlessly any scent that he did not understand.

Grund, stone-still, replied, "Manners, Rew. Manners. You were never good at that, were you?"

Rew shook his head, his eyes still fixed on Vyar Grund's body, meeting the dead gaze, wondering what the king could see through Vyar's eyes, what he could sense through the corpse he had animated and taken control of. Rew wondered how much of Vyar was still there, if any was at all.

"Where is Alsayer?" asked the king suddenly, his sepulchral voice rasping out from behind Grund's leather half-mask. Grund wore the mask to hide the sight of his lips when he uttered his spells or communed with the natural beasts of the world. It was a mask crafted for the purpose of secrecy, and seeing it bar the commandant's dead face, hearing the king's utterance come from that dead throat…

Rew shuddered. Then, he answered, "I don't know."

"You suspect, don't you? Carff? Do you think he is in Carff? You must. Why else would you be walking this way?"

Rew did not respond.

"He took Baron Fedgley's girl," said the king. "I need her. She's—I need her. Kallie Fedgley, the eldest of the line. She must be located. Alsayer is plotting against me, Rew, and the girl is the key."

"Kallie… Alsayer is doing what?"

"Alsayer took the eldest daughter of Baron Fedgley," repeated the king. "I want her. I require the eldest of the Fedgleys."

The king rarely explained himself. He rarely suffered questions at all, in fact, but Rew had to ask. "Alsayer is plotting against you, and this girl is the key? How?"

"That is not for you to know, Rew," scratched a vulgar echo of Grund's voice. It was the king's words, shoved through Grund's dead biology. It was like listening to an animal in its death throes. "Even you know better than to question my reasons or to ignore my commands. It is time you drop this pretense as a ranger. I need your service. Fetch the girl, the elder daughter of Baron Fedgley. Take her alive or dead, I do not care. Bring me her body if you kill her. And then, I need Alsayer alive. I have questions for him."

"He's plotting against you with the girl?"

"You already asked that."

Rew worked his jaw. Not trusting himself to speak, he simply nodded.

"Better," croaked the animated corpse. It stepped closer to Rew, and he fought to control a shiver of fear. "Grund told me much before I killed him, but he did not tell me all."

"You, ah, you cannot learn what he knew, ah, now that he's dead?"

Slowly shaking its head, the corpse of Vyar Grund responded, "No. Alsayer has been careful. He corrupted Grund's mind. He has hidden pieces of the truth from me, but I have learned the spellcaster knows things he should not. I need him alive, and I will find out what else he knows."

Rew swallowed. "Of course. So… Grund was not working for Valchon? He was—"

The corpse cackled, and Rew staggered back a step. "After all of these years, Rew, you are interested in the Investiture? I could feel you fighting it. I thought you might be the one man who could resist. You were always the most stubborn of—ah, the empath. She was caught in the Investiture's snare, and you could not let her go alone. The ancient magic leads us down paths subtle and twisted, but it does lead us all."

Rew shrugged uncomfortably, wondering just how much the king knew about his departure from Eastwatch.

"Grund was working for Valchon, as you surmised. They had Fedgley harvesting wraiths for them. Grund had some of the spirits in his possession when he returned to Mordenhold, powerful spirits, old souls. No necromancer should command such creatures. Grund tried to hide them from me, the fool. The rangers are meant to avoid entanglement with my sons. He knew that, and he paid the price. I began sifting through his thoughts before I killed him, and I learned of the Fedgley girl. Her father had been captured and held in Spinesend. She killed the man and fled with Alsayer. Did you know?"

Rew glanced down at his hands and at the longsword he held. The king had been inside of Grund's thoughts. What had he learned there? If he'd learned anything, Rew quickly decided, then he'd learned enough. Getting caught in a lie by the king meant your death. Rew looked up and responded, "Yes."

The corpse's dead eyes twinkled with merriment, an eerie green glow, some reflection of what the king was feeling. "Grund saw it all. He saw you there as well. And them." The corpse glanced at Rew's companions. "Odd allies, Rew."

"They're loyal."

Grund's eyes, lifeless once again, held his gaze. The ranger's mind raced. The king had looted Grund's memories. Somehow from those thoughts, he'd decided that Kallie Fedgley was the one who'd inherited the baron's necromantic powers. The king was mistaken. He thought—Blessed Mother—Alsayer. Somehow, the spellcaster had planted the notion in Grund's mind, corrupted it as the king claimed. Somehow, that slippery, treacherous bastard had tricked the ranger commandant into believing Kallie Fedgley was the one who could cast necromancy. King Vaisius Morden believed the wrong girl was the threat to his rule!

Rew, very carefully, did not look back at Cinda.

He cleared his throat and asked, "You cannot locate Alsayer or the lass? I would have thought the current of your magic would be tied to the man…"

"Alsayer is more clever than you realize, Rew," responded the king in a rough voice, somewhere between Grund's and his own, "more clever than I realized. He has severed the ties of the Investiture to his soul and to the girl's. I cannot feel them. You know where he is, though, don't you?"

Slowly, Rew nodded. "I know where he went. I can't be sure he's still there."

"Carff?"

Rew nodded again and did not respond.

"Go there and bring them to me. The girl, dead or alive. Alsayer, alive," instructed the king. "Valchon is there, but do not get distracted, Rew. I need the girl. It is imperative you find her. With Grund dead, you are best suited for this role. This is my task for you. Do you understand?"

"Will you… Can you open a portal?" asked Rew. He frowned. "I do not know how it works with Vyar. Can you cast through him? If we can portal there, it will save us—"

"I shall not," replied the corpse. "Alsayer will be prepared for my magic, and he will scamper like a hare the moment he feels it. You must go alone, without the taint of high magic on you or your companions. Find the girl. Find Alsayer. Rew, they have slipped my gaze, but the ties of ancient magic are still upon your soul. Call to me when you have them. I will be waiting."

Rew, his body trembling, kept his eyes locked on the corpse.

"Careful on the road, Rew."

The ranger raised his eyebrow.

The corpse shuffled closer, just half a dozen steps away now. In its hideous, dry rasp, it told him, "My sons are moving their pieces. They are positioning their allies and the strength they can call. There are many dangers on the road you take, both the Dark Kind and men. You can manage it, Rew, but perhaps not while protecting the others. You will watch out for these men, won't you? Little more than bandits to one such as you. You have faced worse. I might have cleared the way for you, but this will be a good test, I think. Follow the trail these men leave you."

"A test of what?" demanded the ranger.

"A test of how serious you are," cracked the undead Vyar Grund, eyes suddenly blazing alight with shimmering green fire. The corpse lifted a hand and pointed a finger at Rew. "Will you run, like you always have before, or will you face who you are? I know you'll find Alsayer and the girl for me, but what then? What will you do then, Rew?"

Rew frowned. A test. Would he run, or would he fight? Had the king guessed his intentions with the princes? Rew's frowned deepened into a scowl. A test. It was a game the king played, and it wasn't the first time he'd played it with Rew. One either succeeded at the king's games, or one died. Those were the two outcomes when dancing to Vaisius Morden's maniacal tune. The last time Rew had been tested, though, he'd chosen a different path. He'd refused. He flipped the board, and he'd disappeared into the wilderness.

The corpse emitted a low chuckle. Without further word or action, Vyar Grund collapsed limply onto the road. No one spoke for a long time. Finally, Rew turned and saw the other four members of the party kneeling, their heads still bowed on the dirt. They were all shaking, too terrified to move.

"We should go," whispered Rew, stooping to collect the two enchanted falchions from the dead ranger commandant. He nudged the body over with his foot, but he saw the rest of Grund's valuables had been stripped away. Why had the falchions been left, what did it mean? "He is gone, but move quietly. Quickly."

Chapter Five

Rew, carrying Zaine's bow, stalked through the tall grass a thousand paces off the highway. Anne followed on his heels, lifting her skirts to her knees so the cotton didn't trail through the low vegetation. The rustle of her movement and her muttered curses almost assured Rew wouldn't find any game, but they'd skipped looking for provisions after the encounter with the undead Vyar Grund, so Rew judged it was worth the attempt to find fresh supplies, even if Anne seemed to be doing her best to sabotage it.

"I'll be back to the camp in an hour if you can wait to talk," said Rew.

"I want to talk away from the children."

Rew sighed.

"The king believes that Kallie Fedgley is the one with the necromantic powers," said Anne, scampering after him as he sped his pace. "Rew, the king is after the wrong girl!"

"I know," muttered the ranger.

"What does that mean?"

"It means, more than ever, we need to find Alsayer."

Anne kept after him, nearly jogging in her skirts, and he

conceded he wasn't going to lose her, so he stopped and turned to face her.

"Baron Fedgley and his wife are dead. Baron Worgon is dead. Duke Eeron is dead. Vyar Grund is dead. Mistress Clae is dead," stated Rew. "That means the list of people who know what Cinda is capable of is growing remarkably short. The princes must know or suspect, but as we've discussed, they won't tell their father. It's one of their plots against the man which started all of this, after all. There is Kallie herself, but she's with Alsayer. That bastard spellcaster is in the thick of it, and he could spill his guts to anyone, but I'm starting to suspect it goes deeper. He's not just a messenger boy for one of the princes. He has his own motivations for doing what he's doing. I just wish I knew what they were."

"So if we find Alsayer and Kallie, then we're safe," said Anne, a small grin curling her lips. "Relatively, I mean. It's still the Investiture, but the king shouldn't take any more interest in us, should he? He just wants your assistance finding them because you're a ranger, don't you think?"

"Perhaps," said Rew, frowning at Anne's smile. "I'll be the first to admit I cannot guess the mind of the king. If we can corner Alsayer and Kallie before the king gets his hands on them, we've got a chance... But before you get too confident, remember we don't have them yet, and there's also Prince Heindaw and Arcanist Salwart. We heard the arcanist was missing, and I haven't the faintest idea where he might have gone. He could be on his way to Mordenhold, for all we know."

Anne grimaced.

"It's worse," said Rew.

She frowned.

"Kallie Fedgley showed she has no love for her family. If she talks to the wrong person..."

Anne remained silent, and Rew nodded.

"As long as Kallie Fedgley lives, she's an incredible threat to Cinda," said Rew. "King's Sake, she killed her own father! If she realizes how much danger she's in and how easily she could flip it on her siblings, she will. You saw her eyes, Anne. She'd relish serving Cinda to the king."

"You're right," admitted the empath with a sigh. "She's a threat, at least until the end of the Investiture."

Rew shook his head.

"But when one of the princes attains the throne—"

"They'll be susceptible to the same plot that the king is now. If they're aware of what Cinda is capable of or if Kallie Fedgley survives to tell them, Cinda is still in danger."

"We can't fight the princes!"

"Not all at once," agreed Rew.

Anne reached out and gripped his shoulder, her eyes wide, her mouth open in a perfect oval. "You don't mean—"

"You and the children could still run. Heindaw has as much reason to keep this secret as us. As long as Kallie and Salwart don't talk where word will reach Vaisius Morden's ears, you should be safe. The princes, the king, they'll care nothing for you and the others as long as they don't know Cinda's secret. Together, you have the cunning and the strength to make nice lives for yourselves. It's what I thought they should have done from the beginning. It's what I tried to do myself, long ago."

Trembling, Anne did not respond.

"It's too late for me to hide from all of this," said Rew. "The king sending Vyar as his messenger was proof enough of that. You heard him. The ancient magic of the Investiture is tied to me. Vaisius Morden can find me whenever he wants. Regardless of that, I've run long enough, and it's time I faced my past. It's time I fought for the future."

"The children will never turn their backs on this."

Rew could only shrug.

Anne frowned at him.

"Raif and Zaine don't understand," said Rew. "They haven't guessed what lies ahead. They don't realize that Carff, Kallie, even Alsayer—none of it is the end of this road. Because they don't know, because they don't understand, there is still the chance they could walk away, even if Cinda does not. It's worth a try, Anne, if you really want to steer them to safety."

"But you cannot…" worried Anne. She raised an eyebrow. "And Cinda?"

Rew nodded. "She does not know all, but she is starting to realize how far this road will take us. She's starting to accept that she will have a role to play when we reach the end of it. Besides, while she is with you and the others, there will always be risk. As long as she is who she is, the Mordens will seek her."

"Then there is no choice," said Anne, steel in her voice. "I told you we're bound together. It doesn't matter if the king is looking for the wrong girl. It doesn't matter if he never finds her. It doesn't matter if he realizes his mistake. No matter what, we are bound together, and we will stay together, but we have to know what it means that the king is seeking Kallie! Why does he want her?"

"You've said we are together before," acknowledged Rew, "but, Anne, you should know… I'm not sure we can succeed. I will try, but the odds are we will fail. There is a reason I've run from this for so long. If I do fail, then Cinda and I are doomed. The rest of you do not have to face the same fate. As long as you do not know all, why the king wants Kallie, any of it, then you could walk away." He held up a hand to stall her protest. "We're together. We're family. I understand that, but it's the captain that goes down on a sinking ship, not the entire crew. There's no need for me to put you at more risk than you already are. I know it's frustrating, but trust me. It's for the best."

Anne shook her head. "Your fate is our fate, Rew. If the ship goes down, we all go down. That discussion is over. What matters now is what can we do? We may fail, true, but allow us to help so we've got the best odds we can get. How do we react to the king's personal involvement, and how can we leverage his instructions to you? There's got to be something we can do."

"We find Alsayer," responded the ranger. "That's what we can do."

THAT NIGHT, THEY DISCUSSED THE IMMEDIATE PATH FORWARD. CINDA, as Rew had known she would, simply nodded. She had no more interest in talking about the details than the ranger did. Raif was shaken by the appearance of the king's undead minion, but he remained steadfast about finding Kallie. Behind his back, Cinda's dark eyes met Rew's, but neither of them spoke to Raif about what would occur when they did find the Fedgley's eldest sister. They hadn't discussed it since that night in Bressan's inn, when Cinda had requested Rew be the one who put the blade home.

Zaine, the one who could abandon the quest most easily, simply shook her head and told them she had nowhere else to go. It wasn't the best reason to march straight into mortal peril, but none of them argued about it with her because it was true. The thief knew no one outside of the party except other thieves. Besides, another companion in the party, facing what they had to face, was a comfort.

And none of them pressed Rew for more details about what it was the princes expected Cinda to do and how he knew so much about it. Even Anne, after a long, searching look at Cinda, did not comment. The empath, it seemed, had decided to put her attention to the health and safety of the party and not where they were headed. Rew wondered if Anne and the others had finally reached the point they were not questioning his direction because they simply did not want to know. Some things were too big to know.

"So we're all in this together," said Anne. "How, ah, how are we going to get there? Carff is still hundreds of leagues away, isn't it?"

Rew, rubbing his chin where his beard was growing long and itchy, replied, "If it was just me, I'd keep walking. No offense, but I could cover three times as much ground each day as we can as a group. But we are traveling as a group, and you're right Anne, it's still a long way away. Walking is going to take us several more weeks, and now the king knows where we are and where we're going. Events are happening too quickly for us to dawdle on the highway."

"We should have bought some of those horses back at Bressan's," mentioned Zaine.

Rew ignored her. "A carriage is what we need."

"So we stop in the next town of sufficient size, and we hire one," suggested Anne.

Shrugging, Rew admitted, "I don't think we have coin for that."

"Oh," replied Anne, blinking as if the thought had never occurred to her they might run out of funds. "How much do we have…"

"Enough for provisions for a month or so, a few stays at inns along the way, and ale," said Rew, pulling his coin purse off his belt and bouncing it on his hand. "A carriage ride halfway across the Eastern Province is not cheap."

"We could steal a carriage," offered Zaine helpfully, earning a scowl from Anne.

"If we got jobs…" began Raif. He shook his head. "At common laborers' wages, it would take us the better part of a year to earn sufficient income to afford a carriage. Longer, I suppose, as we'll need to eat and a place to stay while we worked."

"The king's coffers?" asked Anne.

"We'd have to find a town with a large enough bank to recognize the king's account," said Rew. "There's Stanton, I suppose, but few other choices. It'd give us away, walking into a bank, but the king already knows where we are, so I suppose it's worth a try. It's unlikely the princes will have resources to closely monitor activity on the king's account at all of the banks with authority to draw from it. The problem is, we still have to get to Stanton."

They all frowned at him.

"How much are those blades worth?" wondered Zaine, pointing to the bundle where Rew had secured Vyar Grund's falchions. "Could we sell them?"

"They're worth a lot," said Rew, glancing at the enchanted blades that were wrapped tightly and bound to his pack. He'd taken them and nothing else from the body of his former commandant. He was regretting it. The weapons felt cold, tainted by Vyar Grund's betrayal, but the enchanted blades were too valuable, and too dangerous, to leave lying in the middle of the highway where anyone could find them. He wondered why the king had left the falchions on Grund. Had he wanted Rew to use them? The ranger wasn't planning on it. Rew hadn't been able to do more than draw the falchions for a brief inspection. Then, he'd wrapped them tightly and tied them to his pack where he didn't have to look at the things. The hurt of Vyar's betrayal was too soon to consider using the man's weapons.

"That sounds promising," responded Cinda cautiously, but seeing Rew's expression, she asked, "What am I missing?"

He offered her a quick smile. The girl was sharp. "The people who could afford to pay for weapons such as these will be in the cities, not the roadside towns. Even a well-off merchant, if we can find one, might balk at buying enchanted blades. Weapons like these are valuable, but carrying them and selling them entails risk. The people who could make use of the swords might simply take them rather than paying for them, for example. But even if we found someone we were willing to deal with, there's no one at these little villages who could pay a fraction of what the falchions are worth. Not that I'm set on holding out for the best deal, but I doubt there's anyone who could pay enough for a carriage ride to Carff. Not for a pair of swords."

"Well, this is frustrating," complained Raif.

Rew nodded.

"But you have an idea?" asked Cinda, peering at Rew.

"The king told us there were many dangers ahead," said Rew, "both Dark Kind and armed men. Remember his final words to me, his test? He warned us of these threats for a reason, and I assure you it wasn't for our safety. He left Grund's blades on the commandant but took items like the silver box Alsayer captured the wraiths in. There is reason in all that the king does, and I wonder if he meant us to encounter these men. Bandits, I suspect. He could have intended me to use the weapons on them. I may be wrong, but why else would the king place those clues in our hands? If they are bandits, then they may have sufficient coin to get us into a carriage."

"That's pretty thin, Rew," muttered Zaine.

Rew shrugged. "The way he said it, I don't believe the men would be affiliated with any of the princes or their bannermen, which means they must be bandits, right? And if the king didn't want us to find them, why would he mention them?"

"King's Sake, Rew," scoffed Anne. "Zaine is right, that is thin. Maybe the king warned us of the bandits so we could accomplish the task he set for you? But even if you are correct, you want us to… steal from criminals?"

Rew shrugged. "Who better to steal from?"

"No," said Anne. "The answer is no."

"Anne," he said, waving his hands at the empty landscape around them, "the alternative is to walk hundreds of leagues farther, or at least as far as Stanton, which isn't much closer. Or, perhaps you'd prefer as Zaine suggests, we steal a carriage? We could wait in hiding along the road and waylay whatever innocent traveler comes rolling by next."

The empath shook her head.

"We could sell the bandits the falchions, then," said Rew, knowing that she definitely wouldn't agree to that but hoping she'd meet him in the middle. "Bandits ought to have coin, and they can always use a sharp blade."

"Sell weapons to murderers!" snapped Anne. "You cannot be serious. I'd rather walk than make a bargain with bandits."

"Anne is right. We should not deal with bandits," declared Cinda, but then at the empath's surprised grin, she added, "but Rew is right, too. The king mentioned a test, and he mentioned these bandits. He wants us to locate them, though I can only guess what he wants us to do when we find them. The point is, if that is what the king wants, it is what we need to do. Right now, the king is fooled, thinking our sister is the one who threatens him. To keep him fooled, we should avoid his scrutiny, and to avoid that, we need to do what he asks."

Anne grunted, but she did not argue.

Cinda turned to Rew, and he nodded. "Well thought. Well said."

"So we find these bandits, and then we rob them," said Zaine, rubbing her hands together mischievously. "Thieving from the thieves. I like it."

THEY KNEW THE BANDITS WERE AHEAD OF THEM, BUT IN THE WIDE world, that was little help. They narrowed down the area, though, when they stumbled across the site of an attack which was obviously the work of men and not of the Dark Kind. Rew spotted signs on the road where a fight had occurred, and when they followed them, they found half a dozen armed men who must have been guards and a man and a woman who Rew took to be merchants. They'd suffered before they had died, the woman in particular. Grimly, Rew kept looking around, assessing the evidence. The bodies were lying two hundred paces off the side of the highway, tossed down behind a hill to hide them from view.

"So they are bandits," murmured Cinda.

Rew nodded. The bandits had made some effort to hide their work, but for the King's Ranger, there was little difficulty spotting where an attack had occurred on the highway, where the bodies had been dragged, and the trail the bandits had left when they'd fled with the wagons they'd stolen from the merchants.

Rew had circled the scene and determined that the incident had taken place two days earlier. Had Vaisius Morden known of this, and had he alerted them about it as part of the test? The ranger judged the encounter with Vyar Grund and the murder of these people had happened at almost the exact same time.

Scratching his beard, Rew had spent long moments studying the site, hoping for some clue as to why the king would want them to pay particular attention to this attack. He found nothing that spoke of anything other than opportunistic men with no moral code, who'd taken advantage of a lightly guarded merchant caravan.

They followed the trail the bandits had left after the attack across rolling hills, through thin copses of trees to where the wagons had been emptied of valuables and discarded. They kept following the signs from there, through more stands of trees, over hard packed earth, and half a league down a brisk stream. The bandits were skilled in woodcraft, but not as skilled as Rew.

He figured there were two dozen of them, all men from the depth of the impressions their boots left. While they had some skill at staying hidden—walking through the stream was a nifty trick—there were too many of them, and they were too burdened, to leave no trace. Rew followed them easily. He knew simply keeping on the trail of these men was not the test which the king had spoken of, and he worried about what lay ahead.

Rew suspected that the bandits were returning to their lair, and soon enough, his suspicions were confirmed. The party crested a short ridge of rock then quickly moved back. In the distance, they saw a looming, ancient stone fortress. The place looked as if it hadn't been occupied in ages, but after closer study, Rew saw fires glowing from within, and some of the roofs of the buildings showed signs of recent repair.

They moved around the terrain looking for a better vantage, and Rew identified several locations he thought lookouts might be stationed. The place was isolated and well protected. The men inside would not have taken such pains unless they meant it to be a long-term base, which meant they were serious about conducting their banditry. It was possible, even, that the leader of the bandits meant to establish himself as a local warlord and would attempt to rule the surrounding area. It wouldn't be the first time land had been seized rather than granted by the king.

With Duke Eeron dead, no one officially ruling Spinesend, and Prince Valchon evidently uninterested in restoring order, it was the perfect time for such a thing. The more he thought about it, the more Rew believed the bandits were more than simple thugs.

It left him wondering how much the king knew about them and why. Vaisius Morden ruled with an iron fist, but he respected strength in others as well. There had been occasions in the past when the king had allowed a man to carve his own piece from the kingdom's hide, though Rew doubted the bandits understood that once they'd established themselves and fought off any challenges from the local nobles, their real problems would begin. The king respected strength, and there was no one stronger than him. He left no question what consequences landholders would face if they did not show him proper deference and send in their tithes.

After enough of a look at the fortress to determine they weren't going to deal with the bandits that night, Rew led the others half a league away, in a different direction than they'd come, and found a small canyon back amongst some hills and within a thick, pine forest. Their tracks to the canyon were easy to obscure, and they did not light a fire when they settled down. Rew didn't like the idea of boxing themselves in, but the surrounding area didn't have many options for concealment, so they took what they had.

As soon as they all ate a cold meal, Rew set them a schedule for a watch. Then, he slipped away, going back toward the bandit fortress. At night, he would have an easier time approaching the place and scouting the defenses than he would during the day. There was only so much stealth even he could employ on a wide-open grass expanse in broad daylight.

The bandits, it seemed, had prepared to be followed. In three locations, Rew spied hidden stands where a lookout was stationed. He slunk close to one of them and observed the man inside. The man was dressed simply in leather armor and neutral clothing that looked to be consistent with the southwestern corner of Duke Eeron's duchy. He wasn't clean shaven, but his hair had been trimmed in recent weeks, and he'd bathed since then. He had a shortsword that looked to be cared for, and in his lap he cradled a crossbow that gleamed with fresh oil. A quarrel was set in the device, the tip shining in the moonlight. The man, contrary to everything Rew believed about bandits and their lookouts, was wide awake. The watcher moved little while Rew watched, but the man's open eyes reflected the low light from the night sky. He was a professional.

Rew estimated that it would be impossible for Raif or Cinda to approach the lookout unseen. If they were to come to the fortress, he would have to take out the watcher before they got there. Moving like a snake slithering through the grass, Rew passed by the lookout and approached the fortress.

Along the crumbled battlement, there were no lights, but Rew detected several shadows that could have been more guards, and from within, he saw the orange glow of a fire. It flickered intermittently, as if people were passing back in forth in front of it. There seemed to be a lot of activity for hours after sunset in an abandoned fortress in the middle of nowhere.

Rew reached the walls of the fortress and put a hand against them. The stone was weathered, ancient, placed there by some forgotten family centuries before. It was old enough he thought it could have been from before Vaeldon was officially formed by the rise of Vaisius Morden. Perhaps the family had fallen on hard times when the king's highway passed half a day west of their keep instead of skirting closer. Such places dotted the lonely parts of Vaeldon, forgotten monuments to an earlier age.

Rew trailed a hand along the stone as he circled the fortress. There were no traps laid, no obstacles in his way, but there was no obvious egress into the place, either. In spots where the walls had started to fall down, the bandits had made repairs. Even the sewer spout in the back of the wall had been covered by a steel grate, that, with a quick touch, Rew couldn't feel a speck of rust on. He kept going and found several locations with fresh mortar, and when he'd circled all of the way around and came to the gates, he saw they'd been built of new pine and bound with steel. It wasn't as sturdy as the gates of Spinesend or Falvar, but for an out-of-the-way fortress that few people would ever see, it was stout enough.

He'd been right. These men were bandits, yes, but they had more ambitious plans than that. Someone inside was intending to carve out their own chunk of the world during the chaos of the Investiture. That meant that there were likely far more of the bandits than the two dozen men they'd followed from the road. Several times that, Rew guessed, unless the men were more fool-hardy than their preparations implied.

He looked around and considered retreating back to the canyon to tell the others what he'd found, but so far, he hadn't found anything noteworthy. He sighed, circled the walls until he found a quiet-seeming place, and began to climb.

The walls of the fortress were only a dozen paces high. Too tall to jump up and grasp the battlement, but not tall enough to give him any trouble. He peered between the crenellations and saw a narrow walkway atop the battlement and simple empty towers at the four corners of the fortress. They were open to the inside, just wooden posts and roofs covering them, and they were occupied. Rew could clearly see a man in each of the towers to his sides. Both guards appeared to be looking out at the terrain around them instead of at the walkway, but it was difficult to tell in the dark, so Rew hung on the outside of the wall, his body pressed close to it.

Inside of the fortress were a dozen buildings, some small and dark, others larger. In the center was a great hall, and as he'd guessed, warm light spilled out of the doors and windows. It was clear there was a lot of activity going on inside. Storing takings from the highway or preparing another outing? Rew couldn't tell, but he could hear the murmur of voices from within and gathered that it was at least somewhat full. Fifty men?

He frowned. The activity in the building was not what he would have expected. It was late at night, hours past sunset. Why were so many people awake? It wasn't a raucous celebration. He could hear no singing or boisterous jests that accompanied the kind of festivities men like these enjoyed. If these were simple bandits or even a warlord staking territory through violence, what could they be doing in there if not enjoying the spoils from the merchants? Rew couldn't guess the purpose of the building from outside the walls, but one thing he decided, this was the king's test.

A handful of quietly spoken words caught his attention, and Rew glanced left. A second shape had joined the first in the tower, this one standing. In seconds, the second man started walking, coming along the walkway Rew was hanging beside.

Quietly, the ranger lowered himself and hung flat against the wall. Unless the guard on patrol looked straight down, he wouldn't see Rew, but the care of the bandits was disturbing. At least five men were on watch and patrolling the battlements. Several more outside the walls were stationed in outposts. It was a great deal of security for a fortress in the middle of nowhere. Not even a newly minted warlord needed to take such precautions. It wasn't their mere presence these men were guarding. It was whatever they were doing inside.

Rew listened to the soft tread of boots on stone as the guard passed him by. He pulled himself up again. At night, he couldn't see enough detail to figure out what was going on. He climbed higher, crouching in a crenellation of the battlement, waiting for a chance to slip inside of the fortress. Then, the door to the hall opened, and a dozen armed men walked out, illuminated by the light within and a scattering of burning brands they carried. Soft voices reached him, and Rew heard one man giving the others instructions. The men spread out and began to work. The lights of their torches revealed a large pen, like for livestock, that they'd built in the middle of the courtyard. It was twice as high as it needed to be for domestic animals, though, and the men were placing boards and hammering them around the edges. A second group came and inserted reinforcing struts.

An open air prison? But from what Rew could see, there was nothing inside. Bandits wouldn't take hostages unless it was a nobleman they could ransom, and there was room for an awful lot of nobles in that pen. Any other captives were an expense they would avoid. Even if they had overbuilt for livestock they intended to steal, why put the thing inside? Anyone who'd ever been around animals would fashion their paddock outside of the walls, keeping the smell and the noise away from where they were sleeping. Shaking his head, Rew realized that while he could clearly see what these men were doing, there were no clues as to why, and with so many of them working below, it was too great a risk to try and get closer.

He dropped soundlessly outside and carefully snuck back past the watchers in the outposts then into the pine forest and to the canyon the rest of the party was camped in. It was midnight, and as he approached, he smiled to see Raif pacing back and forth across the mouth of the canyon. The boy had removed his armor, and on the thick carpet of pine needles, he was moving about as silently as he ever had. He didn't have the casual alertness of the bandit watchers, but he was awake, and he was ready.

Rew ghosted toward him and called out softly when he was a dozen paces away.

Raif jumped in surprise, not having seen the ranger approach. He stepped closer and whispered, "Well?"

Chapter Six

In daylight the next morning, Rew diagramed out what he'd seen the night before around the fortress. He marked the outposts where he'd found watchers. He sketched in the buildings within the walls and explained the patrols he'd observed. He was careful to avoid mention of any sewers, as he'd learned where that would get him. The others watched him closely, and when he was finished, they all looked at him expectantly. Sitting on his haunches, he shifted.

"What's your plan?" asked Cinda.

Rew rubbed the top of his head, thinking it was time for a shave. He responded, "Seems every time I offer a plan, you all disagree with it."

"Spinesend was our mission," said Cinda. "We've said that we're going to find our sister, but… Now we're following you, Ranger. It's your path we walk, and only you know where it will take us."

Raif, his lips pressed tightly together, nodded. Zaine simply gestured to his diagram when he looked at her. Anne shrugged.

Sighing, Rew told them, "These are serious men, and they're not afraid of violence. If we walk into that fortress and attempt to barter Grund's falchions for coin, they're going to kill us. We could attempt to utilize Zaine's skillset and sneak in there and lift whatever coin we can find, but I wasn't able to identify a treasure room if they have one, and the place is well guarded. Even at night, there were dozens of men awake and alert. We'd be taking a big risk for an uncertain payout. In addition, I'm convinced there is more to these bandits than what I was able to see. This, whatever it is, is the king's test. He wanted us to come here, and my guess, he wanted us to either investigate or attack these men. That means it's more dangerous than we expected. It's worth considering walking away."

"If it's the king's test, can we afford to ignore it?" wondered Cinda.

"That's what I usually do," admitted Rew. "How do you think I ended up in Eastwatch?"

"So we'd just... leave them alone?" wondered Raif.

"That's the safest option," said Rew. "Somewhere between here and Carff there will be an easier way of getting coin. Or, worst case, we just keep walking until we get to Stanton. If the king is wondering what we'll do about these bandits, walking away is an answer. It's possible it may encourage him to leave us alone."

"Or to visit us again," challenged Zaine.

Rew shrugged. She was right, but long ago, he'd decided that guessing the mind of the king was a game far too difficult for him. Instead, he'd relied on his own instincts, and that had worked for him most of his life, more or less.

"This journey, to Carff and beyond, is about making the kingdom a better place, isn't it?" asked Cinda. "I mean, if that's not what we're about, we could head somewhere and hide until the Investiture is over, right?"

Rew nodded.

"It's a big goal," remarked Cinda, "and there's no certainty we'll succeed, is there?"

Rew nodded again, watching the young noblewoman, suspecting where she was going but letting her take them there on her own. She'd claimed it was his path they walked, and there was truth to that, but she was the one who'd need to do the work when they got to the end. Anne had been right. The children were not ready for what was to come. He and the empath didn't have time to train Cinda and the others, but they had to try. Cinda was the key to it all. For her, and them, to succeed, she had to learn how to take initiative, how to fight for what mattered. Rew watched her, and she smirked at him.

"There is evil in this kingdom—some of it in Mordenhold, some of it right here. I know what you'll say, Ranger, that if we get distracted helping every sod who needs it, we'll never find Alsayer, confront the princes, and solve the bigger problem. You're right, but that doesn't mean we overlook everything, does it?"

"Look, there is no practical way to get coin from that fortress without violence," said Raif. "We don't have any authority here in these lands. Unless you're suggesting we turn vigilante…"

"Maybe I am."

Her brother frowned at her.

"Keep in mind that Rew is the King's Ranger," said Cinda. "We're not on your territory, Ranger, but you are still the king's agent, right? He, ah… that thing seemed to believe so, at least. He wouldn't have mentioned the bandits if he wanted us to ignore them. You believe they are his test, don't you?"

Rew snorted. "Aye, I suppose I am still the King's Ranger. Somehow. And while I hate to guess the mind of Vaisius Morden, this is probably the test he mentioned."

"What would you do in these circumstances if it wasn't for us?" pressed Cinda.

Rew scratched his chin, honestly unsure. "Well, I'd alert the nobleman who's territory we were in—"

"But he's dead," interjected Cinda. "What would you do about these bandits if they were threatening Eastwatch?"

Rew laughed a cold laugh. "I'd kill them."

"I have no objection to that course of action," declared Cinda.

"We saw what these men did to those merchants and their guards. They're bad men, and they deserve whatever comes to them."

"They are murderers," agreed Raif, suddenly warming to the idea of a confrontation, "and Rew is an agent of the king, so his authority extends across all of Vaeldon, doesn't it, Ranger?"

Rew shifted, glancing at Anne out of the corner of his eye to see what she thought of where they were going. "It does, but killing a man is not to be done lightly, even when they deserve it. We should not talk ourselves into this simply so we can take the coin from these men. Not to mention, we're making a great leap to assume we'll be successful in the first place. There's more to these men than simple bandits."

"What more?" asked Raif.

Rew shrugged and did not respond. He did not know, but if it was the king's test, he knew it would not be easy or straightforward. While he couldn't put his finger on what exactly it was, there'd been something terribly wrong about the great hall the night before. It did not make sense the way the men were acting, if they were bandits or even thugs of a warlord. What possible reason could they have for constructing the pen in the courtyard?

"If we don't stop them, what will they do?" asked Zaine. "Attack more merchants, a town? How many will die before they're stopped?"

Not responding, Rew looked around the group, seeing the resolve on the children's faces. It wasn't their battle, but they were willing to make it so because they thought it the right thing to do. They weren't wrong, but Cinda hadn't been wrong either when she'd said each little distraction took them further from what they were meant to accomplish, and just because the king offered them a test did not mean they should actually do it. Rew had spent the last decade avoiding that man's tests, yet now it seemed the children were eager to take the king up on it. Was that the test itself, to see how far they were willing to go? Or was it a test to see how far he would push them? They weren't ready for this sort of thing, or for what was to come, but the children never would be if they never faced serious situations.

Anne cleared her throat. "We've a difficult road ahead of us. Terrible challenges, incredible danger. You've faced such circumstances before, Rew, but the rest of us have not. Not until we left Eastwatch with you, that is. Do you think we, as a group, are prepared for what is ahead of us? Not just our skill, but our willingness to do what is needed?"

Rew met Anne's look, and they held each other's gaze for a long time. Just like her, to guess what he'd been thinking and to voice it, to confront him with what he knew but chose to ignore.

The others stayed quiet, watching the ranger and the empath. Anne, a nurturer by nature and practice, never would have advocated for this, no matter the bandits' crimes, except for what it meant for the children. She was right, whether she was simply guessing at his own line of thinking or if she had decided the matter herself. The children weren't prepared for what was coming. Anne wanted them sharpened, hardened, and annealed in the fires of violence. He wondered how much she suspected they would need that bitter edge. He wondered how closely her intent mirrored that of the king and what she would think of it if the same thought occurred to her.

"It is a balance, Rew," she said, "and none of our choices are good ones. Do we spare these evil men and allow them to continue their ways? Do we ignore what is happening in this region to focus on a grander evil? I don't know the answers to that. None of us do. I don't know how we'll get to Carff in reasonable time if we keep on walking, either. The questions of these bandits, of what we are doing on this journey, are too big for us, too much to consider. I and the children will leave that to you. But we can focus on what we can manage. Those men in the fortress are killers. We know because we saw their handiwork. They will keep killing until someone stops them. Who else is there but us? It's the same logic as your grander plan, isn't it? It's the same reason we'd stand against the Dark Kind who murdered the other group."

Nodding slowly, Rew grunted then agreed. "Very well. There are between fifty and one hundred men in that fortress, and we have to assume they are all experienced with their weapons and are willing to kill. The five us cannot assault the place and hope to survive. Instead, we've got to take them out in small groups or one by one."

"Assassination," said Zaine.

"Tactical warfare," grumbled Rew. Shaking his head at the girl, he added, "The first thing we need to do is gather more intelligence. When do they leave, where do they go? How many can we catch alone, and are there chances to take out a few of them before the rest realize something is amiss?"

The others nodded and murmured assent.

Looking down at his crude scratchings in the dirt, Rew surmised, "They must have people who collect food and other goods for them. Unless they're completely foolish, they'll purchase that honestly from the villages around here. It's only travelers on the highway that they'll kill mercilessly. Staying here permanently, they'll need the locals to support them with industry. Their supply runs are what we'll target first."

———

THE BANDITS, IT SEEMED, WERE NEARLY AS CAUTIOUS GATHERING provisions as they were returning from a raid, but moving enough food to feed so many men left signs, and Rew was easily able to locate the tracks from that activity. They followed the path to a tiny farmhouse halfway to the highway. The decrepit state of its gardens was enough for Rew to know that no isolated farmer called the place his home, but someone was there. He could see smoke curling up from the chimney, and in a yard in front of the house, several men were unloading a cart and transferring goods into packs.

"They take the wagons to the markets then transfer the goods here," whispered Rew as they watched the activity from within a stand of elm trees. "That's smart. Anyone following the wagon will find this farm, and I'm certain they'll leave a person here who has a reasonable explanation for why they're purchasing so much food. Then, from the farmhouse, the men can haul the goods on foot, leaving less of a trace. With warning from their watcher and fewer signs to follow, it's an effective protection against any squadrons of soldiers locating the fortress."

"There's just three of them," said Zaine, touching the ash of her bow nervously.

"There will be more," said Rew. "Look at how much is left in the wagon. I'd guess there are half a dozen men around this farm somewhere."

"Too many?" wondered Anne.

Rew frowned then shook his head. "Not too many if we mean to do this, but I suggest we wait until that wagon leaves, and we take the driver first. One man will be almost no risk to us, and we can use any information we get from him."

"Torture?" asked Anne, her voice tight.

"We won't stoop to that," assured Rew. He paused and then added, "But if we take this man, we cannot hold him until the proper authorities arrive. It's possible whoever is doing the supply runs was not involved in the murders of those people we found. It's possible they're simply an employee of other men. It's unlikely, but they may not even know the nature of their employer. I will not cause pain to gain answers, but we cannot leave the man alive if we take him. Letting him go and continuing a quest against the fortress is not an option."

"I find it hard to believe anyone working for this operation doesn't know what's going on," growled Raif.

"Maybe, but we have to consider it," said Rew. "Before we move, we have to be willing to do what is necessary. If we capture someone, we're going to have to kill them or flee. You understand it will not be fair combat? It will be an execution."

"Let's capture them and see," suggested Cinda. "If it turns out the wagon driver has nothing to do with any of it... We'll decide then. If they know what they're involved in, then we've already committed to doing what is necessary to stop it."

"All right, then," said Rew. "I recommend we take the opportunity of them unloading the wagon and move around to the other side of the farmhouse. We can follow the tracks the wagon left and pick a suitable spot for an ambush."

When no one objected, he led them through the elms, skirting outside of visual distance of the farmhouse and then circling around it. They ran some risk of stumbling into a bandit between the farmhouse and the highway, but their greatest risk was being seen from the farmhouse itself.

An hour later, when they'd moved around to the other side, Rew easily picked up the ruts the wagon had left as it traversed the wild hills between the farmhouse and the highway. The party walked closer to the highway until they found a narrow stream that was spanned by several rough plank boards. New wood. The outlaws must have placed them there recently. They'd been working the region for a few months, surmised Rew, from the age of the bridge and the depth of the tracks to and from the highway. Along the bank of the stream was a thick tangle of bushes, and Rew looked at the others with an eyebrow raised. No one said anything. They were all taking his lead on this.

"All right," said Rew. "Whoever is driving that wagon, we don't want to kill them. Not yet, at least. We do want to stop them, though, and if they've a decent horse we can't let them get mounted and riding. I suggest we stop them at the bridge. They'll have nowhere to go from there, and we can surround them to prevent escape."

"Sounds like a good plan," acknowledged Raif.

Rew nodded at the big fighter, and they went to scout the bridge.

They were in luck. The bandits had felled more lumber than they needed, and a wide plank was sitting unused on the bank of the creek. With Raif's help, Rew brought it up and wedged it onto the end of the bridge. He placed it low where it would be nearly impossible to see from afar, but it was wide enough that the wagon wheels wouldn't be able to bump over it. Rew then arranged their party strategically around the bridge. He placed Zaine two hundred paces back toward the farmhouse, in hiding, but where she was visible from the bridge. He put Raif on the farmhouse side of the bank, in the undergrowth beside the stream, and told Anne to wait with the fighter. He took Cinda, and they crossed the bridge and found their own hiding spots there.

The idea was simple. The wagon would roll onto the bridge and find the way was blocked, and then they'd all jump out. If something went wrong, or there were more bandits than they could handle, Zaine would signal Raif and Anne, who could relay the message to Rew and Cinda, who would try to remove the plank to let the wagon pass without being seen. It was simple, but simple was good.

As they waited, a cool breeze cut through the branches of the thicket around them. Rew tugged his cloak tight and thought about why Anne was in favor of this mad plan. Was it truly the same logic the king might have had, testing how far they would go, how bloody they would stain their hands? Rew had to admit he questioned whether the children would do it, and he wondered if the king had the same concerns about Rew's commitment. It'd been a point of contention between the two of them in the past. Or maybe Anne was confident the children were willing but felt they needed an edge. The children did need seasoning if they were going to finish what they—he—wanted to accomplish. It was a necessary hardening, but it came at a high price.

It wasn't that Rew thought they couldn't do it. He thought it likely, in fact, that they could at least thin out the bandits and escape with no injuries to their party. He had no intention of letting the children put themselves at more risk than they could handle. And it wasn't that Rew thought the bandits didn't deserve it. The atrocity on the road they'd witnessed confirmed these men were due justice, but just because the men deserved it did not make it any easier to dispense that justice. The headsman bore a heavy burden, and once they acted, the children would carry that the rest of their lives. Even for the right cause, killing was a weight on all good men.

The children had killed before, but only when their own lives were on the line. Now, while it might be righteous justice, they would kill with pre-meditated intent. That affected a man, or a woman, no matter how much they believed in their cause. They would be changed from the encounters coming over the next several days in ways that Rew hated to hang on them because he knew how it felt. There was a darkness that came with choosing to end a life, and it never left you.

But Anne had agreed.

He glanced at Cinda. "Are you ready?"

She nodded. "You're doing all of the work, aren't you? I'm just planning to watch."

He smirked and did not respond. There was truth to that, for now.

He'd turned back to watch for the wagon when Cinda added, "Raif did not understand the import of what the king said, what that encounter meant for us. My brother thinks it clever that Morden is looking for Kallie and not us. It hasn't occurred to him, yet, that Vaisius Morden is personally interested in me. He hasn't connected that the king wants our sister because the king is scared of what I can do, what you are leading me to do. It's not just a frivolous flight you're leading us on, is it? Part of me hoped it was."

Rew grunted.

Whispering, Cinda continued, "It is all on me, isn't it?"

"Not all."

"But you cannot do it yourself. You do not have necromancy flowing through your blood as I. That is why ten years ago, you could not act, why you hid. That is why the princes need me, why you need me, and why the king fears me. It is on me because I am the one who has the potential. The only one. But I am not ready. That is why we must do this thing, why I must watch you and learn. Not about necromancy, but about death. If I am going to be worth the king's fear, I must know death."

Not looking at her, Rew responded, "I wish you did not have to carry this burden, lass, and I will do everything I can to ease it, but you're right. It's your talent that gives us a chance."

"Why do you not tell me what is expected? Do you think it will frighten me?"

Reaching over, Rew placed a hand on Cinda's shoulder. "Of course it will frighten you. It frightens me. I don't think you'd turn from this path, though, no matter what I told you. No, the secrets I keep are for your protection. We face an enemy who is far more powerful than us, lass, and I know it is difficult to under-stand, but for now, you will be better off not knowing. Trust me in this. In time, you will know, but not yet."

"I understand, I think. Seeing Grund used like that... I am finally beginning to understand the scope of what we attempt."

"Good."

"I'm still nervous, though. I am glad that you, and Anne, are with us."

Pulling her close against his side, Rew assured her, "You've been through a lot, and there is more to come, but whatever happens, we are by your side. Through storm and fire, blood and tears, we are by your side."

Cinda leaned against him, and they waited like that, his arm around her, both of their eyes fixed on the path in front of them. Half an hour later, Rew saw motion in the distance and then heard a man whistling tunelessly and clucking at the horse pulling his empty wagon. It bounced and rumbled across the uneven turf, and Rew saw no signals from Zaine or the others that there was more to worry about than the one man on the wagon.

He felt Cinda tense, and Rew understood why. The wagon driver was bare-headed with a shock of rough-shorn blond hair that bounced in time with the movement of the wagon. He wore a plain tunic and dark wool cloak. He had a kind face, round, rosy cheeks kissed by the cool wind, and would have looked at home in Falvar or anywhere else they had stopped on their journey. The wagon driver did not look like a bad man.

He appeared to be good man, in fact, a farmer driving a cart to market, except a real farmer would have been bringing in produce to the market and returning empty. This man in his empty wagon was on his way to buy provisions for a gang of murderous bandits. He looked like a simple tradesman, but he was not. At the very least, Rew decided, unless he was a particularly thick-headed man, the wagon driver had to know the people he was working for were not engaged in any honest enterprise.

Rew squeezed Cinda's shoulder, and the girl remained quiet, watching the wagon approach. The man driving it was paying little attention to his surroundings, evidently having already become familiar with his route. He kept driving until his lead wheels hit the crude bridge. When the wagon bounced onto the rough boards of the bridge, the driver stood and hauled on the reins. His horse slowed to a stop, the wagon two-thirds of the way across.

"King's Sake," growled the man. He raised his voice and called, "I know you're playing a trick on me. Is this about the dice game two nights back? Come out here, lads! If you've a problem with how I play, then face me like men about it."

No one moved, and the man cursed. He jumped off his wagon to remove the plank from the bridge.

Rew sprang out of hiding, took several quick steps, and was in front of the man before he could cry out or even think to run. Raising a fist, Rew made as if to punch the man, but the bandit simply staggered back, cowering.

"Move the board," said Rew to the others who'd all come out and were now converging around the wagon. To the man, he said, "Get in the back."

The man stood still, shocked. Then, he rose to his full height and declared, "You're making a terrible mistake, stranger."

"Why is that?" asked Rew.

The man paused a breath and then answered, "Because I don't have anything worth stealing. It's an empty wagon, friend."

"We'll see. Get in the back."

The man didn't move until Rew put a hand on his longsword. The bandit clambered slowly into the wagon bed. Rew joined him, while Anne took a seat on the wagon bench. The children moved the plank out of the way then clambered beside Rew, across from their captive in the back.

Anne wasn't an experienced wagon driver, but she knew the basics, and the horse was already familiar with the route it traveled. Anne shook the reins, and the beast started moving. They rumbled along for several minutes until Rew said, "Turn off here. Those trees up ahead."

Wordlessly, Anne steered them off the familiar path and toward the trees. In the back of the cart, everyone was silent.

"Get out," Rew told the man when Anne brought them to a stop.

"This is a terrible mistake, friend," warned the bandit.

"So you've said," remarked Rew. Casually, he leaned over and cuffed the man on the side of the head. Not to hurt him, just to get his attention. "Get out."

The man, eyeing Rew balefully, climbed out of the wagon and stepped away before turning around. Rew jumped down after him then whipped up a hand, blocking the man's wild swing as he ripped a long dagger from behind his back and swept it at the ranger. Rew gripped the man's arm and twisted it, yanking the limb behind the outlaw's back and forcing the bandit to his knees.

The bandit shrieked at the sudden pain, and his hand went limp. The dagger fell to the earth. Rew kicked it aside where Zaine picked it up. He roughly searched the man, finding no other weapons. To the others, Rew said, "Check the wagon. Look for hidden compartments beneath the boards. He'll have coin for the supplies somewhere, and I'm curious what else."

The man glared at him, peering back over his shoulder where Rew held his arm twisted in a painful lock.

"Who's in the fortress? Bandits or something else?"

The man's glare changed to a look of incredulity, and he laughed. "You think we're bandits?"

Rew blinked. "Are you not?"

Grinning malevolently, the man crowed, "I don't know who you are, but you'll die for this, and you don't even know why. King's Sake, man, is that why you ambushed me? You think to steal our coin? You're making the greatest mistake of your life, friend. If it wasn't me you surprised, I'd find it quite funny."

"Tell me why," instructed Rew.

The man shook his head, chuckling harshly.

"We saw your handiwork on the highway," said Rew, frowning slightly at how the man was reacting to his accusations. "You—or your companions—killed some merchants and their guards. You could have taken their merchandise and let them go, but you didn't. You took your time. You enjoyed it."

The man winked at Rew. "Wasn't me, but I heard about it. Raised a glass to toast the lads for that one. Being around—ah, the lads needed a way to release some tension, you know? It's been a long few months, and men like us hunger for action. I wish I could have been there."

"So you admit you are killers and thieves," snarled Cinda.

"Aye," said the man. "I'm a killer. I've been a thief. A whole lot worse than that, too, girl. You don't know what you've stumbled into, and you'd be best served to back away from it." The man paused. "If I was a bandit, what'd you plan to do about it? You mentioned the fortress. You seen it yet? You five think you're going to overrun the place? Pfah. Take my coin and be away. Truth, it is the best way this can end for all of us."

Cinda glanced at Rew, a question in her eyes. Rew turned to see where Raif and Anne were rooting through the wagon.

The empath told him, "Found his coin purse hidden beneath the bench. Decent amount of silver there. More than a farmer would carry. Plenty to buy food for a few days for a hundred men, if that's what he was up to. Found a sword too. It's seen use, Rew. Ah, sorry, I didn't mean to—"

"He's not going to live to tell anyone my name," said the ranger. He tightened his grip as the bandit tried to move.

"There's nothing else here," said Raif, crawling out from underneath the wagon and reaching into the back. He lifted an empty sack and shook it. "We saw what they were doing with this at the farmhouse, and I don't think there's any mystery to that, at least. As we guessed, this is a straightforward run for provisions."

Rew turned back to the bandit and saw there was no suppressed surprise or hidden glee. The man was what he appeared to be—a leg in the supply chain for those in the fortress —but what were those men up to if not banditry?

"Looking to make a name for yourselves?" guessed Rew. "Hoping that in all of the chaos, no one takes time to stamp you out? What'd they promise you—gold, women, land? That's not how it works. Only the boss'll end up with the spoils. If you're lucky, you'll have a handful of silver at best. Certainly no more than you're carrying in that coin purse right now. How about we make a deal? We let you keep that purse, and you tell us what we want to know. You run off and spend it, and we'll forget you were a part of this."

The man shook his head slowly. "You've no idea, do you? My bad luck, eh, to get taken by five adventurers looking to be heroes. Well, you'll all be dead in a day or two and me as well, no matter how this conversation ends."

Rew studied the man, and the man met his look stoically.

"They'll kill me if they learn I was captured," added the man. "They'll kill me if I were to run. King's Sake, they'll kill me no matter what I do. Chances are, they'll take their time, or feed me to the new arrivals. I've seen the way it goes, and I'd rather end it myself than go through that. You folks don't look like you've got it in you to make this messy, and I ain't talking because of a death threat, so make it quick, will you?"

Rew pursed his lips, looked around the group, and then nodded. The man understood his situation as well as they did. "Fair enough."

Rew's hand dropped to his waist, and before anyone in their party could react, he leaned forward, whipped out his hunting knife, and swept it across the bandit's neck. The man hardly reacted. He had no time. Blood fountained down his front. The light left his eyes, and he collapsed.

Chapter Seven

The next day, six distinct tongues of pale green flame danced across the hearth of the farmhouse. It was Cinda's signal. Six men were coming Rew's way. Outside, hidden behind the cart they'd taken from the dead bandit, Raif and Zaine would be seeing the same. Beside Rew, Anne's jaw tightened. She didn't bother to draw the knife at her belt, but she was crouched and ready to run out after Rew. He stood next to the door, watching the flame until all six fingers of spectral fire winked out.

Rew waited a breath then heard a startled scream from outside of the farmhouse. He burst out the door, his longsword in hand. Five men looked at him in surprise. A sixth was kneeling in the midst of them, frantically trying to reach behind his back to the feathered arrow embedded there.

"Nice day, isn't it?" asked Rew.

The five men gaped at him stupidly until another arrow thunked into one of their legs. The man staggered, screaming, and his companions scrambled to draw their weapons. Rew charged.

One of the men was felled before he even drew the shortsword at his belt, Rew's longsword plunging into the man's chest with enough force to burst out of his back. A second man ripped a dagger from the sheath at his side, but Rew released the hilt of his longsword, stepped toward the second man, and grabbed his wrist. He chopped at the joint of the bandit's elbow, forcing the man's own dagger back at him and stabbing it into his open mouth.

The bandit fell away, choking on his own steel, and Rew reached over to slide his longsword out of the body of his first victim, who had toppled down at his feet. The two remaining uninjured bandits faced Rew together, their faces panicked at the surprise attack, but they had time to recover and consider how to react.

Until Raif came pelting toward their backs, his enchanted greatsword raised above his head, a battle cry on his lips. The two men spun, one leaping away, the other staring like he was facing an avalanche. Raif swung, his giant sword cleaving into the startled bandit before the man even thought to raise his own blade in defense.

The second man who'd darted out of Raif's way was equally as surprised when Rew caught him, grabbed a fistful of hair, and jerked his head back. Rew rammed his longsword beside the man's spine. Spluttering weakly, the bandit died.

Zaine's first target flopped down face first, dead. Her second victim was limping away, the arrow sticking out from the back of his leg like a flag. Rew glanced at Raif, who was looking at the man he'd just chopped down. Seeing the boy was lost in shock for a moment, Rew hurried after the limping bandit, caught him quickly, and then killed him.

Cinda and Zaine were approaching from their hiding spots, and Anne was standing near the farmhouse, her arms crossed over her chest. Raif put a boot on the man he'd slain and yanked his greatsword free.

"Well done," said Rew.

He studied the faces of the children, assessing how they were holding up. For now, they were stunned and silent, but he knew the realization of what they'd done would catch up soon, and by then, it would be best if they were away, safely ensconced back in their hidden canyon.

"Raif, help me drag these men into the farmhouse. Anne, can you and the lasses look around and see if we missed anything?"

She raised an eyebrow at him and then nodded, evidently guessing he was trying to keep the girls busy so they didn't have time to consider what had happened.

Rew and Raif dragged the bodies into hiding, the women circled the building, and then Rew led them toward the canyon. He'd considered waiting to see if the bandits would send someone out to look when their supplies didn't arrive on time, but he worried that they might send more than the party could handle. He would avoid a pitched battle as long as he could. So instead, they crouched down in their canyon hideaway, and Rew watched as Anne checked on everyone. They'd received no physical hurts, but killing a man was no easy thing.

"It feels… strange," said Raif, working a cloth over the blade of his greatsword, cleaning away the bandit's blood.

"It felt good to me," murmured Zaine. She saw the others look at her and hastily added, "I've been around men like that much of my life—thieves, rapists, and killers. In the stories, sometimes, they are heroes, taking from the rich to feed their families. What I saw wasn't like that. In the guild, they cared only for themselves, and it was the most vicious and bloodthirsty of them that rose to leadership. They'd stab the rest of us in the guild as easily as they would a mark. Whoever these men were working for, whatever they are doing, they are killers, and they deserve what they got."

"Aye, but do we deserve to be the ones who dispense that justice?" asked Raif. He tossed down the bloody rag he was holding and said, "I killed that man before he even had the chance to see me coming. That wasn't combat, not a fight. It wasn't a legal execution, either. It was a murder. Back in Falvar, it'd be the baron who decreed guilt, set the punishment, and made it legal. Now that'd be me, I suppose, but we're not in Falvar, and I've no right to handle this sort of thing. It... it isn't comfortable, is it? Those men broke the law and committed murder, but so did we."

"Rew is the King's Ranger," retorted Zaine. "If you want to worry over the legalities, he's got the authority, sort of. We're acting as his, ah, deputies."

Raif shrugged, as if weighing her logic, but it was obvious he was still torn. He was a nobleman, a fighter, and he was trying to frame it in terms he was familiar with. Raif was trying to treat it as a solvable question of law, but what the boy was feeling was no question of law. Rew knew that. He'd felt the same, long ago. The boy had attacked a man from behind and killed him in cold blood. It was unfair. That was what was eating at the lad.

"Not all is black and white," said Rew. "There was much about these men that was evil, but most of them would not have been completely evil. There was justice in what we did, for those victims we found on the highway and for those that surely lie in the future, but it's always a question, isn't it? Who has the authority to dispense that justice? Under the king's law, I have the right, but should I? Should any of you? Good and fair questions, but not the ones that matter."

Raif frowned at him.

"Regardless of the king's law, the important question is whether we've the moral authority to do what we just did," said Rew quietly. "It's not just these thieves, you see, but about what we mean to do in Carff and beyond. Because I'll tell you right now, there's no law we can cite to cover what is going to happen. We're not just breaking the law. My intention is to break the institutions behind the law. It's not about what some nobleman scribbled down on a decree a hundred years ago. It is about what we are or are not willing to do in pursuit of what we think is right. What you're struggling with, Raif, is whether you can sleep at night knowing you're doing wrong for the greater good. How far will you go, and can you live with it afterward? Are you willing to do what is necessary for us to finish this?"

The nobleman snorted and picked his rag back up, looking at

the blood which soaked it through. "I've a glimmer of what you're attempting, Ranger. How many, do you think, will die during the Investiture? Either by the hands of the princes and their minions or because of the disruption this chaotic competition causes?"

"Many," responded Rew. "Thousands already have. Could be hundreds of thousands by the time it's all over. Maybe more. To be honest, I have no idea."

"I suppose that's the answer, then," mumbled Raif. "Hundreds of thousands? Doesn't matter if I like this or not. Doesn't matter how I sleep. The cost to us is irrelevant. We can't allow the Investiture to happen. I don't know what your plan is… but I hope it's a good one."

Rew smirked at him. The power of youth to adapt to change. Raif's moral code was far from malleable, but the fighter preferred things simple. That there was a justification was enough for him, no matter the questions it raised.

"Raif is right. The blood we shed will stain our hands," murmured Cinda. "There will be a dark cloud over our souls when we finish, but we have to, don't we? These men killed innocents on the highway, and we all heard the wagon driver. He reveled in it, and it's just a matter of time before they kill again. The princes will do far worse. We can twist words to convince ourselves it is all right, that we're doing good, stopping men who would do bad, but Raif is correct. None of that really matters. Hundreds of thousands may die. We've got to try and stop that, but we'd be just like these bandits if we enjoyed it."

"Wise words," acknowledged Rew. "That we feel guilt is proof of our humanity, but it is still something we must wrestle with. It's something that, I have found, it helps to talk about."

Anne snorted at that, but he ignored her.

Cinda looked down at her hands, slowly fiddling with her fingers. Without looking up to meet his gaze, she whispered, "I will do what is necessary. I do not know what that is yet, but I will do it. The darkness we bring on ourselves, the sacrifices we make, will be worth it. We can bear the burden for those we can save."

Rew grunted and did not respond. Sacrifices. She was closer to the truth than she knew.

"Bad people doing bad things," said Zaine. "It will always be that way, no matter what we do, but we can stop some of it, so we should. I didn't much like putting an arrow into that man's back, but I'd do it again tomorrow if it meant one less party of travelers has to die. The dead we found were someone's parents, husbands, and wives. The families of those merchants will never even know what happened. That's why I'd do it again, and why I'll keep doing it until they stop us. I know we can't get them all, but we can try. The old life, the old Zaine, is gone. This is who I am now, who we are, I think."

Rew offered her a tight smile.

"When we fled for Falvar, even when we left there for Spine-send, we did so because of the crimes committed against our family," said Cinda. "It's bigger than that. I see that now. Our life, what it once was, is already dead. We can't go back to that world, but maybe we can prevent that from happening to someone else. Maybe we can stop that from happening to a lot of families. That's what we're about, isn't it, Ranger? You want to stop the Investiture, once and for all. What happened to us, to our parents, won't have to happen again."

"I don't know if we can succeed, but it's worth trying," murmured Rew.

"I might've been the last one to see it," said Raif, twisting his huge greatsword in his hands, watching the freshly scrubbed steel gleam in the light, "but I see it now as well. There is no normal for us, is there? There's no return to Falvar to take the throne upon which our parents sat. I'm the baron, technically, but I'm not really, am I? I'll never rule Falvar. Not while any of the princes or the king still live. Cinda is right, our old life is dead."

No one responded to him.

"What we were has died. We just didn't know it until today," stated Raif, his voice rising, his eyes burning. "What we will be remains to be seen, but I think I can speak for all of us, Ranger, in that we've had our eyes opened, and we do not like what is there. I didn't like how today felt, none of us did, but it was the right thing. I don't know if that was the test the king was referring to, but it was a test, wasn't it? A test of whether we've the mettle for this, and I think we do."

Anne was busy sorting their food, preparing a meal, and Rew saw her head bobbing, as if she was nodding to herself. The empath forged connections. She cared for humanity. She knew that sometimes before something could be properly healed, it had to be broken.

Rew stood, stretched his back, and smiled at the three children. "We've a hard road ahead of us. Choosing to take this path is difficult. Staying on the path will be difficult as well, but I think you're all correct. It's the right thing to do. As long as killing doesn't feel right, but we are compelled to do it, we're headed the right direction."

"I'm glad that's settled, then," said Anne, chiming in with false brightness. "Let's eat."

The mood of the group was subdued, and Rew ate quickly. When they were finished, full dark had fallen, and the forest around them was pitch black. He stood, brushing his hands off on his trousers. He told them, "I'm going out for a bit."

"I'll go with you," said Zaine quickly, reaching for her bow.

Rew shook his head. "Not tonight."

"It ought to be a joint effort, Ranger," said Raif. "We proved ourselves earlier today, didn't we?"

"You did well," acknowledged Rew, "and you'll have a chance to prove yourselves again in the coming days. We're in this together, but tonight is my time to go alone."

The children made as if to protest, but Anne held up a hand to stall them. "You did what you needed to do today. Let Rew do what he needs to do tonight."

The ranger put a hand on her shoulder appreciatively and said, "Set a watch while I'm gone, will you?"

Then, he vanished into the night.

He'd seen three watchmens' outposts the night before, but he was more careful this time to scout the perimeter of the fortress, and he found two more. Each outpost was manned by one man who was alert but not so alert that Rew figured they'd found the dead bodies in the farmhouse yet. With the wagon traveling at least a day round trip and then transferring the goods, it fit they might leave one day and return the next. Sometime the next morning, though, the bandits would grow suspicious about their missing men and provisions.

That gave Rew one night to work.

He started with the watcher farthest from their encampment in the canyon, hoping the outlaws took that as a sign of which direction he was coming from in case they discovered the results of his work before he finished. Like a shadow ghosting across the landscape, Rew moved silently and approached the first of his targets.

The man was sitting on a stump, hidden behind a screen of bushes. He was facing outward, so Rew snuck up behind him, in between the man and the sparse light from the fortress. The ranger was careful to keep himself out of that low light, so that there was no chance the watcher would spy his shadow. The watcher was alert, but Rew was the King's Ranger.

He stepped on quiet feet a pace behind the man then lashed out with his hunting knife, burying the steel through the bandit's neck, piercing his throat and vocal chords, killing him silently. Rew removed his blade, wiped it clean, and then leaned the man against one of the sturdier bushes so that, from a distance, it would appear he'd fallen asleep. Rew moved to the next one.

This man was standing, shifting his feet, evidently struggling to stay awake on the cold, quiet night. Rew flicked a throwing knife at the man's dark form and smiled grimly as it thunked into his eye socket. The outlaw fell backward, landing with a soft thump on the lush grass.

Two more men fell to Rew's hunting knife, and each one was placed carefully on the off chance there were other wanderers in the night. Each of the watchers had a sword of some kind and a well-oiled crossbow. Rew took the crossbow from the last man he killed and aimed it at the fifth when he approached him. That man was sitting in the crook of a tree branch a few paces above the ground. Like the others, he was looking outward, and he had his crossbow in his lap.

Rew lowered his own weapon and glanced back at the fortress five hundred paces behind them. He stalked closer to the watcher, and in a flash, leapt up and gripped the back of the man's tunic. Rew yanked and spun, hauling the man down off his perch, spinning and flinging him against the ground. The man gave a startled squeak. There was a loud crack when his head impacted the dirt, bending his neck and snapping it.

Picking up the man's fallen crossbow and standing, one weapon resting on each of his shoulders, Rew waited to make sure no one had heard the commotion. When all remained quiet, he started toward the fortress.

He crouched down, twenty paces from the wall, and watched. No one seemed to have noticed the violence which had taken place at the outposts, and the schedule of the watchers on the wall was the same as he'd observed before. There were four men posted at the corners of the fortress, and there was one man walking a slow patrol between those towers. The sounds of activity on the inside traveled on the cold night air, but it was subdued. Men finishing their supper and preparing for bed, he guessed. Whatever they'd been constructing in their courtyard, it seemed they were finished or had paused work for the night.

There was no way to know how many men could be inside— enough that he couldn't fight them all—but he could continue to thin them out a little more. Shortly, they would find the results of what he'd done in the outposts, and after that, they would discover the bodies at the farmhouse. Within hours, no matter what he did, the chance of stealth would be gone.

Rew cradled one of the crossbows patiently. The guard on patrol made his way back around to the tower closest to Rew. The guard paused there, sharing a quick jest with the man stationed in the tower. Their bodies were dark silhouettes, illuminated only by the glow coming from within the fortress.

Raising the crossbow, Rew sighted at one of the men and pulled the trigger. The weapon thumped, and the quarrel flew up to the tower, taking the bandit in the chest. He stumbled back out of sight.

The second guard stepped to the battlement, peering out into the darkness and calling out loudly, as if checking on his fallen brethren without understanding what had just happened. Chuckling to himself, Rew dropped the first crossbow and picked up the second. He sighted again at the dark shape staring out futilely into the black and pulled the trigger again. This time, his aim was off, and the bolt flew low, skipping against the top of the battlement and flying up into the guard's groin. The man let out a high-pitched, keening wail, and his hands grasped his wounded manhood.

Rew blinked in surprise. Sounds of alarm were rising from within the fortress, but Rew's eyes were fixed on the wounded guard. The man was stone still, his hands clasping his crotch and the quarrel that protruded from there. Tight, pained sounds were coming from him, but he didn't seem to be able to form words. Shaking his head and whispering a half-hearted apology to the man, Rew threw down the second crossbow and retreated into the night.

Fourteen of the outlaws were dead or incapacitated. He wondered how many were left.

Chapter Eight

They got some indication the next morning.

Rew had returned to their canyon, checking to ensure it was hidden from any nighttime patrols that came out following his attack, and had then gotten a brief rest. By dawn, he was up again and had taken the party with him to observe the reaction at the fortress.

Their strategy was predicated around the outlaws not hunkering down inside of the walls. They needed some of the men to come out to investigate, but not too many of them. With just five in their party, there was no way Rew and the others could assault the fortress. Even without the advantage of the walls the outlaws would have, there were simply too many of the bandits, and unlike a commander during normal warfare, Rew couldn't risk losing a single member of his party. They'd agreed, if it came to an outright fight, they would flee. The danger of taking on too many of the bandits at once was too high to be considered.

That didn't mean they were in no danger, of course. As they watched through the gentle mist that rose off the grass in front of the fortress, they saw two dozen men atop the walls. They all clutched bows or crossbows, and every one of them was highly alert.

"Well, that was to be expected," murmured Rew to the others. He handed Zaine his brass spyglass. "You've the best eyes. What else can you see?"

Hiding behind a tree, she leaned out, peering through the spyglass at the fortress and the land around it. "Not much. I'm trying to count, but they're moving. Twenty-five, thirty of them on the walls, all heavily armed, though they don't seem to have much armor. I can't see anything inside, and I can't see any—ah, I think I see one you killed last night. There, behind the bushes?"

Rew saw where she was looking. "Good eye."

"What do we do if they don't come out?" wondered Cinda.

"Every few days, that wagon was going back and forth for provisions, which means they don't have a stockpile of food in there," surmised Rew. "They can't last long without fresh supplies. The question is, do we wait a few days, picking off those we can, or do we move on? The coin we took from the wagon may be enough to get us a ride on a carriage, assuming we can find one. It'd get us to Stanton at least, and from there, we might be able to access the king's account at a bank."

"We've started this, and we ought to finish it," declared Raif.

Cinda absentmindedly summoned and released her necromantic fire, the white-green flames reflecting in her eyes. Or were her eyes changing? Rew frowned. Her gaze stayed locked on the fortress in the distance. "My brother is right. I don't want to leave them here, angry and prepared to take it out on locals or travelers on the road, but on the other hand, we can't wait forever. How long do you think they'll hold before they have to come out? We meant to kick the hornets' nest, but could it have been too much? Not knowing who we are, we could have scared them into a panic. You have to admit, killing the guards on their walls last night was bold. Maybe it was too much, and they're hunkered down now?"

"I think they'll venture out today," guessed Rew, scratching his beard. "The leader of an outlaw crew cannot appear weak or timid, so they'll have to come looking for us. How would it look to the men that we've killed fourteen of them and they've got guard duty tonight with us still out here? I guess half the force will come out during daylight to scout the surrounding terrain, while the other half remains inside and on watch. That's too many of them for us to assault, but we can keep a close eye and hope an opportunity presents itself. If they split up further while they're searching for us..."

"We're not going to finish them unless we take some risk," remarked Raif. "I'm not saying we try to assault that fortress, but we've got to find a way to take on anyone coming outside."

"Surviving this is more important than winning the fight," chided Anne. Meeting Rew's look, she added, "We've proven what we meant to prove, and we've gathered enough coin to speed our journey. This was just a test, remember? We've more important work to be doing."

"It's all guesswork until we see how these bandits react," said Rew. He looked around then pointed to another clump of vegetation several hundred paces to the side of them. "Let's reposition there. From that vantage, I think we'll be able to see inside the fortress when they open the gates. It's not a perfect view, but if we spread out a little and have different angles, we should see most of the area between the gate and the main building if they open wide. There's something odd about the great hall and the stockade they were building in the courtyard. I want to get as good a look as we can at what's going on in there."

They retreated and moved well back out of visual range of the fortress then approached the new location. Rew, moving cautiously, placed each member of the party in a fan so that they all had a different line of sight. He kept one eye on the walls of the structure as he moved, watching to see if anyone detected the movement within the woods. He didn't think the guards would be able to see them, but if the party was spotted, they only had a quarter league of a head start if it came to a chase. Not enough that he was comfortable with their odds of getting away cleanly.

It was two hours past dawn when they finally saw action from within the fortress. The gates cracked open, and three men strode out. They were armed like foresters with long bows and short-swords. Rew held his spyglass to his eye to peek inside the fortress, but he saw nothing there before the gate started to close. He turned and watched the three men. It was apparent they were following the exact same path the men did on the supply run. They had to be going toward the farmhouse.

Rew glanced back to the fortress to see if the three men had been sent out as bait, if maybe someone on the walls would be watching to see if anyone would follow or attack, but all appeared as it had earlier. The guards on the wall were still vigilant, but none were taking any more interest in the countryside than they had been except to watch their companions headed to the farmhouse.

The gates thumped shut, and from Rew's observation point, he could not see anyone else leaving the fortress. Was it possible someone had already snuck out before dawn? He frowned. Men could have been sent out to look for him in the night, but they hadn't moved the bodies of the guards in the outposts, and the party hadn't seen anyone near the canyon or in the fields since daybreak. If there was a patrol out there looking for them, they weren't doing a very good job of it.

Feeling nervous, Rew collected the others, and they moved back away from the fortress. He was guessing where the three men were headed and did not follow them. Instead, they circled around wide, figuring the men would go to the farmhouse, find the dead, and then scurry back to the fortress. Rew aimed to bring his party to the trail about halfway between the two sites and set an ambush for the bandits as they returned. Just three of them ought to be quick work.

Hiking briskly cross country, he asked Cinda, "Ready to take a more active role?"

"I'll do what I can, but don't count on my casting."

"If you're feeling shy…"

"Not shy, Ranger. As I said yesterday, I'll do what is necessary.

It's a concern about whether or not I can. I've gotten comfortable summoning the funeral fire, but casting enough of it far enough to hurt someone is a different matter."

Rew gripped her shoulder but did not respond. The girl needed a mentor to guide her through casting necromancy. He could not serve in that role, but he could make sure she got some practice. Even if her fire did not harm the bandits, it would startle them something fierce, and it would prove what Cinda was capable of. That had to be worth something.

Two hours later, they reached the path the supplies had moved along, and Rew stopped the group. He bent down, looking for fresh signs of passage, and found them. Footsteps through the dew damp grass were obvious. He scratched his beard, warned the others to keep a sharp eye out, and then followed the trail. They moved another two hundred paces before he paused again. He'd found a bare patch of soil and could identify three different boots that had recently passed. He glanced back behind them. When they'd followed the bandits to the fortress, the bandits exhibited incredible caution. They'd hidden the people they'd killed then separated the remains of what they'd stolen. They'd passed through a variety of terrain including the stream to obscure the signs of their passage. Now, after several of their companions had been killed in the night, these men had strode right through a muddy patch of dirt? A child could follow these signs.

"What?" asked Anne nervously.

"It's too easy," muttered Rew. "They're going right where we expected, and there's still just the three of them. That doesn't make sense, does it? King's Sake, it's like they're asking us to take these men."

Raif shrugged. "They are bandits, not tacticians or scholars. These men aren't trained like you train your rangers. I do trust your instincts, and if you feel something is wrong, we should proceed cautiously, but we won't get a better opportunity than these three men out here so far from the fortress."

Rew grunted, dropping his hand from his beard to the bone hilt of his hunting knife. "Why only three men? One is sufficient to relay information to or from the farmhouse. I killed seven of them last night, so they cannot think three is enough to fight us off."

"You say there are just the three tracks, though?" questioned Cinda.

"Three that I can see," said Rew, frowning down at the boot-prints in the mud. "But just because I can't see something doesn't mean it isn't there."

Cinda shrugged, as if to say that he was the King's Ranger, and that if he couldn't see it, in her opinion it wasn't there.

"They're outlaws," remarked Zaine. "They don't care about their losses. Three is enough to see if anyone is still out here. If those men don't come back, they'll know. These men are sacrifices to gather intelligence, nothing more. Believe me, Ranger, whoever is leading these bandits doesn't care a fig for the lives of his men or the risk they are in. It's how thieves think. No loyalties except to gold."

"Assuming they are simple thieves," grumbled Rew. "I am not sure we should pursue this any longer. As Anne said this morning, we've proven what we came to prove."

"It's about more than just completing the king's test," argued Raif.

Cinda nodded. "If we leave off, these men will still be here, and how many more innocents will die because we didn't act? Let's follow a little longer and see what we see. Our eyes are open, and if it's too dangerous, we turn away, but let's be sure of it."

Rew glanced over the rest of the party, and all but Anne nodded. He guessed the sour expression on the empath's face was very close to what he wore on his own.

"If you don't want to follow these men, let's lay in wait for them," suggested Raif. "It's likely they'll come back this way after they reach the farmhouse, and we can take them then. If there are more than the three we expect, we can simply let them pass."

"Very well," said Rew, and he led them along the path the three had taken, looking for a suitable spot to stage an ambush. Ahead, he saw a copse of trees, thick with undergrowth, just three dozen paces from the trail they were following. "Perfect. That's close enough we can be on the path in seconds, but the bush is thick enough all five of us could disappear without—King's Sake!"

In the copse, he saw movement. It appeared as if a shrubbery had detached itself from the soil and strode out of the brush. The shrubbery knelt and raised a bow.

"Ambush!" cried Rew.

Behind him, he heard a clang like a metal spoon had been rapped against a pot.

"Blessed Mother, that stung," growled Raif.

The camouflaged man who'd emerged from the trees fired his bow at them. Rew ripped his longsword free from the sheath and slashed at the arrow, catching its wooden shaft and knocking it away from their party.

Raif yelped, and Rew saw him stagger forward, a line of crimson blood leaking from his cheek. Another arrow hit the fighter in the back, punching shallowly through the armor and lodging there. Raif, crying out, spun, trying to reach the arrow with one hand and draw his greatsword with his other. Men were rising from the grass like shadows, and Rew cursed. He'd been looking for a place the children could hide and had overlooked spots where more skilled woodsman lurked. King's Sake, how had he not seen them? It'd been as if they were invisible. He growled, looking around for a way out. The bandits had turned their own plan against them!

"Follow me," instructed Rew. He reached out and grabbed Raif, dragging the boy after him as more arrows flew toward the fighter. "We've got to find cover."

Zaine cried out and stumbled. Anne and Cinda clutched her and dragged her onward. A feathered shaft sprouted from the back of the thief's leg. The bandits' bows didn't have the force to knock clean through Raif's armor at long range, but the shafts would be deadly enough to the rest of them. Rew imagined the arrow that had struck Zaine was embedded in the bone of her leg, which must have been terrifically painful.

The girl soldiered on, half-hopping, half-carried by the other women. The fear of death was in her eyes, and the continuing hail of arrows was all the motivation Zaine needed to hurry.

Rew dragged Raif to the side, knowing the two men would draw most of the arrows, and Raif at least had some protection. Only a few more shafts fell toward them before they reached a slender creek carved into the wild landscape. The water bubbled in the creek bed well below the ground around it. Watching several incoming arrows arc toward them, Rew shoved Raif down into the creek bed then leapt after him, his soft boots splashing in the ankle-deep water, the bank of the creek rising half a pace above his head.

"Cinda," barked Rew. He turned and saw the spellcaster leaning against the far side, her hands clasped over her ribcage where an arrow was stuck in her torso. Rew hissed, "Blessed Mother."

Anne splashed over to the girl. Cinda's blood immediately staining the empath's hands as she felt Cinda's wound.

Rew glanced at Zaine, who was crouched down, leaning against the other bank of the creek, blood soaking her leg from the calf down. "Fire as often as you can, if you can. Don't worry about hitting anything, just make sure they know you're here. Raif, pop your head up and try to keep an eye on what's coming, but make sure to duck down right quick. Don't leave yourself exposed for more than a breath or two, just enough they know you haven't snuck off. If they're about to overrun you, holler as loud as you can."

Raif nodded, raising his sword, shifting uncomfortably as the arrow stuck in his armor dragged against the dirt bank of the creek.

"You hurt bad?" asked Rew.

"It barely broke the skin," said Raif, "but…"

Rew reached over and grabbed the shaft of the arrow. He wiggled it and then tore it free of Raif's armor, giving the boy freedom to move.

Zaine slung her bow off her shoulder and, gritting her teeth, drew an arrow from her quiver.

"I'll be back," said Rew. He started down the creek, following a bend in the waterway.

Overhead, he could hear the whistle of arrows and shouted commands as their attackers closed the net. They needed to run, but with Zaine and Cinda both wounded, they couldn't. If they had time for Anne to patch the girls up, maybe…

Cursing himself for not being more cautious, and confused at how he'd missed the bandits' hiding places, Rew clambered up the bank of the creek, fifty paces down from the others and behind a thick hawthorn bush. It still had its dark green leaves, and they screened Rew from the dozen men who were stalking across the landscape. The bandits were dressed in a variety of camouflage, some of them sprouting branches and leaves, others merely in a motley of greens and browns. They all held bows, and they were all advancing on the place Anne and the children were hiding.

Rew grimaced. There would be no chance at stealth this time. There wasn't enough cover away from the creek for even the King's Ranger to hide, and he had no time. No time at all. Their attackers were one hundred paces from the creek and were steadily making their way closer, bows and arrows ready. Rew stepped out from behind the hawthorn and began his charge. His feet padded quietly on the grass, and he offered no war cry as he raised his longsword. He couldn't hide, but he didn't mean to give himself away, either.

He was within a dozen paces of the first man before he was seen. The man's companions shouted, and by the time the bandit turned, Rew was there. Swinging his longsword in a wild, wheeling stroke, he decapitated the first man and kept running.

The second attacker raised his bow but didn't have time to loose an arrow before Rew skewered him.

Then, the bandits fought back, and several of them fired at Rew. The ranger dodged to the side, slapping one arrow away with his longsword and taking a painful gash on his arm from another he couldn't avoid.

He reached a third man and stepped close, stabbing him and holding the body upright to shield himself from another arrow, but more arrows didn't come, and Rew muttered a foul curse. His opponents were not fools. They were stepping back, spreading out, and waiting until they had a clean shot.

Rew flung the body of the bowman toward the others and sprinted, arrows raining around him, one slicing across his thigh, another glancing off the bracer on his arm when he raised it to block, the sharp head of the arrow digging a long scar across the leather-covered steel. A third arrow struck his shoulder, but Rew twisted as the arrowhead pierced his skin and swiped the shaft away. It spun from him, ripping his flesh and pulling a stream of red blood behind it. The wound was painful, but it wasn't deep.

He reached another bandit and smashed the hilt of his longsword against the bowman's skull, cracking it, but there were eight more, and the next closest was a dozen paces from him and already drawing his bowstring back to his ear. Rew didn't have time to reach the bowman before he fired, and at that range, the man couldn't miss.

An arrow thunked into the side of the bandit's head, right where his ear was. The bandit blinked slowly for the last time and fell to the side, his own arrow flopping harmlessly a few paces in front of him.

Bellowing, Raif charged from where he and Zaine had just climbed the bank of the creek. Several of the bowmen turned toward the approaching fighter, but others did not, and Rew raced into their midst, taking advantage of the momentary shock to fell two more of them.

Three arrows smacked into Raif, and the fighter went down tumbling, dropping his greatsword and rolling to a stop.

Zaine released again, taking another of their opponents in the abdomen. Then, Rew finished him, crashing into the remaining attackers.

They dropped their bows, reaching for shortswords and daggers, but it was too late. Rew was close now, and these men were not skilled with their blades. One by one, Rew chopped them down until the last fell.

He spun, looking toward Raif, but the big fighter was rolling around, struggling in his armor. Finally, the boy got to his knees and, with some effort, stood. He wiped the blood from his face then winced and touched his shoulder where one of his pauldrons had been knocked askew. An arrow sprouted from his side, near his hip. Luckily, far away from any vital organs. Gingerly, the fighter touched it, but he didn't have the nerve to try and free the missile from his body.

Raif touched his breastplate, where the steel was freshly dented, and rasped, "Blessed Mother. A little more force behind it, and that one would have been in my heart. Pfah, they slipped this one through on my side, though. I think the chainmail slowed it, but King's Sake, the arrow still got through. I thought chainmail was strong enough to stop a shaft?"

Rew grunted. The ignorant invincibility of youth. "That armor saved your life today, lad, but never trust your life to it. Chain may blunt the force, but it can't stop a well-placed arrow. And a good longbow in the hands of a skilled bowman will punch an arrow through solid plate."

Raif was fussing with the shaft in his side, his hands already slick with blood, but he was standing steadily, so Rew imagined they had time to address that injury. The ranger looked to Zaine. She was pale-faced and kneeling on her uninjured leg. She nodded back to him before slumping onto her side, trying to keep the arrow in her leg from jarring against the ground.

"We'd best see to that," called Rew, hurrying over and

kneeling beside the girl. There was a lot of blood, but she hadn't lost enough to kill her. Anne would be able to stop the bleeding and head off any infection, but the arrow had gone deep. It'd require more than a quick patch job, and Zaine wasn't going to be walking far with the arrow in her leg.

"Twelve of them, waiting for us in ambush," murmured Raif from behind where he was studying the bodies of their attackers and shifting painfully, trying to put pressure on the wound in his side. "We escaped un—well, not uninjured, but we escaped. They've written songs about less."

"Aye, but how did they ambush us?" questioned Rew. "I saw nothing until that one man had stepped out of cover. If he hadn't been overconfident…"

"But he was overconfident," retorted Raif. "That's all that matters."

Rew grunted but did not respond. He didn't think that was all that mattered. Then suddenly, Raif screamed, and Rew spun.

The big fighter had been launched into the air. He somersaulted twice before crashing down, his greatsword back where he'd been standing fifteen paces away, a swelling, boiling mound of earth rising beside it.

Rew stabbed the point of his longsword into the soil. He bellowed, "Begone!"

The earth, shifting and rumbling, stopped advancing on Raif and swirled, rocks grinding, specks of dirt showering down as the earth elemental turned to face Rew.

"Begone," hissed the ranger again, shoving forth with the strength of his will, letting the command flow through the steel of his sword and into the soil. The earth stopped moving and then collapsed into a billowing cloud of dust.

Rew knelt, picked up Zaine's bow and an arrow from her quiver, and then pulled the string back to his cheek. From within the cloud of dust, he heard a woman coughing, and when she stumbled clear of the mess, Rew let go. The arrow zipped and took the woman in the chest. She stared down, startled, and fell dead.

"What is going on up here?" barked Anne, climbing halfway out of the creek bed, staring in alarm at the dead woman and the dozen men lying beyond her.

"What just happened?" called Raif, still lying on his back, his hand gripped around the arrow shaft protruding from his side. "Did anyone see that? Blessed Mother, my entire body is going to be one giant bruise, and this arrow feels like it tore me in two. Pfah, I think something—"

"It was an earth elemental," growled Rew. "The woman was a minor conjurer. She must have known enough to hide the ambush from me, but she barely had control over that elemental."

"The woman?" asked Raif, struggling onto one elbow and groaning at the effort. "Who are you—oh. Where did she come from?"

"She was encased within the earth of her summoning," explained Rew. "The elemental cradled her as it moved beneath the surface, and then, it burst out beneath your feet. When it dissipated, she was left behind."

"King's Sake," barked Anne. "What is a conjurer doing out here in the middle of nowhere summoning earth elementals?"

Rew shook his head then nodded toward Zaine. "You'd best see to her, Anne. Where is Cinda?"

"She's in the creek," replied the empath, kneeling beside the thief. "I did what I could in such short time. Help her out of there, will you? She needs more of my attention, but I'd rather do it outside of the freezing water."

Rew walked to the bank and hopped into the creek, his boots splashing for a second time in the cold current. Cinda was leaning against the far bank, her hand clutched over a bloody tear in her robes. The arrow was out of her.

Rew asked her, "You all right?"

"I think so," she murmured. She tried to move and cried out. "I'm not, really. Does it matter?"

"Not much," admitted Rew.

"I can't feel my feet."

"You're going to feel this," said Rew, stepping to help her. "Hold onto my shoulder, and… Anne can take your pain when we reach the top."

Cinda screamed, and Rew grimaced through it all, but he got her to the top of the creek bank. Her wound had reopened, and blood was leaking down her front again. Anne nodded to a spot in the grass beside Zaine, and Rew settled Cinda there, helping the girl press on the injury with her hand.

Anne, already sweating in the cold air, pointed at the arrow in Zaine's leg. "I'm going to need you to pull it out, Rew."

Wincing, and after heartfelt apologies to Zaine, he complied. Anne took the pain from the thief as he yanked the steel head of the arrow out of the girl's flesh. The empath's labored breathing and trembling hands gave away how much it was costing her to shield Zaine from the agony. Cinda watched dolefully, her jaw clenched tight, but to her credit, uncomplaining about Anne working on Zaine first. Or perhaps, she was recalling her own discomfort from when the empath had pulled the arrow from her.

Rew grimaced, looking at the streamers of blood dangling from the bloody head of the arrow.

"Mine went all of the way through," rasped Cinda through gritted teeth. "That's good, I'm told."

"Better than leaving this stuck inside of you," replied Rew. He tossed aside the bloody arrow he'd pulled from Zaine.

They stayed there for an hour while Anne did what she could to speed the girls' healing. Rew tended to his wounds and Raif's. They'd both been banged up badly, and Raif required several dozen stitches. It wasn't Rew's best work, and the boy needed Anne's attention if he was to avoid several nasty scars and days of recuperation, but that could wait until they made it to camp. It had to wait. An hour was the longest Rew was willing to stay. The bandits had set the ambush, and it wouldn't be long before they came to see if it had worked.

"Chew this, and then chew this. Swallow the juice, but not the plant material," Rew told Raif, handing him two pinches of herbs. "The first will lower the risk of infection. The second will numb the pain, but it will wear off by tomorrow. You're going to be hurting and stiff as a fresh plank. Maybe Anne will have strength for empathy then."

Rew stuffed a wad of the first herb into his mouth and, trying to ignore the bitter taste, ground the leaves between his teeth. He made a sour face, like the liquid was stinging his lips, and he swallowed quickly then spit out the masticated leaves.

"Why aren't you taking the second one?" questioned Raif.

"It numbs the mind as well."

"I'm fine, then," said Raif, mimicking Rew and only gnawing off a hunk of the first twist of herbs.

Rew looked at the boy, thinking to argue, but then he put a hand on the back of the youth's neck and squeezed it. "You can change your mind later if you need to. Help me get everyone back to the canyon. It's still the best hiding place I've seen around here, and there's enough cover we won't be found immediately when they come looking." He glanced down at the dead conjurer and frowned. "And I think they will come looking."

Chapter Nine

The party limped and staggered back to the canyon where they'd made camp, and the two girls and Anne collapsed. Zaine and Cinda had marched on heroically, leaning heavily on the others for support, but both of them had taken grievous wounds, and even with Anne's empathy, their bodies needed time to heal.

Raif slumped down on a boulder at the edge of the canyon, and Rew checked his wound. The stitches had held, but blood was leaking from the fighter's side. Rew wrapped it with fresh bandages and instructed Raif to rest, adding, "Perhaps where you can see out into the forest."

Raif grunted and nodded acknowledgement. He laid a hand on his greatsword. "Nothing will get to them without going through me."

Rew patted the boy on the shoulder then looked across the camp to Anne. The empath nodded at him. Standing, Rew told Raif, "I'll be back as soon as I can."

The fighter frowned, shifting as if he meant to stand and then thinking better of it. "You cannot assault that fortress alone, Ranger. Let me come with you."

"You're not going anywhere, lad," said Rew, "but don't worry.

I don't plan to attack, just to watch. If they're coming this way, we'll need all the head start we can get. Listen for me, and be ready to run."

"Ranger…"

"Watch over your sister, Raif."

Raif eyed Rew suspiciously. "You know which cords to tug."

"I do. You'll keep her safe, though, won't you?"

Raif pulled his greatsword across his lap and leaned back against the rock he was sitting on. "I'll watch as long as necessary, Ranger, but don't take too long."

Without comment, Rew checked his weapons and then strode out into the forest. It was late in the afternoon now, and as he walked, he stooped, snatching a handful of mushrooms and then later finding some nuts which he cracked open with his hands. He hadn't eaten since early morning. He knew his body needed the fuel food would provide, but he was having trouble forcing himself to meet that need.

A conjurer sequestered in a remote fortress with a group of what Rew had assumed were bandits. They had attacked the merchants on the highway to rob them, Rew was sure of that, and the men he had killed over the last few days had the look of bandits, but what were they doing with a conjurer? Was she meant to fill out a burgeoning bandits' court in a parody of the arcanists and spellcasters the titled nobles kept? It was possible, but hiring a conjurer of even poor talent was an expensive proposition, and anyone with such coin shouldn't have risked discovery by targeting the merchants they'd found dead near the highway. The bandits who would engage in attacks such as that would flee the area once they'd done their work. For a group planning to stay in the region, it spoke of desperation, or something else that Rew couldn't fathom.

It was all related to the king's test, that much Rew could guess, but why would Vaisius Morden give a fig about some warlord ensconced in a far-off abandoned fortress? Unfortunately, the answer to that question, Rew suspected, would bring him no comfort.

The ranger scowled. The woman had summoned an earth elemental. Her hold had been tenuous, and he'd easily broken her connection by thrusting forward his own anchor to the world in between her and the summoning, but calling an elemental was not the feat of a novice. The woman's blood was mixed with that of nobility, and she would have spent years studying beneath a tutor to have learned such magic.

Why would a woman who had the talent to summon a dangerous creature like an elemental be out here? For someone with her ability, she could make wagon-loads of coin or even earn herself a landholding during the Investiture. It was in the big cities, near the princes and the nobles closest to them, where the opportunity lay. Yet there she'd been, nowhere near anything. She was working with bandits, so it wasn't a moral qualm that was holding her back.

Striding through the forest, Rew was alert, but his thoughts were in turmoil. When he reached the edge of the forest where they'd spied on the fortress previously, his thoughts still swirled like a child on an icy pond, unable to find his footing, unable to keep a direction. He walked carefully before coming within sight of the outlaw's hideout, and when he did, he peered cautiously through the branches and leaves that hid him.

Atop the walls of the place, he saw they maintained a heavy guard but no more than they had that morning. The bandits didn't yet realize their ambush had failed. The gate was shut tight, and from what Rew could tell, the outposts around the fortress still contained the dead men he'd slain the night before. He frowned. They hadn't collected their dead?

There was no honor amongst thieves, but that was particularly cold-hearted. Certainly the dead men had a few friends in the band who would have ventured out to recover the bodies? Rew watched and waited then became worried that there wasn't more concern evident around the fortress. Whoever was leading the group had sent out a dozen assassins to ambush Rew and the others, and those dozen men had failed to return. A spellcaster, for King's Sake, had failed to return! An outlaw band should be up in arms at such a loss. All of them ought to be pouring out like a kicked anthill preparing to fight or to flee, or else hunkering down with every man on the walls expecting an imminent attack. But as the day passed, and the sun sank toward the horizon, there was no motion in or out of the fortress. Rew could see the regular movement of men on watch, but that was it.

An hour before sunset, finally, he saw something. A lone man came trotting toward the fortress from the direction of the farmhouse. Rew held up his spyglass and saw the man was attired similarly to the other bandits they'd confronted, a forester who could have fit in well amongst any of the small villages nearby. Rew turned the glass toward the fortress and observed the men there. They looked agitated, several turning to call down to people inside the walls. A rope was thrown over the edge, and the lone man scrambled up and went into the interior.

A straggler returning from some mission to town? A scout sent to find the site of the ambush? Rew couldn't tell, but he thought it a safe assumption that the bandits knew their ambush had failed. It was likely why they hadn't opened the gate. They were afraid of who was out there, readying an attack, but no one else came or left, and nothing changed atop the walls.

The sun set, and from within the fortress, lights blazed. It was as if they'd lit dozens of torches in the courtyard, casting a low glow on the towers and the men who walked on patrol. Rew studied the guards, waiting, and then, the screaming started.

Deep within the fortress, men cried out, and on top of the walls, he saw hurried movement as the guards disappeared, running down into the courtyard. From the distance, carrying faintly over the empty landscape, he heard guttural cries, the sounds of violence. The light flickered, as if bodies were rushing back in forth in front of it, struggling. The bandits were being attacked—from within.

It was over in a quarter hour. The watchers were gone from the walls. No one had cracked open the gate. The light stilled, though Rew continued to hear the occasional animalistic outburst. The screaming had stopped, but echoes of those terrified voices seemed to hang in the air.

Rew waited, but as the night wore on, the fortress grew quieter, and the light faded until it was only the moon and stars that illuminated the pile of stone and iron. After an hour of hearing nothing, Rew moved down to the fortress wall and climbed it. He sat in the gap of a crenellation and looked down into the middle of the walled space, where the pale silver of the night sky fell on a charnel scene of horrific proportions. The dead were littered like sawdust in a cooper's workshop, not just fallen, but torn apart, scattered around, devoured.

Spread amongst the corpses of the men were those of narjags. Dozens of them that he could see, fallen by the swords of the outlaws, but it was evident who had won the day. There wasn't a man left breathing in the fortress. Rew scratched his beard. From where he was sitting, he couldn't see any narjags breathing, either. Several dozen from each side had fought to the death. Had they all killed each other? If someone was left, Rew couldn't sense their presence inside.

Where had the Dark Kind come from? Their stench, mixed with the scent of fresh killed bodies, filled the place. If there had been Dark Kind there the night before, he would have heard them or at least smelled them. He didn't have a nose like those foul beasts, but he'd faced enough of them in the wilderness that he had no problem recognizing their awful tang, like unwashed sweat and rotten meat. They hadn't been there the night before. He was sure of it. They'd come, somehow, but now, there were no living ones left.

The door to the makeshift stockade he'd seen the night before was open. A pen for the Dark Kind? A pen for the humans? The only thing he was sure of was that the Dark Kind had not been there the day before, but they'd somehow appeared and then vanished.

Disturbed, Rew turned, dropped off the side of the battlement, and headed back toward the canyon where his companions were hiding. He had a creeping tingle like beetles climbing over his back. Had the narjags skirted around him to find his companions? Could a spellcaster have transported the creatures into the fortress and then to the canyon? Neither seemed likely, but he had to know. He had to make sure Anne and the children were safe, and then in the morning, they would return and try to figure out what had just happened.

THE WOMEN WERE STILL RECOVERING FROM THEIR INJURIES AND moving slowly when they arrived outside the fortress. It was clearly abandoned, except for the carrion birds flapping overhead. The rest of the party waited while Rew climbed up the wall once again and dropped down inside to open the gate. There was a heavy wooden bar locking it, and with some effort, he managed to wrangle it out of the hasps. With Raif's help from outside, they hauled open the heavy wooden doors.

Anne looked in, covered her mouth, and turned away. "I'll wait out here."

"As will I," murmured Zaine, hobbling away from the awful stench of the dead.

Raif, shifting on his feet, pale-faced and sweating, looked unsure.

"Will you watch over Anne and Zaine?" Rew asked him quietly. "They should be resting."

Relieved to have an excuse that did not bow his pride, Raif nodded gratefully and guided the women away from the fortress to a place they could all sit.

Cinda looked at Rew and said, "I'll come with you."

"You don't have to."

"I know," she acknowledged then stepped around him to walk inside, her lips tight, her eyes hard. She'd been clutching her injured side as they'd walked from the camp, but as she entered the fortress, she held out her hands, and Rew saw them moving, as if tracing invisible flows. He grimaced as she stepped over ravaged bodies, and her hands rose, like they were following the souls of those recently departed.

Rew touched his longsword for a bit of reassurance and glanced around the buildings on the interior of the keep. He walked to the makeshift stockade he'd seen the bandits erecting and saw it was empty. He knew, in his heart, their answers lay inside the main building that stood with one of its thick doors ajar. The glow he'd seen at night had come from there, and the mounds of the dead around the doorway spoke to what had occurred. But he couldn't bring himself to venture inside, not yet. He was beginning to suspect what he might find, the one logical explanation for what had happened there the night before.

"Shall w-we…" stammered Cinda, looking at the great hall.

"Let's check the other structures first."

They did, though their search was not thorough. There was a kitchen and a nearly empty larder, a dormitory with beds for almost eighty, and rooms for what must have been the officers of the group. They peeked in those, but aside from a finer cut of clothing and privacy, they found nothing to give away the identities of the occupants. There was an armory that was surprisingly well stocked with similar weaponry to what they'd already seen on the bandits. Decent stuff, but it could be purchased in any public market in Vaeldon. Nothing that surpassed the quality of their own arms. They found a treasure room of sorts, though it was almost as empty as the larder. Surprising, given how many men the fortress was supporting.

Still, Rew spent a few extra moments there, taking time to pick a heavy iron lock and throwing open a small chest to reveal it was half-full of dirty gold, silver, and copper coins. He scooped out several handfuls to fill his pouch and then rooted around in the room until he found another pouch and filled it for Cinda. "I can stop buying all of your brother's ales, at least."

She nodded, tying the heavy pouch to her belt, but did not smile.

They left the room, and the rest of the wealth it contained, behind. They needed coin for their travels, but they had filled up their purses with gold, and neither of them had any interest in hauling around the heavy chest and its fistfuls of copper coin. Besides, if the chains anchoring the thing to the floor had been easy to remove, one of the bandits would have stolen the chest long ago.

With nowhere left to explore, they returned to the large building in the center of the fortress. Like the courtyard outside, the floor was covered in dead bodies of both men and narjags. They stepped carefully over them. The stench inside of the main hall was awful. His stomach roiling queasily, Rew saw a pack of dogs in one corner where they must have tried to hide, but like the men, they'd been slaughtered by the narjags. Around the dogs were piles of bones that the men must have tossed on the floor for the animals before the attack. They were mixed with the bones of those men now, and all of them had marks from gnawing teeth. Rew felt the bile rising in his throat.

Beside him, Cinda gagged and looked away. "I don't think I'll eat much tonight."

Rew grunted and kept walking. It was a huge open room, the ceiling high above them supported by thick, wooden beams. The beams were stained with generations of soot from smoky fires that must have burned decades or centuries ago. The corners of the rooms and the walls were thick with dust. There were tables lined with benches where the men must have taken their meals and another section where they could have held conferences. On the far wall of the room, past dozens of dead bodies and wide puddles of blood, was a freshly constructed arch set with glossy, obsidian blocks.

"What is that?" wondered Cinda, ignoring the reams of dead as she marched toward the back.

"A portal stone," answered Rew. "Enchanters make them. They function like… Well, they open a portal. Unlike the invoker's spell, they only allow travel between two distinct points. They're common in Mordenhold, Carff, Jabaan, and Iyre. The king's generals and ministers who can't open their own portals use them to travel back and forth. This explains how the Dark Kind arrived and how they left."

"But to where?"

"That's the question, isn't it."

"Do you know how to work portal stones?" wondered Cinda.

"I do."

"You could open the portal, and we could see what is on the other side."

"It could be an army of Dark Kind," reminded Rew. He crossed his arms over his chest. "It's probably an army of Dark Kind. Whatever survived this fight went somewhere."

"Oh, right," said Cinda, glancing quickly behind them where the dead men and narjags littered the floor like moldy carpet.

Rew followed her gaze, studying the great hall. Aside from the piles of dead bandits and narjags, it looked just as one might expect a bandit hideaway to look. There were filthy plates, discarded food, and ale barrels against the side of one wall. There was evidence of the rough games the men played to amuse themselves while away from the wine and women in the cities. There was no sign that anyone had ever bothered to clean the place. These men had lived in the moment, as their kind always did. They killed, and they feasted. They did not build or maintain what they had because one thought was already on their next move or that the next raid could be their last. There were no clues as to how or why the men had constructed the portal stones. And for a profession which did not have a reputation for building, why had they put the effort into the stockade out in the courtyard? Had they even constructed the portal stone?

They didn't, Rew surmised. Someone else had built the archway, and then tasked the bandits with guarding it. There was no bandit leader in this place. Their leader was on the other side of the portal. It explained why they hadn't mustered a response to his attacks. They'd held out, hoping he would go away, and when he didn't, their master slaughtered them instead of assisting. Was it rage? Or was it because secrecy was a more important concern than success?

Could the pen outside be to hold narjags? Had the conjurer been tasked with commanding them? She hadn't been strong, but perhaps if the creatures had been locked up, she'd have time to bend them to her will. Rew did not know what skill it took to communicate with and command narjags, but if she could summon an elemental, then he guessed she was capable enough.

That was it, he decided. Once the conjurer was dead, whoever was behind it had no use of this place or these men. But why would someone portal narjags to a random fortress and imprison them there in the first place? What could they have been planning to use them for?

Rew turned, studying the wooden frame of the arch and the obsidian set within it. The stones were necessary for such devices, he'd been told. The portal stones he'd used to travel between Vaeldon's capitals were constructed entirely of obsidian. He supposed that was more permanent, and this recent installation wasn't meant to last through the ages. He touched the wood of the arch, letting his fingers trace the grains there.

"What are you looking for?" asked Cinda.

"This is oak," responded Rew. "It's good wood. Strong and durable. It's not found around here, though. Oak isn't native to anywhere within hundreds of leagues of Carff."

"What does that mean?"

"Why would someone construct this portal here, in the middle of nowhere?" asked Rew rhetorically. "I imagine because they didn't want it stumbled over or for it to be detected by any wards that would have been raised near the cities. That makes sense, if they're transporting Dark Kind, but—"

Rew stopped abruptly.

"Why would anyone want to transport narjags to such a random location as this in the first place?" wondered Cinda, echoing Rew's own thoughts. "The odds that we would stumble across such a place must be... I don't know, not very good. There's nothing anywhere near here!"

"What if those odds aren't so long?"

"You think this was, ah, left for us here? The king's test?"

"I don't think it has anything to do with us at all," said Rew, shaking his head. "I mean, what if this isn't the only portal stone where someone could bring the Dark Kind through? There were armies of them outside of Falvar, but they arrived in small groups, remember? Several times, we've heard rumors of the creatures in the area. Even in Spinesend, where no one has seen a narjag for fifty years. Where are they coming from? It's not the wilderness. I would have seen signs of them there. If it was in the regions around the cities, then you would have heard more than rumor. That sort of thing would be on the top of everyone's mind in the keeps, don't you think?"

Cinda nodded slowly.

"Someone is using this portal stone, and probably others like it, to transport Dark Kind into the Eastern Province," said Rew. "That's the only explanation, and there are only so many people capable of launching such an operation."

"One of the other princes attempting to destabilize the region," murmured Cinda, pacing around the room, raising her robes so she could step over the dismembered and ravished body parts. "That's what you are thinking, isn't it? One of the princes is gathering forces for an attack."

"They have to be," said Rew. "What concerns me is that we're finding Dark Kind here, far from Spinesend and Carff. There were Dark Kind in the barrowlands, equally as far from anywhere. Apologies to your family, but none of the princes, including Valchon, give a fig about Falvar. The target isn't some far-flung barony or here in the midst of nowhere. The target is everywhere! What we've seen must be a tiny sliver of what is occurring. My guess, they're trying to destabilize the entire province, keep Valchon putting out fires, while they move against him."

"If there is a portal stone here, and outside of Falvar, you are right. The portal stones could be… could be anywhere," breathed Cinda. "They could be everywhere. Every noble in the Eastern Territory is dead, the cities leaderless. Someone has to do something! We have to do something…"

"There's nothing we can do while we're on the road," said the ranger. "King's Sake, how would we even find more of these if they're hidden in places like this? In Carff, there are portal stones where we can reach the other capitals, including Mordenhold. There's also Prince Valchon…"

"We should go," said Cinda, gesturing at the stone. "If someone killed all of these men because of what we'd done, they could be coming back here. We're not safe anywhere near this thing."

Rew frowned. "The king's test."

"I agree," said Cinda slowly, "but a test of what? Just to see if we'd find this, or if we'd… do what? Do what we did? Everyone's dead. There's nothing else we can do, Ranger. We should go."

"There's one more thing we can do."

Cinda moved away as the ranger raised his longsword. He eyed the portal stone and the giant chunks of obsidian studded along its wooden frame. It was dangerous to mess with artifacts such as these, but all around them were the fruits of what the stone might bring. He couldn't leave it behind, knowing that more Dark Kind might issue from it.

He looked at Cinda. "Step back a little."

Swallowing, the girl stepped over bodies of both man and narjag, backing toward the door.

Trusting to enchantments in the steel that predated even

Vaeldon to protect him, Rew dashed forward and rammed the tip of his longsword into one of the obsidian stones.

The stone shattered like glass, and a jolt like he'd been struck by lightning snapped from the broken pieces, up his sword, and into his arm. Rew cried out in pain, took several breaths, and then struck again, shattering another stone and absorbing another shock as the magic was released. His body was twitching, his muscles quivering with painful spasms. The sword was cool in his hands, ensorcelled by old magic, but it couldn't entirely prevent the kickback from the broken stones. There was power in each of the blocks of obsidian, fresh and raw, and when it was released, it was absorbed into the remaining stones or released violently. Rew gritted his teeth and struck a third time. This time, the blast from the ruined stone knocked him back onto his bottom. He sat there for a long moment.

"Are you all right?" asked Cinda.

"Sort of."

"You're smoking," remarked the spellcaster, coming to stand above him. She waved her hand over his body, stirring the acrid curls of dark gray that drifted off of him. "Are you sure you're all right?"

Rew looked at his palms. They were bright red, but as he flexed his fingers, he decided he could move them enough. He slowly got to his feet and shook his limbs, feeling them tingle like he'd been sitting on them. After a moment, he stooped and collected his longsword where he'd dropped it. The wood hilt was warm but no longer burning hot. The steel was still cold. He frowned at the portal. Three stones were shattered. Two remained. He hoped that was good enough, because he didn't want to think about what a fourth stone might do to him.

"Let's go," he rasped.

TWO DAYS LATER, THEY ARRIVED IN A SMALL VILLAGE AND SETTLED AT the inn there. It had rooms that, while not clean, were dry, and the common room featured ale that was wet. It was all Rew needed. Anne offered a litany of complaints until Rew pointedly inquired whether she would prefer to continue on the highway for several more days until they could find another small, dilapidated inn which might suit her better. After that, she'd retired to the baths without comment, a ceramic pitcher of wine and a wooden mug in her hands. Rew sat in the common room, sipping ale between casual attempts to prod the innkeeper for information.

"Not a lot of carriages on the road these days," the ranger murmured.

The man nodded, happily dipping Rew another ale. The tavern in the inn was empty aside from their party, and Rew suspected he was about to be the man's favorite customer. It'd been two weeks since they had been at Bressan's inn, and a lot had happened since then. Two ales wasn't going to do it.

"Not a lot of wagons, either," continued Rew.

The innkeeper nodded again then asked, "You headed east or west?"

"West," replied Rew, accepting the mug from the man.

"From Spinesend?"

Rew shook his head. "Nah, never been that far. We, ah, we've been moving horses down from Laxton. Cross country because, ah, the horses haven't been shoed yet. Turf is easier on their hooves, you know?"

The innkeeper did not look like he knew, or that he cared. He was frustratingly incurious for an innkeeper manning a small roadside tavern. Rew had spent half his last ale coming up with that story.

"Something happening up in Spinesend?" Rew asked the innkeeper. "How come no one is on the roads?"

"Aye, something happened," said the innkeeper leaning closer conspiratorially, though there was no one else around to overhear him. "Duke Eeron is dead. Killed in his own throne room. They found him holding his own head in his lap, if you can imagine that. Some say his arcanist did it. Others say it was the king himself."

Rew forced a laugh and replied, "The king himself came over to Spinesend, killed the duke in dramatic fashion, and told no one about it?"

The innkeeper shrugged. "Something is going on."

Rew scratched his beard. "That's why there are no carriages, the nobles have fled?"

"They have," said the man. "Lotta nobles passed through a week ago, but those that were gonna run did, I guess. Postal carriage still comes through every other day. Steady as the sun, they are. Work for the king, not these regional nobles, you know. Going to take more than a duke holding his own severed head in his lap to stop them. I figure it's when the post stops that the real trouble begins."

"What kind of trouble?"

The man shrugged again. It seemed he did little else. "Open your eyes, fella. The nobles are running, right? They're running from something, and it ain't the duke, because he's already dead. Maybe it means something to you and me. Maybe it don't. Time will tell. Last I recall seeing so many of them on the road was when Prince Valchon took command of Carff. They all rushed down to kiss the ring. Before that… it was war."

Rew grunted. He drank quietly for a long time, watching the innkeeper meander around the common room, straightening chairs, looking wistfully toward the empty doorway that led to the highway.

"When does that postal carriage come through?" wondered Rew loudly.

"Around sunset, usually. Most of them drivers like to stop over here for the night. Keeps me in business in the slow seasons. Oats for the horses, room and board for the men. Ale on the king's tab, eh." The innkeeper guffawed. "Charge 'em twice what I'm charging you. The king's men never complain about it, though.

Loyalty comes at a price, they say. Sometimes that's an expensive ale that keeps me from closing the doors. Sometimes…" The innkeeper smacked his hand down on the bar like he was squashing a bug. "Those nobles were running from something, my man. I'm telling you. Keep your eyes open."

"Post carriage coming tonight?"

"Tomorrow," replied the innkeeper, standing up straight and peering into Rew's ale mug to see if he was ready for another, "and if they don't, we'll know we're in trouble."

Chapter Ten

When the post driver arrived the next evening, Rew was waiting in the common room prepared to buy the man an ale.

The driver was a slender, confident fellow, his nose and cheeks bright red from the cold wind whipping against his face. He was attired in the coal-gray uniform of the post workers, and as he strode inside, he brushed a hood back, calling to the innkeeper, "Carriage is out back. Send the boy to stable the horses, will you, and an ale for me. What's in the kettle?"

"Soup," responded the innkeeper.

"Put the ale on my tab," Rew instructed the innkeeper, and in a lower voice, he told the post driver, "It's yesterday's soup. It's not very good."

Snorting, the man declared, "I know it's not any good, it never is. And thanks for the ale, mate, but I'm on the king's coin. I don't need you to buy me an ale."

"Then you buy me one," suggested Rew. The post driver eyed him suspiciously. "I need a ride. For myself and four of my friends."

Shaking his head, the driver responded, "I don't know who you think—"

Rew pulled a leather wallet from his belt pouch. It showed years of wear on the patinated leather, but the well-made wallet could survive anything short of complete immersion in water. Such craftsmanship was expensive, but its value was nothing compared to what was inside. Rew opened the wallet and withdrew a thick parchment which he placed on the bar. The document showed creases from where it'd been folded and unfolded numerous times, but the paper was of the highest quality, and the script was clean and easily legible.

The post driver stared at it for a moment before admitting, "I can't read, mate."

"You don't need to read to know what this is," remarked Rew. He tapped the bottom corner of the page where a shining golden seal was embossed.

The driver met his eyes. "How do I know that is real?"

"Do you know it's not real?" questioned Rew. He smirked at the thin man's widened eyes. "Don't worry. It's real. I am Rew, the King's Ranger for the Eastern Territory. No one's going to give you any grief about allowing me to hitch a ride on your carriage."

The post driver nodded thanks as the innkeeper thunked an ale mug on the counter and glanced back down at the parchment. "A ride, you said, for you and four others?"

"A ride for me and four others," confirmed Rew. "How far are you going?"

"Stanton," murmured the driver, rubbing his lips with his fingers, his eyes still on the parchment.

"That will do. Give our party a ride to Stanton, and you'll be done with us."

"Interfering with the post is a capital crime, mate," warned the driver.

"I know."

"I'll have to report to my superiors the moment we arrive in Stanton. I'll need you to go with me and present yourself and this document to them. If I don't, it's my job."

"Understood."

The driver shifted uncomfortably and then reached over and grasped his ale mug. He tilted it up, gulping thirstily. When he put the mug back down and wiped his lips with the back of his hand, he told Rew, "I leave at dawn."

"WE COULD HAVE BEEN RIDING A POST CARRIAGE THIS ENTIRE TIME?" snapped Zaine.

Rew shook his head. "Not secretly. This driver is demanding that we show ourselves at the postal station in Stanton the moment we arrive, and if we don't, he'll have our descriptions in front of the magistrate as soon as he can. I had to show him the documentation for my authority. He has my name, and he'll note descriptions of all of you in his official log. There's no hiding now. If there had been any other way... but the innkeeper was right. We haven't seen another carriage since we arrived here, and I'm not sure if you've noticed, but those oxen-drawn wagons of the merchant trains aren't any faster than our own legs. Outside of the post, any vehicle that can move quickly has already fled the region. Besides, while I was in a bit of a hurry before, now that we saw what was within that fortress..."

Zaine crossed her arms over her chest. "We could have tried tricking him."

"Tricked him how? Only an agent of the king has authority over the post, and the only way I could convince him I was an agent of the king was to tell the truth. I suppose we could have killed him, but I wasn't prepared to do that. I don't think you were, either, lass."

"Stealth was imperative, before," said Cinda, "and Rew is right, none of us would be in favor of killing to steal a carriage. That's the sort of thing we're fighting against."

"But stealth doesn't matter now?" challenged Zaine.

"The king knows exactly where we are," said Rew, "and we're no longer worried about Duke Eeron chasing us down, as he's busy holding his own head in his lap. The princes will still be after us, and maybe they'll have an easier time finding us now, but you saw what happened to the bandits. We need to get to Stanton and warn the baron."

Zaine grimaced. "All we have to worry about is the princes... Still seems like something pretty concerning to me."

Rew shrugged.

"We can't avoid them forever," murmured Cinda, glancing at Rew.

He met her gaze, and shook his head slightly. Cinda knew what was coming, but the others did not. It wasn't time, yet, to tell them.

"We can try," complained Zaine.

"We've agreed it's important to alert Stanton of what is out there, which means if the princes have spies in the city, they'll hear about us no matter what. We have to hope they aren't looking. For now, speed is more important than stealth."

"It's always a balance," murmured Raif. "My tutors said that, you know. I heard them, but I never understood..."

"Aye, experience is a better teacher than us all."

"And what if Prince Valchon hears we're coming, and he's waiting for us in Carff?" pressed Zaine.

"Then I'll deal with him," answered Rew.

The thief blinked back at him.

Anne asked quietly, "Can you?"

Rew shrugged. "I'm not sure, and let's not get ahead of ourselves. It may not matter. The post carriage can get us to Stanton. We've still a ways to go and much that could happen before Carff."

"Confronting a prince, that's a bold claim, Ranger," said Raif.

Rew didn't respond.

Cinda frowned and turned to her brother. "Stanton. Why is that familiar?"

"Appleby," replied Raif. "You recall him? He's a friend of Fredrick, Baron Worgon's son. He'd come visit every couple of months, though more often Fredrick went down to Stanton. He'll see us if we request an audience, but if we do, we can definitely forget stealth…"

"Appleby, of course," muttered Cinda. "Didn't Fredrick mention that Appleby was in Yarrow just before we arrived there?"

Raif shrugged.

"Appleby?" questioned Rew.

"Baron Appleby," said Raif. "He seemed friendly enough when I've encountered him, though he's of age with Fredrick and paid me little mind."

"Baron Appleby." Rew scratched his beard. "Thought that sounded familiar. You know him, then? Would he lend us a carriage? The baron ought to have access to faster vehicles than we can hire with the coin we took from the fortress."

"I don't see why not," replied Raif. "I'm the rightful baron in Falvar now, even if I never take the seat, and courtesy requires nobility share small favors. I've never had reason to think ill of the man, and I don't believe he thinks ill of us. As long as he hasn't been turned against us, he should lend us a hand, and if nothing else, he could help facilitate finding transportation. I've never been to Stanton, but I understand the city is of a size with Falvar. Someone ought to have a carriage there."

"To Stanton, and Baron Appleby," said Rew.

The group looked glum at the prospect of shedding their secrecy, but Rew was sure they were making the right decision. If someone really was flooding Dark Kind into the countryside to undermine the region, they needed to tell someone, and they weren't going to do that quickly unless they got off their feet. Besides, it was already done. Now that Rew had identified himself to the post driver, their secret was coming out no matter what, unless they killed the man.

But the next morning, as they were piling into the post carriage, Rew thought back and realized they hadn't even begun to look glum.

"WHO HAS SO MUCH TO WRITE ABOUT?" GROWLED ZAINE, PERCHED precariously atop the carriage.

"It's double the normal load," drawled the post driver, a wry grin on his lips. "Big shake up in Spinesend. Duke Eeron is dead, haven't you heard? Nobles, merchants, people with relatives—if they can't afford to flee the city, they're sending letters. Thick ones, too. People are scared or greedy. Happens like that, you know?"

Rew nodded and then glanced back at Zaine and Raif. "You on?"

"Sort of," muttered the nobleman, his hands gripping a low rail that ran around the edge of the carriage's roof.

"Hold on," instructed the driver. He slapped his reins, and the vehicle lurched into motion.

There was a squawk inside and the thumping of a rolling body. Rew winced. Anne and Cinda had been stuffed inside the carriage on top of a mountain of letters and twine-bound pack-ages. Evidently, there was enough room still that one of them had managed to go crashing toward the back when they started rolling. Rew hoped, for all of their peace of mind later that evening, that it wasn't Anne.

"Thought about what you said," mentioned the post driver as they rumbled away from the inn, speeding up as they reached the hard-packed dirt of the highway. "King's Ranger but of the Eastern Territory? Didn't think there was much east of Yarrow, just monsters out in the wild, but I suppose that's where you come in, eh? What are you doing here on the highway, Ranger?"

Rew smirked. "You didn't have so many questions last night."

"I slept since then," said the driver, reaching over to tug on a bell that rang merrily, alerting a plodding wagon ahead of them that they were coming.

Whether because of the bell or the pounding of the horses'

hooves that pulled the carriage, the wagon swung to the side of the road, and they rumbled by it.

"I've got business to attend to," said Rew.

"The Dark Kind?" wondered the post driver. "That's the business of your sort, ain't it?"

"Dark Kind?" questioned Rew, looking at the man out of the corner of his eye.

"Narjags, ayres, valaan," said the man. "People been seeing them all over. Surely you know—ah, I see. Of course that's what you're up to, ain't it? Makes sense one like you would be out here now. Monsters come outta the wilderness, so do the rangers. It's good you're here, mate, and I'm sorry I gave you such a hard time last night with the papers and all. Times like these, you gotta be careful. You understand, one king's man to another?"

"Where have people been seeing the Dark Kind?" questioned Rew.

"All up and down the highway, Ranger," responded the post driver. He frowned. "That is why you're out here, ain't it?"

"Aye," said Rew. "I've been hearing the rumors and seen some things that are more than rumor. I mean to do something about it, but it's been years since I've traveled this highway. I'm more familiar with the wilderness now. I also haven't had a chance to talk to many people who cover as much ground as you do. I figure you've heard more rumors than anyone else on the road, haven't you?"

"Well, there have been plenty of rumors," said the driver. "More'n just rumors, as you say. Down south of Stanton, it's gotten bad. Some say all these packs of narjags are converging there. Glad it's not my route. I know post drivers who run that territory, and they're doing it with mounted guards at their side. Nobles aren't going to spare an arm and a sword unless they have to. They're real worried down in Stanton, mate, real worried. Pfah, that's not what I signed up for."

Rew rubbed the top of his head, feeling his cold scalp. "You said valaan. People have seen valaan, truly?"

"Aye, I thought they were a myth, to be honest, but enough people say a thing, you start to believe it. Heard it from some of the soldiers in a little village about a day south of here. Serious men, Ranger, and they wouldn't'ta told me unless they believed it. Now, I ain't seen 'em myself, but you're not like to find anyone who's seen a valaan and is still drawing enough air to tell you about it. It's true enough for me. Could be the valaan that's drawing in all of these things around Stanton. I don't know about that, but that's what they did fifty years ago, ain't it, last time we went to war with these awful creatures?"

"How long until we get to Stanton?"

"Two days," answered the driver before slapping the wooden side of the carriage. "Maybe two and a half, seeing as we're loaded heavy. Can only push the horses so hard."

Rew eyed the beasts in front of them askance and did not respond.

———

THE TWO DAYS IN THE POST CARRIAGE PASSED IN TENSE, MISERABLE quiet. The group did not want to speak openly in front of the driver, and they were all uncomfortable riding in a vehicle that was not meant to carry passengers. Worse, though, were the cold stares they received as they breezed by small villages and other travelers. The farther south they got, the more evidence they saw that things were not right. Backing the post driver's claims, close to Stanton, some of the villages had even erected temporary fortifications—wicker fences, wagons drawn up to block gaps between buildings, and the like. How much of the rumors were true, and how much farce, remained to be seen, but entire villages did not erect makeshift walls around the place unless they had good reason to. Rew and his companions had seen the portal stone. They'd seen what the Dark Kind did in the fortress, and he suspected similar incidents had happened nearby. As he'd feared, it wasn't an isolated event. It was an overarching strategy to destabilize the entire province. It was madness.

As they drew close to Stanton, Rew's mood darkened. With each passing village, he saw more and more evidence that while these people were scrambling to protect themselves, they were woefully unprepared for what was coming. The fortress had held fifty armed killers, and every one of them had died. These people were farmers, tradesmen and women, holding the tools of their crafts. Children, barely old enough to apprentice, were now standing guard.

They were all in grave trouble.

Chapter Eleven

W hen they finally reached the outskirts of the city, Rew saw it was of a similar size to Falvar and Yarrow, but instead of being ringed by walls, it had a sprawl of empty paddocks and marketplaces. The city had grown because it was halfway between Spinesend and Carff, but it thrived on regional trade that didn't reach those two cities.

As they drew closer, Rew could see that trade had dried up to nothing. Only some of the markets showed robust business, and most of the paddocks were empty. The herders, knowing it would be impossible to flee with their charges before the Dark Kind, would avoid the place at all costs. Small merchants would take greater risks but only if there were still customers to purchase their goods.

Instead of vigorous enterprise, Rew saw a steady stream of men moving around the city on patrol. They were heavily armed, and most had decent armor, but they didn't enjoy the benefit of the walls the party had seen in the Eastern Territory cities. Here, on the highway to Carff, it'd been ages since Stanton had needed to defend itself, and whatever walls it had once hidden behind, it had absorbed through the years. Rew imagined any walls that ancient rulers had erected were now part of the city itself, serving as sides of buildings or torn down and completely reassembled. It gave Stanton a disorganized, ramshackle look, as its markets and streets spilled out into the land around it.

The post driver knew exactly where to go to cut through the confusion, and he expertly guided their carriage toward the gate, bouncing out over the turf on the edge of the road to avoid the line of people who were slowly trudging toward Stanton and waiting to get inside.

"Won't be long before they have to seal the place," said the driver, expertly eyeing the line of people, though Rew doubted the man had any expertise in such things.

From inside the carriage, Raif bellowed a curse, and Rew grinned. The way over the turf beside the road was not smooth, and inside of the package-filled carriage compartment, it would be like shaking the beans in a child's rattle. It would be good for the nobleman, Rew thought, to see how the commoners rode when they were fortunate enough to find a place in a carriage.

There was no proper gate barring entry to the city, but there were two dozen men standing around a point in the road where it passed between two stone buildings. There were barrels beside them, which Rew guessed must be meant to block the way if there was an attack, but the defenses were close to laughable. Narjags could scramble over such obstacles in a matter of heartbeats, and unlike human attackers, they'd be driven by hunger and by valaan who'd care nothing for how many of the creatures died in the attack.

The guards recognized the post carriage, if not its driver, and stepped back to allow passage. They did not check to see who was inside the carriage or why several extra passengers were riding with the driver atop of it. Another sign it'd been ages since they'd faced a real threat, thought Rew.

There would be nothing easier than stopping a post carriage on the way into town, killing the driver, and using it as cover. Of course, he supposed, it wasn't spies or assassins the people of Stanton needed to worry about. It was a tide of Dark Kind appearing out of nowhere in the countryside, headed to the largest city of any size to rampage.

THE POST DRIVER DISCHARGED THEM OUTSIDE OF BARON APPLEBY'S keep, and he watched closely as they spoke to the guards and were escorted inside. The man was still concerned about his career and what his supervisor would think about him granting a ride to strangers, but evidently, the decision to stop at the keep was enough to let them go without delay. Given what they'd been told about the Dark Kind plaguing the highway, Rew thought concerns about his job should be the least of the man's worries. The least of everyone in Stanton's worries.

In the two days of riding on the post carriage, Rew had time to consider everything that they'd seen and everything that they'd heard. The Dark Kind represented a threat to any and all, and they would sow chaos even if it had been only rumors of their presence. Clearly, someone was attempting to upset the order in the entire Eastern Province. There was only one man capable of such a feat—Prince Calb.

It had to be his work. He was a conjurer of incredible renown, though Rew had never suspected the man would be quite so vicious. The prince was the middle of the three brothers striving for the throne, and he was the one who kept the most to himself. Evidently, in that time he spent alone, he'd been preparing a flood of Dark Kind to assail Prince Valchon's lands. Rew doubted Calb believed Valchon would fall to a swarm of Dark Kind, but it could distract the older brother, and it might weaken Valchon enough that Prince Heindaw would move against him. It was the way these things went, each brother trying to cut the other, wound them badly enough that they were vulnerable. That thousands of innocent people would die as collateral damage didn't seem to bother any of the princes.

"I cannot handle this myself. We must get word to Valchon,"

said Baron Appleby the moment they'd been escorted into his throne room and relayed their theories to him. The crisply dressed noble was stalking back and forth across the marble dais at the head of his great hall, his hands clasped behind his back, thick wrinkles bristling from his forehead as he creased his brow in anxious thought. Wrinkles on his neatly tailored suit coat mirrored his forehead, implying it wasn't the first day that the man had wrestled with the weight of the Dark Kind surrounding his city.

"What would you have the prince do, m'lord?" asked a dry voice from the corner. Lord Fredrick, Baron Worgon's son, stood and took a step toward the pacing Appleby. "These are your lands, are they not?"

Anne frowned at the nobleman and whispered, "Where did he come from?"

"Yarrow," responded Rew quietly, glancing curiously at the nobleman. He'd been in Yarrow when they'd left there, just a day before the man's father had been ambushed and killed. Why in the King's Sake was Fredrick now in Stanton?

Appleby stared at Lord Fredrick for a long moment and then said, "I cannot fight the Dark Kind alone. The reports of the narjags come in every day, and that's not even counting what I can only hope are rumors of valaan. We have no idea how many there are, but it's clear to me there are enough. My men are not trained for warfare like this."

Fredrick shook his head. "The Mordens respect strength, cousin. If you go running to Prince Valchon, you'll look weak. He has no use for weak men."

Appleby threw up his hands. "What would you have me do? Wait until the narjags are storming through this very room? I don't care what the prince thinks! Without him, we'll lose it all. Maybe if we'd solicited Spinesend earlier—"

"The duke is dead," interjected Fredrick. "I was just there a week and a half ago. There's no help from that quarter, I'm afraid. I'd planned... It doesn't matter. No help was to come from there, so there's no use dwelling on what may have been."

"You wanted Duke Eeron to name you Baron of Yarrow," said Rew suddenly. "That's why you're here. With Eeron dead, you've continued toward Carff."

Lord Fredrick turned to look at the ranger. "I was going to Carff. It seems the road has grown rather dangerous."

"You left Yarrow alone and without your protection?" asked Rew. "The Dark Kind attacked Falvar. They're here. They'll be threatening Yarrow as well."

"That will be my concern once I'm named baron," said Fredrick. He shrugged his narrow shoulders. "Until then, Yarrow has walls and swords, and they can fend for themselves."

"Can they?" demanded Rew. "You know we were with your father. We saw what happened to your men. How many are left after that battle? Surely not enough to defend against a large pack of narjags."

"Not all of Yarrow's strength accompanied my father," retorted Fredrick with a tight smile. "My father was a fool. I am not. We retained enough men to guard the city until my return."

"But your magic c-could—" stammered Raif, the big fighter staring in consternation at Fredrick.

Fredrick raised an eyebrow. "What magic? Like you, Fedgley, I wasn't gifted with my father's talent. You of all people must understand what that is like, but I suppose you do, don't you? That's why you're here, isn't it? Traveling south to Carff, just as I, seeking the favor of the prince to name you Baron of Falvar? The prince, granting us dominion over our ancestral homes. Pfah. There should be no question we are the rightful heirs to our cities. A foolish formality, yet the prince has not done it. What are we to do except seek an audience?"

Raif worked his mouth, shaking his head. "You shouldn't have left."

"You left," retorted Fredrick scornfully. "That is just like the Fedgleys, to scold me for what you yourself are doing. You've always considered yourselves better than everyone else, haven't you? That's what got your father in trouble, isn't it?"

"That's not... We left Falvar to save my father. He, ah—"

"Save him? Lot of good that did."

Raif stood, seething. Whether because he was simply too angry to speak or because he'd learned a measure of maturity since Falvar, he did not rise to Fredrick's bait.

The older noble waited. Then his tone warmed as he continued, "Tell me, boy, when you petition Valchon, have you considered what approach you will take? Both of our fathers were loyal subjects to the prince, but we know that did not help them. Unfortunately, that means we are at a disadvantage because of our fathers' failures. Valchon abhors weakness. Perhaps if we petitioned him jointly, we could make a... a strategy, I suppose, to show how the two of us will bring the Eastern Territory back under Valchon's wing, how we'll stamp out the treachery Duke Eeron and his ilk fomented, and grant the prince the support he needs. He's interested in the Eastern Territory, you know? He had plans for the strength your father could bring. I overheard it. He'd promised great things for the Fedgleys. Did anyone tell you? No? Of course my father would not share such tidings with you. It doesn't matter, you can work with me now, and we will keep both of our houses strong."

Raif grunted.

"Pfah!" growled Baron Appleby, flapping a hand at Lord Fredrick. "Can you not save your machinations for another time? It's all moot if we're trapped here by the Dark Kind."

Lord Fredrick steepled his fingers, ignoring Appleby and studying the two Fedgley children over the long, thin digits. "You have thought about it, have you not? What was it, do you think, that made Prince Valchon so interested in Falvar? My father did not know, but he knew it was critical to Valchon's plans."

"Your father used to do that," said Rew suddenly, breaking his quiet. He held up his hand to show the nobleman what he was talking about.

Fredrick blinked at him and quickly dropped his hands to his sides.

"An unlucky turn, wasn't it," said Rew, his gaze locked on the nobleman, "that your father and his men were ambushed with the assistance of a glamour. That was your role in the court, was it not, to watch for low magic tricks? Unlucky for him you were not there that day, but lucky for you he didn't march with Yarrow's full force. Surprising, isn't that? Deciding to challenge Duke Eeron without all of his men at his side?"

Fredrick frowned at Rew. "What are you suggesting, Ranger?"

"Nothing," said Rew, giving the man a sharp smile. "How soon after your father fell did you leave Yarrow? It couldn't have been very long. Did you go to Spinesend, hoping to solicit the duke's blessing to rule so shortly after the man killed your father? That was a bold choice, Fredrick. If it was me, I'd be quite worried the man who killed my father had just as much reason to kill me."

"I'm properly called Lord Fredrick, but you are right, I was worried. Of course I was, but Yarrow needed a ruler," snapped Fredrick. "These are trying times, Ranger. Even out in the wilderness, I have heard there is a growing presence of the Dark Kind. It seems, like the rest of us, you've left your post—"

"Aye, I go where the Dark Kind go, and it seems they are here. Don't worry, I communicated with the king just days ago. He knows exactly where I am and what I'm doing. I am his agent, after all. Why, may I ask, are you here? Why stop in Stanton?"

Hissing, Lord Fredrick pointed a finger at Appleby. "I came here, Ranger, so that I could return to Yarrow quickly. My cousin had an invoker in his court who could've opened a portal to Carff. I'd be there in moments. The prince could return me after confirming my title as Baron of Yarrow. Coming to Stanton was the quickest way to fulfill my duties to the kingdom and to the Barony of Yarrow. You've no knowledge of the ways of the nobility, so I'd thank you to keep your razor tongue and your suspicions locked inside of your mouth."

Rew blinked and turned slowly to Appleby. "You have a spell-caster in your employ who can open a portal?"

"I did," responded Appleby gruffly, showing some frustration that the conversation seemed to have turned entirely from his city and its needs. "He's dead now."

"How? Why did this spellcaster not go to Carff already?"

Baron Appleby shrugged uncomfortably and told them, "Rumors and suspicion, that's all we've had to work on. With no intelligence of what we face, my commanders can't even prepare our defense! Should we expect attack from the east, the west? Will there be an attack at all, or will these monsters seek easier meat in the surrounding villages? Had we run to Valchon, what would we have told him? We've all heard stories, but none of my men had actually put eyes on what is out there. We had to know, so I sent one hundred of my best men and my invoker to learn what they could. That was four days ago. Two days ago, the party was discovered by a band of adventurers. Every one of my men was dead, including the invoker. The adventurers reported they gave as good as they got, much better even, but there were too many of the Dark Kind. Even with the backing of my strongest high magician, they were overwhelmed. So yes, Ranger, my invoker is dead. It has left us little option except to hunker down and offer hope to the Blessed Mother."

"If he'd portaled to Carff..." murmured Anne.

"I know," snapped Baron Appleby. "We could have gone to Valchon for help, but like I said, we didn't know what we faced. Fredrick is right. The prince hates weakness. All of the Mordens do. My seat in this barony is tentative enough. If I'd gone running to the prince to save us, the first thing he would have done is throw me out of the keep and tear my family's title into shreds." The baron cursed then glanced around the party. "I wish I'd had the courage to face that, but I didn't. It's my burden, my guilt, and I acknowledge it. I may have cost the people of Stanton our lives, but dwelling on that grants us no succor. I've sent messengers, but they've turned up dead, too. We heard from the last of the merchants who made it through from the south. It's been a day since anyone's arrived from that direction. The adventurers... maybe they'll go. Though I've little trust in such men and women, I have no other ideas."

Rew scratched his beard. "A band of adventurers?"

Appleby nodded curtly. "That's what they call themselves. Mercenaries, anyone else would call them. Who am I to complain? I've hired them for Stanton's protection and wrestled with whether to keep them here to bolster our defenses or to send them with our grim tidings. Stanton is a peaceful place, Ranger. Even fifty years ago, we didn't have to face more than scattered remnants of the Dark Kind's forces. No, my ancestors have dealt with bandits, runaways from other territories, the occasional rabble that thinks they don't owe their taxes, and that is it. It's been generations since we've engaged in full-scale war. We've never needed to. I hoped these mercenaries—adventurers, what-ever—I hoped they would help, but they've been as useless as I have. I don't like admitting this, believe me, but I'm afraid that it is too late, and I have failed."

On the side of the throne room, Lord Fredrick crossed his arms over his chest, as if condemning Baron Appleby. A fine position to take when he was hundreds of leagues from his own city, thought Rew.

Rew turned back to Appleby. "What of your own skill? We saw your soldiers on the way in. With your help, couldn't they—?"

Appleby snorted. "I'm an invoker of small talent, Ranger, and I've only got two hundred men left under my command. We've wealth that I collect from merchants on the road, but most of it is spent securing that road, and what's left over fattens the prince's coffers. I and my people are not a military or a financial power. We've survived holding these lands for generations because we're not strong enough or rich enough to draw the eye of the princes and their minions. For five generations, we've never attempted to rise above our station. Now, it seems, I'm to pay for that, our people as well. I don't have the men to protect this city, and my messengers cannot get through. Not even the king's post drivers will venture south now. I was in communication with Duke Eeron, and he'd promised support, but it never came. He's dead, as you said. His remaining commanders and courtiers have sent polite declinations. They won't march to our aid. They've their own problems, they claim. To be fair, it's probably true."

"You have to do something," barked Cinda.

"What?" asked Appleby, spinning to face the noblewoman. "What would your father do, if he hadn't been taken from his own throne room and killed like a dog in Spinesend? Burn a few narjags with the breath of death? Animate his soldiers when they fell to continue the fight? Pfah. I don't care to be told what a dead man would have done in my place."

Cinda blanched, and Raif growled under his breath.

"I've made mistakes, just as your father did," muttered Appleby. "I own that, but don't think to question me unless you've a solution."

"Prince Valchon," said Raif, shifting uncomfortably and glancing at Rew. "A thousand Dark Kind... The prince could handle that. Only he could handle that, right?"

Appleby's lips twisted. "I'm sure that he could, boy, but how to get ahold of him? My invoker, Duke Eeron... it seems that anyone who can open a portal east of Carff is dead. I told you, my last team of messengers turned up dead. Eaten, boy, they were found eaten! King's Sake, I know that Valchon is our only hope, but what do I do with that?"

"These adventurers who found your men, did they say how they were killed?" asked Rew.

The wrinkles on the baron's forehead bunched into even sharper ridges, and he nodded. "Narjags, of course. My men killed hundreds of the foul beasts before they were finished. My invoker, Blessed Mother watch over his soul, managed at least one hundred on his own, the adventurers claimed. I shudder to think how many of the Dark Kind they must have faced. It's unprecedented, so many narjags working together, but my men are dead, and there's no arguing with that. You've more experience with this than I, Ranger. How do so many narjags work together?"

"Valaan," hissed Rew. "The post driver said there were rumors, but I wasn't sure I believed him. It's the only way so many narjags would coordinate an attack like this."

"My family spent little time training me in the art of war, but I studied the histories," said the baron. "I couldn't tell you the first thing about facing a valaan, but I know what such creatures will reap if they assault the city."

"We have to do something," insisted Cinda, looking imploringly at Rew.

"A single valaan is one thing," said the ranger, scratching his beard, "but valaan along with thousands of narjags? You need spellcasters, or you need an army. Both, really."

"W-What about—" spluttered Cinda.

"Thousands of narjags!" interrupted Rew. "All commanded by beings just as cunning as human commanders. If all Appleby has is a couple of hundred untested men and his own paltry skill..." Rew shook his head dolefully before turning to the baron. "Sorry, m'lord, I don't mean to offend."

Appleby waved a hand dismissively. It was offensive, but he'd already admitted it was true.

"You'll want to arm the citizenry, of course," continued Rew, "but most of them will break before the onslaught of so many Dark Kind. The valaan will know that and will use it. A war of attrition is your best bet. Spread your people out. Don't get caught in the open. Fortify as many buildings in the city as you can. Hide the people and let them fight in pockets. It's dangerous because no one will be able to run, and many of those pockets will collapse and the people will die, but if they take enough Dark Kind with them, some of your citizens may survive. It's a better option than flight, I think. You're already surrounded, and the narjags will be on your people every night if you're in the open. Some could slip away, but there's no help within one hundred leagues of here. If the valaan have ayres in their command, you'll never outrun them. No, the buildings of Stanton, as insufficient as they are, are your only advantage."

"Aye, some of my advisors have suggested flight, but…" Baron Appleby shrugged. "I'm told even under the influence of valaan, narjags are difficult to control and prone to emotions. You don't think if we armed the citizenry, put up a good show, we might frighten them off? At least disrupt their attack enough to give us a chance? Perhaps the women and children could slip off in the other direction…"

"Without veterans and able commanders to put some iron in your lines, your men would crumple on the field," said Rew, shaking his head. "Believe me, when they see thousands of narjags racing toward them, the people will run. When they do, you'd be finished. You can't turn your back on Dark Kind. It will be a bloody mess but spreading the fight across the city and cutting them at every street and doorway is your only hope. Behind walls and barred doors, your people can give better than they get. And I hate to say it, but you'll force them to fight to the end. It's an awful truth, but there's no quarter against Dark Kind. It's better to die facing them with a weapon in hand than to be taken."

"But, Rew, y-you must…" stammered Cinda. "Can't you do something?"

He held up his hands at a loss. "Fight a thousand narjags? No, lass, I'd just be one more sword on the line, and that's not what Stanton needs."

"What about me?" asked the noblewoman. "I can stand against them, just like I did when Worgon's camp was attacked."

Lord Fredrick turned to the girl in interest, but Rew didn't wait for the nobleman to ask his question. Instead, Rew challenged Cinda. "Thousands of narjags, lass. They don't have the same fear that men do, and they don't have… They aren't a source of power. You'd have to kill enough of them that it'd give Appleby's soldiers a chance, and to do that would take enormous power, which would have to come from… you understand where this line of thinking goes? Others have thought the same, Cinda, but I don't want to see you go down that path. You know where it leads."

Cinda's eyes were burning, reflecting green in the bright light of Appleby's throne room, but burning with what, Rew did not know. Fear? Hunger? But in a moment, that fire faded, and she nodded curtly. She understood. The power she'd cast in Worgon's camp came from hundreds of souls departing. Baron Appleby didn't have that many men to risk, so the alternative was to put the city's citizens in front, as a sacrifice that Cinda could draw upon. The bitter calculus of necromancy meant gathering strength to fight required many to die.

"If there's a chance…" murmured Raif.

Cinda drew herself up, but before she could speak, Rew said, "There is not."

The noblewoman deflated like a sail with no wind.

"You need Valchon," said the ranger, looking to Appleby. "Without him, I'm afraid barricading the citizens within their homes is your only choice."

"I know," said the baron. He looked away. "I know, but we've sent our fastest riders. I've sent my guard captain in my own carriage, and none of them—"

Shaking his head, the ranger said, "The noise of a carriage will draw narjags like bees to a flower, and if they block the road, it's over. A fast man on a horse is a roll of the dice. If a lone horseman encounters a pack of narjags, or worse, ayres, they'd have no chance to fight them off. You need a group small enough they can adjust and move off the road to evade the narjags, but strong enough to prevail if they're forced into a fight. A carriage or one man on a horse won't do it."

Appleby crossed his arms over his chest and held the ranger's gaze.

Rew glanced around their party and then said, "With your leave, we'll go fetch Valchon for you. Your men don't have a chance out in the country against the narjags unless you send the bulk of them, but I do. I'm the King's Ranger. Dancing with the Dark Kind is what I do."

"YOU REALLY THINK PRINCE VALCHON IS STANTON'S ONLY HOPE?" asked Anne quietly.

Rew scowled and did not respond.

They were walking arm in arm along the low battlement that surrounded Appleby's keep. It wasn't much of a barrier. A dexterous man could leap up and catch the top of it, and Rew or Zaine could scramble over it in the space of a breath. But it was a place of calm amidst the hustle and bustle in the rest of the keep, and it was an easy place for Rew and Anne to stroll, looking out over the city of Stanton.

"Rew," said Anne, drawing him tight against her side. "There has to be another way."

He kept walking.

"You're planning to kill him, aren't you? I've seen the look in your eyes. It's been a long time, Rew, but I still know what that look means."

Rew grunted and admitted. "I was planning to kill him. Alsayer went to Carff, and we need to find him for answers, but this road leads to the king and his sons. If we want the madness of the Investiture to stop, then they are the ones we have to stop."

"But you've changed your mind, now that we've seen the threat out here?"

"I don't know, Anne."

They rounded a corner of the keep, nodding to the lone guard who was stationed there, and kept walking. When they were out of earshot, Anne pressed him, "Rew—"

"I don't know, Anne," he repeated. He sighed. "A valaan with several thousand narjags at its command is a terrible threat. It's something I can't face alone. No man with a blade can stand against that. It's not something Cinda can face, either, even if she'd been training for years. That's an army, Anne, and it will take an army to stop them."

"Then we need Prince Valchon."

"Stanton does," admitted Rew, "but it's not so simple. The prince, if left to his own devices, will retaliate against Calb for releasing the Dark Kind here. He'll burn Jabaan and the surrounding territory to the ground. If Calb has spent himself commanding the Dark Kind, his people will be in danger from Valchon's counterattack. Do we help Stanton knowing it will hurt Jabaan?"

"What do we do, then?" asked Anne. "We can't let these people die."

"I know," responded Rew. He paused, pulling her arm so she stopped beside him. "I can't turn my back knowing these people will die, but I can't let Prince Valchon continue, knowing how many he'll kill in his pursuit of the throne. I... I think we need to go to him, tell him of what is happening here, and encourage him to do something about it. Then after..."

"You'll kill him," said Anne, her voice cold.

"You disapprove?"

The empath turned and looked out over Stanton. It was late at night, and the city was quiet, but it wasn't dead. Tens of thousands of people were down there, lying in their beds or in the beds of others. Some of them were still in the taverns. A few of them were working, cleaning the streets of refuse before morning or getting the ovens started in the city's bakeries. Most of the people in Stanton would be good, honest people. None of them deserved to fall to a legion of Dark Kind.

"These people need Prince Valchon," said Anne after a long moment, "but only because his brother conjured evil. In Jabaan, maybe they need Prince Calb, but only because of the threat Valchon poses. I... I've never thought a man deserved to die, but Rew, I don't know what else there is to do. This cannot be allowed to continue generation after generation. And it will, won't it, until someone stops it?"

The ranger nodded, though he wasn't sure if she saw the motion, and then they continued to walk. They were quiet, simply taking comfort in each other's company. They made another circuit of the battlement and paused at the top of the stairwell that led down into the keep.

"There's a missing piece in all of this, Anne. That slippery bastard, Alsayer. He's playing a grander game than any of us, bigger even than the princes, I think. Every time we see him, he hints at something, but I cannot grasp it. I think he's the key to figuring a way out of this maze."

"Do you think he'll talk?"

Rew wrapped an arm around the empath and said, "He'd better, for his own sake."

"Alsayer went to Carff. Valchon is in Carff. Kallie Fedgley is in Carff," said Anne. "There's much we don't know, too much, but we know one thing for certain. We need to go to Carff."

"That's simple enough, at least."

"If you ignore the thousands of Dark Kind that might be standing in our way," she retorted sharply. Then, despite the grim topic and the incredible danger they faced, she looked up at him and asked, "That's no problem for the King's Ranger, is it?"

He laughed, and together, they walked back down into the keep.

Chapter Twelve

The company of adventurers readily agreed to accompany Rew and his party south to Carff where they would deliver a message to Prince Valchon about the threat facing Stanton. Baron Appleby promised the men and women a fat purse to go, and an even fatter one if they returned with word from Prince Valchon.

Rew had the distinct impression that the adventurers had needed little encouragement to flee Stanton. They'd been outside of the walls. They'd seen what had happened to Appleby's spell-caster and one hundred of his soldiers. It'd be unfair to call men and women in their profession cowards, but they weren't fools, either. No mercenary made a long career of it by facing impossible odds. So the moment Appleby broached the subject, there hadn't even been a negotiation on price. The adventurers had fallen over themselves agreeing to an honorable path to safety and enough coin they could take several months off in Carff recovering from what they'd seen outside of Stanton.

The plan to flee south with their tails between their legs did not stop the ten men and women from strutting about Appleby's courtyard like heroes returned from an epic battle. They preened like mating quail, and when they weren't stalking back and forth as if performers on a stage, they were barking unsolicited advice at everyone who was staying behind.

The ranger gritted his teeth and tried to ignore them. He, very quickly, and Appleby, after some hurried convincing, had decided it'd be best if the adventurers knew little about the party they would be escorting. Men and women like them knew the value of a noble, and with two young ones alone on the road, it wasn't unheard of to deviate from the planned mission and turn to one of kidnapping instead. And if they didn't relay the news to Prince Valchon of what was happening around Stanton, it was quite likely that Baron Appleby wouldn't be around long to inquire about the missing Fedgleys.

Lord Fredrick had loftily declared that he would join them as well. The way he put it, he had business with Prince Valchon. Appleby agreed it was a good decision, and Rew found himself unable to come up with an excuse to ditch the nobleman. He wondered if that's why Appleby had been enthusiastic about Fredrick accompanying them, if it was merely a way of getting rid of the man.

Regardless, after a conference with Appleby, Rew had pressed Fredrick strongly about the need for secrecy, and Lord Fredrick had somehow twisted it into a concession that he, as the highest ranking noble, would be the one to lead the party. It seemed he thought that maintaining secrecy around Raif's and Cinda's noble heritage was the easiest way to ensure he retained the position. Rew supposed that if the children's identities were known, they could outvote the older man or something like that. Nobles had strange beliefs about how things should be done, but as long as they were headed to Carff and the adventurers did not know who he was, Rew was willing to let it lay. Besides, Rew was still worried about the adventurers betraying them, so presenting Lord Fredrick as an obvious target to distract from the children seemed prudent.

The next morning as they prepared to depart, Lord Fredrick immediately began commanding the adventurers, who with patronizing smiles, saluted sharply and then kept on doing what they were doing already. Such men and women were used to bowing and scraping to nobles to collect their bread, and as long as Lord Fredrick was directing them on the path they wanted to walk, there would be no complaints. Rew, for his part, hoped to ignore all of them, though that was easier said than done.

The leader of the adventurers was a brute of a man named Borace. He had a thick, black beard, a massive battle-axe slung across his back, and two swords strapped to his side. His booming voice and expansive gestures were just as large as the rest of him. It was impossible not to hear the man if one was anywhere near him. Like all of his band, he wore a motley collection of armor that might have provided a bit of protection, but more likely, it was meant for intimidation. The man had seen action, and he'd survived. Rew granted him that due, but Borace could have just as easily found a second career in the theater. Mercenaries knew that how they appeared before potential clients was just as important as what they actually did once they were hired, and in that part, Borace was a master.

Borace was seconded by a svelte woman of dark hair and complexion, who wore a slender, curved scimitar and armor made of gleaming bronze discs and delicate chain. At first, Rew had thought the woman's armor to be even more impractical than the brute's, but then he began to wonder. By the time he'd decided her kit could be enchanted, he'd also concluded that while Borace was the supposed head of the group, the woman was the one who commanded fear from her peers.

The third man of note in the mercenary band was adorned with the bright red robes of a necromancer. He had sharp features and a head entirely devoid of hair. Even the man's eyebrows were missing. Rew peered at him, wondering if he had eyelashes, but the necromancer had painted kohl around his eyes to give himself a dangerous mien, so it was difficult to tell.

It was largely the same attire Cinda had worn when they fled Spinesend and Rew had insisted she pack away while sheltering at Bressan's Inn. Spellcasters in Vaeldon were a haughty bunch, and they wore their colors broadly. It proclaimed their power and their heritage. Their abilities flowed from blood that their families had been breeding since the start of Vaeldon. Asking them to hide that heritage was akin to asking them to... Rew frowned. He couldn't think of what it was akin to. Even when it was dangerous and likely to get them killed, the nobles wore the colors of their house and of their magic. It was who they were—the core of their identity—and not a one of them ever considered how shallow a thing that must be if they had to wear clothing to prove it.

This particular necromancer did not look familiar to Rew, which meant he was not a member of the primary houses in the Eastern Province. Instead of tracing back centuries, his bloodline more likely traced back to some country inn thirty years before when a passing noble rutted with a tavern wench. The man had no signet to proclaim membership in a house, but he had enough talent to get away with wearing the robes. A skilled bastard. His place in a mercenary company was no surprise, as outside of royal lineage and the creche in Mordenhold, such men and women were considered disgraces. The necromancer had Rew's sympathies for that, if nothing else.

"Don't let him frighten you," said the dark woman, her bronze armor rustling like a snake in the grass as she took the ranger's side.

Rew let himself jump as if in surprise, but he'd seen her approaching out of the corner of his eye.

"Ambrose commands the souls of the departed," continued the woman, stepping closer, her voice oozing through the noise of the crowd like blood dripping onto a floor. "He has little interest in the living."

"King's Sake," muttered Anne, coming to stand on the other side of Rew. "How many of them are there?"

"A few less every time we stumble across one, it seems," responded Rew dryly.

The dark woman blinked at them.

"We've encountered, what, four or five necromancers in the last few months?" Rew asked Anne. He gave the brass-armored woman a tight smile. "Just as many of them are dead."

"It is unusual, isn't it?" mused Anne, tapping her chin with a single finger. "They're crowding the roads in the Eastern Province like farmers headed to market. It's been years since I've seen a capable necromancer, but as you say, we can't seem to avoid them now. Like rats rushing out of a burning barn. Or rushing into one?"

The dark woman turned to eye them seriously. "You've run into four or five necromancers? What is it that you've been doing?"

Rew snorted and did not respond.

The woman studied him for a long moment before offering, "We're meant to work together, are we not? Let us be friends. They are here because necromancers are drawn to the ancient spirits of this region. Before us, there was another race. They were close enough to our kind that the high magicians can still call to them, still command them, but they're old enough that they've grown powerful. I'm told they have peculiarities that are attractive to those who can control them, advantages over the spirits of our kind. Ambrose, others, they are attracted to such power like bees to a petal, particularly in times like these."

Rew grunted. "Ah, of course. Did Ambrose join you recently? Was he in the barrowlands before?"

"In the barrowlands? No, I don't think so. Who are you?" asked the woman. "What do you know of the barrowlands? What are you doing here in Stanton?"

"That's a lot of questions. Let's start with the first. My name is Rew, and who are you?"

"I have no name," claimed the woman.

Rew put his hands on his hips and tilted his head at the woman. "What do you mean, no name?"

The woman drew herself up and winked. "I had a name, once,

but I no longer do. That sounds rather dramatic, I know, but it's true."

"I bet you don't make many friends when you will not tell people your name."

The woman bowed her head as if to acknowledge the truth of what he'd said.

"What should we call you, then?" asked Anne.

"You need not call me anything."

"What do they call you?" questioned Rew, gesturing to the woman's companions.

"I see how you feel, Rew. That's a lot of questions, but you've answered none of mine."

"I told you my name."

The woman smiled but did not respond. She walked off toward Borace, rolling her hips saucily as she did to keep Rew's gaze on her. She seemed to be encouraging the big man to gather the rest of their band and prepare to leave, but instead, the brute glared back toward Rew.

"That was rude," said Rew, rubbing the top of his head.

"She reminds me of you," claimed Anne.

He turned to glare at the empath, but she looked away, and he couldn't tell if she was being serious or if she was jesting.

Evidently noticing the adventurers were preparing to leave, the children clustered close. Rew told them, "This group has been in Stanton and south of here, so most of them should have no idea who we are, but Cinda, I worry the necromancer may be able to guess your identity. I think you should avoid—"

"He already recognized me," replied Cinda. Rew blinked at her. Cinda continued, "He worked for my father. He was one of the ones trying to harvest wraiths in the barrowlands. I don't know if he knew my face or if he could sense my talent, but he approached me. Don't worry, though. He won't tell the others who we are."

"Aye, that woman thought he'd come from somewhere else. Did he give any indication why he's being secretive?"

"I'm not sure, but the man is hiding something deeper than his failure in the barrowlands. For what it's worth, I'm confident he's no more interested in his secrets being shared than we are in our secrets coming out."

"King's Sake," growled Rew. "Secrets? Half of them know who we are already."

"Fredrick and Ambrose won't talk," said Anne, watching the mercenaries huddle together with the nobleman peering over their shoulders. "Those men are ruled by their fears."

"Fears and ambitions," retorted the ranger. "Fredrick would trade us the moment he felt he had a good bargain, and Ambrose will be as loyal as a scorpion."

"Then you need to make sure their fear of you is more powerful than any reward they could expect by giving you away," said Anne, smiling at him. She winked. "Just like that. Every time they look at you, show them that expression."

Sighing, Rew adjusted his pack and prepared to depart Stanton.

THE WALK OUT OF THE CITY FELT LIKE THEY WERE ROWING AWAY FROM a burning ship with the lone rowboat while the rest of the passengers were still wondering just how bad the fire was going to be. The people of Stanton paid them little regard. Their eyes were searching for men and women in Baron Appleby's service, though there were some who seemed to recognize the adventurers. Rew supposed the mercenaries had been in the city for some time, and they'd left and returned before. All the same, each time he met the gaze of a citizen of the town, Rew felt raw. No one knew when the Dark Kind might strike, so there was no guarantee he and the others would make it to Carff in time. Even if they did, there was no guarantee that Prince Valchon would act. Logically, Rew knew that rushing south was the only way to save the city and that he was the most suitable candidate to do it, but in his heart, it was difficult to watch the city's children scampering in and out of the alleyways playing. He knew they'd have no chance if he failed.

He tried to absorb as much of Stanton as he could, purposefully memorizing scenes and faces. A mother laughed and tossed a knotted ball of rags to half a dozen children who took it and ran gleefully into a park. A blacksmith's face was lit by the fires of his forge. A group of young men in an open tavern lifted mugs of wine and winked at a group of young women who were walking by. The adults on the streets wore forced smiles and tried to ignore the cloak of worry that hung on their shoulders. The younger people, who hadn't been alive during the war with the Dark Kind or the last Investiture, beamed with life. Stanton, when not surrounded by narjags, was a prosperous city if not rich like the capitals, and life must have been good for many of the citizens. Rew wondered if it would be good again.

These people were going to suffer because of something they did not understand, something that most of them would never have heard of. The Investiture was a game of the nobility, and while plenty of those nobles would fall during it, it was the innocent citizens of Vaeldon who Rew felt sorry for. Like horses in a cavalry charge, they were spurred and whipped, rushing toward a danger they could not comprehend and spoils they would never enjoy.

It was a relief when the group finally cleared the last buildings of the city and moved down the highway into open land—a relief and a torment. Rew felt guilty that they weren't doing more, though he didn't know what else they could do. It was the same way he'd felt ten years prior, when he'd first fled to Eastwatch. It'd been cowardice then, to turn his back on the knowledge he had, even when he knew there was nothing he could do. He was having difficulty convincing himself it wasn't the same cowardice now.

"Do you think the prince will come?" asked a dry voice, like a snake slithering across fallen leaves.

Rew looked at Ambrose, the necromancer, out of the corner of his eye. The rest of the man's companions were walking ahead. It seemed they'd taken Ambrose on for his high magic and not for his company. Rew felt the same.

Ambrose raised an eyebrow, waiting for a response. It was creepy, as the man had no hair there.

Hoping it'd get rid of the necromancer, Rew told him, "These are the prince's people."

Ambrose snorted.

"You don't think he'll come?"

Shaking his bald head, the necromancer responded in an affected lilt that Rew supposed was meant to make him seem wise. "The prince has other concerns. You know that as well as I."

"What other concerns?"

Scoffing, Ambrose leaned closer and whispered, "The Investiture, Ranger. Yes, that's right. I know who you are. When I realized who the lass was, it was no great leap to guess your identity as well. I know all about your little group, and I know all about the grand game the nobles are playing. Nobles like your friends, eh, and their father?"

"Yes, and I know about you as well. You were in the barrowlands doing Fedgley's bidding when Falvar was attacked," said Rew, only half guessing. He was suddenly struck by an idea. "You don't know why Fedgley was taken and then killed, do you? Any noble you might hire yourself to could be a part of the plot, and they may not be finished. That's why you haven't told your companions who you are and who you were working for. That was probably wise. Borace looks like he wouldn't demand more than enough coin for a good night's drinking to sell your secret. You should know, necromancer, that I do know who killed Baron Fedgley and why, and you were right to think that they are not finished. I think it best if we keep each other secrets, don't you?"

The necromancer granted Rew a thin-lipped smile and shrugged as if to acknowledge they were both in the same boat.

Rew kept walking, trying to ignore the man. It was annoying, but Ambrose was right. They both had their secrets from Borace and the rest of the mercenary band, and they both had their reasons for maintaining those secrets. He was certain the necromancer would not do anything to reveal who they were, but Rew hated equating himself with such a person.

Ambrose's grin grew, as if guessing Rew's thoughts.

His face twisted in a sour grimace, Rew kept walking. In his experience with those who had magical talent but no title, the one thing they held sacred above all was their own safety. Rew was confident of that, if nothing else. And since he was not worried the man would talk to the others, Rew had nothing else to say to Ambrose, and didn't think anything good would come of getting to know him. Very rarely did anything good come of becoming friends with a necromancer.

Evidently, Ambrose didn't feel the same way. He kept walking beside Rew. He warned, "Do you think the prince will protect the children? He won't, Ranger. It's not the way it works in Vaeldon. He may be their liege, but that only means he has expectations. Valchon, like his brothers, cares about those who are useful to him —and only those who are useful. You'd best keep that in mind. I told Lord Fredrick as well, but he's a fool. He thinks his low magic, his glamours and his trickery, will earn him the prince's favor. Pfah. The prince has as much need of Fredrick as I do a barber."

Ambrose rubbed a thin-fingered hand over his bald pate. Rew forced his own hand to still, to not mimic the man and feel the stubble on his own scalp.

"Fredrick means to offer the prince his services? What services are those?"

Unblinking, Ambrose gave Rew a smirk. "You must suspect how Worgon managed to put himself in such a precarious position. I heard enough while I was still in the territory to make my own conclusions."

Rew grunted, looking to where Lord Fredrick walked at the head of the mercenaries, speaking closely to Borace.

"The nobles, the prince foremost amongst them, see us as no

more than a means to an end. They'll use us, Ranger, and then discard us. My advice? Look at them the same way. Get what you can from Prince Valchon, but don't expect a single copper coin more. The only currency the prince uses is betrayal."

"You know the prince well, then?"

Ambrose giggled and replied, "No better than you."

Rew wasn't sure what that meant or how much Ambrose knew about him, so he didn't respond.

Several moments later, his voice pitched slightly higher and bordering on a squeak, the necromancer blabbered, "Wait, do you know the prince? How would you... You met him in Mordenhold when you were training to become a ranger?"

Not answering, Rew looked out over the rolling hills that lay south of Stanton. Unremarkable landscape that would quickly become boring, if it wasn't that those hills could be hiding hundreds of Dark Kind behind them. Rew frowned, wondering if the Dark Kind were attempting to form a perimeter around the city to prevent flight or if they were merely amassing nearby. Narjags didn't have the discipline to do either, but valaan...

"Ah, you were lying, then," accused Ambrose, apparently trying to interpret Rew's silence and his frown. "You don't know the prince. Take my advice, Ranger. I mean it as—"

"I did not answer you."

"So you're claiming you do know Prince Valchon! You've met him, at least? Tell me, Ranger, so that we can be open with each other. We can work together and... You're tricking me, trying to make me think you're more knowledgeable about all of this than you are. You've never met him, have you!"

Rolling his shoulders, Rew kept walking, wishing the necromancer would go bother someone else. He had hoped that by not answering, Ambrose would get frustrated and leave, but it seemed the necromancer was using Rew's silence to twist more and more intricate suspicions. Still, Rew had no interest in getting to know the man, so he remained silent.

"I have ways of learning what I want to know, Ranger. Save us the time, and just tell me."

Rew ignored him.

"Ambrose!" barked Borace from the front of the line. "Come. I need your council."

The necromancer scurried ahead, and Rew watched him, shaking his head. He couldn't help but think the man was going to keep trying from there until Carff. Rew was not looking forward to that.

"I overheard. Trouble, do you think?" wondered Cinda, coming to walk beside him, watching Borace gesticulate and flail, evidently physically compensating for keeping his voice low enough they could not all hear it.

"Not from Ambrose," said Rew. "That man is frightened of his own shadow. Whatever he guesses, the truth or complete fiction, there's no way he'll risk speaking to the others about it. I've no doubt he'll keep prying to try and learn more from us, though. We just have to set ourselves to ignore him."

"What of his own secrets?"

Rew snorted. "He has none that I care to learn."

"We're safe, then?" wondered Cinda.

"Not safe," responded Rew, shaking his head. "Never safe, but for the moment, our bigger concern is the Dark Kind. The valaan will be holding them half a day from Stanton, if not more. Much closer and the scent of man would be too strong, and even a valaan would have difficulty keeping the narjags from rampaging. Valaan are cunning, but narjags are brutes. They're ruled between their appetites and their fear, and with the smell of food, eventually those appetites would rule the fear."

"Food. You mean us?"

Rew nodded.

"How far do you think we can trust Ambrose?"

Rew stumbled, looking at Cinda from the corner of his eye. "I don't think we can…"

"With only Anne to teach me, do you think I can learn what I need to know?"

Sighing, the ranger replied, "There'd be a great risk, asking for that man's help. He'd want something in return, for one. Maybe we could accommodate him. Maybe we could not. What I really worry about is what he'd do with knowledge of your talent. If he's teaching you, you can't help but show him your strength. He won't tell Borace, Lord Fredrick, or the others, but who would he tell in Carff? He survived the barrowlands, so he has at least some cunning. I think he'll avoid as much risk to himself as he can, but what would the prince give to learn it is you and not Kallie who has a talent for necromancy? King's Sake, I need to talk to Fredrick again. Or maybe I shouldn't. Pfah, we can't let that man know how interested Valchon might be in your talent."

"Ambrose recognized me, Ranger. He has to know I inherited some of my father's abilities. He knows enough of our secret that he poses a risk, so don't you think it better we keep the man close rather than distant?"

Rew muttered a curse under his breath and kept walking, his eyes scanning the hills around them.

"Someone has to teach me," insisted Cinda quietly. "Do you think we'll soon find another more trustworthy necromancer?"

"I'll talk to him," conceded Rew.

He found himself gripping the bone hilt of his hunting knife, and he forced himself to release it. He wouldn't trust Ambrose as far as he could throw the man, but Cinda was right. They weren't going to find any necromancers he trusted more. Ambrose was there, and they had some leverage over him. Perhaps those were the only qualifications that mattered.

For another half hour, they walked together, both of them looking at the group ahead, lost in their thoughts. Cinda startled Rew when she asked, "That woman, the one who won't give her name, she's quite beautiful, isn't she? I don't think I've ever seen anyone like her."

Rew blinked at the noblewoman. "You, ah, you fancy her?"

Cinda laughed. "Of course not."

Rew shrugged.

"Do you?"

"Of course not," he said, grinning at her. "I thought, well…"

"You thought I'd make Zaine jealous?"

Rew stumbled, nearly falling onto his face.

Cinda caught his arm and leaned close. She whispered, "I see her looks. I know what she wants… That is to say, I think I do. I've no experience with such things, Ranger. I don't think she does, either. Maybe if the circumstances were different, we could… Ah, but they are not, are they? If I was back in Yarrow or in Falvar, I'd steal wine with my friends in the keep and we'd gossip and laugh about it. It seems ages ago, but it was just months. That's a life we've left, Ranger, a life I'll never have."

"You might, someday. You fancied Bressan's son, didn't you? I'm not completely blind."

She gripped his arm tighter as if to chide him. "I was… curious about Bressan's son. It's a nice dream. It's good to have dreams. Good for Zaine, good for my brother, but I no longer dream. Not like I once did. Our stay at the inn taught me that. I no longer feel the tingle of excitement that I once did. When I sleep, which is becoming rare enough, my dreams are troubled. They have been since Spinesend. I do not think that will change, Ranger. A door has been opened. Whatever happens in our future, I don't think I'll sleep peacefully again."

"In sleep, you are closer to death."

"Yes. I can feel that. I can feel something, at least. The appetites I used to have, for rest, a laugh, for pretty boys, they are fading. I hardly recall what that used to feel like. At Bressan's… I tried to make myself feel what I once did, but I could not. Something has replaced the curiosity I had—and the dreams—but I don't know what it is. I know there is power there, power we need, but it feels like I'm walking through a room in complete darkness. I don't know which way to go, where the hazards are that I may stumble over. Stumbling isn't the right word, though. If I stumble in a dark room, I'll bang my knee. With this, a stumble means my death and likely the deaths of others."

"I said I will talk to him," replied Rew with a sigh. "Whatever it takes, I will make him teach you what he knows. You're right, it's the only choice we have. Trust him with as little as you can, though. The less anyone knows about you, the better. Cinda, I mean it. Do not show him your full power. You saw the king— Vyar, I mean—and you know what is at stake if the wrong people learn your potential. Tell no one what we've discussed and what you've begun to guess at."

"Even our friends?"

Rew nodded curtly. "In some ways, especially our friends."

"Time and time again, Ranger, we find ourselves in trouble because of secrecy. Do you think that maybe we should be open with each other? My brother, Zaine, Anne, they want to help. If you tell us what your plans are—tell me what it is you expect me to do—then we can help."

"One day, but not today. Cinda, it's for the best. You know what you need to know right now. The less everyone else knows about the future, the better."

"You are a frustrating man. Do you know that?"

"I know that you've been spending too much time with Anne," declared Rew crisply. They walked on a bit longer, and then he told her, "You have an inkling of what is ahead of us, the danger you will face. You know Carff and Prince Valchon, that is just the beginning. If your brother suspected as you do, do you think he'd allow you to keep going?"

"He could not stop me."

"He could try."

They kept walking, eyes ahead. Cinda said, "You're right. Raif is a fighter, but he fights to protect me and our family. If he thought… You are right. He would do everything he could to stop us."

"In time, he will understand," said Rew, "but not yet."

———

FOR A DAY, THEY WALKED AND THEY SAW NOTHING. NO DARK KIND, not even signs of the Dark Kind. Rew extended his senses, finding the wild land south of Stanton different from his wilderness home but close enough he could get the feel of the place. In the wilderness, he could detect the disturbances the Dark Kind caused from far away, but here, he felt nothing except for a lingering unease. They were near but not close.

Borace loudly declared that the battle they'd stumbled across was several leagues off the road and that the narjags wouldn't come to the highway. Rew saw nothing that disputed the man's claims, though none of the Baron Appleby's messengers had gotten through, so at least some of the Dark Kind must be trekking across the highway. He thought Borace's idea had some merit, though. The valaan could be holding their minions back until they could muster enough of the foul creatures to assault Stanton. It made strategic sense, to gather strength as long as they could without giving away their presence. It was possible the valaan did not know the humans were aware of what was happening. There'd been few outright engagements, and if Rew was commanding a force, he would not want to make his presence too obvious by clustering around the road.

He'd be monitoring the highway, though, if he were a valaan, but as a day passed and they saw nothing, Rew began to think they might make it to Carff without encountering a single narjag. He got comfortable, and it nearly cost them.

The adventurers, with loose directions from Lord Fredrick, camped several hundred paces off the road and set a watch rotation that evening. They patrolled the immediate surroundings outside of the campsite. They went through the motions of vigilance, but before Rew could stop them, they'd started a campfire. Growling, the ranger stalked over and demanded they put it out. Borace argued, but when Rew did not back down before the big man's bluster, the adventurers finally doused the fire.

Rew didn't trust Borace and his motley crew, but aside from the fire, he did not distrust them, either. They appeared to have perimeter security well in hand, and they were acting as professionally as any mercenary company he'd seen, which wasn't truly professional, but it was somewhat close. The adventurers knew what was out there, and they wouldn't sleep without adequate protection, but still, Rew elected to set his own watch. Quietly, he gave instructions to the others and told them that no matter what the mercenaries did, they'd be guarding their own backs.

Raif asked him, "You expect trouble?"

Rew's lips twisted. "The Dark Kind are out there. The mercenaries will keep their eyes open, but that's all we can count on. Their kind is as like to flee as to fight."

"Of course," said Raif. He stood, stretching, his armor rustling. "I'll take the first watch, then."

The young nobleman was strong, and the months on the road were giving him the constitution of a bull. He looked wide awake as he began to stroll around the campsite, peering into the darkness and then back over at the mercenaries where Borace was running a whetstone over his giant battle-axe. Raif was alert, but he didn't have a ranger's intuition.

Rew was lying down, rubbing at the stubble on his head in the chill air, yawning and wondering if he'd been foolish to not allow a fire, when he heard a muffled snort. He froze, listening, and heard nothing else, which is what tipped him off. Had it been a mercenary adjusting his crotch before he fell asleep or a man moving on patrol, the sound wouldn't have been cut off so abruptly.

Springing to his feet, Rew yanked his longsword from the sheath and called, "To arms!"

Chapter Thirteen

✦

With his shout, the narjags had no reason for caution, and they attacked. Dozens of them pelted out of the dark, slavering with hunger, ferocious wails cutting through the night like a dull knife. Rew lunged forward to meet them, stabbing a leaping narjag in the chest and flinging it aside, trying to give his companions time to rise, to prepare themselves. His warning, and the narjags loss of surprise, gave them the chance they needed.

The mercenaries were a flurry of activity following his cry, and from the corner of his eye, Rew saw Borace lurching into the thick of the fight, his battle-axe sweeping in terrific blows, cleaving through narjags with ease. The big man's face was split, his white teeth shining as he bellowed with the joy of battle. In the silver light of the night sky, the head of the man's giant axe was black with ichorous blood, and his eyes flared with mad glee.

A berserker. Great.

Rew dispatched another narjag and was glad when Raif joined his side. The boy had been on watch, so he was still fully armored, and even a narjag wasn't stupid enough to run right into the lad's enchanted greatsword when he was ready for them.

Raif's arrival gave Rew a chance to look beyond the first rank of narjags. Several dozen were coming behind the ones he'd already felled. The creatures could move with stealth when they wanted to, but Rew had rarely seen so many working together without direction. When so many gathered, they were as likely to turn on their companions as they were to stalk up on you. Where had the things come from, and who was commanding them? Was it one of the shamans like they'd seen in the wilderness? Rew couldn't see it, but it was dark, and he had other things to look at as a narjag came flying at him, foul teeth barred, a howl erupting from its throat.

Rew smashed his sword into its side, hacking a gaping wound in the beast and sending it flying into the path of a narjag that was charging Raif.

Out in front of the mercenaries, the hulking berserker Borace crashed through half a dozen of the narjags, scattering them as he whipped through, thrashing his huge battle-axe like it was a slender branch. A bloody swath of Dark Kind already lay in his wake. Raif let out a low whistle as the man swept his axe in a mighty blow, catching three narjags at once.

"Did you see that!" exclaimed the boy.

Rew grunted and switched to offense, darting after the berserker, calling over his shoulder for Raif to stay back and to protect the women. There were still dozens of narjags that Rew could see, and who knew how many more in the darkness. If Borace pushed out too far, the man would be surrounded and alone. Cursing, Rew paused to strike down two of the awful creatures then sprinted after Borace.

Zaine released an arrow, the bolt whistling past Rew to take a rushing narjag in the chest. She called, "We'll be fine, Ranger."

They very well could be, but Rew felt better with Raif standing beside them.

Rew chased Borace, who was recklessly punching his way deeper into the ranks of narjags. The ranger paused to slay any of the Dark Kind his longsword could reach, but in the dark, the creatures had an advantage. They'd camped near enough to the road that the land was open, and the light of the moon shone down, but Borace was charging downhill, into the shadows where the narjags could see and he could not. King's Sake. It was dark enough that dozens of the creatures had come within striking distance, and not a one of the watchers had seen them.

Rew spared a glance back, seeing if help was on the way, but near the two campsites, he saw the mercenaries had clustered together and formed a protective circle, steel bristling from them like the spines of a hedgehog. They weren't unskilled, and when the narjags approached, they dispatched them quickly, but they did not venture out. They weren't coming to the aide of their leader.

Lord Fredrick and Ambrose crouched in the center of the formation, either deciding that their strength was not needed or that they weren't willing to expend it to save their companions.

Rew muttered under his breath. While the bulk of the mercenaries were fighting confidently as a unit, the berserker Borace had plowed into the thick of the narjags alone. He was a force with his battle-axe, but against dozens of narjags at night, Rew could see where it was headed. Already, blood was streaming down the back of the man's legs as he twisted and swung, exacting a steep price from any narjag that approached him.

The creatures parted, and Rew shouted a warning. Borace didn't see the valaan coming until it was on top of him, its long limbs extended, talons raking across Borace's flesh with ease.

The big man roared with rage and tried to fight back, but the valaan was frighteningly quick. It slithered out of range and then darted back, leaving bloody gashes everywhere it swung. Borace's armor, more for show than protection, did nothing to stop the Dark Kind's terrible claws. Blood flew as the mercenary spun, and his axe caught nothing but air, as if he was fighting against his own shadow.

Suddenly, the nameless woman was there, her bronze scimitar

slicing out of the night, almost taking the head off of the valaan. It dodged, and she pursued.

Rew raced after them as the fight drifted farther from the comfort of the others. The valaan was retreating, chased by the woman, but there were still fifteen narjags snapping around Borace, and the berserker was bleeding from as many nasty cuts. The big fighter smashed one narjag in its bestial face with the hasp of his axe, spun, and chopped another clean in two, but others swarmed him from behind. One leapt onto his back, sinking teeth into his muscled shoulder. Borace stumbled.

On the other side of the berserker and the narjags, the nameless woman cried out in surprise and came reeling backward. The valaan, caught off guard by her initial attack, had recovered and was now granting her its full attention.

Rew swung hard, hacking into two narjags and hurling them off of Borace. He skewered another, grabbed a fourth around the neck with his hand, and threw it back and then kicked a fifth. He wasn't fighting with enough finesse to deliver killing blows to all of them, but he didn't have time for that. Borace had gone down, and narjags were jumping onto him like rabid dogs. Rew had to give the man a chance to stand back up if the berserker was ever going to stand again.

A narjag lunged at Rew, thrusting forward with its spear. The ranger jerked his hunting knife from the sheath and turned the narjag's strike, directing it into another creature that had its back to him, its mouth fastened to Borace's thigh. The narjag squealed in surprise as its brethren's spear skewered it. Rew rammed his knife straight down into the skull of the spear wielder. He twisted, shoving his knife to his left, dragging the dead narjag with it, using the pitiful creature as a shield. He cut down two more.

The nameless woman cried in pain and staggered back, a gleaming curtain of blood painting half her face, her bronze scimitar whistling in a blur of speed in front of her, but it wasn't enough. The woman was skilled, but facing a valaan was unlike anything she would have experienced.

Shouting curses, Rew barreled into the pile still swarming around Borace, hacking and slashing his way through them on the way to the woman. The berserker was still moving, barely, but his battle-axe was on the turf. One of his swords was missing. He swung his other sword and a balled fist vainly, catching some of the narjags with his strikes, but missing twice as many as they clustered around him.

"Rew!" cried Raif, suddenly pounding up beside him. "We've got this."

An arrow thumped into a narjag's shoulder, and Raif kicked it away before leveling a powerful blow into a narjag on Borace's back, sending the creature spinning into the dark, a trail of dark blood stretching behind it.

"Go!" said Anne.

The empath and Cinda had arrived and were grappling with a narjag that had been a breath away from hacking down on the back of Borace's neck with a rusty hatchet. Anne had one arm, Cinda the other. Rew was on the verge of shouting at them when Cinda released a pulse of green-white energy. It clouded the narjag's eyes. Its body twitched uncontrollably, and Anne leapt away, fervently shaking her hands as it to clear them of something foul.

"Don't do that where someone could see you," growled Rew to Cinda before breaking into a sprint, chasing the valaan, who was chasing the nameless woman. She was fighting with terrific effort, and Rew was shocked she'd survived as long as she had, but when one had not faced a valaan before, it was easy to be surprised by the creature's ferocity, speed, and strength.

When facing a man or one of Vaeldon's natural beasts, it was easy to judge their attributes with a simple look. Bears were big and strong. Snakes were slender and fast. Valaan were different. They were tall and thin, black tinged with blue, like a nighttime sea. They were naked, always, eschewing the peculiarities of the narjags who liked to collect and wear apparel and weapons they scavenged from people. Valaan were above that. They had no clothing, no weapons, just their thin bodies, but that trim build hid incredible strength, and they were as quick as a whip.

The woman, her bronze scimitar and armor flashing in the moonlight, had not expected the creature's speed, and she'd been sent stumbling backward, blood flowing, spattering on the scales of her armor. She was lightning fast, but the valaan was faster.

Rew forgot the woman as he charged the valaan from behind, swiping his longsword at it, knowing the creature would evade the blow. It was like trying to catch a forest squirrel with your bare hands. They might pause, and they might hold still, but when you reached for them, they were away before you could even blink. The valaan seemed to shift, and perhaps it did, using some power that was foreign to Vaeldon, as it was suddenly three paces away, now facing both Rew and the nameless woman.

"Blessed Mother," she growled, "that thing is fast."

"I know," said Rew, standing still, his longsword held up in front of him.

The valaan, its skin gleaming in the night but its eyes reflecting nothing, suddenly lunged toward Rew. It was what he'd been waiting on. It was hell trying to chase down a valaan, so the easiest way to fight them was to let them come to you.

In a blaze of speed his eye had difficulty following, the valaan slashed one of its taloned hands at Rew's head. He swung up, catching the valaan on the wrist with the edge of his longsword and severing its hand. The appendage spun toward him, and he ducked out of the way, narrowly avoiding the razor-sharp claws which still could have left a painful gash on his face.

The valaan was stunned, but only briefly, and struck again with its remaining hand. This time, his longsword out of position, Rew retreated, recoiling back, trying to draw the valaan after him where he could respond to another of its strikes.

The nameless woman leapt at its back, but the valaan ducked, and startled, she toppled over it. The Dark Kind, crouching beneath her, raked its talons on the inside of her thigh where her armor did not cover and spun away as the nameless woman collapsed to the ground.

Rew was after it, hurtling over the fallen woman. He thrust at the valaan. It twisted away again, some preternatural sense alerting it to his blow, but it wasn't quick enough, and his longsword pierced its back, a hand length of steel disappearing in the midnight black body.

The valaan shrieked and surged out of reach. For a heartbeat, Rew thought it might flee, but he'd angered it. Like all Dark Kind, it viewed people as food rather than threats, and there was nothing more infuriating than your dinner sticking a sword in you.

Rew assumed so, at least. It'd never happened to him.

The valaan spun to face him, orange blood pumping from its wrist and streaking down the hole in its back. The ranger didn't know if it would bleed out from the wounds he'd given it. He'd never thought to let one of the things live long enough to see how they recovered from injuries. Even grievously wounded, valaan were amongst the deadliest creatures he'd ever faced.

It came at him in a rush, the stump of its arm and its taloned hand spread wide, its mouth open, displaying teeth blacker than its skin, invisible at night.

Rew swung at its remaining hand, hoping to sever that one as well and disarm it, so to speak, but the valaan had anticipated his tactic and shifted as it charged. He missed its arm as it turned out of range, and now, his longsword was well past it. The valaan hooked its other arm, the one with the severed wrist, around the back of his neck and yanked him close.

He might have been able to fight it, muscle against muscle, but he wasn't sure if he'd win. The thing's cold breath was on his face, and its mouth was opened wide, questing for his throat. In a blink, Rew yanked his hunting knife from the sheath and stabbed up, the sharp steel taking the valaan under the chin a fraction of a second before its jaws locked onto his neck. Rew thrust harder, seeking the creature's brain. It collapsed against him, its tall body falling on him with surprising weight, as if it was made of steel rather than flesh and bone.

Rew stumbled back, staggering under the weight, shrugging the valaan off and yanking his hunting knife free. He watched it, not entirely sure if it was dead or not. Regardless of the damage one did to them, the pain they might or might not have felt, valaan fought to the last breath. Gasping for air, Rew waited until he was sure it wasn't moving any longer.

"Rew, are you all right?" demanded Anne. "You're covered in... blood?"

He turned and nodded. He felt the valaan's cold blood soaking his back. It must have bled all over him when it grappled with him, but all of the blood was the valaan's. Its claws had not scored his flesh.

Raif was standing amidst a pile of dead narjags, his eyes darting to each of the creatures as if surprised he'd already killed them all. Zaine was crouched, an arrow on her bow, looking out into the night in case any more Dark Kind appeared. Cinda was beside the thief, her arms crossed over her chest, scowling at the rest of the mercenaries who were in a tight cluster. They hadn't taken a step to assist their leader. Only the nameless woman had come to his aid. Anne knelt beside Borace, her hands on the big man.

Rew lurched to the nameless woman, who lay on her back, her jaw clenched tight, eyes staring up at the sky above them. Her hands were wrapped around her thigh, and blood leaked profusely through the gaps in her fingers.

"There's an artery in the leg..." she hissed.

"If it'd been more than nicked, you would have bled out already," Rew assured her. Louder, he called, "Anne—"

"I can't do both," responded the empath, her voice already tight with the strain of taking Borace's pain. "This man is as strong and as stubborn as stone, but those things tore into him like a New Year roasted chicken. Rew, help her if you can. Otherwise, we're going to have to choose..."

"Understood," said Rew. "Cinda, get my pack. Raif, Zaine, stay on guard. Shout if you see anything moving out there."

The nameless woman looked into his eyes. "It was so fast. It... I can't believe it. I've never seen anything move like that. It—"

He placed a finger against her lips, silencing her, then reached up for his pack that Cinda had brought. "Some light?"

The girl raised her hand, shifting to hide it from the group of mercenaries behind them on the hill, and the pale white-green glow of her necromantic funeral fire bathed the scene. Suddenly, the light brightened, and Rew saw Ambrose standing on the other side of him and the nameless woman. The necromancer was eyeing Cinda.

"You are your father's daughter."

She didn't respond.

"I appreciate the light, but..." said Rew, not sparing the man a look.

"But you'd rather I had helped earlier?" replied the necromancer. "Perhaps I should have, but I have little skill with battle magic. I might have made things worse."

"Rew," called Zaine, "they're leaving."

Cursing, Rew spared a look at the mercenaries' backs. The remaining men and women were marching off into the dark without a word to their injured companions or to Rew and his party. Lord Fredrick was the lone person remaining near the campsite, his cloak wrapped around him tight, his eyes darting between the departing adventurers and Rew and the others.

"There's no loyalty when you fight for nothing more than coin," said Ambrose. "At least they didn't try to take ours, eh? With the big man down, that could have gotten nasty, but I think you put fear into their hearts, Ranger. They'd rather face the rest of the journey coinless than face you."

Rew ignored Ambrose. He rooted through his pack, searching for his herbs and other medicinal supplies.

Smiling, the necromancer admitted, "Ah, yes. You're right to think I've no loyalty either. I don't have it. Not to you, not to

Borace, but I'm not stupid enough to think I'm better off in the night with those seven fools. I'm staying with you, Ranger. I will help as I can."

"You had better."

"Of course," purred Ambrose, letting the soft glow from his hand brighten, as if the light he was shedding was the big contribution he could offer.

Rew pulled out a packet of herbs, some thread, and a needle. "Can you sustain a fire with heat?"

The necromancer looked down at his hand. "Ah, no. Funeral fire is cool, cold, sometimes."

"Go help Anne with Borace, if you actually can," muttered Rew.

The necromancer turned to go.

Rew ripped up a handful of grass from the soil beside him. He tied it into a knot and he ignited it.

"King's Sake," murmured Cinda.

"Don't tell anyone," grumbled Rew.

The red-orange glow of the burning grass flared unnaturally bright, illuminating the bronze-armored woman in front of them. Her eyes were closed now, and her breath was coming in short, erratic bursts. Her hands and forearms were soaked in blood, and the crimson liquid painted her from the waist down. Rew was growing quite worried that the artery in the woman's leg had been opened wider than he had skill to repair. The light revealed more blood than he'd expected. He studied the woman's leg, between her tightly clenched fingers. He sat down his sewing needle and thread.

Rew drew his hunting knife. He unstopped one of the flasks he'd gotten from Bressan and poured the liquor along the length. Then, he stuck the blade into the fire of the grass he'd lit.

Cinda watched, tittering with worry.

Rew began prodding at the woman's leg, taking care not to jostle her hands or loosen her grip on the injury. If he took time to sew her up, he suspected she'd bleed out, and he wasn't sure he had the skill to do it anyway. The cut was deep, the damage extensive. He had herbs that would help slow the flow of blood, but they took time to be ingested. There were others that could be applied topically, but he'd have to make a poultice, which meant boiling water and several minutes mashing the ingredients together. If Anne could not assist, with the supplies he'd brought and their limited time, there were two choices—a tourniquet or fire.

He pushed the woman's armor aside, feeling her upper thigh. It was thick with muscle, and he grimaced. He thought he could likely get a strap around and cinch it tight enough to stop the bleeding, but he wasn't sure. If it wasn't tight, if it didn't stop the bleeding, the woman was going to die. If she didn't die right away, she might lose her leg if they had to keep the tourniquet on long, which given their precarious situation, was just as good as dying. He needed Anne's advice, but she'd already told him they would have to choose.

Quietly, Rew told the woman, "I'm going to try and cauterize the wound. It's going to hurt."

The woman opened her eyes and looked at him where he was kneeling between her legs. "Last time a man was there and said it was going to hurt, he was wrong. I gave him the night of his life, and he was the one aching the next day." The nameless woman's eyes flicked toward Cinda. "You blushing, lass? What's this ranger been teaching you?"

Rew figured if the woman could jest, she could live. "Move your hands, and don't bite off the tip of your tongue when I do this."

She closed her eyes again and moved her hands, her jaw clamped tight.

Immediately, Rew snatched his hunting knife by the bone hilt and slapped the fire-hot steel against the woman's dark skin where the valaan had slashed her open. Her flesh sizzled, and she screamed, her back arching, her body convulsing. Rew leaned on her, holding her leg flat on the ground as he pressed the scalding blade against her, burning her flesh, sealing the wound.

"Rew?" called Anne, shouting over the woman's screams. "Is everything all right over there?"

"Not really. Give me a moment," he yelled back, nearly thrown off by the woman's twisting and thrashing. He looked down at her. "Your first time?"

She spasmed once more and then passed out.

Chapter Fourteen

⚜

As dawn broke, Rew's hands were clamped firmly beneath his armpits, his cloak wrapped tightly around him, and he was moving in a slow circuit around what they were calling their camp, though it was only a place in the grass where they'd dropped their packs and fallen asleep. It was one hill over from the scene of the battle—as far as they'd been able to take the wounded.

His breath billowed from his mouth, thick with vapor, then trailed behind him like a flag. He could feel walking through the tough grass that he was following a path he'd already worn, but he could hardly see his soaking wet boots when he looked down. They were hidden beneath a heavy layer of mist that clung to the top of their hill and obscured everything else around them. It was as if they were stranded on an island out in the sea, the mainland lost in the distance. He grunted. The analogy felt too close to the truth to be comfortable.

Rew kept walking, following the circuit he'd trod crowning the top of the hill. The path he walked would be obvious to any trackers looking for them, and he would have chastised his rangers for doing the same, but the two-dozen dead narjags they'd left in a pile several hundred paces away weren't exactly hard to find, so he'd forgone his normally cautious habits when it came to leaving traces of his presence. It was luck, not stealth, that he was trusting to keep them safe.

The night before, Lord Fredrick, after receiving stern admonishments and vague threats about how they could not defend against another attack, had cast a glamour about the hill. The nobleman had been reluctant to admit he was capable of such a feat, but Rew strongly suspected he'd done just the same, except on a much larger scale, to conceal the attack against his father's army. Rew didn't mention that theory, as he hadn't wanted to antagonize the nobleman, but he figured if Fredrick could summon enough low magic to hide an army, he could hide their small group.

Fredrick, when he finally agreed to try, had firmly insisted that while his magic could steer away human eyes, he did not believe it would fool the Dark Kind. Even though he still demanded the man cast the spell, Rew had to admit that was a fair point, which was why he was on patrol.

He exhaled, and the cloud of his breath joined the mist that clung to the land like a blanket. Around them, finally with the glow of the sun, he could see caps of other hills shouldering through the fog, and he could see the faint smear that was the road, cutting through the land and off into the gray beyond his vision. It was quiet, the thick air stifling any sound. Not even his own boots were audible as he walked. A dozen armies of narjags could be circling them, and he would have no idea, except that he felt nothing. Nothing at all, except for the flickering warmth of life on the hill in the center of the circuit he walked.

There was a rustle, and he turned to see Zaine rising to her feet. She was picking at her clothing where the dew had dampened it and the fabric clung to her. She bent and gathered the blanket she'd been sleeping beneath. She wrapped that around herself, though Rew guessed it was just as damp as the rest of her attire. With the silent steps of a thief, Zaine left the others and came to join him on his patrol. They both looked out toward the horizon, where the sun was lighting the mist like a sea of flame. Staring across toward the horizon wouldn't do them much good if they were attacked, but Rew couldn't see anything at the bottom of the hill anyway, and the sunrise was pretty.

"You think she'll survive?" wondered Zaine, nodding toward the sleeping figures of their companions.

Rew shrugged.

"I saw you fight that… thing."

"The valaan."

She nodded. "It moved so fast, like… like I don't even know. I don't know how you did it."

"Clean living, faith in the Blessed Mother…"

Zaine snorted then caught herself. In a fierce whisper, she said, "I don't know how you did it, but I know it wasn't that."

Rew grinned at her.

"How long do you think before we can travel?" asked Zaine.

He felt his lips curl down, and Rew shook his head. He didn't know. Too long, though, if he had to guess. They'd killed a valaan and two dozen narjags, but Baron Appleby was worried about thousands of the foul creatures, and if there were thousands of narjags, that meant there had to be plenty more valaan, too, since the one they'd faced had been with a small patrol. If the valaan were limited, they wouldn't waste their numbers on patrol. They would use narjags, like the shaman the party had faced heading to Falvar. That this valaan accompanied the patrol itself, rather than a deputized narjag, was terrifying. That their group almost fell to the one valaan and a handful of narjags made it worse. Against a bigger group of the Dark Kind, not all of them would have survived. King's Sake, he wasn't sure they all had survived. The nameless woman had been teetering on the edge of life for hours, and now, they wouldn't have the questionable help of the other mercenaries. The mercenaries they did have were injured, more a hinderance than a help.

Lord Fredrick would be little help as well if his glamours didn't work on the Dark Kind. If he had other skills, he hadn't admitted them. The nobleman tried to appear mysterious about his ability, but Rew guessed the man truly had no other magical talent. In the time the children had spent in Yarrow, and during the battle against Baron Worgon, he hadn't shown anything other than illusion and a willingness to stab someone in the back.

Rew put the necromancer Ambrose in the same category. Supposedly, he had been collecting wraiths from the barrowlands for Baron Fedgley, so he must have some skill, or he wouldn't have lasted a day in the barrows, but he hadn't lifted a finger against the Dark Kind. One possibility was that the man needed the fresh power of the recently departed to cast his magic. If that was the case, it meant by definition, Ambrose's help would come too late.

Evidently, Zaine must have felt much the same. She was staring at the necromancer like she meant to stick one of her daggers into him. "Do you think—"

Rew waved a hand to shush her. "He's awake. Their kind rarely sleeps. It's quite possible he's listening to us."

Zaine glared at the necromancer, and sure enough, he rolled over, and his eyes blinked open. Ambrose yawned, pretending he had just woken. Rew waved for the man to join them.

"Can I help you?" asked Ambrose innocently when he finally wriggled free of his bedroll and moved to walk beside them, the damp chill of the morning giving him no bother.

"Next time we're under pressure like that, you'll help," said Rew, convinced that the man had been eavesdropping, which did nothing to improve the ranger's opinion of him.

"Well, as you know, it's not so simple—"

"You'll help, or if I survive, I will kill you myself," interrupted Rew. "Everyone in this party will do everything they can to protect all of us, or they're not welcome. And keep in mind, you know too much for us to leave you behind, don't you think? Do not test me, Ambrose."

The necromancer pouted.

"And as we find time," said Rew, pointing a finger at the man, "I expect you to tutor Cinda."

"Hold on—"

"You could try and slip away to join your former friends out there," said Rew, gesturing out at the rolling mist, "but I doubt they'll get far before they encounter more Dark Kind. You spent some time with them. How do you think they'll fare against a valaan? Maybe that will make them better company. You could do a little necromancy, eh? Go the rest of the way to Carff with a gaggle of animated corpses walking in your wake?"

He wiggled his fingers under Ambrose's nose.

Stepping back, the necromancer held up his hands in protest. "You leave me no choice, but even if I had one, I'd stay with you, Ranger. I'll stay, and I'll help. I'm one of yours now, through and through."

Rew snorted, shaking his head at the man's claim. He asked him, "One of mine, is it? Tell me of the woman, then."

Ambrose blinked at him. "She's ferocious in bed, so I've heard. Overheard, I should say. Quiet nights at our lonely camps weren't so quiet or so lonely for her. I've seen her fight exactly as often as you have, and it was impressive. She carries herself with confidence, so that was no great surprise. Truth, even before yesterday, I would have wagered on her to best Borace in battle or the bedroll. She gave him more than she got, that's for sure."

"That's not what I'm asking. Tell me where she's from, what was she doing with the group? She's no more a professional adventurer than you are. Why was she with Borace and the others?"

"I don't know," said the necromancer with an unconvincing shrug. "She's not quiet, but she is secretive. She didn't tell me anything about her past, where she came from, or why she had joined the others. I wasn't with them long, you know. She joined sometime before me but perhaps only by a week or two. In Spinesend, I think. Really, Ranger, I know almost nothing."

"What do you suspect, then?" pressed Rew.

Ambrose pursed his lips and crossed his arms over his chest.

"I feel like we got off to a poor start," said Rew. "We're not really understanding each other, are we?"

Before Ambrose could respond, Rew reached out, grabbed the front of the man's scarlet robes, and then tossed him down the hill.

The necromancer uttered something halfway between a cry of surprise and a curse on the soul of Rew's mother before the rolling fall pounded the breath from his lungs, and all they could hear were grunts and thumps as the man tumbled out of sight into the thick mist.

Zaine stared after him, openmouthed.

"Let's hope that when he climbs back up here, he's more forth-coming," said Rew.

"I'm glad we weren't standing on a hill when you first met us," said Zaine. She turned to Rew. "You really have a thing about throwing people down hills, don't you?"

Rew grinned at her. "Just spellcasters, usually. You're lucky you're a good deal younger than Ambrose or Worgon, and you had no idea who I was. They know who I am and ought to have known better. I suppose you're also lucky none of you were necro-mancers, except Cinda, and that only Raif was a prick."

Zaine laughed, and between her mirth and the approaching sound of Ambrose's curses as he climbed back up the hill, the others started to stir awake.

THAT DAY, THEY DIDN'T TRAVEL. BOTH BORACE AND THE NAMELESS woman had been on the cusp of death, and while Anne had given what empathy she could, it wasn't enough to bring them back so quickly. Anne herself lay on the turf wrapped in her blankets, sleeping more often than she was awake during the day. She insisted she was fit to travel, but not a person in the party took her at her word. Rew and the children sat apart from the wounded and Anne, on the opposite side of the crown of the hill, so their conversation did not disturb the others.

"Feels good to not be the one lying there injured," muttered Raif.

"For once," said his sister with a grin.

He winked at her and patted his greatsword. "I'm learning the use of it."

"Don't be overconfident," warned Cinda.

Raif rolled his eyes at her, but before he could voice a response, Rew remarked, "She's right. Don't be overconfident and overextend. You did well, Raif, and you should be proud of it, but surviving a scrap like that isn't just about swinging your sword. It's about knowing how far you can push yourself into the fray and when to retreat. Against the narjags, you struck when you had the opportunity, but you didn't rush into any trouble you couldn't get away from. That's just as important as how you use your blade." The ranger gestured toward where the berserker Borace was lying. "A lesson on what happens when you push too hard, if you need one."

Raif nodded, looking thoughtful. He grinned, and said, "He was impressive, though, wasn't he? I counted fifteen, sixteen of the creatures that he felled. Imagine telling that story in a tavern, eh?"

Rew grunted and did not respond. Instead, he turned to Zaine. "And you did well also. You selected targets where you had a clean shot and refrained from firing too close to the rest of us. You didn't panic, and best of all, you hit what you were shooting at."

"Most of the time," said Raif, brushing a hand over his head as if to make sure an arrow wasn't there, stuck in his hair.

Zaine reached over and punched him in the arm. "I may have missed that narjag, but I didn't hit you either. Stop complaining."

Rew grinned. "The shots I saw were well-aimed."

"Next time," assured Cinda, "I'll do better. I won't hesitate, like I did yesterday."

Rew shook his head. "No, lass, you did the right thing. Your power is still new to you, and it's no shame to admit you've difficulty controlling it. That's understandable. Necromancy is a dangerous art, and while I expect you'll come into it, you haven't yet. It's better to hold back, to wait until you're certain of what you can do or certain there's no other choice. Also, yesterday, when you sent that pulse into the narjag, you risked showing the others in our party what you're capable of. Remember, lass, the king believes it is your sister who has talent. It's worth all of our lives to keep that secret from him."

Tight-lipped, Cinda nodded.

"That reminds me," muttered Rew. He stood and gestured to Ambrose.

The necromancer was sitting with Lord Fredrick, halfway between the wounded and Rew and the children, as if the two men weren't sure of their welcome in either group. Fredrick was sitting stiff as new paper, attempting to ignore everyone else, and Ambrose was pouting. Apparently, the necromancer was still put out from when Rew threw him down the hill. Ever since he'd gotten to the top, and Rew had shaken some information out of him about the nameless woman, the necromancer had been sulking by himself or in the company of Lord Fredrick, which, given how much the two of them conversed, was still essentially by himself. No one bothered to try and comfort Ambrose, as even the simplest of friendly comments were met with icy regard. The necromancer had not been pleasant to be around that morning, although when Rew considered it, he conceded that very few necromancers were pleasant to be around ever.

Rew waved Ambrose over. He told the necromancer, "Today, while the others are resting, you'll begin teaching the lass."

Ambrose bared his teeth at Rew. The ranger glanced meaningfully down the hill.

"You don't earn loyalty through violence and intimidation," muttered Ambrose.

"Did Borace have your loyalty? You didn't lift a finger to assist him when he was swarmed by narjags. From what I've seen, I'm not missing much."

"Yet you ask for my help." Ambrose looked away and sneered toward the resting berserker. "The man ought to have known what would happen when he charged out alone. I cannot protect everyone."

"You didn't protect anyone," reminded Rew.

"I help those who deserve it."

"Did Baron Fedgley deserve your help?"

Ambrose didn't respond.

"Twice, I witnessed Fedgley call wraiths," said Rew. "Five of them the first time. Then, I believe it was three, the second time. The first time, they were captured by a powerful spellcaster using an enchanted box he'd prepared for them. The second time, the lass banished them. She banished three wraiths from the barrowlands."

Ambrose's eyes popped open wide, and his jaw dropped.

"With the right breeding, the child is always stronger than the parent," said Rew. "The lass is capable of more than her father, but she's untrained. I don't care if you think she deserves your help or not. She needs it, and you're going to teach her what you can, just as we discussed."

"She banished three wraiths? You're certain?"

Rew nodded.

"How?" demanded Ambrose, staring into Rew's face, as if afraid to look at Cinda. "The wraiths Fedgley summoned from the barrowlands are ancient apparitions, terribly powerful. Managing a creature like that…"

"It was instinctual. She has the talent, but she needs it refined. I hate to say this, but she needs your help."

"Has she cast spells other than the funeral fire that I saw?"

"Death's flame."

"An early one, typically," said Ambrose, reaching up and scratching his bald head. "One of the most common for an untrained caster to fling. I, myself, began using it when—"

"She killed another necromancer with it," interrupted Rew, "one in Duke Eeron's service. There were three of them. Did you know them?"

Ambrose opened his mouth and closed it. "I, ah, I was familiar with Eeron's minions, yes. She... truly, she killed one of them with death's flame? I tried to contact them in Spinesend, but I learned they hadn't survived the battle with Worgon..."

"She killed one," Rew confirmed. He leaned close and whispered, "I killed the other two." He waited a breath and asked, "You'll help her, then?"

Ambrose swallowed. "I will do as you ask, but you should know, with strength like hers, she will quickly exceed my own ability. There are things, spells, that are beyond me, which she will become capable of. Necromancy is a dangerous art, Ranger, and we have few of the tools and reference material that is necessary for study. Someone like her, working like this... There is much damage that she could do."

"I know it's dangerous, but it's what must be done. Teach her what you can and advise her of what is beyond you. That's all I ask." Rew crossed his arms over his chest, looking down at the other man. "You didn't actually collect any wraiths for Baron Fedgley, did you? I'm guessing you didn't even breach a barrow. That's how you survived? You lived because you did nothing?"

Ambrose shifted uncomfortably. "Those spirits are ancient. They're beyond me, beyond all of us. Only Fedgley himself could control them, and even he..." Ambrose glanced at Cinda and shuddered. He looked back to Rew. "The others were fools, and they did not understand their own limitations. Fedgley did not employ us to control those monsters. He employed us simply to open the doors and set off the traps. I think he was surprised every time one of us survived what came out of those barrows."

"Teach her," said Rew, nodding to acknowledge Ambrose's honesty, "and I'll trade you no more barbs about loyalty. As long as you're teaching her, I'll treat you as one of us, and I will do what I can to protect you."

"Fair enough," said Ambrose. He turned, shaking out his bright red robes, looking ethereal in the morning sun as the mist billowed away from him.

Rew figured the man would have been quite pleased with the image, though he certainly did not intend it to look that way.

The necromancer drew himself up, tilted his chin toward the sky, gathered his robes high, and gave Cinda an oily smile. "Shall we, then?"

Rew offered Cinda an apologetic squeeze on her shoulder and said, "Raif, take the watch while the two of them talk. Zaine, you're with me. We're going scouting."

"Scouting for what?" asked the thief.

"Anything," said Rew, putting a hand on the hilt of his hunting knife. "Anything at all."

REW LED ZAINE DOWN INTO THE MIST THAT CLUNG BETWEEN THE hills, the early morning sun merely warming the air above, doing nothing to cut through the pervasive moisture. Most of the day, Rew suspected, the white shroud would hang between the hills around them. They had no choice but to stay put because of their wounded, which meant they were sitting there waiting for Dark Kind to come by and smell them. Lord Fredrick claimed his glamour would do nothing to hide their scent, and Rew figured the nobleman was likely correct. Low magic worked on the caster's connection, and Fredrick would have no connection to the Dark Kind. They were foreign to the world, and it made them resistant to magic. It helped some that the mist and the still breeze would prevent the party's scent from carrying far, but all the same, Rew would feel better after doing a bit of scouting, looking for tracks and seeing what else was around them.

They went first to the site of the battle they'd had against the valaan and the narjags. They found the creatures still there and, unsurprisingly, still dead. Rew's visibility was cut because of the mist, but the wet grass was impossible to move across without leaving some sign. It meant he could see what had come in the night, and there were fresh tracks there.

Zaine grunted as they circled the scene of the fight. Rew didn't need to tell her what the trampled emerald green blades meant. Others had come and surveyed what occurred and then left. Narjags, Rew could tell, and he guessed that Zaine suspected as much. The Dark Kind had left, though, and that was unusual. Narjags wouldn't hesitate to eat their own dead, and these bodies were undisturbed.

"Another valaan," surmised Rew. "Leading another patrol, I'd guess, and it kept them moving when they found the bodies. Narjags have poor eyesight, and it's possible they missed our tracks, or that they decided to follow the mercenaries instead. We got lucky, their nostrils would have been filled with the scent of… this, and they didn't detect us nearby. Valaan… I don't know. It's rare to see them at all and even rarer for someone to survive the encounter. It could be they didn't see where we left either, or maybe Fredrick's magic is actually working on them."

"You can see the valaan's tracks?"

He shook his head. "They pass nearly as lightly as I do, but narjags will eat their own if there are no other food sources, and with several thousand of them in the region, they will have already stripped most of the wild animals from the area. The only reason they wouldn't feast on their fallen brethren is if the valaan wouldn't allow it. If we had better light, perhaps I could find where the valaan walked, but there's no need. I'd rather keep moving than waste our time here. We've seen what we need to."

Zaine turned, holding an arrow nocked on her bow, looking into the mist, clearly worried the valaan and the narjags were going to leap out at any moment. "Why wouldn't a valaan allow them to eat?"

"Because it wanted to keep them hungry and eager."

"Stanton."

"Aye, that'd be my guess."

"You're right. We don't have much time, then."

Rew led Zaine away from the dead Dark Kind. There was nothing else to see there. They traveled in a broad circle around the hill where the rest of the party was encamped. A quarter-league north, parallel to the highway, they saw more tracks of the Dark Kind, far enough away that they wouldn't elicit any notice from people traveling the road, but it was enough of a sign that Rew was certain everything they'd heard from Appleby and what they'd suspected was true. It wasn't a handful of randomly scattered groups. This was planned, and they weren't just waiting to come in through the portal stones. They were already there. The Dark Kind were still traveling in small groups, though, several dozen of them together. He suspected that was how they'd arrived, trickling in wherever the portal stones were located, allaying suspicion that it was a mass gathering. That they were still in smaller groups meant they weren't ready to move on Stanton yet. Waiting for more of them, maybe, or something else?

By mid-afternoon, Rew had spotted signs that could be from hundreds of Dark Kind, all roving in packs of one to two dozen.

"There are more valaan but not many," he mused. "They can't be worried about attack from the men in Stanton, so they've split up the narjags so they don't fall upon each other. They'll wait until it's time then assemble all of these groups into an army. When they do..."

"Then Stanton will have no chance," finished Zaine.

Rew nodded. "We, on the other hand, do have a chance because of this. We could face two dozen narjags and have a hope that most of our party would survive."

"Most of us? Well, that's good to know," replied Zaine dryly.

Rew winked, and they kept moving. It wasn't until later that he realized there was another reason the valaan might be keeping the narjags spread out. It'd make it harder for Valchon, or any other spellcaster, to deal with them. It didn't change anything for Rew's companions, or for the people in Stanton, but it demonstrated a level of coordination and planning that was horrifying.

As they moved along, they found more tracks from the narjags, but they did not find any of the creatures themselves. Most of the tracks were a day or two old, with just a few places they could have been left the night before. Toward the highway, Rew spotted the tracks of the other mercenaries.

"Looks like more than just seven men," remarked Zaine, pointing to the trampled grass.

Rew knelt and showed the thief where the boots of humans had pressed the soil and then where the bare feet of the narjags had followed. "Those mercenaries are in for a rough night, if they still live. Not much we can do about that, unfortunately. They'll be a full day ahead of us by now. No ayres, though. That's one bit of good news."

They finished their scouting and returned to the hill.

Chapter Fifteen

❧

The next morning began with a shout. Ambrose, who Rew had put on watch because the man needed only a few hours of sleep, screeched a shrill warning.

Rew kicked off his blanket, scrambling out of the tangled fabric, and rose with his longsword. The camp was cold, his companions barely visible in the pre-dawn gloom, the stars and moon already having faded away. Ambrose was standing on the edge of the hill, his hands smoking as he frantically tried to draw power.

"Watch the backside," Rew growled to Zaine, who'd sprung to her feet almost as quickly as he. The rest of the party was struggling upright, blinking sleep from their eyes and, in the case of the wounded, moving as if they'd aged fifty years since the days before.

Rew took Ambrose's side and saw that a dozen narjags were charging up the hill. The creatures' bestial features were twisted in glee, thinking they'd stumbled across an easy meal. In the gloom, Rew saw nothing beyond the first wave, so he raised his longsword.

"Backside is clear!" shouted Zaine.

"Stay there," Rew called back in response.

Raif joined them, and Ambrose retreated, the vapor of death's breath still curling around his fists, but there was little of it. Was the man that useless, or was he merely pretending to be?

"I'll break them up. You finish any that keep coming," instructed Rew, shaking his head and shoving thoughts about Ambrose away.

Raif nodded.

The giant berserker Borace appeared. The man paused, resting his weight on the head of his battle-axe. The haft sank into the turf, and his chest rose and fell with labored breathing. He rumbled, "I should go first."

"You're still recovering," argued Rew.

The man opened his mouth to disagree, but the time for talk was over. The narjags were almost to the crest of the hill, so without bothering to discuss the matter further, Rew plunged down into the Dark Kind like a stabbing knife.

Narjags, without a valaan to guide them, act almost entirely instinctually. When they see food, they try to eat it. When they're afraid, they run. They were startled by Rew's attack, and anything that startled them frightened them. They split in front of him, which was the first bit of their undoing.

Rew, wielding his longsword in one hand and his hunting knife in the other, cleaved into the narjags that were too slow to avoid him, and as they were all scrambling away, he spared no effort for defense. He simply lashed out, raining blows on exposed flesh, killing some, wounding several. He passed between them like a scythe, and half a dozen narjags were down when he skidded to a halt on the hill and spun.

Above him, Raif and Borace had not waited. Raif, twirling his greatsword above his head, unleashed a devastating attack on a narjag, hacking into the thing and sending it flying as he continued the stroke. The narjag pitched down the hillside, cart-wheeling head over heels before it landed.

Borace, bellowing a war cry, swung his battle-axe with every-thing he had behind it. The giant head of sharp steel smashed into a narjag, cleanly cutting the creature in two, and then it carried into another and parted that one as well. Borace, weakened from his ordeal the day and night before, spun off his feet and lost his balance. He fell to the turf, but the narjags around him were fleeing backward, evidently having no interest in the man or his giant axe any longer.

To their dismay, when they turned to flee, they found Rew. With calculated thrusts, he slayed the remaining Dark Kind. It was over in the space of a few breaths, and twelve narjags were dead. Rew stood ready, scanning the early morning landscape around them, but he saw nothing. The fog wasn't as thick as the day before. He didn't think it could hide a large group nearby, and it hung motionless. Nothing moved in the gloom except their own party.

Rew ascended to where Raif was helping Borace back to his feet. The big lad said breathlessly to the berserker, "I cannot believe you did that. Injured as you are, you still took down two of them. A well-swung blow, truly."

Borace grunted and put one of his big paws on Raif's armored shoulder, nearly knocking the boy over. "We're fighters, lad, and fighters fight until the day we rise no more."

Nodding vigorously, Raif helped the giant berserker up to the top of the hill, whispering admiration for the way the man had swung his axe, the way he'd attacked with no fear.

Rew rolled his eyes and then glanced down at the narjags. No valaan this time, but he spied a narjag wearing a peculiar head-dress. Rew moved back and squatted next to it, frowning at the dead narjag. It was small, unlike the creatures he'd suspected might be shamans near Falvar and in the wilderness, but its arms were covered in a network of scar tissue. Wounds it'd gotten fighting its kind for dominance, guessed Rew. It had no staff, but there were trinkets on its wrists and waist. Bangles it could have stolen off the body of a prostitute or actress, he thought. Worthless, just colorful stones and grimy tin. Enough to catch the eye of a narjag, evidently. In the fight, Rew hadn't noticed the creature commanding the others, and it certainly hadn't cast any spells. Were they shaman, or something else?

Sighing, Rew stood. It was evidence enough that the narjags had some sort of hierarchical leadership. Months ago, he would have spent countless hours musing over the matter with his ranger mentor, Tate, but Tate was dead, and Rew had other concerns now. He gave one last look around the bodies of the narjags then went to join the others.

At the top of the hill, Anne had risen from her bedroll and was prodding at Borace where his wounds had reopened from the vigor of the one swing he'd managed in the fight. The others were standing as well, looking nervous.

The nameless woman had her sword out, but she didn't appear eager to use it. Unlike Borace, she could probably guess the damage she would do to herself by joining the fight. "I suppose you don't need us, then?"

"We handled it," barked Borace, stepping away from Anne, even though the empath was tugging at him, evidently not done patching him back up again. "You can lay down and get a bit more rest, if you like. Mayhap in a bit, I'll lay down with you?"

The woman snorted and looked around. "I don't suppose anyone thought to bring coffee? If I must listen to this jackass braying all day, I'm going to need something to keep me awake."

"The offer stands," cackled Borace.

Rew shook his head at the two of them. "No time for a fire, no time for coffee, no time for… anything else. We've killed two packs of narjags within a couple of hundred paces of here. Fredrick's glamour clearly didn't work against them, and they can smell their own dead. The smell is probably what brought this last batch to us, and it will be more pungent now. If a breeze picks up, they'll find us again in no time. We've got to get moving, get to the highway. Our only hope is to get some distance between ourselves and here. If we stick around, sooner or later one of these groups is going to be too big to handle."

The children moved quickly to begin packing their gear, used to following Rew's orders. Ambrose and Fredrick started packing their kit as well, though not as quickly as the children, and the nameless woman and Borace moved as slow as cold honey. Sighing, Rew gestured for Raif and Zaine to help the two injured mercenaries.

"That's quite a talent you have," the nameless woman said to Anne. She collected a pair of fresh trousers from Zaine and, without modesty, began to change. Rew looked away then hissed at Zaine so that she did as well. Raif hadn't noticed. Cinda seemed uninterested, and the other men watched while pretending they were not. Continuing to Anne, the woman nodded to her thigh. "An impressive scar for my future lovers to find. A bit of a conversation piece, eh? May have been smooth skin there if the ranger hadn't gotten to it with that knife of his. I could tell the lads that—the King's Ranger left his mark on me. What do you think, Ranger? You marked your territory, eh? When are you going to claim it?"

Rew tried to ignore her while across the camp Borace fumed.

"It's not completely healed," warned Anne. "It should hold for a hike along a flat road, but that leg won't do you much good in a fight. Won't hold up well under any vigorous activity, you understand?"

The nameless woman's grin split her dark face, revealing gleaming white teeth and a twinkle in her eyes that Rew hadn't seen before. "Aye, I hear you. What do I owe you for the healing?"

"Nothing," said Anne, glancing at Rew.

The nameless woman followed the look then boomed, "If he's yours, then you oughta claim him. It's not often a man gets between my legs and doesn't want to come back. You've my respect, empath, and whatever you ask, I owe you, but I've needs..."

"He's not my man," said Anne, flushing.

"No?" asked the woman, turning toward Rew. "Well, then."

"Woman," snapped Borace, his meaty hands clutching his giant battle-axe.

Her eyebrow arched, and she stuck out one hip in a saucy pose. "We ain't married, Borace."

"Aye, but…"

"You want my company? You need to earn it," snapped the nameless woman. "You're not our leader anymore, and I'm not falling for any of your lies. Look here, the lass is packing my bedroll. Maybe she's the one who oughta share it."

Zaine, stuffing a roll of blankets into the woman's pack, nearly fell over.

Rew rubbed his head, feeling the prickly hair there standing on end like the hackles of a dog. King's Sake, these mercenaries were worse than the children. Couldn't anything be simple? Anne paused beside him on the way to her own gear, brushing his shoulder with hers, and then, they both prepared to leave.

THE REST OF THE DAY PASSED UNEVENTFULLY EXCEPT FOR THE discovery of the ravaged bodies of the seven mercenaries who'd run away. The mercenaries had made it within fifty yards of the highway and had been set upon there by a pack of narjags. They hadn't gone easily. There were twenty of their foes who'd joined them in death, but once they'd fallen, they'd paid a horrific price for defeat.

Evidently, there wasn't a valaan in the party of their attackers, so there'd been nothing to stay the hunger of the narjags. They'd feasted messily. The Dark Kind had ripped the mercenaries apart, tearing off their clothing and sinking teeth and sharp-nailed hands into their flesh. They'd torn it away and consumed it, taking the meaty bits of muscle and certain organs which presumably they thought were delicacies. All of the mercenaries' skulls were cracked open and hollowed out. Their big bones were shattered as well, and the marrow sucked from them. It was a horrific sight.

Zaine, feeling no need to prove her masculinity, staggered

several steps away and lost her breakfast. Cinda and Anne both turned away. Rew, Borace, the nameless woman, and Ambrose looked over the tableau of broken, torn flesh in disgust.

There wasn't much to see once it'd been determined what had happened. Any items of use had been stripped from the bodies by the narjags, and when the Dark Kind had departed following their feast, they left a clear, bloody trail the direction they'd gone back into the hills.

"Well," said Ambrose, breaking the silence, "I'm glad I didn't go with them."

Rew snorted then led the group past the dead mercenaries. The ranger did not need to ask if anyone wanted to try and scoop the mauled bits of flesh together and bury it. The mercenaries hadn't lifted a finger when they'd all faced the first pack of narjags together, so after Borace searched through the remains collecting the coins and other valuables the narjags had left behind, the dead were given the level of respect they'd earned.

Once the party reached the road, they cut through the moors south of Stanton at a much quicker clip. The highway curved sinuously between the hills, but it was hard-packed, and there'd been little rain in the days before. It was easy hiking, but even then, they stopped well before sunset. The nameless woman, some hours before, had begun limping terribly, and Rew had offered her the support of his shoulder. She'd gritted her teeth and accepted his aid. When the giant fighter Borace started dragging his feet as well, Rew called a halt. Borace was several stones heavier than even Raif, and with his armor and over-sized battle-axe, none of them would make it far supporting the huge man.

They camped like before, atop one of the hills beside the road, and no one bothered to look for firewood. They had no idea how far out from Stanton the Dark Kind might be roving, and no one wanted to give away their position to the sharp-nosed creatures.

Lord Fredrick, after arguing sulkily with Rew about it, cast his glamour over the hill again. The man had a point. His magic had not prevented the Dark Kind from finding them, but narjags were not the only danger so far from civilization. Besides, the nobleman's petulant objections were irritating, and they only served to make Rew more insistent the man cast his spell.

Once the glamour was in place, it was still just late afternoon, and the sun shone brightly. Rew encouraged Raif and Zaine to practice their sparring. The two were unevenly matched, but they were comfortable enough to give each other direct feedback and advice. They worked through their movements, their words just as pointed as their blades. It wasn't long before the berserker Borace hobbled over to them and settled against a rock that had thrust from the side of the hill. He began giving his own brusque instructions. Particularly with Raif, Borace offered firm corrections coupled with incredible stories of how he'd used each move in deadly combat.

The berserker's tales were peppered with other claims of conquests, and Anne's face soured at the lewd descriptions the big man gave. Both Raif and Zaine hung on every word.

At one point when Borace offered a recommendation, Raif glanced at Rew, and the ranger shrugged. He hadn't seen Borace following any of his own advice during the battle with the narjags, and he doubted any of the man's stories about his own prowess were true, but from what he could hear, the mercenary captain's advice was a good fit for the way Raif fought, and instruction from another point of view could be valuable. Any instruction was worth something.

Rew frowned then leaned back and pointed a finger at Ambrose. "You too."

Grumbling under his breath, the necromancer shuffled closer to Cinda and began speaking to her in low tones, as if sharing secrets the rest of them shouldn't hear. As if anyone would want to overhear the vile things necromancers discussed. Rew cocked his ear enough, though, to ensure what the necromancer was telling Cinda was accurate. Rew knew little of necromancy, but he knew more than nothing. At the very least, Ambrose was using the correct terminology and seemed to be explaining real techniques. Rew had been worried the man was a complete fraud, but it seemed he did know something of the art.

Between scowling at Borace's back and muttering at the man's more colorful tales, Anne started supper, and the nameless woman scooted toward Rew. With a furtive glance in Lord Fredrick's direction, she asked Rew, "The lord thinks he leads this party, but you've got them all working for you, haven't you? Been that way since Baron Appleby sent us on our way, hasn't it?"

Rew did not respond.

Lord Fredrick, across from where Anne was working, pulled a skin of wine from his pack and began to drink it. He didn't offer to share. His gaze was fixed somewhere halfway between the arms practice and the discussion of necromantic theory. It wasn't clear if he'd heard the nameless woman or not.

"What did Ambrose tell you about me?" asked the nameless woman, lowering her voice so there was no chance the necromancer could hear her.

"Nothing," replied the ranger, more or less telling the truth.

"If you're curious, why don't you just ask me yourself?"

He blinked at her. "I, ah, I did. You wouldn't even tell me your name."

"Fair enough," she acknowledged, granting him one of her cat-like smiles. "A lady is entitled to some secrets, don't you think?"

"If a lady wants to keep her secrets, she shouldn't be so obviously hiding something," muttered Rew. "Everyone is attracted to a good mystery, after all."

"You're attracted to me? I'm blushing, Ranger," she said, not blushing at all. "What is this alluring mystery you think I'm surrounding myself with?"

"You weren't part of Borace's band for more than a month or so, were you? Joined them in Spinesend, I bet, and when they sensed things were getting heated, you left with them toward Carff. But you all got stuck for a few weeks in Stanton, working for the baron. Why? Why not keep going south on your own when it became obvious Stanton was in trouble? What were you doing with Borace and his minions in the first place? You're not like them, that's obvious, and while he's commenting often enough on your history with him, I get the impression that's not it either."

"I've expensive tastes," claimed the woman, "and a girl needs coin to support herself."

Rew pursed his lips and shook his head. "You've enchanted armor and an enchanted sword. Your kit is worth more than what Borace's entire band would earn in a decade, two decades maybe, depending on the properties of your gear. You could travel to Carff and sell your armor in the market and never have to work again, if that was your goal. Pfah! What was Borace even paying you to join him? Certainly not what you could command from a nobleman or a proper mercenary company."

The woman plucked at the delicate chainmail beneath her brass breastplates. "I told you, expensive tastes. Not much good this armor did me, though. That valaan was a hair away from taking my life."

Rew watched Raif and Zaine spar, Borace now circling them, barking tips and tricks as he did. The young fighter listened intently, but unless he was telling one of his ribald stories, the thief ignored every word from the berserker's mouth.

"What of you, Ranger?" asked the woman. "The King's Ranger of the Eastern Territory, I hear, yet we're not in the Eastern Territory. You're not walking this way to Mordenhold, so why are you headed to Carff? I was told your kind report directly to the king, that not even the princes have authority over the rangers. Is that true?"

"There's more than one way to get to Mordenhold."

The woman frowned at him. "A portal stone?"

Rew quieted and did not answer. Knowledge of portal stones was not common, but she was right. There was a portal stone in Carff that led directly to Mordenhold. He'd meant merely to distract her, but with the portal stone... No, not yet. Cinda wasn't ready yet, not to see the king. But was it foolish to waste the chance to get there? Valchon wouldn't stand in the way of him going to Mordenhold. If anything, the prince would help. Rew turned to Cinda, where she and Ambrose were still in close discussion. Would she ever be ready to face the king? What would they do if she wasn't?

"What are you thinking about, Ranger?" asked the nameless woman.

He let his head roll on his neck so that he was looking at her again. "I'm wondering where you came from."

"Spinesend."

"Iyre?" he guessed.

The woman was silent.

"There's a group of warrior-priests who serve the Cursed Father in Iyre," he continued, absentmindedly drumming his fingers on his leg. "They've dark skin, like yours. Membership is hereditary, I believe. Marriages are arranged within the community, and while they serve the Cursed Father and those who are joining his embrace, they keep to themselves. All are men, though. Odd they'd have armor wrought like that for a woman, but they must have. Enchanted armor, crafted just for you. Do those warrior-priests sound familiar to you? What role do you serve in the priesthood to earn such a gift?"

"You didn't get all of that from Ambrose."

Rew shrugged and did not respond.

"You didn't, because he doesn't know. Hmm. A ranger for the Eastern Territory, but you're familiar enough with Iyre to know about the Sons of the Father? Why should I answer any of your questions if you won't answer mine? How do you know Iyre and the Sons, Ranger?"

"Rangers like to walk. I did a lot of walking before I was assigned to the eastern wilderness."

The woman snorted and stood, leaning heavily on her uninjured leg and waving his hand away as he moved to help her. "You're a frustrating man, you know?"

"Tell it," said Anne from a dozen paces away.

The woman granted the empath a shallow bow then stalked toward where Raif and Cinda were sparring. Borace gave her a big grin, but the woman's attention was on the children.

Rew lay back and closed his eyes, letting the last of the afternoon sun warm him. He let his mind drift, extending his senses, listening to Ambrose instruct Cinda on marshaling her power for the death's breath spell, and to Anne as she rustled about with the food, and then to Borace and the nameless woman as they instructed Raif and Zaine on the finer intricacies of combat footwork.

The camp was peaceful, everyone playing their role except for him. He lay there with his eyes closed, half-listening, half-thinking. A portal to Mordenhold. They could be in the capital in days. They could be anywhere in days, if he knuckled his forehead and behaved himself in front of Valchon. They were going to see the prince on behalf of Stanton, and Rew had his own business with the man, but what to make of the chance the portal stones provided?

Should he confront Valchon or go to Mordenhold? Or perhaps west, to one of the other capitals? Calb and Heindaw would never expect Rew to appear from one of the portal stones. Did it make sense to face one of them first, while Valchon dealt with the Dark Kind? Cinda was learning and growing, but could she learn enough to face the king?

Vaisius Morden thought it was her sister, Kallie, who held the power. If Rew told the king it was his own sons behind the plot to use the Fedgleys, then the king may take care of the princes for them, but he'd take care of Cinda and Rew as well. Besides, would it be any good to eliminate the princes if the king remained upon the throne? Rew figured he could convince the king to act against the princes, but was it possible to keep Cinda's power and his own involvement from the king? What else would the king do in pursuit of his sons? Vaisius Morden was not known for his restraint, and it wouldn't be out of character if he destroyed the princes' cities just to get at the men inside. Rew hoped he could face the princes, but he wasn't sure he'd prevail. The king... The king could handle all three of them.

With tortured thoughts, Rew succumbed to the exhaustion that had been chasing him for days, and two hours before dark, while Anne was still cooking his supper, he fell asleep.

Chapter Sixteen

The hike south was mercifully free of Dark Kind, which Rew suspected meant that the creatures were clustered close around Stanton, and they were likely going to attack soon. He felt it like an ominous cloud behind them, the danger to the city and his impotence to do anything about it except to hurry, to rush toward Carff, and to plead with Prince Valchon to save his own people.

But as much as they wanted to hurry, they made poor progress. Anne recovered in time from the energy she'd spent healing, and the others could easily handle her chores around the campsite, but Borace and the nameless woman were slow to regain their vigor, and Lord Fredrick spent as much time dragging his feet as he did lifting them. When he wasn't speaking in hushed tones with Cinda, Ambrose drifted along like a wraith, just as quiet but only half as creepy. Getting them all going was like shepherding a pack of turtles.

Rew prodded and chided, but there was only so much he could do when the two warriors were simply incapable of more. He'd considered leaving them, but after a quick word with Anne, he dropped that idea.

"When an empath heals, a connection is forged," she'd

reminded him. "I feel them, and I feel for them. They're exhausted, Rew. It's not laziness. It is true, bone-deep exhaustion. Whether I want to or not, I care for their well-being. If we push them too hard, they'll collapse. If we leave them, who knows what could happen to them. The roads are as empty as I've ever seen them, which means soon enough, they'll be filled with bandits and worse."

Rew grunted. "We didn't ask them to accompany us."

"Does it matter? They're with us now."

"It's like the children," said Rew, keeping his voice low. "You're going to tell me they're family next. We can't afford it, Anne. They've their own motivations, their own reasons for being on this journey."

Anne scowled.

"She's a priest of the Cursed Father," whispered Rew.

"No, she's not," retorted Anne.

Rew raised an eyebrow.

"Priests of the Cursed Father are always men," said Anne, "and that woman is very clearly a woman. I thought you'd seen that when—"

"She was bleeding out! You know that's not what happened. And you're right about the priests, but she as much confirmed it to me." Rew frowned and lowered his voice. "How do you know all of the Cursed Father's priests are men? It's only the Blessed Mother I've heard you offering prayers to, and you've never been to Iyre, have you?"

"No one prays to the Cursed Father," replied Anne. "Not even the Sons of the Father."

Rew's eyes lit up. "The herbalist in Spinesend. I knew it."

"She was a woman, if you recall. As I said, there are no female priests of the Cursed Father."

"But she's affiliated with the cult, is she not? I saw the totems she was selling, the artifacts and the bones. She's a purveyor for those who seek the favor of the cult. Did... Were you..."

"That's not why I knew her," muttered Anne. "She's involved

in other, ah, other matters. She helps people, women, who need a place to go. You recall the beds in her loft? Some women are in terrible situations, and need help slipping the chains that their men or others have put upon them. She helps them. I once did as well."

"The girls in your inn."

Anne smiled bitterly. "Aye, them, and many more like them before we came to Eastwatch. Those girls were sent to me, and I made them a safe place to regain their footing and their pride."

"Why didn't you tell me?"

"Because you would have tried to solve the problem, Rew, and some problems like that cannot be solved. Not by one man with a sword."

He grunted, then asked, "But what was all of that in the woman's shop, then? The bones and artifacts?"

"She sells herbs, too, or did you miss those? She… She had to have a cover, and what better cover than an affiliate of those who worship the Cursed Father? Believe me, nothing sends a man running like a description of what some of those powders in her shop can do to…"

She winked at him, and Rew let it drop. Anne, once she took someone under her wing, wasn't going to leave them behind. It didn't matter how often Rew made comments about how many people had been in Stanton and the risk to them if the party didn't move faster. Anne cared for those she could see and that she could touch. It was who she was, and he'd learned he wasn't going to change that. He didn't want to change that.

And like it or not, she'd taken in the nameless woman. He could argue with her about it, but he knew he'd be wasting his time.

So because the others couldn't push too hard, they paused early each evening. They couldn't hike, but Rew took advantage of the adventurers' knowledge and their presence. He had Borace and the nameless woman instructing Raif and Zaine, and Ambrose was sitting with Cinda each evening. Lord Fredrick,

Rew left alone. Allegedly, he was a talented low magician, but Rew and Anne had no interest in trying to convince the man to share what he knew. It seemed the only talent the nobleman wanted to display was bemoaning his place in life. As the days passed, Rew found a new sympathy for Fredrick's father, Baron Worgon. Rew didn't quite forgive Worgon for his actions, but he thought he understood the baron's put-upon outlook every time his son's name had come up.

The exposure to other tutors was good for the children. Raif seemed to listen to Borace more closely than he ever did Rew, and Zaine had become enamored with the nameless woman. Borace was the type of fighter Raif aspired to be—a bull of a man who relied on his strength and ferocious attacks but certainly not his brains. Raif was like his calf, following him with his eyes when they were not in close discussion and emulating the giant berserker in all aspects. More than once, Rew had to still Raif's sharpening tongue with a pointed stare. He thought it ridiculous that the young noble was looking up to the larger fighter, but no one had ever argued about the wisdom of youth. As far as Rew was concerned, the one-time they'd seen Borace in real combat, the berserker nearly died. It wasn't about the size of one's axe, Rew had declared to Raif, but how one used it.

At least, he'd tried to say that until he'd been interrupted by Zaine's cackling. He'd attempted to rephrase, but the moment was lost. The thief's admiration of the nameless woman, at least, Rew could better understand.

The nameless woman strutted as if she was a fierce warrior princess, and when the light hit the woman's armor in the evenings, she looked the part. The gleaming bronze plates and tightly woven chain shone like she spent an hour a day polishing it, because she did. After every sparring session, regardless of whether she'd been touched or even dirtied, she would clean her armor and her blade. Caring for your equipment was important, but the woman's kit was enchanted. It would hold up without constant attention. Over the days they traveled together, Rew decided it was more the need to complete a ritual than it was a need to clean her gear. There was something about the movements which the woman wanted to hold onto, something or someone she honored with that ritual. When he asked her about it, she merely stared at him. While she was unabashedly strange, Rew had to give her credit. The nameless woman knew what she was doing with her blade. She moved like the wind and struck like lightning. The tips she gave Zaine, and her ability to translate those words into demonstrations, were valuable for the thief. In a few short days, Zaine's confidence with her daggers began to grow.

Ambrose, on the other hand, had earned no one's admiration. It turned out he was exactly as they'd expected—a necromancer of marginal talent who'd only survived as long as he had by scurrying away beneath a rock every time someone looked at him sideways. He was a helpless coward, but he did know more of necromancy than Rew or Anne, so that was something. Rew could only hope the hours Cinda spent in his company were worth it for the girl, and that through Ambrose's cycle of preening and sniveling, she found some knowledge she could use.

There were times Rew worried the necromancer was just teaching her parlor tricks with half a mind to annoy Rew. Most of the hushed discussions between the two happened dozens of paces away from the others and lasted well into the night as the two necromancers slept fewer hours than the rest of them.

One night, while Rew took a shift at watch, he was startled by a terrified shriek of surprise from Cinda. He dashed toward where she and Ambrose knelt together away from the others. He skidded to a stop. In front of the two of them, a foul-smelling opossum teetered uncertainly on its four legs. Half the fur on its face had sloughed away, and Rew saw bugs clinging there where they'd feasted upon the opossum's corpse. It'd been… dead.

"Yes," hissed Ambrose, "yes, you've got it. Now, push your thoughts through the link, and move the right—pfah! You lost it."

The dead opossum flopped onto the dirt, motionless.

Rew, looking over the shoulders of the two necromancers, thought he was going to be sick.

"I felt… It was like a part of me, a part of me that was confused. I—It wanted to run."

Stroking his smooth chin and nodding, Ambrose replied, "Naturally."

Cinda reached up and clasped her head. "I still feel its terror."

"Animal instincts are powerful," responded Ambrose sagely. "They're more powerful than human emotions. Their thoughts are simpler, though, and the passage of their souls more fleeting. It is easier to bind an animal than a person, but more difficult to command them. Getting an animal such as this to retain instructions without constant maintenance through the link is virtually impossible. Because people have better developed capabilities for memory and because you share a common understanding of how to communicate, people are more useful vessels. When binding large groups of souls, always use human corpses, as you'll find you cannot continue instructing more than two or three base animals."

"I see."

"Animals are good for practice as dead ones are easier to come by," murmured the necromancer. He glanced back over his shoulder at Rew. "They garner less scrutiny from those who do not appreciate our art."

Rew grunted.

"When Worgon's camp was attacked," murmured Cinda, "I cast death's flame, and one of, ah, one of the men… I held him, for a time."

"How long?" queried Ambrose.

"Seconds."

"That's good," said Ambrose after a sharp intake of breath. "People make better vessels, but they require more power to bind. They can fight it, you understand? If your hold on their soul is not secure, they'll slip away. But once you've got them, it's easier to keep them in thrall. I... I should tell you, I have never bound a person. I do not have the strength."

"Well, I did not do it for long."

Ambrose looked back at Rew and said, "Binding a person with no training is... unheard of." He shuddered and then pointed at the dead opossum. "Let's try again, Cinda. Raising the dead, like all things in life, improves with practice."

Without speaking, Rew left them. He sat on the other side of the camp where he could not hear their discussion, and even after Ambrose and Cinda turned in for the little bit of rest they required, Rew kept watch until dawn. He was deeply discomfited by what he'd seen, and he would not be able to sleep.

Chapter Seventeen

⚜

As the days progressed, they traveled farther and farther before having to stop each evening. The warriors had regained much of their strength, and it was only Lord Fredrick's constant stream of complaints and woes which ground them down to the point none were willing to push harder. No amount of chiding the man about the risk to Stanton would get him to move any quicker, and Rew couldn't leave the purported leader of their group without Borace learning of their secrets. And if there was one thing that could be said of the berserker, it was that once he knew a secret, he did not keep it for long.

What made it worse, was now that Borace was no longer on the verge of collapse, he put his remaining energy each evening into pursuit of the nameless woman. She rebuffed his attentions, which only seemed to inspire him to louder and more ludicrous attempts. The nameless woman weathered the commentary with aplomb, but Anne was seething. More than once, she snapped at the giant berserker, who seemed to find her anger amusing. Rew moved to intercede and perhaps teach the giant man a severe lesson, but Anne stopped him.

"That woman is quite capable of defending herself," she hissed, "and it's only her taunts that fuel his ardor. I suspect that with a man like Borace, if she left him alone, he'd leave her alone as well. I can't claim to understand it, but she's enjoying it as much as he is. It disgusts me, and I'd like to see you put your fist into his face or, even better, see her gut that vile man like a fish, but it's not our fight. She can handle him, if she wants to, and we should leave it at that."

Rew grunted and left it alone as Anne requested, but periodically, the empath could not follow her own advice. Borace laughed uproariously, thinking to goad Anne as he did the nameless woman, until Anne promised him that next time he required her healing, she would not grant it. That shut the berserker's mouth, at least when it came to Anne and the rest of the party. The nameless woman, a cat-like grin curling her lips, took the opportunity to speculate on how soon it would be before Borace would need some of that healing.

The bickering kept on, grating on Rew's nerves, until they were a day outside of Carff. The landscape had changed, and they entered a forest of tall, slender pines. The soil had dried over the days and become sandy. Traffic on the road had picked up, and it was rare they would go longer than a quarter hour without seeing fellow travelers, but the party remained quiet and did not speak to the others sharing the road. It'd been some time since they'd heard rumor of Dark Kind, and so close to the capital, bandits and other worries were nonexistent.

Near Carff, Rew wanted to avoid conversations where someone might guess the identity of the party. The mercenaries and Ambrose were content to comply with his desire for secrecy, Ambrose because he'd bow to anything Rew demanded, and the mercenaries because they did not want to spread rumors and spoil their chance of collecting payment for bringing tidings to Prince Valchon. Lord Fredrick eyed everyone they passed, as if seeking those of his status to share laments, but he saw no one, and he would not deign to consort with even more people below his station after weeks in the company of their party.

Rew felt little sympathy for the man. The nobles who buzzed

around Prince Valchon's court like flies around offal would not be leaving for a trip along the highway now, not during the Investiture. They'd be busy burying their heads in the prince's backside, just as Fredrick hoped to do. Even in peaceful times, the nobles of the court would rarely venture out into the province. They considered the lords of the Eastern Territory and the other remote regions as near-savages. Rew grinned, wondering if Fredrick was aware of that.

For the most part during the journey, Rew had attempted to ignore the nobleman. Lord Fredrick was traveling hundreds of leagues from his home so that in the midst of war, threats from the Dark Kind, and the deaths of every leader of every city in the territory, he could be formally named a baron. It was the sort of self-interested calamitous disregard for anything other than their own gain that defined the nobility, and Rew wanted nothing to do with it.

A week before, he'd decided that because Anne had not needed to heal the nobleman, there was a chance to ditch the man, but day after day, he could not find the opportunity. Fredrick did nothing but complain, so he was always ready to leave in the mornings. While they were cleaning the pots and dishes from breakfast, the nobleman was waiting and grouching. In the evenings, he sat glumly near the campfire, and the bulk of their party was never out of his sight. Whether or not it was intentional, it was certainly inconvenient if they were going to try and slip away.

So it was, one day from Carff, Lord Fredrick, the mercenaries, and Ambrose were still with them. The afternoon sun was high overhead, and its light was broken into shards by the thin tree trunks that rose around the highway. A damp, wet wind was blowing north, coming off the sea south of Carff, and it filled the forest with the smell of salt and open water, a pleasant change if they'd had time to appreciate it.

There was a small village ahead that Rew recalled from previous journeys to and from the capital of the Eastern Province, and it was situated exactly one day's walk from the city. It was a place to gather oneself before plunging into the madness of the big city or a place to ease into the quiet when one left. It had a number of quality inns, and it would be their last chance to plan the arrival into Carff. Rew, still tormented with what to do once they were brought in front of Prince Valchon, needed that time to discuss the options with Anne and the children. He couldn't ignore the fact that anything he did would involve them as well.

When they arrived at the village, Rew suggested they stop, and no one argued. There was a comfortable tavern at the edge of the village which wasn't as fine as where Lord Fredrick wanted to stay and wasn't as raucous as where Borace wanted to stay, but Rew made the choice and ignored their objections. Lord Fredrick had glared at him until Rew asked the man if he was afraid to venture out on his own, just a day from Carff. The nobleman had puffed up like a pastry from the oven.

"Afraid?" sniffed the nobleman. "Of course not. In fact, I don't plan to stop at all. I only suggested it as a courtesy to the women and the children. I will continue on to Carff and find my bed there."

"You won't find it before midnight," remarked Rew then quickly bit his tongue, cursing himself for offering the man a reason to stay with them.

"Perhaps, but without the rest of you to slow me, I think I shall make good time." Fredrick glanced over the party, his gaze lingering on Raif and Cinda. He turned on his heel. Over his shoulder, he declared, "Tomorrow morning, I shall be conferencing with the prince."

"I should have tried that sooner," muttered Rew, watching Lord Fredrick stride down the street and then out of the village toward Carff. Rew turned to Ambrose and the mercenaries, hoping they followed in the nobleman's footsteps, but to his dismay, none of them left. Rew sighed.

Borace laughed a harsh chuckle. "Ranger, I have a powerful urge to be paid for our time, but I don't fancy walking in to see the prince on my own, and I don't reckon Prince Valchon has any interest in speaking with a fool like Fredrick. I think it best we stay together until our business is done. You're the King's Ranger, eh. You're the one who can get us an audience, and as soon as you do and we're paid, you'll be done with us."

Grumbling, Rew admitted to himself the man had a point. Even with deadly tidings, a mercenary like Borace had very little chance of actually getting to see the prince in person, and without that, Borace stood very little chance of getting paid the rest of his share by the prince's staff or by Appleby once it was all over.

"At least that dour-faced nobleman is gone," said the nameless woman with a wink.

"I'll raise a tankard to that," boomed Borace. He leaned toward the woman. "How about we raise a tankard together?"

The woman rolled her eyes.

"Your new friends are going to leave us in a few days, woman. You won't have a choice then."

"There's always a choice."

"Not when it's just the two of us, there won't be."

"Enough of that," snapped Anne, stepping between them.

Barking over Anne's shoulder to the nameless woman, Borace warned, "Just one more day of the empath protecting you, then it's you and me."

The nameless woman strode toward the inn without responding, Borace following quickly on her heels. Shaking his head, Rew went after the big man, the others dragging their feet behind him.

The place he'd chosen served hearty fish stews, fresh baked bread, and cold ale, and so close to Carff, the wine was a far better terroir than anywhere near Eastwatch. Anne, not exactly pleased but satisfied with the cleanliness of the place, perked up when she took her first sip. Rew settled in, contented. If Anne were to order a second mug of wine, he would have free rein for as many ales as he wanted, and he wanted a lot. The tavern was warm but not hot. It was filled with the murmur of conversation but not unpleasantly loud. With so many days on the road together, everyone appreciated hearing some other voices for a change.

Rew sipped his ale and ate his fish stew quietly, waiting for the right opportunity to discuss his plans with Anne and the children. Ambrose knew who Raif and Cinda were, but Borace and the nameless woman did not. Rew counted himself lucky their identities hadn't been given away on the road, and he didn't want to spoil that now. Besides, while Ambrose knew who they were, he didn't know why the party had been headed to Carff in the first place. He'd inquired in his slithering, roundabout away, but Rew had held him off with claims they merely wanted to fulfill their duties to Baron Appleby. He doubted Ambrose believed it, but as a cover story it had the advantage of a kernel of truth. Whatever happened after, Rew had decided they needed to inform Prince Valchon of what was occurring outside Stanton. The people there deserved his help.

Once they'd finished their meals, Borace and the nameless woman began a game of throwing knives at a target on the wall. The woman was far more skilled, and she seemed to take great pleasure in taunting the berserker with that fact, but Borace laughed it off and claimed it was because he hadn't loosened up yet. They were like two feral dogs who couldn't help snapping at each other, but wouldn't stay away from each other, either.

As they played, Rew saw that, unsurprisingly, the big man had a prodigious thirst for ale that eclipsed even the ranger's. Rew watched as the giant berserker downed a pitcher and kept challenging the woman to larger and larger wagers.

Her knives thunked into the wooden board they were aiming at, and his knives thunked into the board or the wall in the general vicinity of the board. The big man kept laughing, though, and evidently, his pride suffered no wound. Ambrose moved to sit near the game, nursing a pitcher of wine and watching sullenly, as was his wont.

Raif made as to move toward the game of knives as well, but Rew caught his arm. "We need to speak, alone."

Grunting, the fighter sat.

"I've been thinking," started Rew. "This surge of Dark Kind is certainly the doing of Prince Calb, whereas your father's capture and imprisonment by Arcanist Salwart and the duke have Prince Heindaw's boot marks all over it. Your sister fled with Alsayer, who we know was communicating with Dark Kind north of Falvar and was the one who actually took your father. The point being, as far as I can tell, that treacherous spellcaster is in the employ of both Calb and Heindaw."

"No one will want Alsayer dead more than Prince Valchon," surmised Cinda.

Rew shrugged. "Perhaps."

"King's Sake, why are we here, then?" barked Raif. "If our aim is to find that man and Kallie, then why look in the one place that's most dangerous for him? He's a spellcaster. He could portal anywhere."

"Alsayer and Kallie did come to Carff. I'm certain of that," said Rew. "You'll see when we get there. The scent of the place is distinctive. You don't forget it once it's been in your nostrils, and I've never encountered that smell anywhere else in Vaeldon. They came here. There had to be a reason, and it could be a strong enough reason they stayed."

Raif glared at him, unconvinced.

"Where would you have gone instead?" Cinda asked her brother. "The only logical choice was Carff. Perhaps we find them here, perhaps we do not, but we had no other leads to follow so it's a moot point as far as I'm concerned."

"Exactly," said Rew, taking a sip from his ale. "There's also a possibility that's been growing on me. What if Alsayer convinced Prince Valchon that he's on the prince's side? He's acted in ways that imply he's supporting the other princes, but he hasn't been very successful at it, has he? And if one wants to turncoat and try to work two of the princes against each other, why not complete the picture and add the third? Believe me when I say that fits Alsayer's profile. I've been wondering if he's truly aligned with any of the princes, and instead, is playing his own game. I think it's possible the man did go to see Valchon when he came here, and because Stanton gives us the excuse to see the prince, it's the perfect place to start our search in the city for your sister."

"That's thin reasoning, Rew," warned Anne. "There's too much we don't know."

"We can twist ourselves into knots all evening," replied Rew, "but we can't plan based on what we don't know."

Anne frowned at him.

Cinda leaned closer. "I thought you said I should never come in contact with the princes, that it'd be very dangerous for me. What has changed, Ranger? Why not, like in Spinesend, we enter the city and gather intelligence before we make our move? Or, as I thought was your plan, you inform the prince of what is happening in Stanton, and we use the distraction to search for my sister in Carff. There's no reason all of us need to visit the palace, is there?"

"She has a point, Rew..." mumbled Anne, fiddling with her wine. "We've all agreed Valchon needs to know what is happening in his province, but not all of us need to be there to tell him. Why take the risk?"

"Because we're meant to do this together."

Anne raised an eyebrow. "I'm not saying we part ways. I'm just saying you be the one to enter the palace, and we can begin searching the rest of the city. We set a place and a time to meet up later."

Rew sipped his ale again and cleared his throat. "I, ah, I'm not sure that's going to work."

"You're planning to kill him, aren't you?" asked Anne suddenly. "You're not afraid for Cinda because Valchon will be dead. What about Stanton? What about Kallie Fedgley? If Valchon is dead..."

"I didn't say I planned to kill him."

Anne narrowed her eyes.

"Fine," snapped Rew. He looked around the group. "We've all

agreed this has to end, and it won't end while the princes continue their sport. Anne is right. I've decided I'm done running, and it's time to face... to face the princes. We'll tell Prince Valchon about Stanton, and with luck, he'll act to save the people there. After he's finished, I'm hoping I'll get an opportunity..."

"You think you could kill the man in his own palace?" asked Raif, his eyes wide. "King's Sake, Ranger, he's a prince!"

"I might need help," replied Rew. "I don't know what's going to happen, but I know our chances are better together, and I know if it goes sideways we may have to change plans on the run. It puts you all at risk, that is true, but we've always known there'd be risk. I think it's worth it this time."

"If we sit back, the princes will kill each other, won't they?" asked Zaine. "Seems to me like the path of least resistance is simply doing nothing, and then if you want to take on the survivor, so be it."

"They'll kill each other along with how many others?" retorted Rew. "Stanton will just be the beginning. King's Sake, not that I harbor a love of nobles, but all of those on the thrones in the Eastern Territory are already dead. That's a good example of what is to come."

"Good point," said Zaine, sitting back and lifting a mug of wine to her lips.

Rew frowned. Where had she gotten wine? Had she stolen it from Ambrose? From Anne?

"We've known this was coming," remarked Cinda, glancing around at the other children, "or at least we suspected it. I know you told me to keep the secret, Ranger, but I could not. We—Raif and Zaine and I—have agreed to see it through. If this is what we must do, this is what we will do."

"I think it was more like you told Raif and I that we were going to see it through..." corrected Zaine.

Cinda shrugged.

Raif coughed and added, "My sister is right, Ranger. You might be able to sneak through the woods as quiet as a mouse, but you haven't been very sneaky about your intentions. I heard enough here and there between you and Cinda or you and Anne. If you think bringing Cinda before the prince is worth it… I'll trust you. We'll do what we can to help, but don't think we've forgotten our sister. I want to find Kallie."

Rew grunted. "Alsayer is our only lead to Kallie. Carff is our only lead to him. And who knows more of what's happening in Carff than Prince Valchon? I understand Kallie is your priority, but what we must do is still aligned. Rest assured, whatever happens between Valchon and I, I still plan to find Alsayer and your sister with him. At every turn, that bastard has shown up, and I suspect he will again. I don't plan to let him slip away next time."

"So, to be clear," said Raif, "your plan to find our sister is to tell Prince Valchon about Stanton, hope he does something about it, and then kill the man? And all the while, we cross our fingers and pray to the Blessed Mother that Alsayer walks around the corner and then decides to tell us where Kallie is?"

"Yes, something like that," said Rew, "and in truth, I won't mind if Alsayer takes a little persuading, if you know what I mean."

Raif grinned and lifted his ale mug in salute. "I'm with you on that. Once we find Kallie—"

Cinda reached over and put a hand on her brother's arm. "It's about more than that, now, Raif. We'll find her, but when we do, it's not over."

"It's not?" he asked, raising an eyebrow. "It could be over for us, couldn't it?"

Cinda held his gaze. "Not for me."

Raif looked away. Rew wondered what Cinda had told her brother or, more like, what he had heard. Sometimes, it was easier not to know.

"I've got to see this through," insisted Cinda. She paused and asked, "Are you with me?"

"We're family, aren't we? Of course I'm with you," grumbled

Raif. He reached over, took the ale pitcher in front of Rew, and filled his mug. "Kallie is family, too. Don't forget that."

Cinda studied her brother, and for a moment, Rew thought she was going to disagree. She'd been clear, weeks before speaking to Rew, how she imagined the meeting would go with Kallie. Their older sister had made her feelings known, and then she'd stabbed Baron Fedgley in the back. Family or no family, there were some things you could not come back from.

"Pfah," said Raif, "enough of this talk. If you've no more, I'm going to watch them throw knives."

"Don't drink too much of that ale," warned Rew. "We've a big day ahead of us tomorrow."

"You're not my father, Ranger."

Scowling, Rew watched as Raif stood and left to join Ambrose.

"He didn't mean anything by it," Cinda told him. "He's infatuated by Borace, but he'll see the man for what he is sooner or later."

"He didn't mean anything by what?"

"Nothing."

They sat quietly, watching across the room as Borace and the nameless woman flung their knives. The woman was quite good. A number of other patrons had turned to watch as well, many of them placing bets and howling encouragement or heckling as the pair took their turns. Borace was not as good, and it seemed to compensate, he was flinging his blades harder and harder, which only made him even less accurate.

"Will Prince Valchon know what my family is capable of?" asked Cinda, scooting her chair closer to Rew. "Even if, like the king, he believes Kallie is the one, will he be able to tell..."

The ranger scratched his beard and then answered honestly, "I don't think he will be able to sense your power, but I cannot be sure."

"Do you think, Ranger, that since tomorrow I will be presenting myself to a man who may want to kill me, it is time to explain what this is all about?"

Rew poured himself another ale. Anne pretended she was not listening, but it was clear she was. Zaine likely was as well, but the thief was better at hiding it.

"I don't think Prince Valchon will immediately attack you," said Rew. "He probably doesn't understand why his brothers would be interested in you. Heindaw was always the more cunning of the brothers. He's the deepest thinker, the one who constructs the most twisted plots. Valchon's style is more… direct."

"But if Valchon does know…"

"If he knows and he fully understands, he'll probably attempt to use you just as Heindaw did your father, that or immediately kill you. That's the risk we take."

Cinda frowned. "And how was Heindaw planning to use my father? What is it about us, about our talent, that these princes are seeking?"

"Necromancy is an art of capturing the power that resides in every soul. Some spells channel that power into physical manifestations, such as funeral fire. Other, more complicated expressions of the art, manipulate those souls by tying them back to their corporeal body. You know about that now, don't you?"

Cinda's face grew pale, but she nodded and had no comment. Rew wondered if she was thinking back to the opossum she'd animated or if there was more that he had not seen. He should ask what Ambrose had been teaching her, but he would not. Like Raif had decided, sometimes it was easier not to know.

After a moment, Cinda frowned at him and said, "These things are basic necromancy. Even Ambrose is capable of those feats. Why me, Ranger?"

"What if a soul was attached to a different body?"

"I don't know if that is possible," replied Cinda. She brushed a lock of dark hair behind her ear. "The soul recalls the body, Ambrose told me, and what I've felt matches his explanation. There's a familiarity between soul and body. When a necromancer animates a corpse, they are binding a soul to a vessel it already inhabited. When done at the moment of death, it's easier because the soul does not yet know it has departed. Even when done after some time, the soul always remembers the old vessel, like a former home, and it yearns to return there. I... I'm not sure it could be done, tying a soul to a different body."

"It is possible," said Rew. He let that statement settle before continuing. "That's not to say it's easy or that it has often been accomplished. There has to be a true connection, for one. That is the element of the low magic hidden within what you do. Not any soul can inhabit any body. Blood—a familial line—is the only connection I'm aware of which makes it possible. A part of a parent is in each child, you understand? In addition, the necromancer must learn much about their subject, and both parties must be willing to consummate the bond. Immense power, naturally, is required for success."

"Why are you telling me this?" asked Cinda. "What does this have to do with me or with my father? Are you saying that my father somehow could have bound a soul to a body different than its own?"

"No, I do not think your father was capable of such a feat."

Cinda frowned. "It was said my father had no equal outside of the royal line."

Rew nodded.

"Rew..." said Anne.

He held up a hand to silence her. "For both parties to be willing, presumably one must be ignorant, don't you think? A necromancer of high talent would not likely be fooled and agree to the casting. But one who was not a necromancer, who believed they were participating in a ritual which would grant them immense power..."

"I don't understand," said Cinda.

"I began on this path years ago," said Rew. "I learned that during the first Investiture, when three sons competed to inherit the throne from Vaisius Morden the First, just as they do now, one of them was a necromancer. He won over his brothers, but he never took the throne. That is the only time the winner of the Investiture did not ascend. It's not common knowledge, but it has been passed down through ranger lore. Never since then has a necromancer competed."

"But all of the Mordens have the talent for necromancy, do they not?" argued Cinda. "For hundreds of years, the Mordens have been the most powerful... Hold on. Talent for high magic is passed through the blood. The princes... Valchon is an invoker, yes? Calb, you said, was a conjurer..."

"And Heindaw is an enchanter," completed Rew.

"King's Sake," spit Cinda. "How then... But none of them should have any affinity for necromancy, unless you are saying... No, that cannot be."

"When they ascend the throne, they suddenly gain the talent?" asked Anne. "I don't understand."

"We say talent is passed through the blood as a convenient way of explaining something we do not understand," responded Rew. "It is hereditary, that is true, but it's more than the physical nature of one's blood. It has to do with one's soul and how it melds with the physical vessel."

"Blessed Mother," gasped Cinda. "None of the kings have been necromancers until they take the throne. You're... you're saying there has been only one Morden! That they're all... Oh my."

Rew nodded.

"Wait," said Zaine, turning around and giving them her full attention. Lowering her voice, she hissed, "Are you implying that the king is the same... that there has only been one king? Someone would know!"

"Who? How would they know?" asked Rew. "These things are not written in books. They're not stories the nobility tells each other. No bard would survive long singing tales of the Mordens' dark secrets. Even within the royal family, none know all of the pieces. The king takes on a new body, so to any casual observer, it's impossible to see the difference. Those close enough to the former prince to observe a change in behavior—primarily his brothers—are dead. Other nobles and servants that don't fall in the Investiture are removed from the king's presence by granting them far-flung titles or killing them. Even if someone did suspect, what would they do about it? How does one challenge a necromancer who has survived the last two centuries by inhabiting other bodies?"

"He's... he's immortal," breathed Cinda.

Rew nodded.

"If they knew, someone would do something," said Zaine.

"They would run," said Rew. "They'd run and they'd hide. Believe me on that."

"There's only been one Vaisius Morden," whispered Anne, "one soul taking over the bodies of his children... Blessed Mother."

"I think," said Rew, "that the Blessed Mother has little to do with this."

"What does this have to do with me?" asked Cinda. "I have a talent for necromancy, but not like this, surely not..."

"It's my thought that your bloodline branched off from that first child of Vaisius Morden," said Rew. "The princes do not have children now. Valchon, Heindaw, and Calb are all childless. No surviving children, at least. I believe that's because Vaisius Morden learned from his first attempt at this foul game. The first generation had children, and I suspect they sired your line. Since then, Vaisius Morden has been carefully pruning his heirs for two hundred years. He's developed strength beyond imagination, but your line is pure as well! Of all of the noble families in Vaeldon, only the Fedgleys have fostered a true talent for necromancy. The others with the skill are like Ambrose, bastards. Think about it, Cinda, have you ever heard of a nobleman who had the talent of your father? His ability was unique in Vaeldon. If it wasn't for the need to monitor the barrowlands and the ancient souls which reside there, I think Vaisius Morden would have stamped out your line generations ago. As it is, he's left himself vulnerable."

Cinda worked her mouth, unable to come up with the words she was looking for.

"Your blood, descended directly from the king himself, may have the strength to face him. I only began to suspect when your father was captured. I've thought about it, and I think it's the case. Heindaw, of all of the Mordens, would know. You are unique, Cinda, in your ability to face the king and to end his dark ritual."

"But how?" asked Anne. "We can't… Cinda can't just walk up to him and fight him, can she?"

Rew shook his head. "Of course not. I have an idea, but it's not for tonight. If Cinda is willing to do this, then that is a discussion for another day."

"Why?" demanded the empath. "If we know Morden's secret, then why should we not learn the rest? What else could there be? Rew, we are in this together, and that means we should keep no secrets from each other. You have to tell us what you know."

"Because if Valchon, Calb, or Heindaw understand the possibilities, they may not understand the mechanics," said Rew. "Knowing something could be done is not the same as knowing how it's done. There's a reason Heindaw did not act immediately when he captured Fedgley."

"But…"

"Anne," said Rew, reaching across the table to put a hand on hers. "The world of the king does not end at death's door. The world of the living is not the only plane he has skill to inhabit. Even when you die, he can reach you. Death is not what you should be concerned with. If you know the way Vaisius Morden passes his soul from one body to another, if you know how it could be stopped, then you'll never be safe. Not in this life, and not in the next. Do you understand me? Your soul may pass to the realm of the dead, but there you are in even more peril! Vaisius Morden could call upon you, and he will imprison you so that no one else may reach you. There is nothing—literally nothing—that man would not do to destroy this knowledge. He has the power to trap your soul for all eternity. His sons, his own children, have been in his thrall for hundreds of years. Those first children and all since then are completely powerless against his whims. The princes that prevailed in the Investiture know his secret, and because of that, he will never release them. If he is willing to imprison his own children, think what he will do to you. But as long as you remain ignorant, he has no reason to hold you. It is once you know the truth that you could be doomed for eternity."

"Oh," said Zaine. She stood, steadying herself with a hand on the table. "I, ah, I need to go to the watercloset. I think I'm going to be sick. Or a drink. I need a drink. I'll be sick and then a drink."

"Anne, can you follow her?" asked Rew as Zaine staggered away from their table. After the other two were out of earshot, he turned to Cinda. "Perhaps I should not have shared even this with you. It is difficult to know. I do not believe the king would hold you, not for what I've told you tonight, but I can't be sure. I hope this is enough, though, for you to understand what is at stake. You were right, Cinda. You could be in grave danger meeting Prince Valchon. I can't put you into that situation without you knowing why, without your understanding and agreement, but I also can't seal your fate with the rest of what I know until I'm certain we have a chance to stop the king. Until we know there's a chance, it is safer not to have this knowledge. Do you understand?"

"I understand," rasped the girl. "I… I think I might like some wine."

"Of course," said Rew, reaching to grab Anne's mug and scooting it toward the girl.

Cinda, her eyes blank, like the world around them had ceased to exist, stammered, "I-I… It is good we know this, though it terrifies me. I had faith in you, Ranger, that this was important, that we were following you to a worthy destination. I didn't realize… Blessed Mother, watch over us all."

Chapter Eighteen

The tavern, which had started the evening relatively quiet, was growing rowdy, thanks in no small part to Borace's decision to buy ale for anyone who asked. The berserker, his purse fat with the coin he'd gotten from Baron Appleby that he no longer had to share with seven dead mercenaries, was celebrating. Rew wondered if Borace's pride had suffered at the loss of the nameless woman's company and as the one who'd taken the most grievous injuries during their fight with the narjags, and now the big man was trying to salve that hurt with enough ale to quench a house fire.

The nameless woman's continued barbs did not seem to be helping, as Borace's expression got more and more surly as the two of them started another round with the knives. It seemed the giant brute was having difficulty reconciling the idea that she used to share his bed, but that she'd changed her mind. Eyeing the man, Rew thought that surely it couldn't have been the first time the berserker had experienced such a thing, but maybe as a mercenary who spent his time on the road and was only in the cities following a large payment, perhaps he had not. He wouldn't be around long enough for any one woman to empty his purse or to grow tired of his antics.

Drowning his frustration in ale seemed a terrible idea, but Rew was certain the berserker wasn't going to listen to him if he advised slowing the pace of the drinks, so he didn't bother. Raif, enamored with the giant berserker, had raised plenty of those ales to join the celebration and kept encouraging more. It seemed the nobleman was throwing himself into the big man's wake, perhaps to forget the earlier conversation about the princes and to find some rock that he could hold onto and understand.

"My brother is going to be sick," worried Cinda, watching as Raif and Borace finished a raucous song and then tilted up their mugs, the muscles of their throats working as they drained every drop.

Rew, who was supposed to share a room with the boy that night, looked on sourly.

"You should tell him to slow down," advised Anne. "Sometimes men need a reminder that they're drinking too much."

Cinda did not respond, so Anne turned to Rew.

"He's not going to listen to me," said the ranger, shaking his head. "Maybe you ought to try? You're the most experienced at that sort of thing."

Anne reached over and punched Rew in the shoulder. "Aye, and my experience tells me that if I try to talk to him, it will only remind him that I'm an empath, and tomorrow morning, he'll be begging me to take the pain of his headache. Sound familiar?"

Rew felt it best to stop talking.

"I'm his little sister," declared Cinda. "There's not a chance he'll listen to me."

All eyes turned to Zaine, and despite themselves, they burst out laughing at her terrified expression. It wasn't the first drink for any of them, and Raif wasn't the only one who would benefit from making it their last.

There was a roar across the room, and they turned to see Raif was now engaged in the knife tossing game, except it appeared the loser was required to quaff whatever ale they had remaining in their mug and buy another round. The woman was assembling an impressive array of full ale mugs, while Raif, staggering and belching, had enough empties that the serving women couldn't keep up clearing them away.

Shouts from the other watchers heckling Raif for losing to a woman were starting to get under the boy's skin, Rew could tell, but when Borace started in on the lad, his booming voice thundering around the interior of the tavern, Raif's face glowed beet red.

"Beat by a girl? No, you throw like a girl!" roared the giant berserker.

"Oh, no," murmured Cinda.

Rew made to rise, but instead of swinging a closed fist at Borace's chin, Raif merely shook his head and shouted back, "Aye, she's beating me, just as she beat you every time you threw against her! I've still got a better record against her than you do because I haven't lost as many. Pfah. Whether it's a game of knives or a fight, I don't think I've ever actually seen you win anything."

Borace stumbled back as if he'd been struck. "What?"

The nameless woman sauntered in front of the men, spinning one of the throwing knives in her hand and offering them her cat-like smile. She purred something at them, but Rew couldn't hear it over the noise in the tavern. The ranger glowered at her. She might not be enjoying the berserker's bed any longer, but she did enjoy teasing him about it. Surely she could see that was not helping matters.

Ragged chanting broke out amongst the onlookers, and Raif, encouraged by the display, pulled out a handful of gold coins from his share of the purse they'd taken from the bandit fortress. "Eight, ah, nine gold that she beats you two times out of three!"

A raucous roar went up from the crowd. Nine gold was more than many of them would have ever held at one time. Rew rubbed his hands over his face, feeling that perhaps the others had been right, and he should do something about this. Before he could, Borace, half a barrel of ale sloshing in his belly, the shouts of several dozen onlookers encouraging him, took the wager, and the crowd parted, giving room to the woman and the berserker to throw their knives.

Borace went first, and it was lucky that everyone had backed far away. Only one of his three knives actually struck the target, and it wasn't as close to center as all three of the woman's tosses which followed seconds later.

Shouts and catcalls erupted from the tavern, many of the spectators riding on the river of Borace's free ale. Rew began to wonder just how much Appleby had paid the man and if Borace had coin to survive the rest of the night at this rate. Amidst the tumult, in a questionable display of masculine bluster, Borace demanded another pitcher of ale and suggested doubling the bet with Raif. The nobleman, perhaps still smarting from the ribbing Borace had given him earlier for losing to the nameless woman, offered to triple it.

"If Raif loses, he's going to be asking you for the coin," Zaine quipped to Rew.

Rew grunted. "Raif isn't going to lose. The question is, what does Borace do when he loses?"

The black-bearded berserker was turning up the new pitcher, his throat working mightily to handle the deluge of ale that poured mostly into his mouth, though plenty dripped into his beard and off his chin.

"Thirty gold!" yelled Borace over the cacophony in the tavern. He shook the pitcher upside down to prove it was empty and then leaned toward the nameless woman, his voice carrying throughout the room. "When I win, how about I lay you down on a bed of that gold?"

The nameless woman, with no gold at risk and having not yet lost a match to either man, laughed spitefully in Borace's face.

Rew wondered, if given her history with the berserker, she was enjoying this more than she should. She waited a moment, as wagers were made, silver and copper flashing as coins changed hands or were slapped down on tables. As soon as it seemed the bulk of the wagers had been placed, the nameless woman turned and flicked three gleaming steel knifes at the board. They all thumped firmly into the target. From the distance, Rew couldn't see exactly where they'd struck. He didn't think it was the best trio of throws she'd made, but he suspected it was better than any Borace had flung so far that night.

After the audience tallied the nameless woman's score, the bearded berserker walked forward and yanked the knives from the board. He stalked back and prepared to throw. A rictus of a grin split his lips, as if it was carved there from wood, or as if he was afraid to let it slip for fear he'd never get it back again. He no longer showed the teeth-baring glee he had minutes before, and Rew suspected that even Borace could do the simple math and realize how difficult a time he would have matching the woman's throws.

A skinny man lurched from the crowd. Clearly, he'd been imbibing more free ale than was good for him, and he smacked a hand against Borace's chest. He slurred, "I bet gold on you, big man. Don't you go losing it to a woman, now."

"I won't," snarled Borace, shoving the man away, but in the din of the tavern, Rew could tell the berserker's voice had dropped an octave. He was subdued as he took his position, clearly mulling over the fact that he had no particular skill at throwing knives and that perhaps he'd wagered far more than was wise when all signs pointed to him losing the match, again.

But pride is as slippery as a fish, and it stinks just as awful. Borace cocked his arm and flung a knife, which missed half a pace to the left of the board. Howls of laughter greeted his throw, and the man's chest heaved with angry breath. He raised an arm and flung the second knife, and this one was well-thrown, more out of luck than anything else. The crowd in the tavern went wild, and Rew could no longer hear what was being said.

Raif approached Borace, and Rew and the others could see the big man shaking his head. Raif was pleading with Borace, grasping at the berserker's arm, but Borace shook the nobleman off.

"He's offering a way out of the wager," guessed Cinda.

"He thinks he'll lose?" asked Zaine, wide-eyed. "That last one was nothing more than luck, and even if Borace wins this match, he cannot win another. It was best two of three, wasn't it?"

Shaking her head, Cinda explained, "I don't believe Raif thinks he'll lose his money. I believe he thinks Borace cannot pay. Raif is trying to avoid a scene, though it doesn't look like he's having much luck."

"Your brother has come a long way since I first met him," acknowledged Rew.

"You've seen him during unusual times, Ranger. You haven't seen the best of him. My brother doesn't always think through his actions, but he always acts with honor. He's learned a lot, too, meeting people who don't automatically bow when he walks in the room, watching you…"

They turned back and saw Raif backing away, his mouth tight, his eyes on the nameless woman. She pranced toward Raif and settled standing close to him. Borace tore his eyes away from the pair and stepped up for the last throw of the round.

He missed the board, by a lot.

Again, the tavern erupted, most of the patrons laughing at Borace and those foolish enough to have bet on the big man. The nameless woman's eyes were hooded as she watched. Raif had his arms crossed over his chest, and while he'd just won a fortune and there were scores of witnesses to attest to it, he didn't seem eager to attempt collection.

It seemed that the small, thin man who'd drank too much of Borace's ale was on the losing end of many of the bets, and no one was shy about asking him to make good. People were shoving the man, jostling him and ripping his purse from his belt. From the look of it, Rew guessed the purse didn't contain nearly enough coin to cover the little man's wagers. Hands were bunched into fists, and several men were fingering their belt knives. Rew thought the small man ought to be running as fast as he could, but instead, the little fellow staggered toward Borace like a fighting rooster. The berserker was at the target, drawing one knife from there and two from the wall.

The small man slammed a finger into Borace's chest, and he appeared to be demanding compensation, though why that should be the case, Rew couldn't fathom.

"He's going to get that finger broken off if he's not careful," murmured Zaine. "I don't think Borace is one to take demands kindly, especially when he's sore about losing."

The rest of the room quieted as well, particularly those who had won bets from the little man. It looked as if they weren't going to need to rough the man up, that the giant warrior he was accosting was going to handle it for them. But instead, Borace shoved the three knives into the slender man's hands and said loud enough to be heard around the room, "You want your coin back? Then you throw against her. I'm done. She's beat me."

Shaking his head, the thin man said, "Nah, mate, I want my coin from you. You lost. You owe me."

Laughing, Borace shook his head and looked out at the crowd. "That's not the way it works. Hey, anyone want to take care of this little fly? I've got a wager to settle, and it looks like he does, too."

A man, a scar cutting down half his face, across one eye, and twisting his mouth into a disgusting sneer, laughed. "No worries, my man. We'll handle the little fly for you. The rule round here— if you don't pay in coin, then you gotta pay in blood."

"If you say so," growled Borace, pushing past the small man toward Raif. He coughed into a fist and asked, "Don't supposed you'd, ah, like to throw for the balance? Double or nothing?"

"You don't have double," remarked Raif.

"The woman, then," said Borace, gesturing to her. "She's yours for, ah, a week if you can beat me."

Raif shifted uncomfortably and shot a look toward Rew and the others.

"Two weeks?" asked Borace.

"I'm not yours to offer," hissed the nameless woman.

"Silence!" barked Borace, and he raised a hand as if to slap her.

"Hold on," snapped the small man. He grabbed Borace's arm and, with surprising strength, tugged the giant berserker around. "You're not going to leave me to these animals. I bet on you. You owe me."

"I don't owe you a thing."

All around, the other patrons cackled in bloodthirsty glee. It reminded Rew of nothing more than a pack of narjags circling their prey.

Borace gripped the front of the smaller man's tunic and shook him hard. "I've got a woman to deal with, so get out of my face, fly. You're on your own, and best of luck with that. It looks like you're going to need whatever grace the Blessed Mother spares you. I'd say I care, but I don't."

The small man swung his fist, the three throwing knives still in his hand. The points of the blades plunged into Borace's neck. The small man staggered back, his mouth a perfect oval of surprise. He wasn't as surprised as Borace, though. The giant berserker reached up and gripped the handles of the knives.

"No!" shouted Rew. "Don't pull those—"

Borace did, and three geysers of blood fountained out from the puncture wounds, staining his shirt and everyone unlucky enough to be within half a dozen paces of him. The small man finally decided to run, and no one thought to stop him until the door banged open and he was out into the cold night.

Standing in the middle of the room, Borace looked down at the bloody knives in his hand in confusion, while blood spurted in sticky jets from his neck.

Rew glanced at Anne where she was sitting just as still as the fighter. She did not look away from the berserker, but she did not stand and run to him, either. Rew put an arm around her shoulder, and she raised her wine mug to her lips. Barely audible, she whispered, "I think I'll have another after this."

Chapter Nineteen

It was a subdued journey the next day into Carff. Borace had been an ass who had rarely displayed any consideration for anyone other than himself, but in some ways, that made it worse. It was hard to blame the man for being a selfish prick while not caring about his horrible demise. If he was guilty, they were as well.

Raif took it the worst. For a week, he'd been practicing several hours a day with the giant, and to see Borace felled in the opening salvo of what never became a drunken tavern brawl was difficult. The mercenary captain had strutted and preened as if he was the greatest warrior to walk Vaeldon's soil, but he'd been nearly killed by the narjags in the only real combat they'd seen him face, and then he'd been stabbed to death by a reed of a man all because Borace was terrible at throwing knives and making wagers. Raif had taken the man at his word when he'd bragged about his prowess, and it was a hard thing to admit you were wrong about a person. It didn't help that Raif's admiration of Borace echoed how he'd felt about his father, and both men had died from daggers wielded by those they would have considered their inferiors.

The nameless woman had taken Borace's death the best. While she was polite enough not to share her disdain for Borace in front of Raif, she made it no secret to the others she thought the world was better without such a man. And perhaps it was. The mercenary had gladly taken Baron Appleby's gold to leave Stanton and its people behind. He'd laughed when he'd discovered the bodies of his companions who'd fled without him only because he'd been too injured to follow. He'd cackled at spending his fallen companions' share of the spoils on ale, which of course, led to some rather unwise assumptions about how skilled he was at throwing knives and how dismissive he should be to a man holding them. Was the world better off without the berserker in it?

Rew cursed to himself. He didn't give a fig about Borace, whether the man was dead or alive. He'd been mulling the question over only because they were hours from Carff, where they hoped to find Prince Valchon, another boastful man who'd wrought much sorrow in the world. Though in Valchon's case, the prince had earned his confidence. If Borace did not deserve his death, then did Valchon? And the most difficult part, what right did Rew have to judge such matters?

In the early afternoon, Rew found himself walking beside the nameless woman, and no one else was around them. He asked her, "You didn't know him long, but you knew him well, did you not?"

She glanced at the ranger out of the corner of her eye. "I had a fling with him because we were off in the middle of nowhere, and there was nothing better to do. He made me regret it ever since. What, you think I ought to be sobbing like a child that the man is dead?"

Rew shrugged.

"It's because I knew him well that I've no tears, Ranger. You didn't see him taking time to say words over his mercenary friends, did you? That's how he lived. He didn't care about the living or the dead, and we've no reason to care about him."

"But doesn't that make us the same as him?" questioned Rew. "Borace being a heartless man doesn't justify our heartlessness, does it?"

"You think too much, Ranger," she said, patting the hilt of the brass scimitar hanging from her belt. "Care about your family and your close friends. For everyone else, there is this."

"He was part of our group..." reminded Rew.

"Not really."

Rew frowned at the woman.

"Ask the empath. She feels the ancient magic that courses through this world. She knows. Borace was physically with us, but he was never a part of us. Not even a part of me, Ranger, and I got closer physically to the man that I imagine you would ever want to be. If he'd been a true part of our group, she would have healed him, wouldn't she? Why do you think she just sat there, Ranger? She knows."

They walked on for a bit longer, neither of them speaking. Rew decided to do as the woman suggested. He stepped to the side of the highway and waited for Anne.

She raised an eyebrow at him in question, and he asked her, "Borace was with us, but was he one of us?"

Understanding his meaning, Anne shook her head. Rew nodded and began walking again at her side.

"The question is, does that matter," said Anne. "Does it matter he wasn't one of us? Does it matter he wasn't a good man? I've healed hundreds of people that I never learned the names of. They could have been killers for all I know. Some of them probably were. Maybe I should have tried to save Borace. I think I could have, had I been quick."

"That's not... I-I didn't mean you," stammered Rew. "Anne, no, you can't blame yourself for that man's death. King's Sake, the only one who should be blamed is Borace."

"It was my decision not to heal him."

"No... Don't put that on your—"

"You've been so wrapped up in your own head that you've been ignoring everything else," Anne chided him. "You're worried about how you should feel about Borace's death when I'm the one who chose not to heal him. But that's not what you're really worried about, is it? Rew, you're tearing yourself up over a decision that you've already made, that all of us have already made. Maybe it's right. Maybe it's wrong. That's too complicated for either of us to know. What we do know is what we feel, the nudge that the Blessed Mother grants us. You can feel the nudge, Rew, just as I did with Borace. The decision has been made. That's my point. Right or wrong, it's done, and rather than stewing about it, we ought to be moving on. It's bigger than us, and I won't claim to understand what is happening, but I don't have to because I have faith. Faith in the Mother, and faith in you."

Rew frowned.

"If you don't confront Prince Valchon, he'll kill thousands of people," said Anne. "You worry that if you do, he won't save thousands of people. Those are huge, complicated tangles that you'll never be able to tease loose. What you do know, and what you can get your arms around, is what he'll do to you, to Cinda, and to me. That's the nudge the Mother has granted. Is there any way we all walk away from this and the king and the princes ignore us? It's too late, Rew, which in your heart you know. The choice has been made. We've decided what road we're to take. All that's left is to walk the path."

"I never thought you'd ask me to kill a man."

"I'm not asking you to do or not to do. You know what you're going to do already. Nothing I say will turn you from the path, and despite the guilt and horror I feel about such a thing, I wouldn't turn you from it if I could. Walk your path, Senior Ranger. You're going to kill Valchon. The only question is when."

They walked on for a while before Rew asked, "What about how?"

"Stop complicating things, Rew."

WITH SURETY OF WHAT HE NEEDED TO DO BUT NO PLAN OF HOW OR when to do it, they arrived in Carff. Seeing Valchon was a gigantic risk, but it was Heindaw who'd imprisoned Baron Fedgley, so Rew believed it possible, even likely, that Valchon did not know it was Cinda herself who was the lynchpin in it all. If the king could be fooled into looking for Kallie, then why not Valchon?

Besides, without going to Valchon's palace, they were at a dead end. And worse, they'd be signing Stanton's death sentence as well. The people there had no chance if the prince did not come to their rescue.

Despite wrestling with it from every angle and deciding it was the best plan, Rew's stomach roiled in protest, and his hands ached from clenching them as the sprawling walls of Carff came into view. Laughing bitterly to himself, he admitted settling on a plan to challenge the royal family shouldn't be the kind of thing that set one's mind to ease.

When they got to the gates of the city, they were still almost a league from the coast and the expansive harbor which had earned Carff's place in the world. Over the noise of the city, they couldn't hear the lapping of waves or the calls of the seabirds, but Rew knew from experience that when they reached Prince Valchon's palace, they would. From the prince's expansive rooftop gardens, there were places of quiet contemplation where one could absorb the energy of the sea, spaces where one could look out over the harbor and the activity there, toward the city itself, or take in the industry that stretched along the coast. Some of those gardens were quiet glades where no sound but the wind intruded. Others were filled with tinkling fountains and hidden musicians, and some were positioned to appreciate the cacophony of the city.

The gardens, long before Valchon occupied the palace, had been designed strategically to grant whatever impression the master of the house wanted to show visitors. The palace had dozens of faces, and the prince could decide which was his that day. The building, Rew had always thought, reflected Valchon perfectly, as if it had been designed with the chimerical prince in mind.

As they plunged into the chaos of Carff's main thoroughfare and the noise rose around them, Rew gestured for the others to keep close. It was easy to get lost in a place like Carff. There were calls from vendors who lined the blocks around the city gates, selling all manner of items that newly arrived travelers might need, and just as many items that Rew couldn't fathom anyone wanting or needing.

The air was damp and heavy, like a wet blanket, but it wasn't as cold as they'd felt on the way there. So close to the coast, a breeze blew off the water and brought warmth with it. The city seemed to generate its own heat as well, with so many people and animals packed tightly together.

Rew led them on, taking the main avenue that cut from the gates to the market square that crouched in the middle of the city like a spider at its web. Beyond the markets and the bustle around them was Valchon's palace, hugging the coast with its back turned to the city.

There were all manner of strange and exotic sights to catch the eye, and while Rew tried to hurry the others along behind him, he quickly found he couldn't. Every half dozen steps, one of the children would stumble, staring openmouthed at some new wonder.

There were street performers of a stunning variety, wearing colorful costumes and calling songs and chants designed to capture the interest of passersby. Behind them was block after block of a dazzling array of shops and kiosks. They were stuffed with goods, and there seemed to be very little organization to it all —tailors beside bakers beside potters. The main thoroughfare of Carff was meant for strolling, and each vendor displayed their wares to catch the eye.

Even more interesting than those seeking the attention of visitors were the visitors themselves. Carff and her port drew people from all over the world, and for the nobles and Zaine, used to the remote Eastern Territory, there were people unlike anyone they'd ever seen. The streets were a kaleidoscope of the world's people. The babble of dozens of different languages filled the streets like water in a river. Rew tried to get the others to grab ahold of each other's belts so they were not separated, but getting their attention was proving futile.

"That woman just swallowed an entire sword!" cried Raif. "Right down her throat!"

Rew coughed, bug-eyed. He was looking at a woman wearing a black veil and headdress, skirts of the same loose, billowing material, and nothing else. She was perched at a ground level window of a house of pleasure, and her eyes and bare chest offered an invitation to what happened inside.

"Rew!" snapped Anne. "He was talking about an actual sword-swallower."

Rew turned and saw the empath clutching Raif's arm, dragging him away from a woman who was slowly drawing a length of gleaming steel from her throat.

"Lead us on, Rew," growled Anne low in her throat. She seemed to be trying to move Raif before he realized what sights awaited on the other side of the street.

Rew leaned over and wrapped his hand around Zaine's arm, the same way Anne was pulling on Raif, and hauled the thief after him.

"Did you see that?" asked the thief, a flush reddening her cheeks. "She was... right there on the street."

"I know."

"Ah, Carff," said the necromancer Ambrose, following quietly in the wake of the others. "A city of wonders."

"Come on," said Rew, pulling Zaine onward as the thief tried to look back at the half-naked woman and stumbled.

"I was meant for that life, once," Zaine whispered. "From

here… it doesn't look bad, does it? It's what takes place behind those walls, in the rooms…"

"It's a good thing you took up thieving," barked Rew, looking back at the woman in the window and then cursing and dragging Zaine along with him. "We all have our vices that we indulge, and more often than not, trouble comes with them. It's best when you find your own trouble, on your own schedule."

"That woman was something, though, wasn't she?" asked Zaine, finally coming after him so that he could release her arm. "I've seen other women in the baths, of course, but never like that. I wonder, how much do you think—"

"I need an ale," grumbled Rew, interrupting the thief and gesturing for her to hurry after him.

"Rumor has it that the prince has the finest wine cellar in Vaeldon," said the nameless woman, elbowing Ambrose aside to walk beside Rew and Zaine.

"It's no rumor," acknowledged Rew.

"You think we'll see him, the prince?" questioned the nameless woman. "I know that is your plan, but do you actually think he'll agree to an audience? Fredrick told me it could be weeks or a month before he'll deign to visit with us. Without the nobleman, I wonder if we'll see Valchon at all. The tidings of Stanton could be passed to an aide of the prince, and then what reason does he have to see us? Surely he has bigger concerns than a ranger from the Eastern Territory."

Rew did not answer. He wasn't sure if that was true—whether or not the prince had bigger concerns.

"Do you drink wine, Ranger?" asked the woman.

He glanced at her and sighed, figuring answering some of her questions was the easiest way to avoid more pointed, probing inquires. "I do."

Nodding, the woman said, "I as well, but I'm afraid the prince's finest vintages will be wasted on me. I can tell a good mug from vinegar, but that's about it. Still, it'd be nice to say you sat in a palace, drinking the grapes of the nobles, eh?"

"Why are you still with us?" asked Rew suddenly, looking between her and Ambrose. "Both of you. You've made it to Carff. You took what was left of Borace's payment from Appleby, and we'll warn the prince of what is happening. You've coin to spend, and you don't even know our plans after we finish with the prince. There's no reason you should stay with us."

"That's rather rude, isn't it?" asked the woman.

"Sorry, I don't mean to be—" Rew cut off, shaking his head. He had meant to be rude. "Rude or not, why are you with us?"

Ambrose cleared his throat and said, "Find trouble on our own schedule, was that what you said? I think, perhaps, that is good advice, and I will take it rather than accompanying you to see the prince. Men like him collect men like me for sport. Hear me, Ranger. The way to survive this world is to never climb higher than you ought. You've ventured from your wilderness, but do not venture too far. I don't claim to know what you're up to, but I know enough. You should turn away from this and disappear. Ranger, I hope you hear me—there are worse things than death."

Rew stared at the necromancer and replied, "Good luck, Ambrose."

The necromancer granted Rew a shallow nod then turned to leave. The crowd parted as Ambrose strode into their midst. Those of Vaeldon knew the meaning of his crimson robes, and those who did not knew to avoid what everyone else was avoiding. Rew watched the man go, wondering grimly how much wisdom Ambrose had meant to share. Things worse than death. He shook himself, then turned to the nameless woman.

"Do you know why the priesthood of the Cursed Father only allows men?" she asked before he could speak.

Rew scratched his beard. "No."

"Because the cult of the Cursed Father is a mirror to the reign of the Mordens. There are only male warrior-priests because there are only princes. I have overheard a little of what you and the others have discussed, enough to know you must have realized there are no women Mordens. Did you know there was no Cursed

Father two hundred years ago?" she asked him, dodging around a group of singing men, their arms linked over each other's shoulders, their breath heavy with the clove-spiced wine the commoners in Carff drank. "Did you know that? Of course not. You weren't alive then, and neither was I. But like you have stories, the priests of the Cursed Father have stories as well. There's no god of death, Ranger. There is no sentient force hungering for our souls. The Cursed Father is no more than a story!"

Rew stopped dead in his tracks, frowning at the woman and ignoring the scowling pedestrians who had to swerve around him. "What?"

"Come on, Rew!" called Anne from ahead of them. "I need your help. If I lose those two in this market, we'll never find them!"

Rew began walking again, drawn into the swirl of Carff's spice market. There was no Cursed Father?

The scent of the spices hung over Carff like a cloud, but within the market itself, it was more like a tornado, and it blasted into Rew, whipping away his questions for the nameless woman. Peppercorns and chilis. Cinnamon and nutmeg. Earthy cumin and acrid tartar. Spices Rew did not know described in languages he did not understand. Bundles of fresh sprigs harvested locally and dried sheafs traded from afar. Jars of it, piles of it, all spread across hundreds of tables and sheltered by linen awnings. Behind the tables, boisterous men and women stood, bellowing the quality of their goods, and disparaging everyone else around them. Behind them, wheelbarrows filled with sacks were wedged in, filled with more of the spices.

It made one's eyes water on the first inhale, and tears poured down your cheeks before long, but then you became accustomed to breathing in and out the heady scent. The heat of the peppers, the acerbic sting of spice from south of the sea, and the comforting allure of rosemary and thyme that reminded Rew of Anne's cooking. It was a lot to take in, and for the moment, the blast of sensation washed away his shock at what the nameless woman had said, what she was implying. When he'd gathered himself, Rew saw the woman had fallen back several steps and was smiling at him coyly, well aware of the storm she'd caused.

"Cinda went that way!" cried Anne, pointing into the crowd. "Get her before we lose her, Rew."

Rew took hold of Zaine's hand then plunged into the thick of shoppers, threading between locals garbed in loose tunics and robes, northerners bundled in furs and wool, adventurers in armor, women, men, and children. Some were pushing their own wheelbarrows through the crowds, knocking aside those who got in their way. Others were hauling heavy sacks, getting bounced around and jarred every time they passed another person. Wagons filled with spice coming in from the harbor were depositing new bags from all over the world. Shoppers for the largest inland merchants strode about with strings of assistants in tow, and mothers purchased small pouches for their own kitchens, always keeping a hand on their children.

Rew and Zaine caught up to Cinda, and Rew grabbed the noblewoman's sleeve. He turned and fought his way through the current of people to where Anne was bending Raif's ear, scolding him for running off into the crowd without her. The big fighter had the sheepish look of a child caught by his mother with his finger in the honey jar.

"I'm not a child," Rew heard the big lad complaining, despite how it looked with Anne jabbing a finger at his face and chastising him. "I wasn't lost."

"Oh, you know the way to the palace, then?" snapped Anne. "Were you going to meet us there later, perhaps? Such a big man, taking care of himself, ignoring everyone else around him."

"I'm not a child," repeated Raif. "I can take care of myself."

Rew shoved a little closer to the two of them and remarked, "Raif, someone has stolen your purse."

"What!" exclaimed the big youth, his hands patting vainly at the two strings where his purse had hung from his belt.

"Watch the urchins," advised Zaine. "They'll be the ones working strangers in the market."

"King's Sake," muttered Raif. "I had twenty gold in that purse! That's half our coin, Cinda."

"Good day for the thieves, then. I told you to stash your valuables out of reach," said Rew. He nodded toward the south end of the market. "Let's clear out of here."

"W-We have to tell the authorities—" stammered Raif.

"Tell them what, that you've never seen a big city before and you didn't protect your purse, or that you didn't listen to me about keeping only a token amount there while the rest was safely hidden? You didn't see the thief, did you? And even if you had, the guards would just laugh at you. A thousand purses are cut in this city by a hundred pickpockets every day, Raif."

Rew turned to find the nameless woman still lingering behind them. He opened his mouth to ask if she was coming but then shut it. There was no Cursed Father? Was that true, why had she told him that?

The nameless woman gestured toward the palace, and Rew grunted. He led the group through the swirling spice market, pushing against the flow, trying to avoid being sucked into its center.

From the spice market and off the commercial streets that wagons used to haul cargo from the harbor to the market, the crowds thinned, partly because the boulevard widened, nearly twice as broad as the road to the gate and partly because there were fewer people. The palace saw a great deal of activity, but those who did not belong stayed away. From time to time, a visitor to the city would venture too close, but they were quickly discouraged. It was always that way, but during the Investiture, the expansive, palm-lined road to the palace seemed nearly empty except for the heavily armed guards walking on patrol.

Even if the commoners of Carff did not know that the Investiture was going on, they knew what it meant when instead of revelers, it was armed men and women coming and going, and instead of feasts, the prince was hosting councils. The prince was preparing for war, and it was obvious to anyone who was paying attention. Valchon's men, in squads of ten, walked by them every few minutes, the guards attired in unbleached linen and copper breastplates, with wide scimitars hanging from their belts.

"I appreciate the choice of weapon," remarked the nameless woman, "but that armor won't stop a heavy blow. Copper? No soldier has worn that in a thousand years."

"It's not swords the prince worries about," said Rew, glancing around to make sure no one could overhear what he was saying. "Prince Valchon has armies twice the size of his brothers, so Calb and Heindaw won't march against him, not out in the open."

"You said Calb was the one who'd called the Dark Kind, right?" asked Raif. "That's an army of sorts, isn't it?"

"Fair enough," Rew conceded as they passed another squad of the soldiers. "Recall the cave we found you in, Raif? Copper is a natural barrier against high magic. What those men are wearing may not be enough to stop a serious practitioner, but it's better than no protection at all. I told you, Valchon worries little of swords and daggers. It's magical attacks that concern the prince."

"I'm just glad to see a man who doesn't dress his armsmen like they were vomited out from a rainbow," said the woman. "These are fighting men, not decorations. Back in Iyre, some of the minor nobles would… Well, I'll go visit the menagerie if I want to see a peacock."

"Aye, you could look at it that way," responded Rew, "or perhaps Valchon just doesn't want the men to take away from his own display."

He waved ahead of them to where the palace was coming into view, and it was not a study in modesty. The walls of the palace were those of a keep, but the way it sprawled across their entire field of vision earned the more impressive title. Fifty paces high, thick, sand-colored stone rose like a mountain range, blocking the view of the sea from much of the city. Atop those walls, men moved on patrol, but what caught the eye was beyond those guards where lush gardens were bursting with life. The vegetation sprouted from several dozen places around and on top of the palace. It was thick and dotted with colorful flowers, raised on a steady diet of sea air and regular rain that blew in over the harbor.

There were palms, which towered above the rest like stern uncles, a plethora of fruiting trees and bushes, and flowers that spilled over the walls hanging like sheets, their brilliant colors exploding into a visual feast for anyone who could peak past the stone barriers that surrounded them. A block from the palace, the scent of the flowers warred with that of the spice market behind them.

Zaine turned to Rew. "I finally understand how you knew exactly where they'd headed."

He nodded. "Nowhere else smells like Carff smells."

"Kallie's in there, somewhere," remarked Raif, looking up at the towering stone walls of the palace.

"She came here," corrected Rew. "We don't know if she's still here."

"How do you plan to find out?" questioned the nameless woman.

"I'm going to ask Prince Valchon," responded Rew.

The woman's jaw dropped, as if she'd been doubting the entire journey that his plans were exactly what he'd been saying they were.

Rew led the party to the gate. It was a towering barrier made of pale, foreign wood, bound in verdigris copper, much like what the soldiers' armor was made of, but this metal had been binding the gates for ages. It looked bright, cheerful almost, but the men arrayed in front of it were not. They held their pikes as if looking for an excuse to use them, and they glared at anyone who came within half a block of the gate. Rew ignored the looks and marched toward them.

"Halt," called a man who had the flared helmet of a captain. "The palace is closed."

"We've come to see Prince Valchon," declared Rew.

The captain stared at him. "Did you not hear me, friend?"

The man did not look as if he was trying to make friends.

"Tell Valchon that Rew is here to see him."

"Rew. Lord of…?"

"Of nothing," responded the ranger. "Just Rew."

The guard laughed and then frowned when he saw Rew was not making a jest.

"Your plan is going rather well, don't you think?" whispered the nameless woman to Rew.

"It happens this way more often than you'd think," said Zaine from Rew's other side.

"Send a runner to the prince, and he will agree to see us," instructed Rew.

Before the guard could reply, likely to say no, a small postern gate opened beside the main one. A liveried man stepped out, a valet dressed in Prince Valchon's colors, wearing the same stern, disapproving expression that all men of his profession wore. The guards seemed to know him.

"These, ah, these adventurers are to come with me," declared the man.

"Who sent for you?" demanded the guard captain. "We haven't told anyone they are here. King's Sake, I haven't figured out who these people are yet. He says he's from… He hasn't said."

"My instructions came from the prince's office," reported the valet.

The captain backed slowly out of the way, making room for Rew and the others to walk to the postern gate. Rew guessed the men at the palace were well aware of Prince Valchon's magical powers, but it gave the ranger a titter of nerves as they walked inside. Valchon could have laid a ward near his palace or, with effort, even all the way around the city. He could be alerted of their arrival, if he'd been looking for them, but why would he have cast such a ward? Had he known they were coming? Had the prince been waiting for them? Frowning, Rew wondered if Lord Fredrick had somehow managed to make his way to the prince. He doubted Valchon would see such a man, but how else had their arrival been noted?

They followed the valet through Prince Valchon's extravagant palace. The floors were covered in rugs woven by the hands of Carff's finest artisans or cut from the skins of exotic animals from all corners of the world. The walls were hung with tapestries from Carff and paintings Rew suspected were from the northern capital of Iyre. There were arrangements of flowers in gleaming gold and silver bowls, elegant candlesticks, and statuettes inset with sparkling gemstones. It was a nation's wealth, concentrated in the palace of one man. Carff was the mercantile capital of Vaeldon, the primary point of trade with nations beyond, and gold collected in the prince's coffers like dew on grass. A common joke, amongst the nobles, was that any prince residing in Carff spent so much of their wealth on valuable trinkets because they'd run out of room to store the coins in their counting house. It wasn't true, but there was a true element to it.

The valet led them deep into the heart of the palace, several floors below where the prince received guests in his gardens and quite a distance from where Rew knew was the throne room. It was a nice space the valet led them to, though. Long and wide, thick wooden beams in arches supported a ceiling covered in intricately inlaid, glazed ceramic tiles. Two huge stone fireplaces bracketed the room, but only one was lit. Couches and stuffed chairs were scattered about the floor, sitting atop piled rugs. Cases of books were staggered against the walls. Flags hung there as well, between the shelves, a myriad of color catching the eye in the stone and wood room. Some of the flags were recent. Some could have predated Vaeldon. Fallen realms. Strange that Valchon would display such artifacts on his walls. Strange that they'd been brought here at all. Rew did not recall ever having seen the room before, and in years past, he'd been a frequent visitor to Carff.

He spied a table filled with decanters of wine and spirits. They'd been set out recently with care by highly trained staff, but in other corners of the room, he saw dust and grime that never would have been allowed had it been a room the prince regularly occupied. The ranger frowned. He was becoming certain that this room was not one in which Valchon entertained, which meant... He wasn't sure what that meant.

Rew turned to question the valet, but the man had slipped as quietly as a shadow back out of the door. So instead, Rew drew himself up and then strode toward the drinks. Carefully, he did not look at Anne or give her time to chide him. He poured a glass full of wine and leaned back against the table. It was quite good wine, probably. He was more of an ale man, but there wasn't any ale, and one did what one had to do. They'd been in the palace mere minutes, and already, he was surprised and off balance. He needed something to steady his nerves before he had to face the prince. All of their fates hung on that meeting.

Anne glared at him and his drink, but the others went to join him, helping themselves to Prince Valchon's largesse. The nameless woman began shamelessly sniffing at the necks of the various decanters, speculating about the vintages and the terroirs, giving lie to her earlier claims about how little she appreciated wine.

"I don't believe Prince Valchon regularly uses this room," said Rew quietly but loud enough they could all hear him. "He could be meeting us here because he doesn't want us noticed, though there are plenty of other rooms scattered throughout the palace that regularly serve that purpose. If he really wanted to hide our presence, he would have sent us away then found us in the city later for a more clandestine meeting, or, since he evidently knew we were coming, he could have intercepted us before we even reached the gate. Since we've already walked through his halls... I don't know. I don't know why he wouldn't make use of the dozens of spaces set aside. It makes me nervous."

"We should be prepared, then," muttered Raif, reaching up to touch the hilt of his greatsword, reassuring himself the giant blade was still there.

"Have no worries, my friends, because it is not Prince Valchon who had you brought here," drawled a honeyed voice.

"Ah, King's Sake, it's you," muttered Rew, setting down his glass and drawing his longsword.

Chapter Twenty

"Cousin!" cried Alsayer, holding up his hands. "You do not need that. Not yet. Not for me."

"I'm not so sure about that, Alsayer," growled Rew, stalking toward the spellcaster.

Alsayer lowered one hand and began tugging on his goatee with the other. "Is this about what happened atop the tower in Spinesend? Or, ah, no, about the throne room in Falvar? Of course you are upset about, ah, those events. I apologize, Rew. I really do. I knew you weren't going to be killed by a wraith, and I had to slow you down. Cousin, you weren't going to listen to me, so I had to do it."

Rew got to the spellcaster and grabbed a fistful of the man's black robes. He shook Alsayer, raising his longsword menacingly.

"Rew, be civilized," demanded Alsayer. The spellcaster made no move to attack.

Rew's hand trembled. Desire to bury his steel in the man's arrogant face was consuming him. Alsayer deserved a sudden, brutal death, but Rew had questions that only Alsayer could answer. There were so many mysteries, and the spellcaster was near the heart of all of them. Rew gritted his teeth, and instead of stabbing his longsword through his cousin's throat, he shook him again.

"We're not enemies," snapped Alsayer, cutting off Rew before he could speak. The man's voice was tight with forced calm.

Rew flung the spellcaster across the room, and Alsayer tumbled, crashing into a bookshelf and wailing as the volumes rained down upon him. Rew was on him in a breath and yanked the man to his feet before he could react. He threw Alsayer again, smashing the man into the shelves, splintering wood. Rew reared back with his sword while Alsayer was looking down, spitting blood onto the pile of books at his feet. Growling, barely able to restrain his fury, Rew smashed his fist down, clipping Alsayer on the ear with the hilt of the longsword. The spellcaster fell to his knees, but he still did not defend himself.

"He's mine," said Raif calmly from behind Rew.

The ranger glanced back and asked, "Are you certain?"

"He killed my mother and kidnapped my father. He made my sister kill… He's the reason for all of it, Ranger. Singlehandedly, he brought our family down. The spellcaster is mine."

Stepping out of the way, Rew reminded the big fighter, "We need answers, Raif. Only he can tell you where Kallie is. Only he can tell us what all of this is about."

Snarling, Raif stepped forward. "Oh, don't worry. I'm not going to kill him, yet."

Wiping blood from his mouth, Alsayer growled, "I came to talk to you, Rew, not to fight with you. Stop this foolishness."

Raif raised his enchanted greatsword and strode forward.

Alsayer flung out a hand, and a fist of solid sound whomped into Raif's chest, flinging the fighter backward. Rew charged, but a terrible reverberation began, and he staggered. It felt like he was a gong, a heartbeat after being struck by a mallet. Stunned, he barely got his arms up in time to interrupt the wall of sound that crashed into him, but as it did, he felt it didn't have the fury of the last one Alsayer had cast his way. This one forced him back several paces and then vanished. Alsayer was speaking, but all

Rew could hear was a ringing drone in his ears. He raised his longsword, all thoughts of questioning the spellcaster vanishing. Alsayer was too dangerous to interrogate. He shouldn't have let Raif approach the man. Whatever answers they would get, they would have to get after Alsayer was dead.

"Rew, I'm here to talk! Blessed Mother, don't you want to know what all of this is about, why I came here to meet you? King's Sake, Cousin, if I was going to attack you, I wouldn't have brought you here and announced myself. You want answers? Then stop and listen!"

The ranger paused, seething.

Alsayer eyed him cautiously.

"Well, talk then," snapped Rew. He adjusted his grip on his longsword, thinking of how he could distract Alsayer and pull one of his throwing knives from his boot. The man would be difficult to get close to for a killing blow, but if he wasn't expecting it, a thrown blade might do the trick.

But Alsayer was right. The spellcaster had the answers. As much as it pained Rew, as much as it screamed against his every instinct, they needed those answers.

The spellcaster stood and straightened his robes. He turned his eyes, looking over the group in the room. "The Fedgley children, of course. I knew I could trust you to care for them, Rew. Well done. The thief, I should not be surprised. The innkeeper, ah yes, but so much more, aren't you? I learned of what you're capable of, but I never learned how Rew found you. Be careful, will you, because if I've learned of what you can do, so will have the other players of this grand game. The necromancer… Where is he? I know he entered the city with you. Pfah, the man was better off not showing his face here, but we cannot leave loose ends, Rew. He knows too much about you, so we're going to have to snip his thread. I don't have time now, but soon. And you, miss, who are you?"

Alsayer was looking at the nameless woman, and she was returning the look, stunned.

Raif struggled to his feet, cursing. With his free hand, he touched the throbbing bruises Alsayer's magic had left on his body. From his face, Rew could see that the boy was surprised it wasn't worse and that nothing had been broken. Alsayer, for whatever reason, had pulled his punches. He really did want to talk.

Everyone stared at the spellcaster, waiting.

"You always had such odd friends," murmured Alsayer, turning back to Rew. "Who is she?"

"That's not what you wanted to talk about," responded Rew, raising his longsword. "Tell me what you want to say before I change my mind about listening."

Alsayer touched a finger to his ear where Rew had cuffed him with the hilt of the blade and then looked at the wet blood on his fingertips. His eyes rose toward Rew, and he said, "I want you to wait to kill Valchon."

Rew shifted uncomfortably, fighting the urge to look behind him, toward the open door to the rest of Prince Valchon's palace.

"Don't worry," said Alsayer, wiggling his bloody fingers. "I've sealed the room. No sound will escape."

Rew looked skeptical.

"No guards have come to investigate the ruckus you caused. As long as I maintain my barriers, they will not come."

Shrugging, Rew nodded, conceding that Alsayer had a good point. If the guards weren't drawn by the booms of the magic the spellcaster had released, they weren't going to be drawn.

"You're aware of the Dark Kind mustering in the east?" asked Alsayer. "Surely you saw them on your way here. I think by now it is impossible to avoid the creatures in between the cities, not that I would deign to make that walk. The narjags are like mosquitos in summer. We need Valchon to deal with them, Rew. That is why I ask you to wait to kill the prince. It's not the time, yet."

Rew stared at the spellcaster, at a complete and utter loss for words.

Alsayer waved a hand. "Yes, yes, I know you have many questions, many accusations, but in moments you must go visit with dear Valchon. I cannot hide my presence here for long. When you see him, you need to encourage him to deal with Calb's minions. There is no one else who can—or at least, no one who will. Rew, the alternative is to seek help from the king himself, and your guess is as good as mine how he would react. For my part, I think I'd rather legions of the Dark Kind than the king's undead. And that's if Morden doesn't understand the import of your present company."

"The import of my present company? What are—"

"We play a deep game, Cousin," interrupted Alsayer. "I must go before Valchon realizes I'm here. Tell him, if you want, that I'm the one who wrecked his library. He can't want to kill me any more than he already does. All I ask is that you hold off on your own plans until he's dealt with the Dark Kind." The spellcaster glanced at Cinda. "Valchon doesn't know her capabilities. You cannot believe how difficult it was to lead both him and the king astray. I recommend you continue my charade. She's safe as long as you keep her necromancy quiet. The moment either of them understands what she's capable of... you know what will happen."

Shaking his head, Rew didn't know how to respond. He spluttered, "The king... you were the one who tricked him?"

"Of course. Rew, we will see each other again soon enough, but it is time for me to go." Alsayer reached out and turned his hand, and the gold-swirled purple of a vortex began to form. "Wait to kill Valchon. Just wait. That's all I'm asking of you. Think of the people in the east. Think of what the Dark Kind will do to them if you do not solicit Valchon's help. Once he's dealt with the narjags, as far as I'm concerned, the prince is yours. They all are."

"Where is my sister?" bellowed Raif.

"She's safe, lad," claimed Alsayer, stepping toward his portal. "If you survive the next few days, you'll see her again."

"I don't want her safe. I want her—" Raif stopped when the

spellcaster stepped through the swirl of purple and gold and let the opening shut behind him.

"Blessed Mother!" snapped Rew, punching a shattered bit of bookshelf beside him. "That man is infuriating."

THE VALET EYED REW SKEPTICALLY THEN TURNED AND LET HIS GAZE linger on the damage in the room. "A small disagreement?"

Rew nodded. "Gambling debts, you know?"

"I, ah, I'm not sure that I do."

"We've got it sorted, now," assured Rew, reaching over to slap Raif on the shoulder.

The valet stepped back out the doorway of the library. Rew guessed the man was thinking of the safest way he could call to the guards. He'd walked by the room on his way to somewhere else, had stopped after noticing the extensive damage, and was now clearly regretting it.

The ranger growled, "Take us to Valchon."

"The prince will not—"

"He knows me well, and believe me," said Rew, gesturing around the room, "this isn't the strangest thing he's heard of me doing."

The valet coughed, glanced both ways down the corridor, and evidently saw no guards nearby to call for help. With a brisk spin, he started down the hallway toward wherever the prince was, or maybe he was leading them to the barracks or a coterie of spell-casters. Either way, there was nothing Rew and the others could do except follow.

Rew could feel the others behind him almost physically over-flowing with questions about what Alsayer had said and how Prince Valchon could possibly know the ranger so well. There was no time to talk about it, though. The valet had arrived moments after Alsayer had disappeared, and even the nameless woman had kept her mouth shut in front of the mousy man.

The valet led them past a legion of armed men and spellcast-ers, gesturing curtly at Valchon's people to fall in behind, before arriving in an expansive gallery. Evidently, he really was taking them to Valchon. One wall was open to a marble-tiled balcony that overlooked the sea, and the other walls were plain stone dotted with dark, wooden doorways. At each doorway was a pair of armed men, looking curiously at the new arrivals. There were more armed men out on the balcony. A group of spellcasters was sitting in a tight cluster, and they surveyed the party with suspi-cious looks as the valet led them past. Prince Valchon was at a Kings and Queens game board across from another man. Without looking up, he flicked his wrist, and the man stood and departed.

"You've redecorated," drawled Rew, pausing twenty paces from the prince.

Valchon stood and stretched, still glancing down at the game board. They waited while he studied the positions of the pieces. Then, he glanced up and smiled a broad, wolf-like grin, showing no surprise at finding the ranger standing there in front of him. "I've been simplifying my life these last years, Rew. The musicians, the dancing girls, most of the scholars, they were a distraction that I did not need. I run a leaner court than when you were last here, and I've gotten rid of many of the accoutrements of my station as well. The tapestries, the golden bowls, I've had them taken from all of the rooms I frequent. What's the point of them, Rew? As you know, after I left Mordenhold, I surrounded myself with the luxu-ries we were denied. The trappings of wealth, pleasure in all of its forms… but I found I no longer saw those fine things. They'd become invisible to me, and let us be honest, they were useless. Who eats from a golden bowl? Perhaps if we were a merchant family, and we wanted to show our success to the world by displaying the finest items our treasury could afford, but I could buy all of the golden bowls in the kingdom if I wanted to. Believe it or not, I began to feel the same way about women. Part of the allure of a beautiful vessel is how difficult it is to obtain. When I came to Carff, every woman in the kingdom would throw herself at me.

The thrill of the chase was theirs, no longer mine. These days, I lead a simple life. I'm sure you, of all people, can appreciate that."

Rew glanced at the guards and the cluster of spellcasters. "Simple?"

Prince Valchon laughed and reached up to brush his long, dark hair back from his face. "The cost of doing business, Rew. Come, your companions look cold and hungry. There is food and drink in the next room, and if it's not already burning, we'll start a fire on the hearth. In truth, there are some comforts I still enjoy. I've made sure to keep employing the best chefs and sommeliers in the kingdom. Please, join me."

The prince loped across the room, looking like a predator trotting across the plains. He was tall, lithe, and brimming with energy. He wore a stark white shirt, unlaced at the neck. It was loose on his body but not so loose it hid the prince's muscular frame. He wore snug trousers that hid very little at all. He had black leather boots on his feet, and a black leather belt clasped with a simple silver buckle. There were none of the other adornments a man of his station could afford, and Rew wondered if he really had simplified his life or whether it was all an act by a consummate actor.

Prince Valchon had always presented himself like the beaming master of ceremonies at one of Carff's supper theaters, but Rew knew the prince had the blood-soaked soul of Vaisius Morden's child. His appearance was part of his draw, how he gained allies. He was magnanimous, generous with those he called friends, but there was a price for his grace, and it was during the Investiture he would collect.

"You were never much of a player of games, were you, Rew?" Valchon asked over his shoulder as he led them into a long reception hall. "It was arms practice and forestry which interested you."

"I've never liked people," admitted Rew. "I decided to avoid them in the woods, and if I couldn't…"

Valchon laughed as he led them to a table spread with delicacies: dates stuffed with minced ham and pungent cheese; a dazzling array of glazed pastries and confections; roast duck, chilled and glistening with fragrant sauce; crisp toast bracketed by jars of honey and marmalades; fresh fruits sliced and spread; and piles of exotic nuts, half of which Rew couldn't identify. Behind him, Raif's stomach grumbled audibly.

"A light repast. I hope it's sufficient to tide us over until the chefs can prepare something more substantial. It's too bad I did not know you were coming, Rew, or I would have put together a proper welcome. Ah, but you did not want that, did you? Sneaking in under my nose... It startled me, when I sensed you approaching, already within the bowels of my palace. Before you arrived, I meant to spend the evening at the game board, watching the sunset and drinking wine until my opponent could beat me." Valchon waved to a table on the side of the room. "Please, lay down your gear and relax. I'll send word to the kitchen, and supper will be ready soon enough."

A squadron of beautiful female servants, attired in flowing, low cut, sheer dresses, entered carrying steaming piles of hot, damp towels and bowls of warm water scattered with rose petals and lemon.

"You kept a few of the golden bowls, I see," remarked Rew.

Valchon laughed again, but Rew noted the prince's eyes sparkled with something that did not look quite like amusement. The ranger put his pack and cloak on the table, trying to arrange the items to hide the wool-wrapped falchions he'd taken from Vyar Grund. It'd be awkward, Valchon seeing those. The ranger accepted a hot towel from one of the serving women and left his longsword slung over his shoulder and his hunting knife on his side. The others followed suit.

Valchon shook his head. "Here on business, Rew?"

Grunting and making a sudden decision, the ranger slung off his longsword and placed it on the table beside the falchions.

"You must have heard rumors of the Dark Kind assembling all across the Eastern Province?"

Valchon nodded.

"We were in Stanton just a week ago," said Rew. "Baron Appleby believes thousands of the creatures have surrounded the city. From all across your territory, they are converging there. Any moment, they could attack. Stanton does not have the means to defend itself against such a threat, so I've come to ask your assistance."

"Wine?" inquired Valchon, accepting a glass of dark crimson liquid from a woman and gesturing for her to offer it to his guests as well.

"This is important, Valchon."

"Wine first," said the prince. "It loosens the tongue, Rew, and then men such as you and I can speak openly about matters such as these." The prince held his glass to his nose and inhaled. "Ah, a surprising selection. A recent vintage but well chosen. In time, these grapes could grow to be the finest in the kingdom. You are fortunate to taste them while the vines are still young. Drinking this wine is like seeing the future."

Rolling his eyes, Rew took a proffered glass from a comely servant who was carrying several on a gleaming silver tray. The ranger nodded toward the table, giving Raif and the others permission to fall upon the food. It might only be there as a light snack for the prince, but it was the finest table they'd seen in months. Rew sipped the wine and wondered if maybe it was the finest table they'd ever seen. The wine, certainly, was as good as could be found.

Valchon's gaze flicked to Rew's longsword where the ranger had laid it upon the table. "Still carrying that thing, are you? I suppose it's only right. You always were the swordsman. Tell me, what sort of business are you here on, Rew? Surely if you mean to use that tonight, you won't dishonor me by taking advantage of my hospitality first?"

"I told you. I came to warn you about the threat to Stanton."

Valchon scoffed, waving a hand dismissively. "You think I've no idea what is happening within my own province? Maybe you do, thinking you could sneak into this palace without me knowing. Let us cut to the heart of the matter, and tell me what you were doing in Stanton in the first place? Walking to Carff, I assume, but why? It's a bit outside of your territory, or have you been promoted? My father told me about Vyar Grund's betrayal. Are you filling the late commandant's boots, now? I didn't think you'd accept the role if it was ever offered to you. The King's Rangers aren't political, Father tells everyone, but we both know the commandant spends far more time in my court and that of my brothers' than he does trekking through the wilderness. If the rangers weren't political, Vyar Grund would not be dead, eh?"

"Just how much time was Vyar spending in your court, Valchon?"

The prince smirked.

"You feel nothing? You've known the man your entire life. It was his involvement with you that—"

Valchon held up a finger to still Rew's tongue. "Grund's death is a great loss for Vaeldon. We can agree on that, but let us not engage in rank speculation. Unless... What do you know?"

"The king used Vyar Grund—his body—to send me a message."

"Grund should have been more careful," said Valchon, his tone finally losing some of the casual arrogance he'd had since first seeing them. "I should have been more careful as well. I am human. I make mistakes, and Grund paid for that one. Is that what you want me to say?"

Rew frowned at him, and Valchon turned and acknowledged the rest of the party for the first time.

"Baron Fedgley's two youngest children. A priestess of the Cursed Father—I didn't think those existed... Let me guess, a thief? An empath, and of course, two of your companions are missing. A necromancer of marginal talent, found lurking in the city after departing your company, and who is currently enjoying a stay in my dungeons. He really should take more care about where he shows those robes, but men of small power cannot help themselves bragging about it, can they? And Lord Fredrick, who was also a yipping dog but of a different breed." Prince Valchon tapped his lips with a finger. "Curious company, Rew, curious company. If my curiosity could be further piqued by your companions, why, it would be. What possible reason could all of you have for coming to visit me?"

"I told you. Stanton."

Shaking his head, Valchon murmured, "That's what the necromancer said, I am told. What a fool. He served no use to Fedgley, did he? No use to Appleby, either—or you or I, for that matter. The late Lord Fredrick, of course, was looking out for his own interests, but you left him as soon as you could. He, at least, I understand."

"The late Lord Fredrick?"

Valchon nodded and pointed to an arched window opposite the balcony. Rew walked to it and peered through the thick glass down into a bare courtyard. There was a body there sitting in a chair, holding its head in its lap. Rew couldn't see Fredrick's face, but he didn't need to.

"It was him, then," muttered Rew. "I'd wondered…"

"Tell me, Rew," instructed Valchon. "What is it that you think that man did to earn his fate?"

"He cast a glamour on his father, Baron Worgon. He convinced the old man to march toward Spinesend, and then he cast a pall of darkness over the baron's army, allowing Duke Eeron to ambush them. Was Worgon actually working for you, or did he just think he was?"

"Worgon was working for me. He was my bannerman," acknowledged Valchon. He nodded toward the Fedgley children. "As was Baron Fedgley before Eeron and his foul arcanist took the baron into captivity. Not all in the Investiture is a grand mystery, is it? But there are some mysteries. There's been a great deal of interest in these children, for example, and I want to know why."

"It was you who killed Duke Eeron, then?"

"Of course," said Valchon, twirling his wine glass in his hands and studying the liquid as it bled down the side of the crystal. "Eeron pledged allegiance to Calb. He captured Baron Fedgley. He ambushed and killed Baron Worgon. They were my men, in my province, and that sort of thing cannot go unpunished. What do you think, Rew, of his execution? I'm considering making this my signature, displaying the bodies of traitors in such a manner. Is it suitably dramatic?"

Rew meandered away from the window and the sight of Lord Fredrick's decapitated body. He did not respond to Valchon's question and ignored the prince's twinkling smile.

Eyeing the two Fedgley children, Valchon continued, "Baron Fedgley was collecting wraiths for me in the barrowlands. You all know this? Good. Powerful allies, those wraiths. Fedgley had informed me he could harvest them and begged favors from me in exchange. The barrowland wraiths are of a particularly potent vintage, a race our ancestors exterminated before Vaisius Morden the First took the throne. A handful of those wraiths could sweep through an entire army. Spellcasters, except for the purest blood, are helpless against them."

Rew grunted.

"I've told you nothing new?" questioned Valchon, sounding mildly surprised. "For a man so vocally uninvolved in the Investiture, you are remarkably well-informed."

The ranger picked up a stuffed date and popped it into his mouth, chewing the big bite slowly and obviously, so he did not have to respond. He washed it down with an unnecessarily large gulp of Valchon's wine.

The prince grinned at him and waited.

"I passed through Falvar and saw some of the wraiths that Baron Fedgley had collected."

"You know then that Alsayer kidnapped the baron and his wraiths and fled. I tasked Grund with finding them, and while he could not secure the baron himself, he did manage to recover the wraiths. You know that as well, do you not? You were in Spine-send to see it?"

Rew did not respond.

"The king found out about Grund, and unfortunately, the commandant paid the price for involving himself in matters the king's rangers are meant to avoid. The king meant the lesson for me, but I think it applies just as well to you, don't you agree?"

Valchon raised an eyebrow, and Rew scowled at him.

Smirking, the prince turned to Raif and Cinda. "Your father pledged his support to me. Will you do so as well?"

"I-I, ah…" stammered Raif.

"We have little to offer," interjected Cinda. "We were fostered with Baron Worgon for years, and—"

"You have something to offer," interrupted Valchon. "There is a reason my brothers seek your family. I can protect you from them, but in exchange, I need to know what it is the Fedgleys are expected to do. Why are Heindaw and Calb so interested in your family?"

"It's their sister Kallie who carries the family's magic," interrupted Rew. "She is her father's better, I believe. She can control the wraiths you mentioned."

"Interesting," murmured Valchon, his eyes still on the children. "Throughout the years, some offer me their strength of arms, others their strength of magic, but most valuable of all is information. That, I am afraid, is a commodity I'm sorely lacking these days. I'd like to know, for example, where your sister is. Do you know?"

Cinda swallowed nervously and shook her head no, and Rew cursed to himself. The girl couldn't look guiltier. It was hard to blame her. One of the most powerful high magicians in the kingdom's history was staring at her sternly, but if she said the wrong thing…

"Why do you think the king would be interested in your father's wraiths?" questioned Valchon, stepping closer to Raif and Cinda. "The Blessed Mother knows the man can call upon a legion of his own if he so desired. Did he confiscate them as further punishment for making use of Vyar Grund, or something more?"

"Kallie Fedgley is with Alsayer," said Rew, breaking into the conversation again. "I don't know where the spellcaster is now, but they are together. I believe he plans to use her to command the wraiths for his own purposes. There were five, Valchon, five of those ancient spirits. With those at his command, Alsayer will be a potent force during the rest of the Investiture. You know him as well as I. You know the bastard has been plotting this since shortly after he learned to walk."

"I meant to use the wraiths to counteract Calb's incursion," said Valchon suddenly, followed by a deep sigh. "The spirits of our own race are not sated by the souls of the Dark Kind, did you know? But the wraiths Fedgley harvested, from deep within the barrowlands, are from an age before the Dark Kind came to this realm. Those wraiths will consume the Dark Kind as hungrily as they do us. Not having those spirits to call upon is unfortunate, and it will be costly. I dealt with Duke Eeron quickly, but the Dark Kind will be more difficult. They're spread all over the province, appearing like moles from portal stones my beloved brother Calb must have spent years scattering in out-of-the-way locations. We've found and destroyed many of them, but it's clear there are just as many more."

"Why are you telling us all of this?"

"Why should we not tell each other these things?" countered Valchon. "Unless, that is, you mean to use your sword against me?"

Gripping his wine glass tightly, Rew shook his head.

"You took a great risk coming here, Rew," said Valchon, slowly circling the room. He passed by Anne and the nameless woman, and they both took a step back. Then he walked around the table and drew near Cinda. Pale-faced, trembling, the young noble-woman could not take her eyes off the prince. "It is out of character for you to involve yourself in these matters, and even more so to put friends in grave danger, yet here you are, and they are with you. What have you told them of yourself?"

"Nothing," said Rew. He shifted. "Little. Very little."

Nodding, Valchon said, "Very well. I will respect your privacy, but my consideration comes at a cost."

Rew raised an eyebrow.

"Finish your wine, and have another," instructed the prince. He winked and continued, "That isn't my price, but we will discuss it soon. Unless you've changed greatly, you'll want to be drunk."

Slowly, Rew sipped his wine. He said, "You know I'm not one for games. What do you want of me, Valchon?"

"That will come," said the prince. "You came to Carff to see me, so you go first. What is it you want?"

"I want you to intercede before Stanton is overrun."

Valchon shook his head. "I'm afraid that is something I cannot do."

"What?"

"The Dark Kind are scattered, Rew. To track them all down would take me weeks, maybe longer. I don't know. As I said, we haven't found all of the portal stones Calb has scattered across the province. He surprised me, doing that so early. It violated the rules the king has set around the Investiture, but what can one do? Once it begins, there are no rules. The result is that I could be hunting Calb's foul conjurings and portal stones until summer before I found them all, but I cannot do that. I cannot spare weeks or even days. It was Calb's plan to have me do so, I am sure of it. When I am distracted, he'll move, and he will strike at my allies. Heindaw has shown his interest as well, as the Fedgleys have experienced. Arcanist Salwart is his minion. Did you know? Salwart's last act before fleeing to Iyre was to betray Duke Eeron, serving the duke to me on a platter. I wanted to take both of the traitors, but I had to choose one. Whatever Salwart knew, Heindaw knows now, and he'll be prepared to leap at my side as

Calb strikes my other. They've both turned their eyes on me, Rew. They mean for me to be the first to fall."

"You'll let the Dark Kind roam freely, then?"

"Not for long."

Rew scratched his beard and raised an eyebrow.

"I'll let them take Stanton, and I'll trap them there," explained Valchon. The prince shrugged. "That way, I can slay the bulk of the creatures in one blow without having to spend weeks chasing them around and exposing myself and my allies. Both Calb and Heindaw know I've built a foundation of support they cannot match, so they'll try to separate my friends and take them one by one. I will not let that happen. If I can defend myself and those close to me these next weeks, I've the pieces and the strategy to win this game. To my sorrow, the cost will be high."

"You'll... you'll let them take Stanton," breathed Cinda.

Valchon nodded crisply. "Appleby is of little consequence. I'd thought to grant his barony to a stronger ally anyway, once I was crowned. The only reason I haven't already was because I wanted it as a carrot, an incentive for others to prove themselves worthy. I have Spinesend and Yarrow for that, now. Both are greater prizes than Stanton. Nobles, once they are ensconced in a keep, think of nothing but betrayal. It's best not to share the spoils until you no longer need the allies."

"B-But the people..." stammered Cinda.

Valchon looked at her, confused. "There's no army to speak of in Stanton. No spellcasters of note, now. The place is worthless."

"Aye, and that goes both ways," barked Rew. "It appears as liege you have little value to offer Stanton."

"That was unkind, Rew," replied Valchon with a vicious grin. He glanced toward a doorway where a servant had just appeared. "Ah, I believe our supper is ready. Shall we?"

Chapter Twenty-One

D inner was an extravagant feast. Heaps of food were spread like the ridges of the Spine, spilling down a table that was ten times longer than their small group needed. Decanters of wine were proffered in a constant rotation by servants with straight backs, starched livery, and serious miens. It left Rew wondering where the young women had gone who had served wine in the other room. He thought to ask Anne if she noticed the change as well then quickly thought better of it.

When they sat, Rew positioned himself beside Valchon, hoping to steer the man's conversation away from probing questions of the children or the others, and it worked. The prince grew nervous, though not in a visible way. Valchon maintained his haughty but gracious manner. With skill practiced and refined for decades, he made them feel welcome. He inquired about them enough to be polite but not enough to make them squirm as if under interrogation. Then, he quickly excused himself.

Rew had left his longsword with their other gear, but he had not completely disarmed himself. He had his hunting knife and the daggers he kept in his boots. Sitting beside Valchon, he was close enough to the other man that he could reach him with those blades. The prince was well-prepared for such scenarios, but tonight, he had difficulty. Rew was having difficulty with it as well. In the blink of an eye, he could put steel into Valchon, or at least try to. It was what he'd come to Carff to do. It needed to happen, for the good of Vaeldon, but then there was Stanton. If there was a chance Valchon would act and lives would be spared, then Rew had to stay his hand. He told himself it was Stanton's need and not Alsayer's request that kept the peace

To Rew, the tension felt palpable, like steady rain that one could not ignore, but somehow, the others did. Raif set himself to the buffet of savory dishes like it would be the last food to cross his lips, and the nameless woman gave Valchon's wine similar attention. Zaine both ate and drank, but mostly, she marveled at the spectacle of dining with one of the princes of Vaeldon. Cinda and Anne had sat farthest from Valchon, and they ate quietly, hunched down on the other side of the sprawl on the table, clearly hoping to be ignored.

After the first few of many courses, Valchon stood and told Rew and the others that his servants would show them to rooms and baths after they'd dined. No one objected to the prince leaving, but all the same, he apologized profusely as if he was retiring after a grand ball and they were his courtiers.

Before he left, he leaned toward Rew. "One last word?"

The ranger nodded and followed Valchon to the side of the room.

The prince cleared his throat and inquired, "Alsayer?"

Rew raised an eyebrow.

"My servants reported the state of the room you were waiting in," remarked Valchon. "He met you there? That man is like a particularly frustrating fish, always taking the worm from my hook or wriggling mysteriously through the nets I've placed for him. Here, in my own palace? I'll be honest with you, Rew, I don't know how he entered undetected, though I can make an easy guess at how he left. What happened? Did you confront him about Falvar, Spinesend?"

"I did," muttered Rew, speaking cautiously. "It, ah… Sorry

about the damage we caused. Confront is a mild word for what I had to say to the man."

"Every bit worth it, I assume. I'm told you spilled his blood?"

"Not enough of it."

Grunting, Valchon nodded, looking distracted. Rew's fingers twitched, and he closed his fist, forcing himself not to yank his hunting knife free of the sheath. He waited impatiently, wondering if Valchon was finally getting to demanding the price he had mentioned earlier.

"Where is he now?" questioned the prince.

Rew crossed his arms over his chest. "That I do not know. We scuffled. He lashed out at the others which stayed my hand. Then, he fled through a portal."

"What did he want?" pressed Valchon. "Surely he must have had something important to discuss with you if he risked the conversation in my palace! Tell me what he wanted?"

Shaking his head, Rew answered honestly, "I don't know. That man... he keeps popping up unexpectedly, and I've fought with him several times in as many months, but he never finishes the fight. Each time, he's fled through a portal where I cannot follow. He could be anywhere."

"Was he after the children?"

"He has their sister already, and she's the one with talent."

Frantically, Rew tried to imagine a scenario he could turn the encounter with Alsayer to his advantage. Would telling Valchon that Alsayer was interested in Stanton help or hurt the city's chances? He certainly couldn't tell Valchon that Alsayer had asked Rew to wait a little while before killing the prince... But what else would Valchon believe was a conversation worth the spellcaster taking the risk in the palace?

"If I ever get my hands on that bastard..." growled Valchon. He clenched his fist, and Rew's hackles rose, feeling the building charge of high magic. But just as quickly, Valchon released it, and opened his hand. "Which of my brothers do you think he supports?"

Rew shrugged. He didn't know Valchon's angles or Alsayer's, so he elected, instead of trying to manipulate the prince, to tell him the truth. Some of it, at least. "Both of them? Neither of them? I don't know. I wish I did. I think at times, he's served both of them but never faithfully. If it helps, I doubt Calb or Heindaw trust the man, either. He's playing his own game, though it's beyond me what it might be."

Valchon reached up and brushed back his hair. "The Investiture is a tangled weave of alliances and betrayals. Threads of loyalty span centuries or merely minutes. The winner of the contest will be the one who weaves fastest, who accumulates the most allies and positions them correctly. It's like a Kings and Queens game board. One must—ah, you do not play, I forget. It's all about recruiting allies and watching for those who will betray you. I speak to you openly, Rew, which is something I rarely do with anyone these days. I have no idea what Alsayer is up to, and it infuriates me. What does the man want? Coin, land, prestige? Power, of course, we all do, but I can't fathom the twisted path he's walking to get there. You are right. Neither I nor any of my brothers would trust the spellcaster at our backs once this is over. Whoever ascends the throne, they're going to kill Alsayer the first chance they get. I have dreams of killing that man. He has to know that none of us will ever trust him, doesn't he?"

Rew snorted. "Don't trust Alsayer. We all have that in common, if nothing else. What do you suspect he's been up to?"

Valchon threw up his hands. "That's a good question. We should pool our knowledge, Rew. Tell each other what we know, and perhaps together, we can paint a full picture. You go first."

Rew scratched his beard. That was like Valchon, to speak of sharing and then insist the other go first. He looked at Valchon and saw the man's eyes glittering back at him. Rew shook his head. "Valchon, I don't know what Alsayer seeks. The truth? I thought in Falvar he was acting in concert with you. It was certainly risky, operating in your province against you, but whoever he was working for... It's interesting that he did not give them the wraiths he captured from Fedgley, isn't it? He communicated with the Dark Kind outside of Falvar, so I'd guessed that he was in league with Calb, but I believe it was Heindaw he kidnapped Fedgley for... Ah, it's too twisted of a knot for me to unravel. Alsayer fought Vyar. I saw that, so the one thing I'm sure of now is that Alsayer is not working for you."

Prince Valchon grunted, his face as blank as a mask.

Rew eyed him, wondering what that mask hid, and asked, "What do you know?"

"Alsayer is the one who opened the portal for Duke Eeron's army to ambush Baron Worgon. Eeron supported Calb, which is why the Dark Kind threaten everywhere in the province except for Spinesend. So you're right, the spellcaster acted on behalf of Calb. But as you say, in Falvar, he was coordinating with Arcanist Salwart, who fled to Heindaw in Iyre. I suspect it was Alsayer's connection with the duke that fooled Eeron into holding Fedgley in Spinesend, perhaps to confuse myself, or... Pfah! He's thrown his support behind both of them, but who does he truly owe allegiance to? You swear it is not you? You are not working together with the man?"

Rew laughed. "Valchon, there is little trust between you and I, and I don't think either of us believes that there ever will be, but I assure you that I am being honest with you now. If I see Alsayer again, I plan to strangle him with my bare hands."

Valchon grinned. "More and more in common, Rew. Twenty years ago, who would have thought? Good night, Ranger, and—"

"Rethink Stanton, will you?" asked Rew, raising a hand to catch the prince's sleeve but then quickly taking a step back instead. "Those are your people, Valchon. If you don't go and soon, they're going to die."

Losing his grin, Valchon replied, "I know. They are my people, and I'm going to let them down. It's the bitter calculus of what we do, Rew, of who we are. Those are my people, but soon, all of Vaeldon will be mine. If I move to protect Stanton, it will leave somewhere else open, and my brothers will take advantage, and people will die. I can't save it all, so I'm doing what I can."

"Are you?"

"You've seen enough of the pieces on the board to tell I'm playing defense. It is not I surrounding towns with Dark Kind. It is not I attacking barons in their keeps, killing their wives, and imprisoning them. I am doing all that I'm able, but I cannot fight both of my brothers at once. The only way this ends is when they die. That, Rew, is how I'm trying to save lives."

"It shouldn't be like this."

"You could help me."

Shaking his head, the ranger stepped back. "That's your price, is it?"

"We don't have to be enemies, Rew. I offer you no threats, to your person or to your secrets. All I ask is that you think of what I'm suggesting. Calb and Heindaw will kill countless people. You know that. You've seen that! If you want to stop them…"

"Rescue Stanton, and I will seek out your brothers," said Rew quietly, looking away from the prince. "If you want my help, you have to earn it."

Valchon drew himself up, standing half a head taller than Rew, and responded, "I'll think about your offer."

"Valchon, there's not much time…"

"I'll think about it, but remember no matter what I decide, it is my brothers who are forcing this. They are the enemy of us both. In your heart, you know it is not I who released the Dark Kind on Stanton or killed your companions' parents or ambushed Baron Worgon. The blood is not on my hands. If you want it to end, then help me end it!"

"I'm not going to be your assassin, Valchon."

"Then you carry the same guilt as I."

The prince inclined his head, spun on his heel, and left the banquet hall.

Scowling, Rew returned to the table and waved for another glass of Valchon's wine.

LATE THAT EVENING, REW SAT IN THEIR ROOMS, SLUMPED IN A stuffed leather chair. One leg was hanging over the arm of the chair, and a glass of wine was cradled in his hands. The windows were flung open, and the pervasive scent of flowers and spices filled the room. It was a chilly night, but not as cold as they'd been on the road, and with a fire, he was enjoying the contrast. He was staring into his wineglass, watching the firelight illuminating the ruby liquid, making it seem as if it was alive, when the nameless woman settled beside him. He wanted to be alone, so he did not look at her. She did not let that stop her.

"That could have been worse."

Rew grunted and did not respond.

"He said he'd think about it, right?" she pressed. "Maybe tomorrow there's a way you could—"

"What is it you want? Why are you still with us?"

The woman raised a glass. "I told you. I'd heard he had the greatest wine cellars in Vaeldon."

"You did say that," muttered Rew, rolling his eyes. "You also said there was no Cursed Father."

The woman offered him a wry smile. "Perhaps I misspoke. There is a Cursed Father, but it—he, I should say—is not what you think. It's a construct started by the first Vaisius Morden. I don't know why, so don't ask, but I know it to be true. Its lore, Ranger, written in the most ancient histories of the Sons of the Father."

Rew frowned. He'd had too much wine. Vaisius Morden had started a death cult? His thoughts were sluggish. The woman wasn't making sense, and as he considered it, he decided she hadn't answered his question. "What does that have to do with why you've joined us?"

"My father devoted his life to a religion which is nothing more than chicanery. It's a story told by the kingdom's greatest charlatan. Why? Why is that, Ranger?"

"How should I know?"

"I don't expect you to know," she replied with a laugh, "but I expect you to get me into the places where someone does know. The king finances the priesthood. It is his tax revenue that fills the coffers which allows the priests to fill the crypts. Why?"

Rew drank his wine. It felt like following the trail of his thoughts was wading through knee-deep mud. The woman didn't mean for him to answer her, he thought. He wouldn't respond, even if she pressed, because he realized he knew the answer. Why would the world's greatest necromancer establish a cult that was purported to bless the departure of a soul from a body? Who but the world's most powerful necromancer would want crypts full of corpses? Rew didn't need to speculate about the details. The concept was terrifying enough as it was.

He considered whether that made his plans more or less dangerous and decided it didn't change much at all. Morden was already far more powerful than Rew and more powerful than Cinda ever would be. More powerful than anyone would ever be, Rew hoped. It wasn't strength that could give them an advantage. It was trickery. That was had been and would be their only hope. Still… He sighed. That a two-hundred-year-old death cult formed by an immortal necromancer was not more frightening spoke to how difficult their challenge was… and to how much of Valchon's wine he'd drank, Rew admitted. Ten years ago, he'd known with certainty that he did not have the ability to stop the king. Did he have a chance now, even with Cinda? His thoughts were muddled. He wasn't sure.

But what did that have to do with the nameless woman? They'd made it in front of Prince Valchon, and she hadn't said a word about the Cursed Father or any of it. What was she waiting for?

"What else did you learn, studying with the Sons of the Father?" asked Anne.

Rew jerked, nearly spilling his wine over his stomach. Anne

had been sitting quietly beside him the last hour, and he'd forgotten she was there.

"You're worried the Blessed Mother is a fabrication as well?" asked the woman.

Anne shook her head. "No, I am not. The Blessed Mother is real. I've felt her."

The woman shrugged and lifted her wine. "That could be. I don't know. I've never personally felt anything of the sort, but I won't discount those who say they do. In the literature of the Sons of the Father, the Blessed Mother is considered his equal. She's the giver of life. He's the taker. Balance. It's a neat fiction. It resonates with people and gives them answers to what they are seeking, allows them a framework they can use to make sense of their lives. Could part of it be true? I suppose so. I make no claims about the Mother, only about the Father, and he is nothing more than a dangerous fabrication."

Anne shook her head.

"That still doesn't answer why you are with us," said Rew, staring at the woman, trying to pin her down with the weight of his sight. "If you want answers, why are you pestering me and not Valchon? It's his father who... who is the Cursed Father."

"My father taught me about the Cursed Father until we were discovered," said the woman. "It is illegal to share the secrets with anyone outside of the cult—and particularly with any woman, but he persevered. He'd obtained the highest tier in the Sons of the Father, and he didn't like what he'd found. He thought to arm me with both knowledge and skill to survive in a world that was far more terrible than he'd believed. My father diverted funds from the temple to pay for my education in arms. He bought me this armor, and he told me what he knew. His punishment was to be taken by the Father."

"Ah," said Rew, feeling sick. He finally understood what the woman's purpose was.

"In his studies, my father found a way to sever my connections to the world. The king can no longer find me with his magic, but my father could not do the same for himself. The king would have known if he suddenly disappeared, so instead, my father burned the temple down around himself, destroying all traces of who I was and giving me the head start which has kept me alive. You know the king, though, Ranger. You know that death is not the end. In death, the king took my father. He still has him. That, Ranger, is why I am following you. I've been traveling for four years, crossing back and forth across Vaeldon, searching for someone who could help me, anyone who could help me. I found you. Only you."

"Why do you think I will help you?"

"You helped the children find their father, did you not? It seems to be a specialty of yours."

"Aye, and their father is dead now," snapped Rew. "Call it a specialty if you like, but the doesn't mean I'm any good at it."

"My father is already dead," said the woman stoically. "What worse could happen?"

Chastised, Rew murmured, "I am sorry. I didn't mean—"

"I've heard the stories of what this group has done. A spell-caster and the ranger commandant? Imps? Dark Kind? I saw what you could do against those with my own eyes. The valaan…" The woman shuddered. "And then, tonight, your word alone got us an audience with Prince Valchon. He respected you as an equal. I'd planned to confront the man and beg for his help until I saw that." The woman sat forward, her eyes like burning embers in her face. "The others did not understand, but I did. Prince Valchon respected you as an equal. He feared you, Ranger."

Rew turned away.

"I do not need your secrets, but I do need your help," declared the woman. "With you, we will free my father from the Cursed Father and grant him his peace."

"Despite what you may have heard, I am not in the business of saving people's fathers."

The woman opened her mouth to retort, but Anne shushed him and said, "We have matters to attend to. We cannot make you any promises, but we will not turn you away, either. You are free to continue with us as an equal member of our group as long as you respect Rew's leadership and you understand our direction is determined by him, not by you. Perhaps, in the end, your father's soul may be freed. We will assist if we can, but our mission comes first."

The woman sat quietly and thought for a moment before agreeing. "That is fair."

Anne nodded as if something was settled, and the nameless woman stood up and left them.

Rew let his head fall back against the chair. Quietly, speaking to the ceiling, he asked, "Do we not have enough going on already without taking in another stray?"

"She's different," said Anne. "She's not like the children."

"Aye."

"She may help us, Rew. She could not stand against the valaan, but the woman can fight."

"She may help us. She may not," he grumbled. "How does that make her any different from any other stranger we stumble across? If she travels with us, how can we be sure we can trust her? Today, a single wrong word in front of Valchon, and all of us could have been killed."

"She did not say that word. She held our confidence and earned our trust."

"She's a skilled fighter, I'll grant you, but she comes with complications."

"Complications and knowledge," retorted Anne. She put a hand on his leg. "Rew, tell me, can we not use this secret information about the Cursed Father she claims to have? If you mean to... the king... Can you tell me her knowledge isn't valuable?"

He swallowed and did not respond.

"If Vaisius Morden has been stealing the bodies of his children, keeping his soul alive eternally, and he is the one who founded the cult of the Cursed Father, isn't it possible that this woman could be a critical addition to our group? I don't know how you plan to stop the king, but surely an ally brave enough to knowingly walk this path is a boon, and she may be just what we need."

Rew covered Anne's hand with his own and replied, "One does not easily leave King Vaisius Morden's service, Anne. I don't know if her father truly found a way to sever the king's connection to her, it is possible, but there's a reason I haven't done it with my own connection to the man. The king has more ties to her than just his magic. What would that woman do to free her father? Who wouldn't she betray?"

"Oh," said Anne quietly.

"I believe her story, that her father is in the king's clutches and that she's spent four years searching for a way to free him, but it's not so simple," continued Rew. "Fighting the king is hard, but agreeing to serve the king is easy. We cannot trust her with what we do. We cannot count on her when the moment comes to stand beside us instead of stabbing us in the back. While he lives, King Vaisius Morden alone has the power to release her father. Will she seek the king's death or his favor?"

"Blessed Mother grant us your grace."

Rew tilted up his glass and drained it, the empty crystal sparkling in the candlelight—like stars in the sky.

"Should we…"

"You've already told her she can join us, Anne. If we change our minds, the first thing she'll do now is go to Valchon. What does she have to lose? She'd tell him everything she knows and suspects about us. I think we'll regret her joining us, but I'm tired, and I can't think of a way to get rid of her without giving us away."

"Wine?" asked Anne, her voice warbling and plaintive.

He nodded.

"One more then rest," she said. "Whatever happens, I don't

believe we'll have long to wait before Prince Valchon makes his move."

"How do you know?"

"Because we saw the Dark Kind surrounding Stanton. Stanton does not have long, so Valchon won't take long either, one way or the other."

Chapter Twenty-Two

Anne was right.

They slept fitfully in a wing of Valchon's palace, taking turns at guard as if they were out in the wilderness. They did not discuss their plans or their strategy, though. There was nothing to discuss. Either Valchon would help his people in Stanton and elsewhere, or he would not. If he did not… They knew what Rew intended, but he still did not know how he would do it, so he was glad no one asked him.

Rew thought about that as he lay awake much of the night. Valchon implied he wanted to recruit Rew to face his brothers. Was that an opening? Would that get Rew close enough to the other man to slide a blade home? Valchon was still alive because he was no fool. He would be ready for Rew if the ranger struck at him. The dinner, the drinks the night before, it was all an act. It was meant to put Rew and the others at ease, but Valchon would not be at ease. He would be ready for an attack at all times, from any direction. If he wasn't, he would have already been dead.

That meant Rew had to bide his time. He had to wait until the man's back was turned, his guard down, and then Rew would stick the knife in. But he had to do it after giving Valchon the opportunity to eradicate the Dark Kind that were plaguing his land. If there was any chance the man would act to save thousands, Rew had to let him do it.

That part was decided quickly.

There was a knock on the door the next morning as they finished breaking their fast. The food had arrived at dawn, and Cinda, who was on watch, had let the servants in to lay the table in their sitting room. They'd eaten quietly, after Rew assured them that poison was not Valchon's way, and he reminded them they'd partaken of the man's table the night before. They didn't discuss it, but it was understood they weren't going to be allowed to roam the hallways freely. Valchon's generosity would only carry so far.

When the knock came, Rew wiped his mouth on a crisp linen napkin, stood, and with a hand on his knife, answered the door. The plain-looking man who had been across the game board from Valchon the night before was waiting calmly in the hallway. He gave Rew a wan smile, his eyes flicking down to where the ranger clasped his hunting knife. "Prince Valchon wonders if you'd like to accompany him to Stanton?"

"He's decided to act, then? He will protect Stanton?"

The man shook his head, his smile unchanging. "The Dark Kind moved first. They attacked the city last night. The fighting has been going on for hours."

"Blessed Mother," hissed someone behind him, but Rew wasn't paying enough attention to determine who it was. Stanton, attacked by thousands of Dark Kind. Thousands, tens of thousands of people would suffer for it.

"When is he leaving?"

"In a quarter hour from the throne room. If you'd like to accompany him, I can wait for you here."

Rew nodded and looked over his shoulder at the others. "Raif, get your armor. Zaine, your bow. Cinda and Anne... be ready."

He didn't know the nameless woman's name, so he didn't say anything to her, but she'd already darted over and was slipping her bronze chainmail shirt over her head.

Rew turned back to the plain-looking man and saw the man was still smiling at him. "Ranger, you will be with the prince. You do not need your weapons."

Rew grunted and did not respond.

―――――――

PRINCE VALCHON WAS STANDING IN THE CENTER OF HIS THRONE room surrounded by a dozen spellcasters of various flavors and two score swordsmen who had the look of trained killers. His elite guard, no doubt. The men and woman stood poised, ready to sweep their blades out at any threat. Rew worried that in a moment, they would do just that.

Beside the armsmen, there was an arcanist and a woman wearing plain clothing. At a glance, Rew decided she might be the most dangerous one there. She must be an assassin or trained to defend against them.

As the party entered, the spellcasters ignored Rew and his companions. The swordsmen eyed them for a moment then let their gaze rove ceaselessly around the rest of the room, and the plainly clothed woman studied Rew and the others openly. Rew grimaced. The prince was formidable on his own, and attacking him was not short of suicide at any time. Attacking him with this many people around him, all looking for threats, was unthinkable.

The woman caught Rew's expression and granted him a wink and a shallow curtsy. The curl of her lips was an uncomfortable echo of the man who'd fetched them. Both looked as if they knew something that Rew did not. An act? It could be. They were swimming deep waters, and he'd learned long ago that amongst the sharks, one had best have something to hide, and if not, you should pretend that you did. Rew scowled back at the woman, not trying to mask his displeasure at the events unfolding. If the woman was what he suspected, then she already knew he'd pressed the prince to intervene for Stanton, and being upset that the prince had not was a natural reaction. Rew would hide his actual intent by letting the truth of his emotions show on his face. The woman finally turned away.

Rew glanced around and saw their escort had disappeared. Was the plain man another assassin, a strategist, or the prince's companion at the game board who just happened to be available when someone had been needed to collect Rew and the others? Muttering to himself, Rew stared at Valchon, waiting.

The prince did not meet Rew's gaze, but he must have felt it because he declared, "It seems we're all here. Shall we go?"

Without waiting for a response, he raised a hand, and beyond him, a swirling vortex of gold-streaked purple spun into existence. It was three times the size of the portals they'd witnessed Alsayer open, and in heartbeats, a trio of spellcasters darted through, all wearing the black robes of invokers. A gaggle of swordsmen followed and then a pair of green-robed conjurers. The woman—her hair bound back and her dress that of a well-to-do homemaker in the city—strode through the portal with confidence that no homemaker had amongst so many deadly people.

"Watch her," Rew instructed Zaine quietly. He didn't know if the woman was a spellcaster or hid some other skill beneath her mundane presentation, but the fact that she was hiding meant she was the one to keep an eye on.

The prince walked through next, and shortly after, a swordsman waved to Rew and his group. They strode through the portal and found themselves on a hill outside of Stanton. The prince's entourage had fanned out, encircling the hill, while several of the contingent stayed close. Rew couldn't help but notice the woman stood by the prince's side. Her eyes were on Rew, not on the city below or on anyone else.

The ranger returned the wink she'd given him on the other side of the portal when he'd first seen her and then looked down at Stanton. Beside him, Anne gasped and covered her mouth with a hand.

Narjags poured through the streets of Stanton like black floodwaters. People were visible in pockets throughout the city, defending as best they could. Rew pulled his spyglass from his belt pouch and put it to his eye. He saw the defenders of Stanton had erected the temporary barriers they'd seen positioned along the roadways when the party had been there, though many of those fortifications had already been overrun. Some buildings were locked tight, and he could see people firing arrows or stabbing down with polearms from the higher floors. It gave the ranger no satisfaction, but evidently, Baron Appleby had taken Rew's advice and spread his defenses across the entire city.

It meant they couldn't be overrun all at once, but it also made providing support nearly impossible. Street by street, it would be a war of attrition. Lit by the fires of burning buildings, narjags were chasing the people who hadn't found a secure place to hide. In other locations, defenders were ambushing the foul creatures, filling blocked alleyways with dead Dark Kind. In a few spots, Rew saw organized forces of narjags making coordinated assaults against the barricaded buildings. That was where the valaan would be, he knew, but he did not see any of them yet. It was utter chaos, and he guessed thousands of people had already died. He hissed, watching a squadron of one hundred narjags breach a large structure and rush inside. Stanton's defenders were even less effective than Rew had believed they would be. Already, the course of the battle was clear. The Dark Kind were going to take the city.

"Looks like most of them are within the walls," murmured Prince Valchon, pushing his hair back from his face. "Confirm?"

A spellcaster, garbed in the green robes of a conjurer, closed her eyes and wrinkled her brow. They waited a moment silently, the distant sounds of the fighting drifting on the wind and reaching them on the hill. The spellcaster opened her eyes and turned to the prince. "One out of twenty remains outside. I believe this is as good as we can hope for. My advice, m'lord, is to proceed."

Valchon nodded.

"I sense... approximately six thousand, m'lord. The largest gathering in at least fifty years. Is that the extent of Calb's ability?"

Valchon shrugged and adopted a wide-legged stance. He flexed his fingers, and his eyes grew serious. "I doubt that's all he can command, but it's enough for me to act."

"Valchon," cried Rew, lowering the spyglass. The prince glanced at him, his face a blank mask. Rew snapped at him, "You're planning to destroy the city, aren't you? There has to be another way!"

"If I had the wraiths Fedgley harvested, it could be different, but I do not. There are no choices, here, Rew. Observe what my brothers force me to do. Observe what happens when good men —men like you—do not stand against them."

With no ceremony, Valchon raised his hands, and the wind began to blow. It was subtle at first, and Rew only noticed it because he was waiting for it, but soon, the rest of the people on the hill shifted, moving uncomfortably as gusts of warm air stirred their clothing. Others began looking back behind them, and they cringed. Rew didn't look. The moment he felt the first hot breeze across the stubble on his head, he knew what Valchon was calling. It was a spell that hadn't been cast in generations, and the prince must have been preparing it for weeks. It was a statement to his brothers, his father, to all of Vaeldon, a demonstration of what Prince Valchon was capable of. It was the end of Stanton. Rew thought he was going to be sick.

"Blessed Mother," said Cinda.

"What... w-what is that?" stammered Raif.

"He's calling a rain of fire, a maelstrom," said Rew, finally turning to look back behind them.

The sky was like the brightest, fiery sunset swirled with the dark of the worst winter storm roaring in from the sea. Red and orange, split by bands of black clouds, swirled and churned in a massive front that spread past the horizon, but seemed to rise into a soaring point just a league east of them. It was as if all of the clouds and all of the smoke in the Eastern Province was being gathered in a fist and pulled higher, creating a towering formation that, as they watched, raged into an inferno. From where they were standing, they could feel the heat of the clouds and the rumble of thunder. The wind was like a fire elemental's breath pouring over them.

The spellcasters and the swordsmen on the hill were silent. The spellcasters would be awed by the power Valchon was drawing upon, Rew knew. The rain of fire was a story such men told each other when in their cups. It wasn't something they could call upon themselves. It wasn't something they imagined anyone living could call upon except maybe the king himself. But the child was always stronger than the parent, and Valchon wanted to remind all of Vaeldon of that fact.

The swordsmen likely knew nothing of the magic that Valchon was channeling. They didn't know the spell, didn't know what horror Vaisius Morden the Fifth had caused when the maelstrom had first been summoned. But they knew that a burning cloud, towering several leagues above their heads, was going to result in an impressive amount of devastation when it released.

Rew crossed his arms over his chest and gripped himself tightly. The people of Stanton stood a better chance with the narjags raging through their streets. He found his gaze was locked on Valchon's back. He couldn't look up at the clouds like most of the others on the hill. He couldn't look down at Stanton, where the prince's horrific magic was going to rain down. He could only look at Valchon's back. Rew's arms were trembling, his hands twitching.

The plainly dressed woman stepped into his view, between him and Valchon. Her face was calm, her hands clasped behind her back. She faced him and ignored everything else. She was there to watch him, Rew realized. She was there just for him. She was the prince's protection against Rew while Valchon's attention was focused on casting his spell. His spellcasters, his swordsmen, they could look out for outside threats, but this woman's eyes were only on the ranger. Valchon knew, or at least suspected, why Rew had come to Carff. Rew and the woman stared at each other, breathing steadily, calm on the exterior.

Valchon knew why Rew was there, but why was he allowing the ranger to accompany him? What had their discussion been about the night before if Valchon suspected Rew's intentions?

Valchon was distracted, his back turned. Now was the time to end it, but it could not be the time. If Rew struck and killed Valchon, he might save Stanton from the rain of fire, but they would still face the narjags. And with the woman watching him, with a dozen spellcasters surrounding them, Rew couldn't do it. He wouldn't succeed. It was just like ten years ago, when he recognized what was necessary, but understood he didn't have the ability to do it. Rew knew what to do, but he wasn't capable.

The first fireball that came hurtling down from the sky brought with it the terrific rumble of thunder, but the crash of its impact with Stanton was like nothing Rew had ever heard. A bright streak across the sky, and then a block-sized section of the city erupted in flame. The wave of sound was something that even Alsayer would envy, and the ground shook beneath their feet like a wave-battered boat. Cinda fell to her knees, but her brother quickly pulled her back up. She was surprised, not injured.

Moments later, more of the meteors came flashing down, and the individual wail of their flight was lost in the concussive blasts as they landed. Like old brick beneath a mason's hammer, Stanton crumbled. Debris flew with each crashing meteor, carried from the force of the impacts and the hot air that billowed up from the city.

The people below, perhaps the narjags as well, would have been screaming in terror, but nothing was audible above the roar of the falling fire. Beside him, Rew felt Cinda weeping against her brother's shoulder. Zaine stood stunned, too shocked to feel or understand what was occurring. Anne's face was taut, and Rew put his arm around her. They'd been in Stanton, and while she hadn't practiced her healing there, she'd meet Appleby and others. She'd made connections in that city. Though faint, it would be enough that she would feel an echo of what was occurring below.

The horror of the destruction was like thick mud sucking at them, but even more than Anne, Cinda would be feeling the welling departure of Stanton's souls. The potential power would be like a lake she could dive into, if she thought to take the plunge, or perhaps a hurricane, raging in from the sea. Unavoidable, its overwhelming strength and destruction inevitable. The rush of that power would be like razors, dragging along her skin, but pleasure as well, the nails of a lover on her back.

Rew understood, suddenly, why Valchon's coterie contained no necromancers. He understood why Ambrose had been imprisoned for the sole crime of entering the city. Valchon knew what kind of power the day's events would provide to one who could tap into it. This was the surest confirmation that Rew could ask for, that the prince had no idea it was Cinda who held her family's powers. Even untrained, one with her potential could have unleashed terrific magic on the prince, and with his back turned, he wouldn't have a chance to respond. Death's flame could scorch the prince, his guards, and his spellcasters with a fury that none of them could stop. If Cinda understood, if she seized that power...

There was no reason to wait, now. Stanton's fate was sealed.

Rew twitched again, and his gaze flicked between the plainly-dressed woman, Stanton, and back. Would Cinda act? He couldn't risk looking at her, couldn't risk prodding her. If Valchon's guardian saw, she may understand in an instant. Could Cinda, untrained, master such a geyser of power quickly enough to lash out against all of those on the hill? Rew wasn't sure, but he knew if he looked at her, they would lose that precious surprise.

Valchon stood still as stone, his arms raised high. The woman, his most trusted protector, never looked away from Rew. She grinned at him.

After several minutes, it was over. Cinda had not struck, and Valchon's spell was spent. The clouds, still hot and boiling, began to dissipate slowly, and the rain of meteors streaking down into the city trickled away until only a few small, whistling missiles crashed into the billowing heat and smoke. What was left of Stanton was engulfed in flame and black clouds. Rew knew when those fires finally died down, the buildings, the narjags, and the people would be completely obliterated.

Without question, no one had survived the attack. Nothing had. Any trace of what Stanton had once been was gone forever. There was nothing to rebuild, nothing to start over from except blasted ruins. The monument to Stanton would be there for a hundred years, and as Valchon turned to look at Rew, the ranger saw the prince had planned it that way. Valchon had wanted this. Maybe he'd told the truth about the wraiths, and he would have used them if he could, but without them, he'd made a show of destroying his own people, his own city, as a message to all others —not just his brothers, though they were a part of the audience. Valchon wanted everyone in Vaeldon to know what had occurred there that day, to know now, and to know in the future, when he planned to take the throne and rule as king. Stanton was Valchon's promise of the type of king he would be.

Bile was rising in Rew's throat at the sight of the man looking at him, a man he'd known for years, a man who'd... There was a finality to it. Before, Rew had planned to kill Valchon and his brothers. He'd thought to find a chance to slide a blade home. He'd wondered if that chance would arise and what he'd do if it didn't. He'd stayed his hand at dinner the night before. He would not do that again. Rew couldn't live in a world where these men ruled, where they even existed. Chance or no chance, Rew couldn't coexist with such evil. They had to be stopped. Nothing else mattered.

The plainly-dressed woman stepped closer to the ranger.

Over the distant cracking of heat-shattered stone and roaring flames in Stanton, she demanded, "Has the girl not seen death before?"

Rew, for the first time since Valchon had begun calling his magic, looked to Cinda. She was bone-white, quaking, only able to stand because Raif had an arm wrapped around her. Her eyes were blank, as if she could not see anything around them. Now that he was looking at her, Rew heard tiny whimpers. She hadn't cast her magic because it was too much for her, more than she could manage. It'd been their opportunity, but she was a novice. She hadn't been ready.

Rew cleared his throat and loudly declared, "She's a sensitive soul."

"Is she?" wondered the plainly-dressed woman, taking another step toward Cinda.

"She's my apprentice," claimed Anne, putting a hand on the girl's shoulder.

The woman looked at Anne curiously and then grinned, her teeth flashing white. "Ah, yes, the empath. I've heard of you. A unique talent, we have been told. You must feel what happened below. You passed through Stanton a week ago, no? Was that enough to forge a connection? Tell me, does it hurt? Could you feel them dying?"

"You've heard of me?"

"It's my job to know who comes before Valchon," responded the woman. She turned her gaze to Rew. "It's my job to stand between him and danger, whatever form it might take. Are you satisfied the threat of the Dark Kind is over, Ranger? Was this what you wanted?"

"You have us at a disadvantage," responded Rew, his voice cracking. He kept his arms locked across his chest to prevent himself from drawing his longsword. "You know much of us, but I'm afraid I know nothing of you. Who are you, to be so trusted by the prince?"

Behind the woman, Valchon opened a portal back to his palace in Carff, and like before, a trio of spellcasters led the way, followed by swordsmen, and then the prince himself.

The woman held her position between Rew's party and the portal until Valchon was safely through. Smirking, she said, "I would not be very good at my job if you knew who I was."

"Odd, then, that you chose to accompany the prince today. It's not often you see a spymaster out in the open."

"No, I suppose not," said the woman, her cruel smirk growing broader. "But for the right occasion—"

Behind the woman, through the open portal, there was a scream. A screeching wail was followed by a bestial shriek and then shouts as swordsmen and spellcasters responded to an attack. The woman spun and sprinted toward the open portal.

"After her!" cried Rew, shoving Raif and Cinda before him and spinning to grip Zaine's arm and haul her after. "If that closes, we're stuck a week away from Carff!"

The rim of the vortex, purple with crackling gold, began to close. Not the violent snapping shut they'd seen before, when a caster ended their spell, but a closing because the caster was distracted, under attack, and had lost concentration on maintaining the portal.

The prince's spymaster seemed to flow between the swordsmen and spellcasters trying to force their way through the slowly closing opening, displaying a supernatural grace that ought to have been impossible.

Rew moved after her through the swordsman and spellcasters like a lawn bowling ball crashing through a set of pins. He shoved and flung men out of his way as he led the party toward the portal, and when they got there, he paused a breath to make sure his companions were still on his heels.

"Stay behind you. I know!" shouted Raif.

The fighter and the nameless woman were bringing up the rear, and as Valchon's minions realized they'd been pushed out of the way, they suddenly surged forward. Raif swung an elbow back into a man's face. The nameless woman tripped another and stepped over him. Rew charged through the portal, his companions and several of Valchon's people rushing in behind him. Half the remaining people on the hill squeezed through, and then the portal winked out. Rew looked around the room they'd stormed into.

He quickly regretted the decision to use the portal.

Prince Valchon stood in the middle of his throne room, his arms raised, whips of lightning trailing from his fists. He was lashing them about, wrapping the crackling strands around hulking imps and charring them to cinders with a pulse of blazing energy.

His spellcasters had spread out and were locked in their own battles with a horde of imps that were pouring through the windows and the doors of the throne room. Invokers were flinging heaving globs of liquid fire or thrusting out hands and launching jagged spears of ice. Conjurers were smashing vials, releasing captive summonings of their own, and sending their imps into the midst of the battle, where no one would tell which side which imp was on—including the imps themselves—so they simply began killing everything they could get their claws into. Swordsmen raised their blades valiantly and, for the most part, died where they stood.

Rew tugged Cinda tight and shouted in her ear, "No matter what, you do nothing! Cinda, do nothing!"

They'd missed their chance to take down Valchon with the flow of power from Stanton, so now all Cinda could do was give herself away. Rew glanced at Anne, who stood on the other side of the noblewoman, and she nodded understanding. Prince Valchon—and the king—thought it was Kallie Fedgley who was the necromancer that Heindaw wanted. Valchon had proven that by allowing Cinda to witness the destruction of Stanton, and if the king had any doubts, they would be assuaged if he learned of the event. The Mordens didn't realize Cinda was capable of necromancy. It was worth her life to maintain that fiction.

Rew, Raif, and the nameless woman formed a triangle with the others inside. Zaine fired an arrow, catching a giant imp in its muscular shoulder. The creature, the size of an overgrown bull, snarled in rage. Then, it charged.

Rew wanted to curse at Zaine for drawing attention to them but didn't have time. The imp was to them in two gigantic bounds, and the ranger rushed forward to meet it. He didn't want that thing within arm's reach of the others.

The imp swept a huge, clawed hand at him, and Rew ducked beneath the blow and came up swinging, hacking into its tough hide with his longsword before deciding he should have taken more care and delivered a killing blow.

The imp spun, smashing him with the back of its arm, and Rew went tumbling across the marble floor before springing back to his feet and lunging. He rammed his longsword into the imp's chin, plunging the blade into its brain. He fought free then leapt at the back of another imp that was battering Raif.

The fighter had fallen to his knees as the creature's heavily muscled arms flailed against him. Blood streamed down one side of his face, but Raif kept his greatsword up, meeting each of the imp's ferocious strikes.

Rew stabbed his longsword into the creature's back, and at the same moment, the nameless woman's scimitar flashed across its neck.

"We have to get our backs against a—pfah!" cried Rew. They needed to get their backs to something, but the imps were still cascading in through the windows and the doors. The space along the walls was covered by a rain of muscles, claws, and teeth.

Another imp came screaming out of the boiling conflict, and Rew stepped in, slashing at its face to stall it. Raif lunged forward, putting his weight behind a thrust and skewering the beast through the chest.

"Nicely done," called Rew as they both backed away toward their companions.

A dozen paces away, an invoker gripped the arm of an imp, its flesh smoldering where he tried to cast enough heat into the beast to finish it, but before he could summon the power, the imp grasped his head with its other hand and dug a clawed-finger deep into the man's eye. The imp wiggled its finger, scrambling the man's brain, then threw his body aside.

The imp turned toward Rew and the others, but before it could attack, Valchon's spymaster came spinning gracefully through the madness, wielding two gleaming silver poignards. She plunged one into the side of the imp then moved on, drawing the slender blade free. The poignard shone in the wicked light from the spells being cast all around them. It was spotless. Rew watched in awe as the spymaster fell upon another imp, felling it with the same casual ease. Whatever the woman's other skills, it was obvious the two blades she wielded were imbued with deadly enchantments.

In the center of the room, Valchon roared and spun, his lightning whips churning wildly around him. His people had fallen away, evidently deciding they faced better odds near the imps. None of those creatures had reached the prince, but it was difficult to tell in the insanity of the room which side was getting the better of it.

A cloud of ink black speckled with shimmering stars blew through the room a dozen paces away, tearing through three imps and one swordsman like they were made of soft clay.

Rew spun and saw Alsayer stalking down the stairs at the front of the throne room and joining the battle, waving his hands like he was orchestrating a stringed quartet playing for some pretentious nobleman. Around the spellcaster, space cleared almost as much as it did around Valchon. Alsayer laid waste to the nearby imps.

"You!" bellowed Rew, pointing at his cousin with his longsword.

"I don't have time for this!" shouted Alsayer, his voice barely rising above the tumult of the battle. He flung his hand up and sent a burning jet of fire past Rew, catching an imp in the chest, igniting the thing like a pitch-soaked brand.

"Watch them," growled Rew to Raif and the nameless woman. He took a step toward Alsayer.

The spellcaster was killing the imps, but Rew couldn't believe the man wasn't somehow responsible for all of this.

"I don't have time," cried Alsayer again. He raised his hands, palms up, and the marble floor beneath Rew's feet shattered, tilting wildly and throwing Rew sideways where he slid a dozen paces across the slanted surface.

He rolled down the sloped floor and jabbed up with his longsword into a small imp that had sprung after him. He shoved it off and staggered to his feet. Alsayer cast one of his black clouds into another pack of imps, shredding them and two of Valchon's spellcasters in the process. Alsayer pursed his lips in a frown, as if pondering whether sacrificing the two spellcasters to kill a few imps had been a good bargain. Rew started toward Alsayer, hoping to catch the man while he looked the other way, teetering on the edge of the shattered flooring.

Alsayer sensed him coming and twisted, sending a hissing jet of fire at Rew.

The ranger dodged, but his cloak caught flame, and orange and red sparks trailed him as he twisted out of the path of the spellcaster's attack.

Then, Valchon was beside Alsayer, and the two men began unleashing a spiraling matrix of white stars, battling in a coordinated fashion that was impossible to believe was spontaneous. The stars they released gleamed too bright to look at and spun too fast to be tracked even if you could. In a blink, afterimages were burned into Rew's vision. He looked away, but it wasn't difficult to follow the path of the destructive spells. They spun in a circle around the two spellcasters, and where they went, flesh and bone was hewn.

Imps roared and screamed as they were shorn apart. It was like a dozen giant saw blades from a lumber mill had been sent rolling around the room in ever-expanding circles. Arms, legs, and torsos were severed, and heavy chunks of flesh cascaded across the marble floor. The stars were directed, to an extent. Many of Valchon's men survived, though plenty died as well. The survivors stood where they were, too terrified to move, and Rew saw more than one man stain their pants as they lost the battle against pure terror.

Flapping his cloak to extinguish the flame that kissed the hem, Rew stalked toward the prince and the spellcaster.

"The portal stones," Alsayer was shouting. "That's where they're coming from. We have to shut them down."

Valchon turned to the entrance of the throne room, and Alsayer risked grabbing the other man's sleeve. "By the time we fight our way there, even more will have come through."

Alsayer pointed down, and the prince nodded curtly.

Rew crouched, prepared to spring at the backs of the men. He hefted his longsword and offered a hope to the Blessed Mother. Valchon or Alsayer—he hadn't decided yet. He had a chance to take one of them but likely not both.

He pushed off a raised ledge of shattered masonry, launching himself toward the men, his longsword raised above his head to chop down with a devastating blow. Then, the floor in front of Valchon and Alsayer exploded, and Rew was hurled back. The ranger, thrown like a leaf before a storm wind, cartwheeled and rolled across the floor. He slid into the wall and lay there, crumpled.

"King's Sake," he groaned, opening one eye to see Valchon and Alsayer standing at the opening they'd created through the floor of the throne room. It seemed neither man had been affected by the explosion. As one, the two spellcasters jumped down into the hole before them. Rew repeated, "King's Sake."

Anne rushed toward him, falling to her knees and sliding against him. She put her hands on his body, but Rew shoved her away.

She looked at him, astonished, and he gently took her wrist. "I'm all right, Anne."

"You don't look it."

"No empathy," muttered Rew. He tried to stand but wavered.

The empath stood, and he braced himself against her arm. Together, they dragged his battered body up so he was on his feet.

"This is madness, Rew."

"No empathy," he said again then began stumbling toward the hole in the floor where Valchon and Alsayer had disappeared.

Without the two spellcasters, the fight in the room was turning against the men. Imps were still pouring in, though not as quickly, and their opponents were tired and shocked. More soldiers pounded in through the main doorway, but the floor of the throne room was scattered with huge chunks of shattered marble and broken bodies. The soldiers stepped inside, and their enthusiasm waned the second they saw what they were dealing with. It appeared most of Valchon's spellcasters were already engaged or dead.

Rew glanced around frantically and saw that the rest of their party was still intact, though Raif had blood dripping from his face onto his armor and walked with a limp, and the nameless woman held one of her arms close, as if she was worried it was broken. Cinda and Zaine seemed all right, though the noble-woman's face was pale as milk. She held her belt knife in her hand, and from the distance, Rew could see it gleamed with blood. Zaine only had two arrows left in her quiver, but one was nocked on her bow, and as Rew watched, she fired it at an imp that was leaping onto the back of a soldier.

She touched the arrows at her side and called to Rew, "I'm saving these two in case I get a shot. Did you see? They jumped down into that hole, wherever that goes."

Rew gave her a quick nod. "Let's go after them."

"Rew, are you sure?" called Anne, crouching close to the others, looking around wildly as the battle raged throughout the room.

He gestured around them and said, "Valchon can't get any more distracted than this, and you saw what he's capable of. I don't want him to see me coming."

Leading the party toward the yawning hole in the floor, Rew tried to steer them around the tangled swarms of imps and battling swordsmen and spellcasters when he could, and he cut their way through the fighting when he could not avoid it. They reached the edge of the hole in the floor, and Rew saw that beneath the throne room was the chamber which housed Carff's portal stones. A dozen arches that linked to the other major cities in the kingdom and wherever else Valchon wanted to dispatch his minions in a hurry. In the center of the room, Valchon and Alsayer were surrounded by dead imps, and one by one, the portal stones were flickering quiet as the spellcasters sealed them with their magic.

Rew saw a flash of light in the corner of his eye, and he spun, chopping down a hand and whipping his cloak up.

The spymaster smashed into him, her weight and the momentum of her charge sending him sprawling backward, over the edge and into the hole to fall down toward the portal room.

Rew arched his back and flipped the woman over him. She gulped in surprise. One of her wrists was caught in his grip, her enchanted poignard held safely to the side. The other blade had stabbed into his cloak, and as they spun in the air, he twisted the cloak, cushioning the gleaming steel as she tried to turn it toward him. They fell, weightless, and then slammed hard against the stone floor of the room below. Rew had flipped her, so she landed first. He landed on top of her.

He felt her ribs flex and then crack beneath his weight, and wrenching pain lanced into him as his shoulder was jarred out of its joint. Gritting his teeth, Rew braced his arm and threw his weight down, slamming the bone back into its socket. Agony froze him, and tears watered his eyes, blinding him momentarily. Beside him, the woman lay flat on her back, pathetic whimpers escaping her lips. She was too injured to move.

Rising slowly, Rew turned to face Valchon and Alsayer. "Allies, then?"

Valchon chortled. "I was suspicious as well, Rew, but he played you right into my hands."

Alsayer shrugged. "I've been telling you the truth, Rew. I told him the same. We do not have to be enemies in this."

"I disagree," said Rew, and he raised his longsword in his trembling hand. His shoulder throbbed in pain, and he knew half the rest of him would be covered in bruises and small cuts, but he could fight, he was pretty sure. He had to fight.

"The portal stones are all sealed now," said Valchon. "Carff is cut off from the rest of Vaeldon."

Rew frowned, and behind the two spellcasters, a blaze of purple and gold spun into view. One of them had opened a portal.

Valchon swung his hand up and then jerked it back. Anne, Cinda, Raif, and Zaine came tumbling off the edge of the floor above like they were being hauled on a rope. Valchon flicked his wrist, and the group of them slammed together then went flying through the air toward the portal. It flickered, and they passed through it.

Rew stared, jaw hanging open.

"They're in Jabaan," explained Alsayer, "in Calb's palace. In the same room he's holding Kallie Fedgley, in fact. He'll be distracted for a time attacking Valchon, but as soon as he realizes his plan has failed, his mind will turn to defense, and your friends will be in grave danger."

"What have you—"

Alsayer, speaking over him, continued, "Kallie agreed to serve Calb, to perform the act Heindaw tried to force her father to do." The spellcaster's eyes flicked toward Valchon and then back to Rew. "The children wanted to see their sister again, no? They're seeing her now, Rew, but they only have until Calb returns or until Kallie uses her powers against them. Rew, she is a necromancer, and she is in the service of Prince Calb. When he returns to Jabaan, the necromancer will be in his thrall. Do you understand?"

Rew, stunned, stood stock still. But Kallie—Cinda. Alsayer was telling Valchon that Kallie had the necromantic powers, but to Rew, the bastard was talking about Cinda. Alsayer had served the girl up to Prince Calb!

"On a game board, Rew, you must make use of every piece available," drawled Prince Valchon. "Even when they do not want to be involved. I know you'll never forgive me for this, but I need you to kill my brother. Go through that portal and finish Calb, Rew. It's the only way to save your friends. He's weakened. He would have thrown every conjuring he could get his hands on against us. It's your opportunity, but the chance we are giving you cost a great deal. It won't come again. You have the element of surprise now. Calb will not suspect you lurking in his palace. Do not waste this on some foolish heroics."

Shaking his head slowly, Rew could not find the words to respond.

"We all knew it would come to this," said Valchon quietly, his voice barely audible above the chaos on the floor above. "Even Father knew. He wanted it, I think. The king hungered for you to compete, but all you wanted to do was run. It's too late now, Brother. You're involved, and there's no running from this. Vaisius Morden always gets his way."

"Not always," growled Rew, raising his blade.

Valchon threw back his head and laughed. "He'd love that, Rew. He can't wait to see us kill each other. Don't you get it?"

A low rumble and a cascade of screams echoed down the hallway, and they heard the sound of men being torn apart. The imps were coming.

"Rew," bellowed Alsayer, commanding the ranger's attention. "One of us is holding the portal open. If you kill either of us, there's a coin flip on whether or not you'll see your friends again. How long do you think they'll last, with Kallie Fedgley, in Calb's palace?"

Rew glared at the spellcaster, and the walls of the room shook as something giant crashed in the hallway that led to the portal room.

"Whatever is out there," said Valchon, pointing at the entrance to the room, "is going to take every scrap of magic Alsayer and I have to stop it. When it comes through the door, Rew, the portal will close, and your friends will be alone."

The building thundered again, and dust spilled down from above them. Rew could hear the hungry wails of the imps and the panicked shouts of men.

"How do I even know they're in Jabaan?"

"You don't," said Alsayer, "but you know they went through that portal, and you know that if you kill us you won't be joining them."

"You're a bastard, you know."

"Aren't we all?" crowed Valchon.

Rew walked by the two spellcasters, a pace away from them, his longsword clutched tight in his hand. He ached to reach out, to swing that blade into them, to ram his steel through their flesh. Calb would be weakened, but Valchon was as well. This was Rew's chance. Valchon had paid a heavy price to draw out his brother Calb. There might never be another opportunity to take on the prince so weakened, but Alsayer was right. They'd outmaneuvered him. It didn't even matter if Rew guessed right and killed the one who wasn't holding the portal open. Whichever one he killed, the survivor would turn their magic on the ranger. No matter what, if he didn't go through the portal, they would close it, and there was no other way to reach Jabaan in time to save Anne and the children. Stranded in Calb's palace, facing a sister who'd delight in betraying them, they'd be dead in minutes without Rew.

"Good luck, Rew," said Alsayer. "Do what you need to do to stop Calb from controlling the necromancer, and remember, we do not have to be enemies."

Not looking back at his cousin, Rew stepped into the shimmering field of the portal, and it felt like he was walking through a curtain of broken ice. As his heel cleared, he felt the sensation vanish, and without looking, he knew the portal was closed.

He blinked and saw Kallie Fedgley standing at the far side of a room, a dagger in her hand. Cinda and Raif were facing her. Blood dripped from Raif's wrist where Rew guessed his sister had slashed him.

"Blessed Mother," groaned Rew.

"Anne's been praying to her since Stanton," quipped Zaine. "It's not working."

Thanks for reading!

✦

My biggest thanks to the readers! If it wasn't for you, I wouldn't be doing this. Those of you who enjoyed the book, I can always use a good review—or even better—tell a friend.

My eternal gratitude to: Felix Ortiz for the breath-taking cover and social media illustrations. Shawn T King for his incredible graphic design. Kellerica for inking this world into reality. Nicole Zoltack coming back yet again as my long-suffering proofreader, joined by Anthony Holabird for the final polish. And of course, I'm honored to continue working with living legend Simon Vance on the audio. When you read my words, I hope it's in his voice.

Terrible 10... Always stay Terrible.

Thanks again, and hope to hear from you!

AC

YOU CAN FIND LARGER VERSIONS OF THE MAPS, SERIES ARTWORK, MY newsletter, and other goodies at accobble.com. It's the best place to stay updated on when the next book is coming!

Made in the USA
Las Vegas, NV
01 August 2022

52531929R00187